Red Crystal

Clare Francis is well known for her work on television and her voyages across the oceans of the world. She has written three non-fiction books, COME HELL OR HIGH WATER, COME WIND OR WEATHER, and THE COMMANDING SEA. Her first novel, NIGHT SKY, which is also available in Pan, was an international bestseller.

Also by Clare Francis
in Pan Books

Night Sky

Clare Francis

Red Crystal

Pan Books in association with
William Heinemann

First published 1985 by William Heinemann Ltd
This edition published 1986 by
Pan Books Ltd, Cavaye Place, London SW10 9PG
in association with William Heinemann Ltd
9 8 7 6 5 4 3 2 1
© Clare Francis 1985
ISBN 0 330 29384 2
Photoset by Parker Typesetting Service, Leicester
Printed and bound in Great Britain by
Hunt Barnard Printing Ltd, Aylesbury, Bucks

For my parents

PART ONE
Spring 1968

One

Gabriele Schroeder chose her clothes thoughtfully.

What did one need for such an occasion?

Running-shoes certainly. Jeans. A top which wasn't so bulky that it would impede her arms. At the same time it would be cold waiting outside the hotel. She pulled on a sweater and took a scarf from the hook on the back of the door. With a leather jacket, that should be enough to keep her warm.

She made a half-hearted attempt to tidy the area around her bed, stuffing some clothes into a holdall, and then gave up.

A broken mirror sat on the mantelpiece. She looked at her reflection. Hair dark, shoulder-length, slightly wavy, parted severely in the middle; skin pale; eyes dark and hollow. She still wasn't used to herself without make-up – she'd worn it for years: the pale white foundation, the thick eye-liner and heavy mascara. A slave to fashion. But who needed make-up? That was for manufactured women who didn't know who they really were. She could see that now. But it had taken her long enough to realise. She was twenty-five.

Finally, the hat. It was a woollen one that came down over her forehead. After a moment's thought, she removed it, fastened her hair to the top of her head with a pin and replaced the hat. Better: now her hair wouldn't get in her eyes.

The complete political activist.

A small tremor of nervousness tugged at her. She'd never done anything like this before. Nor had the others. Nor had *anybody*. Demonstrations in Britain were usually orderly, good-humoured, well-behaved. *Passive*.

This was going to be different.

She ran downstairs to the kitchen.

The others were there. Eight in all, including Max and Stephie.

They were sitting round the room, drinking and smoking joints. No one looked worried. They seemed to think it was rather a lark. Gabriele relaxed a little.

Someone asked, 'Do we know who'll be there, Max?'

Max's thin, intense face was expressionless behind the wire-rimmed glasses. 'The American ambassador. A whole collection of dons—'

'A *disgust* of dons.' It was a boy with bright red hair. Gabriele recognised him from meetings on the campus at Essex. His name, she remembered, was Paul Reardon.

'— and maybe someone from the Foreign Office.'

'No cabinet ministers?'

Max shook his head. 'They didn't say so.'

Gabriele knew that Max's information came from his friends at Oxford, the organisers of the demonstration. The occasion was the Oxford Anglo-American Society Dinner.

Someone said, 'Pity.'

As they collected their banners and placards, Reardon came over to Gabriele. 'Linda, isn't it?'

She gave it a second to let her annoyance pass, then said firmly, 'No, it is not. The name is Gabriele, Gabriele Schroeder.'

He stared at her. 'Sure. Sure . . .'

To ease the moment along, she added, 'It's my *real* name. Linda was . . . Linda was just something I called myself for a while. Okay?'

'Okay.'

At five they set off in a single mini-van. It was rush hour and it took half an hour to get from Kentish Town to Paddington and on to the Westway. Gabriele began to worry about being late. But then the traffic improved and they were clear, bowling along the A40 towards Oxford.

There was plenty of time. She should have realised. Max, for all his apparent vagueness, was an efficient organiser. In their undergraduate days at Essex, it was Max who'd arranged transport to Ban the Bomb marches, who'd joined the International Socialists, and made the first demands for student rights. Now he and Stephie were two of the six permanent residents of the house in Kentish Town. It was more of a community than a shared house, really. There were always people coming and going. Every two weeks meetings of the Kentish Town Housing Action Group were held in the living-room, and sometimes homeless people stayed on mattresses on the floor. Victims of oppression, as Max called them. Gabriele was proud of helping the homeless; it showed that one really cared. It was the practical application of one's beliefs: praxis.

At twilight they came into the centre of Oxford, and turned north on to the Banbury Road. After half a mile, Max pointed to the right. There was a sign: The Linden House Hotel.

They looked in through the gates. Already there was a large

crowd outside, chanting loudly. There were also some blue uniforms.

They did a U-turn and parked. Everyone was silent. Gabriele got calmly out of the van and slid her placard out of the back. It read: US MURDERERS – OUT OF VIETNAM.

Max said, 'We'll give it till eight-thirty. Then they'll all be in the dining-room. And the pigs might have gone away.'

Someone giggled nervously. 'They won't even realise what's happening.'

The tension eased. There was a flutter of conversation, and they walked jauntily through the gates to join the crowd of shouting demonstrators. Gabriele hoisted her placard and took up the chant of the crowd – *Fascist killers*! and *Win, win, Ho Chi Minh*! She began to feel high, as if she'd been drinking, yet her mind was perfectly clear.

Although the crowd numbered at least two hundred, Gabriele counted only six policemen keeping the doorway to the hotel clear. As the dinner guests arrived, prominent in their evening clothes, the crowd waved their banners and roared abuse. But it was all very good-natured. No one tried to press against the police or jostle the guests.

After ten minutes a large limousine drew up. The American ambassador. A faint mask-like smile on his face, the ambassador walked quickly into the hotel, professionally oblivious to the screams of the crowd. The cool indifference was irritating.

The stream of guests trailed off. The demonstrators looked bored and started talking in groups. Gabriele saw Max slip away, towards the van.

She followed and found him sliding a long metal crowbar from under a seat. 'To get in with,' he murmured.

Gabriele viewed it with surprise. She hadn't thought anything like that would be necessary. The idea of using a weapon-like object made her feel uneasy.

As they walked back towards the hotel she decided not to say anything. After all, a new strategy required new tactics. She wasn't going to be the one member of the group to be faint-hearted.

Stephie, Reardon and the others were waiting, with about fifteen of the Oxford contingent. Silently, they slipped away from the other demonstrators in ones and twos until they were gathered at the side of the building. Gabriele took a quick look back. The police were hidden from view by the remains of the crowd; they

11

had seen nothing. But then they weren't really looking.

A high wall with a closed gate barred the way to the floodlit hotel garden beyond. However the gate was unlocked, and they filed straight through into the garden and hid behind some large shrubs. The dining-room looked out on to the lawn and the diners were clearly visible through the tall french windows. The top table, Gabriele noted, was to the right. She decided to make straight for it when the time came. She gripped the handle of her placard more tightly. She wanted to wave it right under the ambassador's nose.

Max ran forward, followed by Stephie and Reardon, and pressed himself against the wall to one side of the windows. He seemed to be examining the door locks. He reached out and tried a handle. Clearly it was locked.

He strode out in front of the windows. With a slight shock Gabriele realised what he was going to do. He was swinging the crowbar in a great arc. It came forward and hit the glass with a bang. A small hole appeared in the window with cracks running in several directions.

Max twisted his head to look questioningly at Stephie, as if he couldn't understand why the glass hadn't shattered. Then Stephie stepped in front of the window and lobbed something heavy from her shoulder. A brick-like object hit the window with a great crash. Max put his hand through the glass and the next moment the window was open.

The sound of protesting astonished voices swelled out from the dining-room. The next moment the rest of the group were running forward, whooping and yelling. Gabriele caught the exhilaration. She pulled her hat further down over her face and, letting out a great shriek, ran for the window.

Inside, Gabriele almost fell over a huddle of people be.. ver something on the floor. She side-stepped them neatly and made for the top table, passing behind a long line of angry, startled, bemused faces. A man rose up in front of her, shouted 'Outrageous!' and put out his arm. Fending him off, Gabriele dived past, rounded the corner of the room and, placing herself behind the ambassador, held up her placard and began to shout: '*US out! Hands off Vietnam!*'

There was uproar. She saw Reardon on top of a long table, stepping none too carefully across the china. Stephie was running round the far side of the room, waving her placard like a maniac. The others were parading up and down, shouting their slogans above the din. Some held chairs in front of them, herding startled guests into a corner. But most of the guests sat stunned, waiting in impeccable British style for somebody to do something.

The surprise was total. Gabriele almost laughed at the guests' incredulous outrage.

The noise rose to a crescendo. A table was turned over; there was the crash of breaking china and cries of alarm as the diners shot to their feet and examined their clothes, dripping with wine and hot greasy food.

Gabriele danced along behind the top table, enjoying the sight of the appalled faces. A shout rose above the din. Reardon, his hair flaming red under the lights, stood on a table, a wine bottle held high in his hand, and slowly, solemnly tipped the bottle until the red wine spilled in a long stream on to the table and splashed up at the diners, who hastily withdrew, wiping at their clothes with their napkins.

'*The blood of the Vietnamese!*' Reardon screamed. '*Murdered by the US aggressors!*'

Gabriele cheered loudly. She saw Stephie force her way past Reardon and approach the top table. Stephie raised her placard in front of the ambassador who was getting to his feet in an attempt to leave. Seeing her, the ambassador turned his back. With a yell of anger, Stephie raised the placard and, reaching across the table, brought it down on the ambassador's head.

Gabriele saw the ambassador clap a hand to his head, then a sudden movement to the right caught her eye. Uniforms had appeared: three of the policemen from the front door. They went for Reardon, pulling him down from the table head first. Another grabbed Stephie, but she swung at him and clipped him smartly in the eye. He fell back, his hand to his face, and Stephie sprinted away.

Gabriele hesitated: should she fight or run? Through the pandemonium she saw Stephie and Max moving across the back of the room towards the windows.

Time to retreat then. Gabriele turned to run, but stopped dead. A group of guests were standing in the aisle, blocking her way. They looked angry and obstructive, and she had the unpleasant feeling they would try to prevent her from passing. She felt a moment's fear, a clutching claustrophobia.

She fought it and, calming herself, gritted her teeth and rushed them.

All but one, an obese round-faced man, fell back. The man made an attempt to grab her, but she struck out, shooting an elbow sharply into the obscenely large stomach. She heard him gasp.

Now the way was clear and she raced to the end of the long table, rounded the corner and made for the open window. The huddle of people she had stepped over were still intent on whatever lay on the floor. She paused and glanced down. It was an elderly man, his eyes closed, his head cradled in a woman's lap. Gabriele had a vivid image of the woman's lap, bright red, a vast pool of wetness that was obscenely bright against the pallor of her dress.

She hesitated, but then people were bumping past her and Max was dragging her away, yelling. 'Come *on*!' Dropping her placard, she ran for the garden gate.

She arrived panting at the van to find the others clambering in. As the engine fired with a roar, Stephie reached out to pull her up into the front seat. The van shot off and swerved round a corner, the open passenger door swinging wildly on its hinges. Gabriele clung to Stephie, shaking slightly, not yet brave enough to reach out for the door and pull it closed, thinking only of the pale man with the closed eyes and the white dress covered in blood.

But then Stephie laughed, a wild hoot of triumph, and Gabriele realised that she was right to be exhilarated: the demonstration had achieved everything they had hoped for, and more. It was the end of passivity, the beginning of a new movement. *She – they –* were part of it.

But what really astonished Gabriele was that it had been so easy.

They rounded a corner, the door of the van swung shut. She was safe. Catching the mood, she hugged Stephie and began to laugh.

Nick Ryder frowned in concentration and read the passage again. 'Underneath the conservative popular base is the substratum of the outsiders, the exploited and persecuted of other races and other colours, the unemployed and the unemployable. They exist outside the democratic process . . . Thus their opposition is revolutionary even if their consciousness is not.'

Ryder wondered if he was really understanding all this correctly. Did Marcuse mean that the underprivileged could be revolutionary without *knowing* it? Seemed highly unlikely. Or did he mean that their opposition justified *other* people being revolutionary *for* them?

He put the book down and yawned. He was too tired to read this sort of stuff tonight. It was difficult enough at the best of times. Although he was finally beginning to understand some of it. He opened his eyes and looked at the line of books on the mantelpiece. Marx, Engels, Fanon, Guérin . . . In two months he'd accumulated quite a library.

He marked his page and slid the copy of *One-dimensional Man* back among the other books.

Nine o'clock. It was the first time he'd been home before ten that week. It was a pity that nice girl Anne hadn't been free. She was a social worker and about the only one he'd ever met who didn't burst with good intentions or look like the back of a bus. In fact Anne was rather attractive. She'd said she had a meeting that night. He hoped that she wasn't feeding him a line.

He thought: What a suspicious mind you have. But then it went with being a policeman.

A nice hot bath was what he needed. He put on a record – *Traviata*, with Moffo and Tucker, and stood for a moment, letting the soft notes work their magic. Italian opera never failed to move him. His love of music had been the most amazing discovery of his life.

He never let on to the lads, though: they'd find it very curious.

He went into the bathroom and ran the hot water. The gas geyser hissed and roared and finally spat out a minute trickle of steaming water. From bitter experience he'd learnt that the hot water cooled off considerably during the twenty or so minutes the bath took to fill, so he added no cold.

The steam rose in wet curtains. It reminded him of the freezing bathroom at the back of the house in Barrow and his mam yelling at him to get the hell in before the water got cold. He hadn't been home in months, and probably wouldn't get round to it until summer. It was a bit of a chore now anyway. After four years the north seemed a lifetime away.

He went to the kitchen, which was so small you could reach everything while standing in one place, and poured himself a beer. He returned to the bathroom. It wasn't far. The flat consisted of a hall, bedsitting-room, kitchen and bathroom. For some time he'd been meaning to find himself something better. But, being in Lambeth, just across the river from Westminster, it was handy for the office. It was also very cheap.

Though the bath was only half full he was impatient and, undressing quickly, got in. Shivering, he lay back and felt the hot

15

water creep slowly up his body. In another five minutes, when the water covered his legs, it was going to be very pleasant indeed.

The phone rang.

Ryder breathed, 'I don't believe this.'

For a moment he lay still, considering whether to answer it. If it was the office they could go to hell. On the other hand, it might just be Anne . . .

He got out, grabbed a towel and padded wetly across the bedsitting-room to the phone.

A cheery, horribly familiar voice echoed down the earpiece. 'Hello, sport. Didn't disturb anything interesting, I trust?'

'Sod you, Conway. What is it?'

'Oxford. That Vietnam demo. A real fracas. Rampaged round the dining-room waving placards. About thirty or forty of them.'

Ryder sighed. 'The Oxford lads were warned, for Christsake. *Several* times . . .'

'I don't doubt it, mate, but the fact remains that it was a right cock-up. The *ambassador* got hit on the head. And there was an injury caused by a brick. Geezer's all right, but it could have been nasty. There's mutterings about bringing serious charges. Trouble is, they're short of customers—'

'Didn't they nab *any* of them?'

'Two, I think.'

'God, how many lads did they have on the job then?'

'They're not saying, but can't have been many, can it?'

Ryder was silent for a moment. 'I suppose they want some names tonight.'

'You got it.'

Wearily, Ryder went back to the bathroom and got dressed again. He should have known. This had happened before. It was the fault of the structure. There was no national police force, just a large number of county and borough forces, each, Ryder sometimes thought, more stubbornly independent than the next. You could give them all the information you liked, but you couldn't force them to act on it.

Names, they wanted, did they? Well, they were asking a lot. All the same, he was already turning some ideas over in his mind.

In 1968, as much as now, the work of Special Branch was deliberately unpublicised – not to say shrouded in secrecy – and the police liked to keep it that way.

It was generally believed that the three hundred or so officers of the Metropolitan Police Special Branch were merely the legmen for the Security Service – known to the public as MI5 – and indeed one of their main responsibilities was the arrest and charging of spies and subversives previously identified by the Security Service. But in fact Special Branch's brief went further, treading an uneasy line between pure police work and intelligence-gathering. Officially, the Branch had to keep an eye on undesirables – mainly foreign – entering and leaving the country, to help guard government ministers and foreign VIPs, and to investigate foreigners applying for naturalisation. But they were also expected to keep abreast of developments among the 'lunatic fringe' – the anarchists and the far-left and far-right extremists: those who were 'likely to threaten the country's security or to cause a breakdown of law and order'. Whereas MI5 dealt with foreign-linked plots and security leaks – counter-intelligence – the Special Branch kept tabs on home-grown trouble-makers.

Or tried to.

Ryder had transferred from Lancashire CID to Special Branch twelve months before and his speciality was Trotskyists.

He took a number 10 bus across the river and arrived at Scotland Yard shortly before ten. Special Branch was located on the seventh floor of the brand-new metal and glass tower block off Victoria Street that was the headquarters of the Metropolitan Police.

Ryder found Conway sitting in front of a heap of files.

'Oh *there* you are,' Conway said. 'The boss phoned. He wanted to know if this shemozzle was our fault.'

'You told him?'

'Yeah. He was somewhat relieved.'

Ryder took off his jacket. 'Any more news?'

'They've caught a few more. No names yet. But apparently they were local Oxford trouble-makers.'

'What about the two they nabbed?'

Conway handed him a file. 'Haven't got anything on one, name of Lampton, but there's a bit on the other, name of Reardon, Paul.'

Ryder took the file and remembered having seen it quite recently. Unlike other branches of the Criminal Investigation Department, Special Branch kept large numbers of files on people who had no form. In fact almost all the people the Branch were interested in had never been near a court of law, let alone a prison.

The file on Reardon was very thin. One four-line report on a slip of paper. It was no wonder Ryder had recognised it – he'd written it himself.

It read: Reardon, Paul. Date of birth: 17th April 1946. Student at LSE, 1964–67. Failed to sit finals. Feb 1968: Member of SSL Central Committee. Address: unknown as at February 1968.

Since Reardon had no passport, there were no further birth details or photographs, which Ryder would normally have obtained from the passport office.

Conway stared over Ryder's shoulder. 'There could have been less, I suppose.'

'Well, it's a damn sight more than there was before –' He almost said 'before I sorted it out' but didn't. Conway was well aware of the situation. Until recently there'd been quite a gap in the Branch's intelligence on the far left. Marxists, anarchists, and the Communist Party of Great Britain were covered by the relevant Branch sections, but the Trotskyist Section had got into a bit of a mess. The problem was that the Trots were increasingly difficult to keep track of. Some were still pro-Moscow, others vehemently anti-Moscow. The groups were continually splintering and merging, and almost impossible to categorise.

This Paul Reardon was on the committee of the SSL – the Socialist Students' League, a militant Trotskyist group, but violently anti-Moscow. It had been formed by a group of students at the London School of Economics – known in the Branch as the London School of Comics – an institution famous for its left-wing views. In the past LSE students had been revolutionary in an intellectual non-violent kind of way. But the Socialist Students' League was distinctly aggressive. That was why Ryder had opened a file on them.

Ryder examined the main file now and looked at the list of people suspected of membership of the SSL. It was impossible to be sure who the members were because the league was typically disorganised, charging no subscription and keeping no lists.

The list was very short, fifteen names, if that, and consisted of speakers at the two meetings that Ryder himself had attended. He tried another tack.

'What addresses have the two given?' he asked Conway.

'Home addresses. Reardon's in Birmingham. The other bloke – Lampton – in Cheshire.'

'What about occupations?'

'Market stallholders.'

That was a new one on Ryder. 'Oh, yes. What do they sell?'

'Second-hand books, apparently.'

'And they haven't given a London address?'

Conway looked at his notes and shook his head.

So, no lead to the other demonstrators that way. Ryder asked without optimism, 'Anything else to go on?'

Conway made a face. 'Well, the dinner guests did offer some descriptions. For what they're worth. You can imagine the sort of thing – student types, long hair, bearded, unkempt. *Really* helpful. But the assailant – the brick-lobber – was female, and the Oxford boys don't seem to have got her in custody. The description's a bit better.' Conway read from his notes. 'About twenty-five, long mousy hair, pale complexion, very thin, jeans, distinctive patchwork jacket covered in flowers.'

Ryder tried to fit the description to one of the names in the file, but couldn't.

Nothing for it then. It was time to go out and about.

Ten-thirty on a Saturday night was not the best time to find informants. As he left the Yard, Ryder resigned himself to the fact that he was unlikely to find any of his regular sources until late in the night, if then.

He began at the Carlton Arms, a pub off Gower Street, near one of the London School of Economics' halls of residence. Ryder had no trouble passing as a student. His fair wavy hair was down to his collar and he invariably wore jeans and an old denim jacket. He was twenty-six but could have been less. He had the classless anonymous look of a thousand other young men, which was just what he wanted.

The pub was crowded, mainly with students. But neither of the two men Ryder was hoping to see was there. He gave it ten minutes, until just before closing time, and hurried off to the Duchess of Teck nearby.

No one there either.

He didn't like pressurising his informants, and usually took care to make the whole process of giving information so casual that it was almost painless. But he needed those names.

Against his better judgement he went into a hall of residence off Endsleigh Place and asked for one of the men by name. Someone went to look for him. He was out. Ryder was almost relieved.

He found a callbox and phoned the flat where the second student lived. Also out.

It looked as though he'd have to wait until the next day.

Although there was always Nugent. He might be worth a try. Nugent had been at the LSE until he dropped out the previous year. He now lived on social security and, Ryder suspected, was heavily into drugs. Nugent lived in a flat in a rundown house in Upper Holloway and wasn't on the phone. It was a long way to go on the off-chance.

Ryder hesitated then, with a small sigh, set off for King's Cross to catch the Piccadilly Line north to Finsbury Park. It would probably be a wild good chase, but at least he would have left no stone unturned.

It was shortly before midnight by the time he got to the decrepit house where Nugent lived. The front door was open. The sound of loud beat music echoed across the street. Inside there was a party going on. About a dozen people were draped around a purple-lit room, in various stages of intoxication. There was a strong smell of grass.

Nugent was sitting on the floor, his lank Jesus-style hair falling forward over his face. He was smiling benignly. Ryder sat down beside him and raised his voice above the din. 'Hi.'

Grinning stupidly, Nugent made a valiant effort to focus. With a sinking heart, Ryder realised Nugent was more than well away, he was totally gone.

When Nugent finally spoke, it was to utter a stream of gibberish that was hard to make out over the noise, but seemed to involve a forthcoming Ying-Yang uprising and an Inner Space Adventure. Ryder nodded sagely. Then, without much hope, he shouted in Nugent's ear, 'D'you know Paul Reardon or someone called Lampton?'

Nugent made an effort to concentrate. 'Sure.'

'Where do they hang out?'

Nugent's eyes clouded over and took on a look that wasn't so much far away as out of sight.

'Who're their friends?' Ryder prompted.

'Friends, man? Who's got friends . . .?' Nugent giggled and nodded his head in time to the music.

Ryder repeated the question. For a moment Nugent ignored it, then turned abruptly and, his eyes suddenly hard and bright, said distinctly, 'Five smackers.'

Ryder thought: 'You're not so high as you seem, my friend. He said, 'Okay, but I'll want addresses.'

Nugent grinned. 'That's all I got, man. Try a house in Manor Road, Kentish Town. Can't remember the number . . . But the door's sort of purple.'

'Anything else?'

Nugent shook his head.

'What about a girl? Thin, tall, fair-haired. Wears a jacket covered in flowers.'

Someone passed Nugent a joint and he drew on it deeply. Ryder waited. Eventually Nugent mumbled with bad grace, 'Stephie. Same house, man.'

Ryder allowed himself a moment's satisfaction, then paid Nugent his five quid. If the information was good, it was cheap at the price.

Gabriele turned over and closed her eyes more tightly, but the morning light was bright and intrusive and she knew she wouldn't get back to sleep.

She had been dreaming of light, the light she had seen as a child: bright yellow summer light full of promise; the promise of fulfilments and pleasures and freedoms she could barely guess at, but which she knew with absolute certainty that she had to have. In the dream, however, the light was elusive, reduced to a few thin tantalising shafts that managed to find their way between the heavy oppressive curtains in the front room of the house where she had grown up.

Then, as in the dream now, every detail of the room was vivid in her mind. The curtains and the dark furniture pressed in on her, claustrophobic, devoid of life or hope, exuding blank despair. Tea was on the table: scones and heavy cream cakes, a pot of tea for her parents, milk for her. A pervasive deathly quiet, the clock sounding unnaturally loud on the mantelpiece. Her father reading, her mother bent over her embroidery. No one saying a word. Then for some reason Gabriele started to cry – she couldn't remember why – and her mother looked up in surprise. Gabriele asked for something – was it to go out and play? Or just to go for a walk? Or to be told a story? Or just to do something *different*? Whatever, the request was denied. With quiet and relentless patience her mother explained that the next day was a schoolday and she must rest.

And then the silence had closed in again, like a shroud.

Even now Gabriele tensed at the memory of her feelings: the intense frustration, the voiceless rage, the corrosive loneliness.

With an effort she pushed the memory out of her mind.

Opening an eye, she looked at her watch. Not even eight, and she hadn't got to sleep till three. She murmured 'Hell', and sat up naked on the edge of the bed. She reached for a towel and, wrapping it round herself, padded slowly out of the room.

Another memory nagged at her mind. Last night. The red-stained dress, the bleeding head. She still wasn't sure how she felt about that. Not happy anyway.

The kitchen was a mess. Glasses, bottles, saucers of ash lay everywhere. They'd talked for a long time last night. Then Stephie and Max had had a row – she couldn't even remember what it was about – and Max had stormed out. Gabriele wondered if he'd returned.

Her private supply of instant coffee was still behind the fridge where she'd hidden it. She looked in the cupboard for the muesli she'd bought the previous day. The packet was there. Empty. That was the trouble with living in a commune – people were apt to share things. The muesli wouldn't have been any good anyway – there was no milk. She settled for the coffee, strong and black.

Upstairs she tapped lightly on Stephie and Max's door and looked in. Stephie lay curled up in the bed alone. No Max. It must have been a big row.

Stephie was still fast asleep. Gabriele closed the door and went back to her own room. Tuning her transistor to Radio 4, she lay on the bed. The carefully enunciated voice of a BBC presenter talked about farming. An establishment voice. An audible reminder to the lower orders that the ruling class existed and was still firmly in control.

While she waited for the next news summary, she turned the radio down a little and, pulling a suitcase from under the bed, opened it and took out a book. She kept all her books in the case, otherwise they got borrowed and never returned.

She got back into bed and started to read. The book was entitled *The Revolutionary Society* and its author was an Italian philosopher named Petrini. She had already read the book twice. But there were still a number of passages she very much wanted to read again.

From the first reading, Petrini's ideas had impressed her deeply. He had taken the outworn ideas of the old left, discarded those that were flawed or unworkable, and advanced those which were manifestly based in truth. His observations, his logic, his conclusions were faultless. He had made that great leap of the imagination which took his theories beyond the half-baked ideas of the past, to a series of brilliantly original truths that actually related to people's needs.

Society was structured, according to Petrini, to serve the capitalist system . . . The establishment controlled the people's very existence . . . People were not seeing the real world, but what they had been trained to see. They were encouraged to want material things, TV sets, cars and washing machines, because those things effectively subdued them. Their time was filled with empty repetitive pursuits to stop them from thinking . . .

This was all so true that Gabriele could only shake her head and wonder why she'd never realised it before.

The way forward was not to improve the present structure, but to replace it. People needed to rediscover the world as a physical sensual extension of themselves, and to realise they need not be cogs in the machinery of a harshly unnatural and alien world.

To achieve this, all institutions – schools, universities, factories – had to be subverted, so that people would question the existence of those institutions, and see the truth.

Gabriele marked her favourite ideas with a pencil and turned over the corners of the pages, so that she could find them more easily. There was one particular passage that she kept returning to.

It said: 'The way forward for the political activist is to sharpen and crystallise attitudes on the two sides of capitalist society. The social contradictions must be exaggerated, so that people are able to see them for the first time.'

Contradictions must be exaggerated.

Sharpen and crystallise.

Gabriele liked those phrases. It was what the demonstration had been about – hardening attitudes to Vietnam, getting some action. Yes: sharpen and crystallise. She underlined the words twice.

The voice on the radio had changed. She turned it up. The end of a programme. Finally, the news.

It was the third item. There had been a violent demonstration at a dinner in a hotel in Oxford. The US ambassador had been slightly injured . . . Another man still in hospital . . . Five people charged.

Gabriele's first feeling of elation at making the national news evaporated. They hadn't mentioned the *point* of the demonstration. Typical of the Establishment to conceal the facts. She thought bitterly: I should have known. She turned off the radio with an angry snap.

At least the man with the bleeding head hadn't been badly injured or they'd have said so. And as for Pete and Paul, they'd be okay. They'd get bail and be charged with causing a breach of the peace or whatever the quaint terminology was. There'd be a fine and a reprimand. And that would be that. No great deal. In fact, rather a feather in their caps. Neither of them would give away any names, of that she was sure. It was just bad luck – or good luck, depending on the way you looked at it – that they'd been the ones to get caught.

She heard a sound and looked up sharply.

A tall black man stood in the doorway. She relaxed. 'Hello, Tobago. Didn't know you were here.'

'Just short of a bed. So I helped myself to a mattress last night. Hope it was okay.'

She nodded, 'Sure.' Tobago was currently homeless and, when the pressures of the temporary accommodation the council had fixed up for him and his four-child family became too much, he grabbed a mattress on the floor somewhere. He knew where the spare key was hidden, underneath the dustbins round at the back.

'So, what's the news?' she asked.

Tobago came in and sat on the end of the bed and she settled back and half-listened to the long involved story of his struggle with the incomprehensible local authority system.

Suddenly a loud knock sounded on the front door below. Gabriele frowned. Who could it be at this hour on a Sunday?

She said, 'Go and see to it, would you, Tobago? And if it's anyone wanting help, tell them to come back later.'

He went out, pulling the door behind him. She heard him padding softly down the stairs and opening the door.

There were voices.

She sat up, very still, very tense.

A shout and the sound of feet . . .

Alarmed, she jumped out of bed and looked for something else to put on. There was no time. She could hear *dozens* of feet now, hammering up the stairs. Hastily she pulled the towel more tightly round her and tied the ends into a knot.

The door burst open and Tobago came in. 'It's the fuzz!'

She pushed past him and looked out of the door.

Men were streaming up the stairs, running purposefully. Already they were barging into the upper rooms.

Retreating into the bedroom, Gabriele slammed the door and stood there, panting with rage. She should do something. But *what*?

Tobago murmured, 'Shit, I don't need this—!'

The door opened with a bang and two tall figures stood in the doorway.

'Right,' said one, 'I have a warrant to search these premises . . .' He rattled rapidly through the technicalities.

Gabriele watched incredulously. She'd never seen a small-minded bureaucratic Hitlerite in action before. It was unbelievable.

The second man pointed at Tobago. 'You! Downstairs!'

Gabriele shouted, 'Leave him alone. He's done nothing!'

The first one turned in exaggerated surprise. 'Oh? And how do you know that, love?'

The outrage shot through Gabriele. 'Don't you *love* me!'

The policeman took a step forward and said condescendingly, 'Now, let's be a good girl and get dressed.'

'Not with you looking on, you dirty little man!'

'Believe it or not, I wasn't planning to watch,' he said with heavy sarcasm. 'Anyway, I didn't think you lot minded that sort of thing.'

'My God –! Go to hell!'

She went to the bed and, slowly and deliberately, got in.

The first policeman sighed. Gesturing to the other man, the two of them got either side of the bed and pulled her out. Their hands were firm and uncompromising on her arms. Gabriele thought: I can't take this.

She knew what she should do: stay *cool*. And for a moment she did manage to fight off the claustrophobia and stay passive. But then, as they pulled her to her feet, the panic rose in her, white hot and angry, and, catching them unawares, she pulled free and lashed out. There was a brief satisfying *ughh!* as her elbow hit soft flesh. She grabbed for her alarm clock, a heavy round metal one, and swung it through the air. It caught one man on the side of the head and his hand shot up to clutch the wound.

Then both men recovered from their surprise and their hands tightened like vices on her arms. She felt a new wave of panic and lashed out with her feet. But they were pushing her down and down, backwards. The bed came up against her back until she was lying helplessly on the mattress.

Suddenly a weight descended on her middle and with a shock she realised that one of them was *sitting* on her.

'*Get off!* You bastard, get *off!*'

'No chance,' came the reply. 'Not until you promise to come downstairs quietly.'

Gabriele felt the bitter taste of humiliation. She must look like a complete fool.

Four more people came into the room, including two women in plain clothes. One man started searching the room, but the others came over to the bed and regarded her coldly. She realised they were going to move her by force. One of the women asked, 'Well, are you going to come quietly then?'

Gabriele shook with anger. 'If you lay a hand on me, I'll kill you.'

'That's not very sensible, is it?' said the woman. Then, without another word, they went for her arms.

Ryder stood a little way up the street and waited impatiently. It was the right house, he was sure of that. Not only was it the only one with a purple door, but he'd checked on the place very carefully at six that morning, first with the newsagent on the corner, then with an early-rising neighbour. Both knew that the place was inhabited by hippy-type students. The *Ban the Bomb* and *US Out of Vietnam* posters in the windows had confirmed it.

Nevertheless the right address was no guarantee that the brick-lobbing Stephie would actually be there, and he watched the house impatiently.

He wondered what was taking so long. The raiding party – all Special Branch officers – should have got the inmates out by now.

Noise started coming from the house: shouts, some abusive language, and the crash of furniture. A moment's silence then a long agonised scream echoed across the street. Ryder shivered. What the hell was going on in there?

The front door opened and Ryder stood back so that he wouldn't be seen. First a black man was escorted down the steps and into a car. Ryder was surprised. There were no black activists in this group, neither had a black activist been seen at the demonstration. Next came a stream of ragged, jeans-clad individuals.

Ryder counted ten of them. Good God, how many lived in the place? Finally a thin girl with long mousy hair and a flowered jacket came sullenly down the steps. Ryder allowed himself a moment of self-congratulation. *Stephie.* Perhaps she was the one who had screamed.

They were driven away. Ryder ran up the steps and into the house. The remainder of the raiding party would be searching the place by now, and he wanted to see if they had found anything in the way of political tracts and pamphlets.

He pushed open the door and nodded to the officer in the hall. The officer, a constable of about twenty-three, made a face and indicated upstairs. Another scream reverberated through the house and Ryder looked upwards.

A group of four officers, two of them women, were at the top of the stairs, descending slowly, a thrashing figure in their midst. All Ryder could see were some long bare legs kicking out wildly from behind the leading policeman. Then he glimpsed a head twisting from side to side, the long dark hair obliterating the face. The unsteady group finally reached the bottom of the stairs and Ryder stood back. In the space of the hall the group opened up and Ryder saw that the girl was tall and slender and that she was covered by nothing but a towel.

The girl sobbed and writhed and all of a sudden the towel was on the floor. Ryder had a momentary impression of a slim lithe body and a pair of firm white breasts. Then he looked away.

A male voice shouted viciously, 'Leave that!'

Ryder looked back and saw that one of the women was reaching for the towel. The male voice snapped again, *'Leave that!* Just get her in the van!'

Ryder muttered 'For Christsake . . .' as the men half lifted the writhing body out of the door. The girl let out a long low moan, as if in pain, and then she was being carried down the steps and into the street in full view of the staring onlookers. At last she was bundled ignominiously into a police car, and handed back her towel. Ryder felt a spasm of shame.

The officer in the hall was nodding as if the whole thing was to be expected and Ryder realised that it hadn't occurred to him to look the other way. Ryder asked, 'Was that really necessary?'

The man regarded him with surprise. 'She was resisting arrest, sarge. What do you expect the lads to do?'

'I know, but . . .' He shook his head.

'Come on, sarge. She's not shy. I mean it's all free love for them, isn't it?' He lowered his voice. 'Besides, *she* was shacked up with the West Indian. I mean . . .' He gave a knowing wink.

Ryder sighed inwardly. Sometimes he thought he was in entirely the wrong job.

Two

The valley lay behind the downs, a rich pocket of verdant pasture and tranquil woodland tucked between the long ridges of the chalk hills. A narrow road, no more than a lane, ran from the main Salisbury road down into the valley, arriving, after many twists and turns, at Cherbourne St Mary, a pretty unspoilt village built of soft grey Wiltshire stone and boasting a particularly fine early Gothic church.

Victoria Danby drove slowly through the village, which appeared to be totally deserted. But then it was Saturday, and still early. She glanced at the estate agent's directions balanced on her knee. Another mile. At first she thought she'd missed the turning but then it appeared, a rough road off to the left with a large *For Sale* board on the corner.

The track was full of pot-holes and she had to weave the Mini from side to side to avoid the worst craters. She wondered if the estate agent would be there yet.

She angled the driving mirror towards her face and took a quick look. She grimaced in despair. Wild fair hair hopelessly frizzy, an undistinguished nose that she'd always disliked and far too many freckles. An angry spot on her right cheek glowed conspicuously through the cover-up stuff she'd applied that morning, and there were signs of another brewing on the other cheek. It was horribly unfair. Almost as unfair as eating nothing but one bowl of home-made muesli – no sugar, skimmed milk – twice a day and staying at a remorseless eleven stone.

The track ran between tantalisingly high hedgerows that hid the ploughed fields on either side, then threaded its way into the latticed shadows of a delicate woodland. Elms sprinkled with buds of palest green reached overhead in tall archways. As the end of the tunnel grew near Victoria caught a glimpse of sunlit meadows ahead, and then the Mini emerged into the open.

Victoria stopped the car and stared. She remembered the estate agent's details – two lower pastures fed by a stream, two fields of cereals, and some medium-quality grazing on the higher land. Twenty acres in all. Not a lot. In fact it was more of a smallholding than a farm.

But the house!

It lay at the end of a small valley, just above the stream, and was bound on two sides by rising ground. She loved it instantly. It was built of mellow grey stone with two dormer windows set into a slate roof. According to the agent it was a hundred and fifty years old, but it looked as though it had been there for ever, staring serenely across the tranquil valley.

Victoria just *knew* the others would love it too.

She drove on. The track dropped down into the valley through rich pastureland, passed over the stream at a narrow stone bridge, and rose up to the house. She parked in front of the house on rough gravel and, getting out, wandered round to the side where various sheds and outbuildings surrounded a concrete yard. Beyond were hen houses and a kitchen garden full of overgrown vegetables. She strode past the garden and up the hill, climbing higher and higher until she paused, panting, near the top. From here it was possible to see the whole property spread out below. Small, yes – but it had everything they would need to be self-sufficient. Well, *almost*.

High on the opposite side of the valley was the woodland through which she had driven. It had the effect of screening off the farm from the neighbouring property, making it somehow self-contained, almost *secret*. Victoria liked that.

In fact she liked everything about it.

At the same time she must be rational. It was a big decision. But if there was a catch, she couldn't see it. There was work to be done, obviously, things like painting and clearing up and general repairs, but that was part of the attraction, part of the challenge. Anyway, with eight people to do the work nothing would take very long.

She strolled along the side of the hill, picking at wild spring flowers, basking in a sense of contentment and home-coming. This was going to be the best thing that had ever happened to her, she just *knew* it.

The stillness was broken by the sound of a car bouncing down the track to the house.

The estate agent. Victoria ran down the hill and found an earnest young man getting out of his car.

He stared at her and blinked in surprise. 'Miss Danby?'

Victoria said a firm 'Yes', and realised he was taken aback by her age – or was it her clothes? Both probably. She looked younger than twenty-five and she was wearing one of her more psychedelic flower dresses. Doubtless he'd been expecting a farming type with brogues and a headscarf.

She said, 'It was nice of you to come on a weekend.' She offered him a spring violet. 'Have a flower.'

The young man took the flower awkwardly, then nodded in a knowing way, as if the tiny violet gave a clue to Victoria's appearance. News of the flower power movement had obviously reached this corner of Wiltshire.

They went into the house. The kitchen was dark and dirty, but Victoria was delighted to see that it had hardly been modernised at all. There was a coal-fired range, two stone sinks, a cool larder and, best of all, a large scrubbed kitchen table. The two living-rooms each had a ghastly thirties-style tiled fireplace, but these could soon be ripped out to reveal the originals underneath. Upstairs the four bedrooms had dark paint and gruesome wallpaper, but that could be stripped off in no time. Mentally she allotted the nicest bedroom to herself and Mel.

In the main hall was a door which led down some steep stone steps to a pair of large cellars, dark and cool, ideal for storing fruit and vegetables.

They went outside again. Victoria stood back and imagined the house in a year or so's time. Inside, everything would be bare wood and bright paint and Indian rugs. In the outhouses they'd have their craft workshops and storage for the farm implements. On the land they'd have goats and pigs, a few cows, a field of vegetables, an orchard of fruit. They'd work hard all day, and have discussions in the evenings, and music and singing . . .

It would be a real community.

'I'll take it.'

'Pardon?' said the agent. 'Er – you don't want a survey . . . or a look at the yields?'

'I'll take it, just as it is.' She smiled at her own rashness. Also at the pleasure in having surprised this rather straight-laced young man.

As she drove away she stopped and looked back.

Hunter's Wood. That was its name.

Hunter's Wood. Still and benign in the clear morning light.

She thought: I love it already.

Sir Henry Northcliff put down his pen and sighed. He wished that they weren't having to go out to lunch. He would have preferred to have had a light meal at home, gone for a walk on Hampstead Heath, and spent a quiet afternoon by the fire.

There was a soft knock and Caroline put her head round the door. 'We should leave in half an hour.'

He nodded. 'I'll have finished by then.' They smiled at each other. Whenever Henry looked at Caroline he was amazed by his good fortune. It seemed quite extraordinary that this lovely creature should be his wife.

He motioned her in and she came quickly over to the desk. They gripped hands. 'Six months tomorrow,' she smiled.

'And they said it wouldn't work.'

Their marriage had certainly been talked about. The wedding had been as quiet as possible and had taken place a good four months after Henry's divorce had come through, but it had made no difference. All the newspapers had carried the story, some with pictures. The gossips in Parliament and Lincoln's Inn had enjoyed a field day. It wasn't every day that the Attorney-General got married, and to a girl half his age. He knew what people were saying: that he was making a fool of himself. He knew equally well that it wasn't true.

'Will you have to work this evening?' Caroline asked.

There was a pile of legal gazettes which he should glance through, but he was loath to work that evening. With two dinners, a late meeting at Number Ten and a lot of paperwork to catch up on he'd been busy every evening that week. He replied, 'No.'

'Good! I didn't pursue you all these years never to see you at *all*.'

She touched his hand and left. He reflected on her 'pursuit' of him. It was utter rubbish, of course. Caroline was incapable of anything more forceful than calm resolve, and she had resolved to love him quietly and patiently from the time she was eighteen. He hadn't been aware of it then, of course. She was, after all, only a child, the daughter of a friend who had died long ago. But when his empty marriage had finally drawn to its long overdue conclusion, she had been there, quiet and understanding, the one person he felt at peace with. It was a year before he'd realised that she was right about the enormous age difference – that it didn't matter a bit. When they'd eventually married she had been twenty-five, he fifty. They had been exceptionally happy ever since.

The phone rang. It was David Garner, the Director of Public Prosecutions. David took many decisions with only the briefest reference to Henry, but anything with political overtones, anything that might 'develop', anything remotely sensitive, these things were brought straight to Henry as Attorney-General.

Henry had been so busy during the week, working on some proposed legislation the government wanted rushed through, that he and David had not been able to discuss all the outstanding business.

Henry guessed – correctly – that this call would involve the Oxford demonstration which had occurred several days before, on the previous Saturday. He pulled the file towards him and opened it.

'A total of thirty students have been charged now, all on breach of the peace charges,' the DPP began. 'But one has been positively identified with *both* assaults. A girl named Stephanie Kitson, who was seen to throw the brick which broke the window and injured the dinner guest. And also seen to whack the ambassador over the head.'

'And how *are* the victims?' asked Henry.

'The ambassador has a bruise on his forehead, but nothing more. Thank *goodness*. The other guest is recovering, apparently. No permanent damage, but several stitches in his head. There'll be a medical report, of course.'

'So, has this girl caused any trouble before?'

'No, but the police have successfully opposed bail – she's liable to disappear, so they think. She keeps announcing that she doesn't recognise their authority.'

Henry said, 'I see. Now, there were no other assaults. Is that right?'

'Correct. But some demonstrators held up chairs and waved them threateningly, others brandished banners, a table was overturned. So far only two people have been positively identified with these antics – names of Reardon and Lampton.'

'And neither has any previous form?' Henry asked.

'No, nothing at all.'

Henry thought for a moment. Violence during political demonstrations was a relatively recent phenomenon in Britain, one that was extremely distasteful to the average citizen, and he knew that the government were very keen to stamp on it hard. Particularly when an ambassador had been assaulted – and the US ambassador at that. It was politically extremely embarrassing and the press had been making a meal of it both in Britain and abroad.

And yet political considerations weren't really the overriding factor here. The point was, these demonstrators had to realise that they were subject to the law like everyone else, and that their political views did not excuse their actions in any way at all. Innocent dinner guests had a right to dine without being assaulted and abused. Besides, a man had been wounded. That on its own merited a serious charge.

'Right,' he said finally, 'if you're satisfied as to the evidence, let's go for actual bodily harm, assault and criminal damage for the brick-throwing lady. For the two who brandished chairs, affray. For the rest we'll have to leave it at breach of the peace. For the moment anyway.'

'Okay. Oh, and there's another girl out on bail, name of Linda Wilson' – the DPP laughed shortly – 'why are *women* getting so aggressive suddenly?'

Henry grunted in mystification.

'Anyway,' continued the DPP, 'they can't pin her to the demonstration. No positive identification at this stage. But they want to charge her anyway, with assaulting a police officer and resisting arrest.'

Henry asked, 'Where did they arrest her?'

'At a house in North London in the early hours of last Sunday, I think. The place where they found the Kitson girl.'

Henry could imagine it, the police rushing in, waking the occupants, giving them the fright of their lives. In his days at the Bar he'd defended enough people to know the outrage they felt at being hauled out of bed early in the morning, particularly if they were not habitual criminals.

'What sort of form did the assault take?'

There was the rustle of papers at the other end of the line. 'Er – an alarm clock to the head.'

Well, I'll have a look at that evidence in more detail, but my instinct is to forget about that one and concentrate on the offences

33

at the demonstration itself. What do you think?'

They discussed it for a few minutes, and agreed the basic principles.

When the DPP had rung off, Henry considered the last matter of the Wilson girl. Yes, he was sure it was right to drop the charges. The student might have had a vindictive motive for assaulting a police officer but she could just as easily have been terrified out of her life. Besides in the eyes of the public and more particularly the media, dawn raids smacked of fascist tactics, and he didn't want to add fuel to that flame.

It was almost time to leave. He put the papers he'd been working on in his briefcase and tidied his desk. There was an hour and a half's drive ahead, just to go to a lunch with people he suspected he wasn't going to like very much. County types, rich. But they were distant cousins of Caroline's – second cousins by marriage, he seemed to remember – and she'd gone to stay there a lot when she was a schoolgirl. He must put a good face on it.

He went into the hall and found Caroline waiting with his coat. 'It's a lovely day,' she said. 'It'll be nice to get out into the country for a bit.' She shot an anxious look at him. 'I'm sorry if you're dreading it – I hope it won't be too boring.'

'I'm sure it won't.' He touched her cheek. 'Just give me a subtle kick in the shins when my eyes glaze over.'

It was either back to London or home to pick up her record player. Victoria decided on the record player. She could give Mel and the others the news by phone and tell them all the details when she got back to London.

Going home meant seeing her parents, of course. They wouldn't like her buying the farm, not at all. In fact, the thought of how intensely they wouldn't like it made Victoria feel a little nervous. But then she wouldn't tell them, not today anyway. She'd do it by letter during the week.

Cawsley Hall lay half an hour away on the edge of the Cotswolds, near the Wiltshire-Gloucestershire border, an imposing property situated at the end of a long drive in two hundred and fifty acres of park, paddock, and farmland. The house itself was a small but excellent example of early eighteenth-century Palladian architecture and, though the Danby family liked to think they'd lived there for ages, they had, in fact, only been in the house since 1890 when Alfred Danby, the son of a Bristol shopkeeper, made his first fortune from brewing.

As the house came into view Victoria winced. There were several strange cars parked in the front drive. She sighed. Week-end guests. She should have checked. She left the Mini out of sight at the side of the house near the walled garden and went in by a side door. She walked quickly through the gun-room, across the back hall and began to climb silently up the back stairs.

'Tor?'

Victoria spun round, then relaxed as she saw her sister in the hall below. 'God!' she exclaimed. 'I thought you were Mother.'

Diana giggled and shook her head. 'I saw your car. How *are* you? How's – *things?*'

'Are there many guests?'

'About four staying. But there'll be lots more for lunch.'

Victoria made a face and sat disconsolately on the stairs. 'Bother!' She hated parties, at least the sort her parents gave.

'It's all best behaviour stuff,' Diana went on. 'The county's coming – the Lord Lieutenant and Sir Harry Mortimer and the Gordons. *And* the Ranfurleighs! A coup for Mother.' She rolled her eyes. 'And of course there'll be Caroline and Henry—'

'Caro and Henry!'

'They're the *star* guests.'

Victoria was astonished. 'But Mother didn't *tell* me! *Honestly!*'

In the old days Victoria had often asked Caroline home for the summer holidays. Mother had tolerated the visits because Caroline was a distant relation, but there were other school friends she would have preferred Victoria to bring home. Now, ever since her marriage, Caroline was suddenly a bosom member of the family. Sometimes Victoria was amazed at her mother's transparency.

She said angrily, 'I mean, *honestly*, Di – Caro's *my* friend.'

Diana shrugged. 'Maybe. But Mother's been trying to get them down to lunch ever since the wedding . . .'

The sound of voices came echoing down a corridor. Victoria braced herself as Mrs Danby came into the hall carrying a vase of flowers.

'Ah, so you've decided to come after all! *Well* . . .' Mrs Danby looked at Victoria's clothes and made a visible effort to restrain herself.

Victoria said, 'I didn't know you were having a lunch party.'

'Oh yes you did. I told you. *Months* ago.'

Victoria vaguely remembered her mother mentioning it. 'But you didn't say Caro and Henry were coming.'

Immediately Mrs Danby was on the defensive. 'Well, darling, what if they *are*? We're very fond of them. Daddy and I have been trying to get them down for *ages*.'

'But—'

'Goodness gracious! I should have thought you'd be delighted. You haven't seen them in months, have you?'

Victoria dropped her eyes. How could she explain to Mother that it hadn't occurred to her to impose on Caroline's new life.

'Well, since you *are* here,' continued Mrs Danby. 'Daddy and I want to talk to you.'

Victoria had a sudden premonition of what was coming.

'Mr Rawlinson phoned me,' her mother said quietly and firmly, 'and he told me you had some funny ideas about Granny's trust.'

Victoria stared. She didn't think solicitors were allowed to tell tales. She protested mildly, 'But it's nothing to do with anyone else.'

Mrs Danby blinked at her. 'I beg your pardon.'

Victoria drew a deep breath and said with growing uncertainty, 'I can invest the capital in Granny's trust more or less as I like.'

'Well – !' Mrs Danby said with authority. 'I don't think that's true, Victoria—'

'Yes, it is.'

Her mother stiffened. There was a silence. Eventually she said coldly, 'I see. And what exactly are you planning to invest it in?'

'A farm.'

'A *farm*?' Mrs Danby exclaimed. 'Why a *farm* for goodness sake?'

Victoria said earnestly, 'Because I want to work on the land, to create things. To' – she searched for the right expression – 'to lead a meaningful life . . .'

'Ah!' Her mother pounced. 'Now, *wait* a minute. This isn't *you*, is it, Victoria? It's someone else who's been putting these ideas into your head. Am I right? A – *friend* – perhaps?'

'No.' Victoria lied. She'd never told Mother about Mel. Mel had hair down to his shoulders, wore embroidered clothes and had no job. She added defensively, 'Although certain friends *are* going to help me. It's going to be a co-operative.' The word sounded better than a commune.

Mrs Danby sighed long and loud, an expression of exasperation and exhausted tolerance. 'Well, I don't intend to discuss this any more *now*. I've got lunch to worry about. But I really think you're being exceedingly thoughtless, Victoria. *Exceedingly*.'

When she'd gone Diana said, 'Oh dear.'

'She can't stop me,' Victoria said unhappily. 'I can do it, Di. And I'm jolly well going to.'

A loud buzz of conversation was coming from the open door of the drawing-room. Going into rooms full of people had always filled Victoria with dread. She remembered all those agonising parties in her teens when, feeling huge and whale-like in some ghastly unsuitable dress, she'd clung to a wall, totally ignored, or been dragged across the middle of a room by the hostess, like a prize specimen across a show ring, to be introduced to someone who wasn't in the least interested in talking to her.

Some fears never faded. She drew a deep breath and went in. Her mother spotted her and, putting on her best hostess's face, came bustling over. 'Well!' she said tightly. 'Don't you look splendid, Victoria dear. Just like a Red Indian, with that' – she indicated the bright scarlet bandeau Victoria had tied round her head – 'thing! *Very* exotic!' She took Victoria's arm and cast round a little desperately.

At the far side of the room Victoria could see Caroline and Henry in a group of five or six people. Before she could move towards them her mother gripped her arm and, pushing her firmly sideways, said hastily, 'Come and talk to the brigadier for me, will you?'

The manoeuvre was too late; a brittle-faced woman was standing in front of them, waiting for an introduction. 'Ah, Lady Ranfurleigh,' Mrs Danby said with a nervous laugh, 'have you met my *other* daughter?' Then, retrieving the situation triumphantly: 'She's our *exotic* one, you know!'

Victoria thought: I'm going to scream.

Some drinks appeared. Victoria grabbed a gin and tonic and downed it in three. Lady Ranfurleigh was saying how colourful Victoria looked and how the young seemed to think they were the first young people ever to rebel, but of course that just wasn't true. She herself had been a bit wild in her time and worn rather a daring frock to the Savoy.

Spotting her father nearby, Victoria mumbled an excuse and backed away. She stood, uncertain, in front of him and said, 'Hello, Daddy.'

He smiled at her, blinking rapidly. 'Hello, old thing. What a surprise.'

In a surge of affection she reached out and hugged him awkwardly.

'I say, old girl. Well, well . . .' Embarrassed, he pulled gently but hastily back and patted her arm. 'You . . . er . . . keeping all right?'

'Daddy, I –' She looked into his face and grasped at the essential kindness behind it. 'Daddy, can I – *talk* to you later?'

A look of alarm came over his face, one she recognised well. She knew then that it was hopeless.

'A bit overdrawn, are you, old thing? Eh? Need some new clothes? Well, don't worry, I'll look after it . . .' He glanced away. Then, murmuring 'There's a good girl, there's a good girl', he was gone.

She stood still for a moment, working hard to make herself calm, then took another drink from a passing tray. It tasted good. She made her way round the edge of the room, head down to avoid strangers, and found herself in front of some canapés. She wolfed down half a dozen, then a few more, and felt better.

She found Caro and Henry still in a tight group. Someone was talking loudly about government policy on law and order and Henry was nodding vaguely, his eyes glazed with polite disinterest. Caroline was listening intently, her head inclined towards her neighbour. Victoria tugged at her sleeve.

Caroline turned and broke into a warm smile. 'Tor! How lovely to see you. I was wondering where you were. Gosh, it's been *so* long!'

As they talked Victoria was struck, as always, by Caroline's calm assurance. She had a rock-like core of honesty and serenity. Integrity: that was what she had. Victoria thought admiringly: She's everything I'm not.

Someone touched Victoria's arm. It was Henry. 'Well, well, how are *you*?' He kissed her warmly on the cheek. Victoria was pleased and flattered. She'd only met Henry three times, and she'd been a bit frightened of him. Yet here he was greeting her like an old friend. She smiled at him and wondered why she hadn't realised before how very nice he was.

He leant down and whispered conspiratorially, 'Good thing for everybody that you're here. You bring the average age in this room down at least thirty years.'

Victoria laughed and lurched to one side. She recovered, flushing with embarrassment. The gin had gone to her head. Henry looked politely away.

Lunch was interminable. On Victoria's right was the old brigadier. His breath smelled of whisky and stale tobacco. 'I say, rather like the garb!' he kept saying, as he eyed her dress. 'You a *flower* child, are you? Or a hippy? Never quite sure what the difference is meself. Tell me – d'you believe in all this make-love-not-war thing? I mean, it's all very well, but people will never stop being *aggressive*, y'know. Take it from me! I was a soldier.'

Victoria took a second, larger, helping of chocolate mousse and washed it down with more white wine. Her elbow slipped off the table and she realised she'd drunk a little too much.

In a moment of self-honesty of which she was rather proud she thought: No, not a *little* too much, a *lot* too much.

'What are you up to nowadays, Victoria?' It was a young man sitting opposite, the son of a local landowner.

'Setting up a collective farming project.' It sounded wonderful, put like that, except that she seemed to be having trouble getting the words out in a nice tidy row.

'Is that one of these *commune* things?' chortled the brigadier. 'Free love and all that? Gosh, all right if you can get it!' He leered at Victoria.

The young man said loudly, 'I knew a chap once who went potty and gave up everything to live in a sort of commune. Because the world had too many possessions or *something*. But really he wanted to opt out. Couldn't face responsibility. He was nutty as a fruit cake, of course. Quite mad.'

'Oh, I don't know,' hooted the brigadier. 'Got the *free love*, didn't he? Can't have been that potty!' He turned to Victoria and winked.

She stared, aghast. 'You think that's what it's all about! You think we – do it for *that*!' Her anger flowed out, white-hot and unsteady, a long passionate jumble of justification and explanation. Words mixed themselves up inexplicably, syllables jumped out of sequence, but she rushed on. 'We try to *care* about each other which is more than anyone usually does. *Society* – is so selfish an' *money*-centred. An' people pay *lip* service – about caring – but they *don't*. Not *really*. And peace. We care about *peace* and we make an *effort* to stop war. Which is more than any of the governments do. An' as for love – yes, sex if you like – it's open an' free an' *kind*.

Better than being hidden away an' joked 'bout an' *dirty* like *you* think it is . . .'

She suddenly became aware of her own voice unnaturally loud and ugly in her ears. Around her was an eerie silence.

At the far end of the long table there was a frozen, if blurred, tableau. Her mother's face, appalled and reproachful. Lady Ranfurleigh's, averted and embarrassed. And Henry, who was looking sympathetic and a little pained.

Victoria said under her breath, 'Oh shit!'

Conversations started to pick up again and Victoria stared hard at her plate, thinking: I don't care. And knowing perfectly well that she did.

After a few minutes she pushed back her chair and stumbled out of the room.

Caroline found her on her bed, crying miserably, and said quietly, 'Oh, *Tor.*'

'I'm sorry,' Victoria said, with all the dignity she could muster. 'I didn't mean to be an embrass –' she took another shot at it '– an embarr-*ass-ment* to you both.'

'Oh, never mind about *that*. What about you? Is there something the matter?'

'It's just – they were laughing at my farm. They think it's a joke. No one believes – or understands . . . No one's really *interested* . . .'

'But *I'm* interested, Tor. A *farm*? I'd love to hear about it. In fact' – she paused slightly, as if making up her mind – 'why don't you come over in the week and tell me about it?'

Victoria eyed her uncertainly, trying to suppress the dizziness. 'But – surely you're busy. I mean – aren't you?'

'I'm usually free for lunch. And sometimes in the evenings too. Henry often has to dine out. It'd be fun.' She patted Victoria's hand. 'Really.'

Victoria blinked and, gripping Caroline's hand, said, 'You know – you're very kind. Did you know that? Always have been. V-e-r-y kind.' She tried to bring Caroline back into focus, but without success. She shook her head and said in a small voice, 'Oh, Caro. Why's it all so difficult?'

Three

The British people had no idea how lucky they were.

Nick Ryder read the *Guardian*'s front page. He'd already gone through *The Times* and the *Telegraph*. There were serious riots in Paris, and the French had brought out the CRS riot police. The CRS weren't known for their gentleness and consideration – they went straight in with batons and tear gas and walloped you on the head. No British easy-easy tactics there.

But Nick wanted to understand the nature of this trouble. It had been started by the students – but why?

At eleven he went out and bought *Le Monde* from the newsstand at Victoria station. His French wasn't that good but he was able to get the gist of it. Three days ago, on the Friday, someone – either the Rector of Paris University or the Minister of Education – had called in the police to clear five hundred protesting students from a sit-in at the Sorbonne. By nightfall there were running battles all over the Latin Quarter. Hundreds had been wounded and almost six hundred arrested. The next day, Saturday, four students had been given two months in prison: unusually heavy sentences by any standards.

But what had caused the trouble in the first place? Nick ploughed through the editorials and after half an hour had the consensus of opinion. Gross overcrowding in the universities, childish old-fashioned rules, paternalistic overbearing university authorities . . . Yes, that would be enough to set most students off.

But was there more to it than that?

He called the DST in Paris, the French equivalent of a combined Special Branch and Security Service, and, after a long wait, spoke to the English-speaking liaison man, Claude Desport.

Nick began smoothly, 'Just wondered if there was any information you needed? Any way we could help?'

Desport replied wearily that he would appreciate a watch on the ports. 'We already have German, Italian and Dutch anarchists and Trotskyists,' he explained. 'You might as well let us know when your agitators are going to arrive.'

'We're keeping an eye out.' Nick knew from Conway, who'd been weekend duty officer, that the ports had been alerted to look for people on the political agitators list. Nick asked, 'D'you expect this trouble to go on for some time then?'

'Ah! Who can say? But I think – certainly.'

'Is it organised then, Claude? Who's behind it?'

Nick could almost see the Gallic shrug at the other end of the line. 'Impossible to say at the moment. But I think our trouble is our own.'

The moment he rang off, Nick got out the list of political agitators. It included members of anarchist groups, extremists of every political shade, and agitators who could be expected to turn up at whatever event was likely to cause the most trouble – rent-a-mob. There were pacifists who went on Ban the Bomb and anti-Vietnam marches – a lot of well-known faces here: actresses, churchmen, writers – as well as the purely political extremists.

The list was very long. The ports could never be expected to pick up so many names.

He went through the list carefully. Who out of all these people was most likely to cause the French real trouble?

He picked out twenty names from active far-left groups and, telexing them to Dover, Folkestone and Heathrow, asked for a special watch to be kept for them.

It was all he could do. With a bit of luck one or two of them might turn up.

But would it mean anything? He had the unpleasant feeling that there were many more figures in the shadows. Figures that had no names.

The train seemed to have reached the outskirts of Paris at last. Gabriele tapped her fingers impatiently against the window. It had taken a couple of days to scrounge enough money for the trip and now it was Thursday and she was quite certain they were going to be too late for all the excitement.

She turned to Max. 'Are we nearly there, d'you think?'

He didn't answer, but stared morosely at the opposite seat. He'd been in a deep depression ever since Stephie had been arrested two months before. Gabriele sighed, 'Come on, Max. This is *revolution*, for God's sake.'

She knew what was eating him: the thought of Stephie in that remand centre, and his own guilt at not having been caught. But the trial was coming up soon and then Stephie would be out with a suspended sentence and they could all forget about it.

Except that Gabriele couldn't forget. She still had terrifying nightmares. She dreamed that people came for her in the night and stripped off her clothes and took her into a brightly lit room full of cold watching eyes and left her there, naked and vulnerable . . . She woke from these dreams with an overwhelming sense of despair, as if she'd been defiled and raped. It was the kind of humiliation that never left you, even when your mind was occupied with other things; the kind of pain that made you shiver even after the memory of the incident itself had faded.

She'd only been held for two days, of course. And then they'd let her go. At the time she'd been relieved. Only later had she realised her mistake. It would have been much better to admit some part in the demonstration. Then they would have charged her. At her trial she could have defended herself, made a long impassioned speech, got publicity for the cause and shown her contempt for the judicial machinery.

It had been an incredible opportunity. And she had missed it.

Now everyone was talking about Stephie. Already there was a campaign to get her released. Already everyone knew her name . . .

At last the train crept into the Gare du Nord. In the main concourse Gabriele bought a copy of *Le Monde* and read it on the Métro. Thirty thousand people had marched up the Champs-Élysées the previous day in sympathy with the students and had brought Paris to a complete halt. Five Nobel prize winners had asked de Gaulle for an amnesty for the imprisoned students. And – Gabriele took special note – an opinion poll put four in five Parisians behind the students.

Gabriele had talked flippantly about revolution, but she realised with a slight shock that there was a good chance of it really happening. She wasn't sure that she was pleased; she wanted to be involved, to be an essential part of the movement and she vaguely resented the fact that she was not.

They got off at the Odéon and walked into the Latin Quarter. Police were everywhere – in large vans, in cars with screaming sirens, and manning the barriers leading to the Sorbonne, which had been sealed off since the weekend.

At the Students' Union in the Rue Soufflot, they were redirected to the Salle de la Mutualité, a large hall off the Boulevard St Germain.

They arrived to find crowds thronging the doorways. They

pushed their way through. Inside there must have been at least three thousand students, chanting, '*Libérez nos camarades! Libérez nos camarades!*'

Gabriele and Max made their way down the aisle to the platform, where forty or fifty of the organisers were gathered, standing in groups. Max led the way up on to the stage and Gabriele was relieved when he greeted several people by name, and introduced her. She had a fear of being left out.

A young man went to the front of the platform and raised his hand for silence. Everyone sat down.

Gabriele realised that it was Cohn-Bendit himself at the microphone. He began to give a dazzling display of the rhetoric and nerve which had made him leader of the *enragés*, the discontents who had started the protests against the university system. It was Cohn-Bendit who had stepped in front of the Minister of Youth and Sport at the Nanterre campus and asked him what he was going to do about the students' sexual problems – a reference to the strict segregation between girls' and boys' residential blocks. The Minister had replied that Cohn-Bendit should jump in a pool. 'That's what the Hitler Youth used to say,' retorted Cohn-Bendit. The conversation had been widely reported all over Europe and had become a part of student folk lore.

Now, as he talked about immediate reforms, Gabriele caught the electric atmosphere in the hall, the feeling that the changes he was urging would actually take place.

After long and enthusiastic applause a German went to the microphone, pledging solidarity from the students of West Germany. Then came a Belgian. Max whispered in her ear, 'Leader of the International Trotskyists.'

The next introduction was made, but it took a few moments for the name to sink in.

'Antonio Petrini.'

Gabriele tried to reconcile the figure standing at the microphone with the author of *The Revolutionary Society*. She had imagined him to be – well, more dynamic-looking. He was about fifty, and small, with a bald crown surrounded by a fringe of long straggly hair. His nose was large and he wore thick, black-rimmed glasses. Gabriele was disappointed.

But the audience had no doubts. They greeted him with loud applause, some rising to their feet and clapping their hands above their heads.

The moment Petrini began to speak, there was a hush. He spoke for less than five minutes in heavily accented French, pledging his support to the cause. He had a calm dignity and an impassive detachment that gave his words a tremendous authority. Gabriele thought: He isn't disappointing at all.

When he sat down again, she applauded loudly.

One of the organisers came over to Max and spoke in his ear. Max shook his head and, turning to Gabriele, said, '*You* speak.'

Gabriele stared, aghast. 'But I've nothing prepared!'

The organiser shrugged and started to move away.

Gabriele heard herself say, 'Wait – *je viens. Je parlerais.*'

She quelled the mounting panic and walked to the front of the stage, forcing herself to move with exaggerated confidence.

At the microphone she calmed herself and began in her best French: 'My friends, I bring you greetings from the students of Britain!' There was a small cheer. 'We too suffer from a repressive system.' She paused, aware that it sounded dull after Petrini's powerful words. Something different was needed. She licked her lips. 'You are an example to us all.' She raised her voice. 'Only two months ago I had a policeman astride me!' A roar of amusement and mock horror went up; she waited for it to fall away. '. . . The pig was pinning me to the ground, trying to make me see sense. *But*, my friends, all *I* could see was his great' – she searched for the appropriate word and hoped that '*cul*' was right for backside – '*son gros cul!*' They screamed with delight. 'Next time, I will follow your example, and give him a hail of bricks before he ever gets near me! You are our example. Long live the student movement. *Solidarité!*'

She raised a fist to the roof and walked away.

The applause rose in a great wave and roared over her. She grinned in pleasure. As she sat down Max patted her shoulder.

The next speaker went forward, and Gabriele tried to concentrate on what he was saying. After a time she became aware of being watched from the other side of the platform. It was a young man sitting immediately beside Petrini, a dark bearded man, lounging coolly in his chair. As she met his gaze he nodded at her and smiled. She was about to return the smile when she realised his admiration had more than a little suggestiveness to it. He was trying to attract her. She thought: What a nerve.

But she was in too good a mood to be angry. She gave him a brief dismissive smile and looked away.

It was only later, after the meeting had finished, that she realised the bearded man was with Petrini. That changed things considerably. The next time he looked at her, she held his gaze.

Two other men had particular reason to stare at Gabriele.

One was carefully dressed in casual clothes and held some text-books rather self-consciously in his lap. He was aged about twenty-five and had entered the meeting on a forged student identity card. He sat in the body of the hall and stared at Gabriele, trying hard to memorise her face so that he could pick her out from the central DST files back at headquarters. If he didn't find her there one of his informants would give her name and he would check with Special Branch in London to see if she was known there.

The man didn't worry about identifying the other speakers. He knew exactly who they were. Most of them had been on the DST files for some time. Cohn-Bendit, Petrini . . . The Italian had been involved with extremists for years, not just as mentor and guru to left-wing thinkers, but, it was suspected, in more concrete ways. He was known to visit Cuba frequently, also, more recently, Czechoslovakia.

The DST watcher had placed most of the others on the platform too, which pleased him. That was his job: to keep a track on the foreigners. France was a haven for deposed rulers and political refugees and had always been proud of it. Traditionally, these people had been welcome as long as they did not interfere in France's internal affairs. But appearing at this rally was interference of a serious kind, and most certainly would not be tolerated.

He stared at the girl again. Dark, very striking. Yes, he'd remember her face all right. Whether he'd ever manage to discover her name was a different matter. Many of his informants were difficult to track down at the moment.

The second man, also more observant than most, sat in the body of the hall, but further back and to one side. At fifty-four he was far too old to pass as a student, but then he didn't need to. Several of the people on the platform were acquainted with him and regarded him with great respect. He had dedicated his life to a cause of which they approved wholeheartedly. He was the champion of oppressed people, particularly in the Third World; the defender of those under the tyranny of imperialism and dictatorship; the protector of the poor and downtrodden.

He ran an organisation called Aide et Solidarité whose official function was purely humanitarian, helping refugees, exiles and those who were being persecuted for their political beliefs.

That was on the official level.

However, Aide et Solidarité had a second and distinctly unofficial function. It provided arms, papers, liaison, and every sort of logistical support for subversive groups in the free world.

The man, an Egyptian-born Jew named Duteil, was well known to the security services as an admitted communist who'd been involved in numerous liberation movements. He entered France clandestinely in 1953 and had actively backed the FLN, the Algerian nationalist liberation organisation, providing them with papers and arms. He had been imprisoned by the French until the general amnesty of 1962. Since then he had been deeply involved in national liberation movements in numerous countries – Angola, Mozambique, Haiti, Santo Domingo and Kurdistan.

In France itself, however, he had done nothing illegal, nor had he done anything to suggest he was interfering in the country's internal affairs. Thus he remained free to go about his business.

And now he watched. And listened. He knew Petrini well; they were old acquaintances. But he wondered which of these vociferous young people would in the years to come forget their anger and become model citizens, and which would never forget, but move forward to the point where they felt impelled to become active against capitalist society – which of them, in fact, he should get to know. The dazzling Cohn-Bendit? The next speaker, the earnest Belgian theorist? The funny, uncertain young English girl?

The only thing he knew from experience was that you could never tell.

It was four in the morning. Gabriele was in the young Italian's room.

She sat in a chair, regarding him with open interest. He was better looking than she had thought. The beard suited his distinctive features: the rich black hair, the long straight nose and dark hooded eyes. Very physical.

Yes, Gabriele decided, he would round the day off nicely.

His name was Giorgio.

He appeared to be Petrini's helper, his orderer of food and

fetcher of information, a role he played with the lazy amused feebleness of a child humouring a parent.

After the rally she and Max had met the student leaders – Cohn-Bendit, Sauvageot, Dutschke, the Germans, Belgians and Italians – over long discussions at the students' union.

Later Petrini had bought dinner for at least twenty of them. There was fillet steak and spring vegetables and plenty of good wine. Afterwards they went back to Petrini's room to talk again. In a series of brilliant submissions he had argued for the need to polarise the two halves of society and to demonstrate to people how empty and meaningless their lives really were. To do this dissidents had to be properly organised in active units. If necessary they must be prepared to use force to highlight the ruthless repression of the system . . .

Gabriele had followed his arguments carefully, grasping each thought and storing it carefully away in the back of her mind.

Afterwards she remembered one phrase in particular: '. . . people need to have the injustices of the world demonstrated to them, so that their own thoughts, which may be no more than suspicions, shall be crystallised in their minds . . .'

Crystallised . . . That word again.

But now it was four in the morning, and the talking had stopped. Everyone had gone to bed. Max had found a floor somewhere. And she was here, with Giorgio. She had already decided to sleep with him. She liked making these decisions in isolation, at her own whim. That way she kept control.

Now she glanced around the comfortable hotel room. 'This is very grand,' she remarked. 'Do you always live like this?'

'Petrini does,' Giorgio replied slowly. 'So when he pays, I live like this too.' He spoke English with a heavy Italian accent which she liked.

She wandered round the room to show that she hadn't made up her mind to stay. She was still high on the wine and the charge she'd got from the speech, and she wanted him to make a play for her, so that she could hold back and exasperate him a little. It would be more exciting that way.

'Do you work for Petrini?' she asked.

He seemed amused by the question. 'No. I work for myself.'

'Well? What is it you do?'

He shrugged, immediately bored by the question. 'I do what I want.'

'Are you . . .' She hesitated. The question she wanted to ask was difficult to put directly. 'Are you an *activist*?'

He gave her a long stare, as if considering whether or not to take her into his confidence. Then he raised his eyebrows and smiled suggestively. 'Of course.'

She realised he had purposely misunderstood her. She said impatiently, 'I mean, are you involved in a dissident group?'

He sighed. Deliberately ignoring the question he said, 'I'm tired. I'm going to bed.' He turned and walked into the bathroom.

Gabriele stood in the centre of the room feeling piqued. He was deliberately excluding her. Her vanity was hurt. She had almost made up her mind to leave when he reappeared in the bathroom doorway.

'Please,' he said reasonably. 'We've talked enough . . . All of us. Enough for a long long time.' Examining her face he added suddenly, 'But if you insist – *yes*, I am committed to direct action. Of course!'

She blinked, reluctantly impressed. 'I see.' She had a vision of him leading a charge of demonstrators into a line of police. Then she remembered that the Italians had probably gone much further than that and she allowed new images to develop in her mind. She pictured him hiding out at secret addresses; planning a campaign; perhaps even using a gun. The images were attractive and more than a little exciting.

'Okay?' he asked.

She smiled. 'Okay.'

'I am going to bed now,' he said. Then, matter-of-factly: 'Will you come with me?'

A few moments ago she would have kept the matter in doubt much longer, just to show that she had control of the situation, just to demonstrate that she despised his arrogance.

But now there was no need. He understood what she wanted from him: access to the right people, the means to learn. Now it was a straightforward arrangement of mutual convenience. The matter was decided.

The afternoon of the 10th May began quietly enough with a rally in the Place Denfert-Rochereau attended by students, school children, teachers, trade unionists and sympathisers of every age and sort. At six-thirty came news that at long last the government had made some conciliatory proposals. But *not* about the imprisoned students – they were not to be freed.

A great roar went up: *Libérez nos camarades!*', and the crowds marched on the Santé Prison. A mass of police prevented them from reaching the prison walls and they turned away, heading for the Maison de la Radio, the government-controlled broadcasting centre on the Right Bank.

The government ordered all bridges across the Seine to be blocked and then they closed off the Boulevard St Germain – another ill-judged decision. Now the students were hemmed in on the Left Bank. They had nowhere to go: only back the way they'd come or into their own territory, the Latin Quarter.

The student leaders hurriedly conferred and announced their decision.

They would take the Latin Quarter and hold it at all costs.

It was the beginning of the worst violence Paris had seen for thirty years.

The news spread through the crowd like a bolt of electricity and the students ran for the Latin Quarter, fanning out through the maze of narrow streets around the Sorbonne.

Gabriele ran with Giorgio and it was only when she looked over her shoulder that she realised Max was no longer in sight, lost somewhere in the crowd.

They ran until they were short of breath, and found themselves in a small street to the south of the quarter among a group of about two dozen students. Already a car had been dragged into the middle of the street.

Then Giorgio had an iron bar in his hands and was hacking at the ancient cobblestones, trying to lever them off the road. Another car was pushed into the street and was rocked violently until it fell on its side with a loud grinding noise.

Gabriele searched desperately for materials, tugging ineffectually at gratings and street signs. Then she saw that Giorgio had got under the *pavés* and was levering them up fast. She joined the chain carrying stones to the rapidly growing barricade.

Later, when it grew dark, they were joined by more students, trade unionists and sympathisers, until there were over a hundred people in that one small street alone. Food and drink were brought by well-wishers and residents of the quarter. Everyone paused to eat. The atmosphere was warm with comradeship and the exhilaration of shared danger. Gabriele felt an overwhelming sense of achievement and well-being. Impulsively she put her arm through Giorgio's. She thought: I love it all.

A messenger roared up on a motorbike with information from the student leadership. Massive reinforcements of riot police were encircling the quarter.

The group set to work with fresh ingenuity, raiding building sites, tearing down scaffolding and barbed wire, until by midnight the barricade had grown into a formidable wall of cobblestones, cars, wire, and jagged metal. Gabriele armed herself with a metal bar torn from the frame of a shop's window-blind.

The CRS were sighted at two-ten. Gabriele felt her mouth go dry. Slowly, without urgency, the riot police formed themselves into ranks at the far end of the street. They made a sinister sight: the rows of long black coats, the invisible faces, the goggles and helmets, the shields which glinted darkly in the street lights. Someone shouted, '*Pigs! Fascists!*'

At two-fifteen a deathly silence fell, broken only by the sound of shuffling feet. The line of raised shields was moving towards them.

Gabriele took her position half-way up the barricade, adjusted the handkerchief round her mouth and gripped a cobblestone in her hand. She wasn't frightened any more; the adrenalin was making her light-headed, almost euphoric.

A shouted order, and the black line paused. Snub-nosed pistols were pointed in the air and fired. Missiles with long white tails sailed up and over the barricades. The air became thick with sharp pervasive gases . . . Gabriele pressed the handkerchief to her face, but the gas seeped through, stinging viciously at her eyes, stabbing at her throat until she choked.

A low rumble echoed along the dark street. The rumble grew to a clatter, a crescendo of batons beating on shields, and the black line was charging forward, unchecked by the hail of stones, *pavés* and missiles from the student lines. Gabriele stood up and hurled a cobblestone wildly into the darkness, then bent down to pick up another.

Suddenly she realised that the gleaming black figures were mounting the barricade. Dropping the cobblestone, Gabriele reached for the iron bar at her feet and grasped it tightly.

Quickly, so quickly it took her by surprise, a dark shape loomed up in front of her. The figure swung his arm up in a high arc, a baton clutched viciously in his hand.

She lashed at him with the iron bar. The metal made contact and swung back to hit again. The figure swayed as if off-balance. Then it was twisting to one side, the arm coiling back like a spring, and too late she saw the baton coming rapidly savagely down.

She raised an arm against the blow, but it caught her on the side of the head, a dull sickening jolt of pain. She fell back, the sounds of the battle ringing in her ears.

Another blow thudded on to her shoulder and with a cry she rolled down the mound of stones to the ground.

She covered her raging head, but there were no more blows. Through her dim agony she could hear the sounds of the fight: thuds, cries, shouts, boots scrabbling on the stone . . . Then the *whoomph!* of a small explosion and the crackle of fire. With an effort she crawled away, searching for the shelter of a wall, a doorway . . . Suddenly a foot in her side, a body falling over her and running off . . . Cries of pursuit growing fainter . . . Then quieter – just the crackle and spit of a fire nearby.

After some time she felt hands grasp her and started in alarm. But the hands were gentle, the voices soft. They pulled her to her feet and led her to a lighted interior. A cloth wiped her head, soothed her burning eyes . . . Rest, a soft pillow . . . Ah – peace.

She lay still for a long time until the pounding in her head dulled to a sullen throb. Outside, it was quieter. As much as an hour had passed. Dimly she concluded that the fight must be over. She dozed uneasily.

Suddenly there were sharp obtrusive noises: the sounds of heavy vehicles and shouted orders and doors opening.

Confused and alarmed, she opened her eyes and tried to understand.

Harsh voices, boots on the stairs.

What on earth—

The fear leapt into her throat. Through the door came black helmets, faces invisible . . .

She stared incredulously.

It was a bad dream relived, a second nightmare, except it was real again. She thought: *I'll die if they touch me.*

They grabbed her and she gasped. They pulled her to her feet. She yelled, '*Let go, you pigs!*' They were pawing her, searching her. A gloved hand came close to her mouth and she bit it hard, meeting flesh through the leather. There was a cry. She struggled and kicked out. They grabbed at her arm and, catching the wrist, twisted it harshly up her back.

She thought: *I'm going to go mad.*

She screamed and kicked out with her feet, finding a target. There was a shout of anger.

The next moment her head exploded and a wall of blackness closed in on her.

Through the blackness she heard someone groaning loudly and realised it was herself. Then, as if in a dream, she was being half-dragged, half-carried across a hall and down some stairs into the street. A veil of warm wetness covered her smarting eyes and there was a strange sweetness in her mouth. She was hauled roughly over stones and heaved backwards into a van, the metal floor cold and hard on her skin.

She mustered her strength to gasp, 'Fascist Nazi pigs! Fascist bastard pigs! Fascist—!'

Then the doors slammed shut and there was nobody to hear.

The night of the 10th May became known as the Night of the Barricades; over sixty makeshift barriers were thrown up in the streets of the Latin Quarter. From all over Paris thousands of young people, manual workers and professionals, rushed to the students' aid until the CRS riot police were faced with an enormous army of guerrillas. The fighting raged for four hours and was remarkable for its savagery and hatred.

But if the hand to hand fighting was bloody – beaten heads, broken limbs, four hundred seriously injured – it was the mopping up operations which were remembered with most bitterness. The injured dragged from stretchers to be beaten up for a second time; a Negro thrown into a van to emerge with a battered bloody face; girls stripped and taken naked into the street; innocent passers-by attacked. In many areas the police took their opportunities for revenge.

Local residents and onlookers were horrified. So too was most of France. The next day the government tried to mediate, but it was all too late. The workers and the students were united. Within two days there was a mass anti-government demonstration of over eight hundred thousand people. Three days later more than nine *million* workers were out on strike. A student soviet occupied the Sorbonne and several provincial universities were taken over. Even members of the most respected professions – the doctors, lawyers, scientists, musicians – rebelled, questioning the outdated structures in which they worked.

The revolution had arrived.

The hospital room was white and brilliantly lit and hurt her eyes. At least two days had passed, though she wasn't absolutely sure. At one point the police came and demanded her name. She closed her eyes and didn't answer.

They returned with her shoulder bag which she supposed they had found somewhere near the barricade.

They held out her passport.

Linda Wilson.

She smiled because it didn't matter if they knew that name.

Another night came – the third? – and a voice obtruded into her consciousness. It whispered urgently 'Gabriele! Gabriele!' Someone was shaking her.

She stared into the semi-darkness and saw two figures leaning over the bed. One of them was Giorgio. Already they were pulling her out of bed and wrapping a coat round her shoulders.

She said, 'I knew you'd come.'

Four

The weather was blustery but fine, and the coast of France was clearly visible across the straits. On the green, white-flecked sea beyond the breakwater a ferry turned in a stately arc to negotiate the eastern entrance to Dover harbour.

'She'll be docked in about seven minutes,' said the local Special Branch man. 'D'you want to come down to the desk or watch through the window?'

'The window,' Nick Ryder replied. He didn't want to be seen.

He picked up the batch of names and photographs, tapped his pocket to make sure he had a pen, and followed the officer down to the observation room.

The room was sited high in the wall of the immigration hall and had a large one-way window so that it was possible to look down on all six of the channels unobserved. Nick settled down in a chair and spread out the photographs on the shelf in front of him. Picking up a pair of binoculars, he practised focusing them. Below, the local Branch men were stationed behind the immigration booths.

The first passengers came into the hall at a rush, anxious to get to their trains and coaches. Then came the families and shoppers, hampered with children, large amounts of baggage, and trolley loads of French food. Orderly lines formed in front of the immigration booths.

Nick scanned the lines carefully, but there were no familiar faces. At the far end of the hall the slower passengers shuffled in: a group of older people; some young hikers with enormous back-packs . . .

He sat up. And some faces.

Yes. Several he recognised.

He took one at a time, matching each face to the list or, where he had a photograph, to that as well.

Ellis, Bishop, Wheatfield . . .

He tried to remember something about the first two although, as Marxists, they didn't strictly fall into his Section. Ellis: International Marxists and CND; Bishop: International Marxists and Vietnam United Front. The third was Wheatfield, Max. International Trotskyists and now Socialist Students' League. One of his.

Within ten minutes he had fifteen out of the seventeen names. He'd probably missed the other two in the crowd. He watched the last passengers pass through the channels, but there was no one else.

He made his way back to the immigration office and waited. The local man came in and announced, 'All accounted for.'

'I missed two,' Nick admitted.

They checked their lists and decided he'd missed the two who had passed through first.

'Well, that's nice and tidy for once, then,' said the inspector.

'As long as none of them sneak back into France,' Nick pointed out, 'or decide to start something similar here.'

The local man shrugged and put on a look that said don't let's worry about that now.

Nick made a call to Claude Desport at the DST in Paris and said, 'Can't say I'm grateful, but all seventeen have been received. Will there be more?'

'Another nine or ten tomorrow,' Desport replied, and gave him a list of names. 'If we find any more you'll have them within twenty-four hours.'

That's what Nick liked about the French system: any aggravation and it was immediate expulsion, with no chance of appeal.

'But there are – let me see – *three* we cannot send back to you,' Desport was saying. 'Two decided to go over the Belgian border, and a third decided to – er, stay.'

'Stay?'

'She got away. Her name is . . .' There was a pause. 'Wilson, Linda. If we pick her up again, we will let you know.'

Linda Wilson. The name rang a bell, but it took a moment for Nick to place it. Of course. The raid after the Linden House Hotel affair. The girl on the stairs. He had a fleeting vision of her body, long and beautiful, then, with an effort, closed his mind to it.

Three unaccounted for.

Nick reflected that the local men had been somewhat premature. Nothing was ever neat and tidy.

Gabriele forced herself to stand up. A moment later, when the dizziness had passed, she walked unsteadily from the bed to the window. She looked down into the street. It was quiet. There was nothing to suggest that, five days after the Night of the Barricades, the country was virtually at a standstill. Six million were on strike, so the radio said: train drivers, dustmen, car workers, lorry drivers, professional people; and the numbers were still increasing. The uprising had grown beyond the students' wildest dreams.

The street was quiet because the quarter was quiet: this apartment was a long way from the Latin Quarter. Gabriele was restless. She wanted to get back to the centre of things. She had already decided to leave the next day and go in search of Petrini and Giorgio.

Not that she hadn't been looked after. The apartment belonged to a young priest who brought her food and occasional news. A doctor came twice a day and shone a light into her eyes and gave her tablets to take away the pain in her head. Then there was a woman journalist who called every evening, to check on her. It was almost as if these people were part of a well-established organisation. But this was never confirmed and, after asking twice, Gabriele did not ask again.

Now she went back to bed and slept until evening. When the priest returned she told him she would be leaving the next day.

He frowned and suggested it would be unwise to be found on the streets without papers. After he left the room, Gabriele heard the slight ping of the telephone bell. Later, when the priest reappeared with some food, he said, 'You will be collected at three tomorrow afternoon. To make arrangements about your papers.'

Then Gabriele knew without any doubt: there was an organisation. She wondered what else it provided.

She was dressed and ready by three the next afternoon. She felt much better; the worst of the headache had gone.

At half past three the doorbell finally rang.

It was Giorgio.

She said, 'You're late.'

He shrugged good-naturedly and ignored the remark.

As they went down to the street Gabriele cast him a sidelong glance. He had come to visit her at the priest's apartment three days before, but only stayed ten minutes. He'd been restless and impatient, and she'd had the feeling that he was irritated by her incapacity. But now he was bright and attentive, and she was aware that he was trying to please her again.

'Your head is mended?' he asked as they got into his car.

'I'm all right.'

'Ah. That is good.' He seemed relieved.

He drove off fast, ignoring one set of lights that had just turned red, and shooting rapidly into the Avenue Leclerc. There were few cars about and no buses or traffic police. The city seemed half-abandoned.

Giorgio laughed. 'In the car, when we took you from the hospital, you moaned so much I thought you were dying.'

'My head was hurting. But it's all right now.' The memory of the pain was fading. She remembered feeling sick and feverish, but she could no longer conjure up the agony of the pain itself.

But she had forgotten nothing about the Night of the Barricades nor the way in which she had been injured. She had played the scenes of the two assaults over and over in her mind until each moment was etched vividly on her memory. She cherished the details; they were valuable.

Giorgio was driving steadily north towards the Latin Quarter.

She asked, 'Where exactly are we going?'

I was given an address. A photographer's. I was told to take you there.'

'Who by?'

He shrugged. 'Friends of Petrini. But I don't know who *precisely*.'

She looked at him sharply. Was he telling the truth? If not, why

57

was he holding back? He must trust her now, surely.

'What happens after the photograph?'

'You will have papers. You'll be free to move around.' He paused. Looking across at her, he added, 'I am staying in the apartment of a friend; near the Sorbonne. There is room. If you like.'

Gabriele thought: He trusts me after all.

She considered. She wasn't sure she wanted to get too involved with this man. She sensed he was unpredictable, difficult even. On the other hand, his connections were too useful to give up. Particularly since he was in contact with this organisation.

She said, 'All right.' Then added, 'It'll be much more convenient.' She didn't want him to think she was moving in because of him.

They parked to the south of the Latin Quarter and picked their way on foot through narrow streets whose surfaces had been almost completely torn away, and whose sides were still littered with stones and burnt-out cars. Finally they entered a doorway beside a second-hand bookshop, and climbed some stairs. On the first floor was a small photographic studio. A man emerged from a back room and shook hands. He did not offer his name.

He sat Gabriele on a stool in front of a camera and rolled down a plain black background.

'Look straight at the camera.'

There was a flash and Gabriele blinked.

The photographer said, 'I'll need some details.'

She gave him her height and age. 'What languages do you speak?' he asked.

'English, French, a little Italian and German.'

The photographer scratched his head. 'At the moment I can only offer you Turkish, Dutch, or Argentinian. Perhaps Argentinian would be best. There are many people of English origin living there.'

Giorgio said, 'Take Dutch. It's safer. No one speaks Dutch.'

The photographer indicated that it was all the same to him. 'What about names?'

They went through some ideas, and decided Anneke van Duren because it was easy to pronounce. The photographer said, 'It'll be ready by tomorrow evening at six. Will you pick it up?'

As they emerged into the street, Gabriele looked for the house number. Eleven. And the name of the street: Rue Vauquelin. She filed it away in her memory. She still did not know the photographer's name.

They walked back towards the car.

Giorgio said, 'We'll go back to the priest's and pick up your things.'

'No,' she said carefully. 'I'll move tomorrow. When I have my papers.'

He shot her an angry look, and strode on ahead. He drove her back to the Porte d'Orléans in silence.

Outside the priest's she said soothingly, 'We'll have dinner tomorrow night.' She brushed his cheek with her hand. 'It'll be nice.'

He looked at her resentfully. It was his turn to be piqued. She was glad. It wouldn't do him any harm.

Eventually he gave a faint nod of resignation. 'Tomorrow.'

She got out of the car and watched him drive away. The moment he was out of sight she turned her back on the apartment and set off down the street. In the Avenue Leclerc she looked round uncertainly. She knew the buses were on strike, and probably the Métro too. She didn't have the money for a taxi. In the end she put out a thumb and a motorist stopped. He dropped her near the Latin Quarter.

She walked back through the narrow streets until she came to the Rue Vauquelin. She went to number eleven and looked at the name plates inside the front door. *Studio Vincenne – photos commerciales et portraits.*

She mounted the stairs, and listened outside the photographer's door. The sound of voices came from inside. She went down to the street and waited in the second-hand bookshop, browsing through the shelves near the window.

Half an hour later two men emerged from the side door into the street. One of them was the photographer. He shook hands with the second man and walked off.

Gabriele replaced the book she had been reading and went out into the street. The photographer had crossed the road and was walking unhurriedly away with his hands in his pockets.

Gabriele took a brief look over her shoulder and followed.

In the quiet embassy building on the Boulevard Lannes the Soviet Second Trade Secretary scanned the back copies of *Le Monde* for any last scraps of information that might flesh out his report. The report needed all the padding it could get. As the senior officer of the Paris Residency's Directorate K (First Chief Directorate, KGB) it was his job to know what was going on. Normally he liked to think he did. He had excellent contacts in the PCF (the French Communist Party), the FGDS socialist alliance, and the left-wing trade unions such as the communist-controlled CGT. But themselves taken by surprise, they had not been able to tell him very much. This uprising had sprung from small student groups about which there was little information. For one thing, they were newly formed; and for another, the groups were for the most part vehemently anti-Soviet. He had re-emphasised this in his report, both to explain his failure to predict events and to prepare the Centre for a continuing lack of information in the future. He hoped the message had sunk in.

Having said that, he had to try to discover what these students were all about. Over the last month *Le Monde* had carried interviews with most of the student leaders, who had talked of capitalist repression and reactionary forces and of the need for a socialist revolution in the Third World. This, he felt, was the key. This was the spot where they could be reached and their idealism turned further to advantage.

He fiddled with his pen, wondering whether to stick his neck out. Putting forward policy ideas was a risky business – it could earn you credit or a firm slap down and delayed promotion. He hesitated a moment then added a footnote: 'Despite the idealism and independence of the various new extremist groups in France and other West European countries, they are unlikely to be averse to logistical support when it is offered *indirectly*, through pro-Soviet Third World countries whose cause they champion, or by established organisations such as Aide et Solidarité. Help in the form of direct funding will be met with suspicion. It is suggested, therefore, that the support offered by Aide et Solidarité be stepped up to meet the requirements of these new groups.

'It is unlikely that we will be able to exert any influence over these groups either by infiltration or by threatening to control their logistical support. However, this need not be a major concern, since any acts of a disruptive or terrorist nature carried out in capitalist countries will, by their very nature, be destabilising.'

He laid down his pen. It was a fair assessment, though perhaps he had stuck his neck out a bit far on that last statement. Until now Aide et Solidarité had mainly provided support for Third World groups. Now he was suggesting that all other subversive groups, regardless almost of doctrine, should be encouraged. He just hoped it matched the current line of thought in Moscow. He switched a few words round to improve the flow, then sent it to be typed and encoded.

Later he made a telephone call across Paris, to a director of the Banque Commerciale de l'Europe du Nord (BCEN) in the Boulevard Haussmann. 'I have put in a few words for additional funds for your export friends,' the Second Trade Secretary said. 'I feel confident they will get all they need.'

The statement was acknowledged and the call terminated. The bank director wrote a brief note on a pad to remind himself to call the import–export company, which was a customer of the bank's, and speak to one of its directors. There was no point in calling just at that moment, as he knew the director would be out. And there was no secretary to answer the call. That was because the company did very little business.

The bank director knew a great deal about the import–export company because the bank covered the company's frequent over-drafts with loans. The loans were made without collateral and no interest was ever charged. Furthermore, all payments for goods and services imported or exported were made by draft through the bank. Not that any goods were actually transported. They existed solely on paper, and were merely a means of channelling funds into the import–export company. These funds – like the loans – originated from the country which owned and controlled the bank, which was the Soviet Union.

The two directors of the import–export company were both Frenchmen who also kept personal accounts at the bank. One of the few employees of the company was Bernard Duteil, known as Raymond, the head of Aide et Solidarité. In fact, his salary from the import–export company was his sole source of income, and Aide et Solidarité itself existed on funds provided by the import–export company.

On the memo pad the bank director made a further note to tell the director of the import–export company that a back-up request for additional funds had been made.

A board meeting of Aide et Solidarité was held that evening. There were more than twenty people on the board, including a Dominican priest, a Protestant pastor, a famous left-wing political philosopher, and various Paris intellectuals. It was fashionable to be a member of the Aide et Solidarité organisation. It showed that you cared about the worldwide anti-colonial struggle, the current cause beloved by the radical chic.

Many who sat round the table that evening chose not to think about how Aide et Solidarité was funded. For them it was enough that it existed at all. And although some of them knew that the organisation regularly produced false papers for those in need, only two of them were aware that arms, explosives, training and liaison were also provided. One of those people was, of course, Duteil, alias Raymond, and the other his deputy.

The meeting had originally been called to discuss two items: the accommodation of foreign refugees, and the next anti-Vietnam war demonstration.

However, not surprisingly, the discussion quickly turned to the revolt. Despite its rapid progress the final outcome was far from certain, everyone agreed. Admittedly the workers had latched on to the student movement very quickly and had been quick to come out on strike, but their motives were dubious. A great number of them, far from challenging the capitalist state, were perfectly happy with it. All they wanted was a larger slice of the cake. If the government dangled higher wages and the promise of greater representation in front of them the revolt might easily fall apart.

Horror was expressed at this possibility. The radical chic liked the idea of the workers sticking to their principles even if it meant turning down higher wages.

The discussion then turned to support for the revolt. It was pointed out that the organisation had many safe houses. Could they not be offered to students being sought by the police?

Duteil interrupted immediately. 'You all know that Aide et Solidarité cannot and must not help them. If we assist those who are fighting the French government, we will be closed down. We are only tolerated as long as we stay out of French affairs.' He offered a palliative. 'What you do as individuals, however, is your own affair.' Duteil shot a meaningful glance at the Dominican priest. The priest acknowledged it with a blink, unnoticed by the others.

The matter was dropped and the discussion moved on to other matters. Half an hour later Duteil brought the meeting to a close.

The priest stayed behind after the others had gone.

Dueteil shook his head and said wryly, 'I have broken my own rules. I hope I'm not going to regret it.'

'The girl knows nothing.'

'I hope not.'

They walked the short distance from the luxurious offices which were lent to them for board meetings, to the offices of Aide et Solidarité, which were somewhat less well appointed. In accordance with its role as supporter of the poor and oppressed, Aide et Solidarité possessed three shabby rooms, two almost empty and the third with the bare minimum of furniture, including two battered desks, some chairs, two filing cabinets, and a couple of ancient typewriters.

The photographer was waiting for them. His role in the organisation was an important one. Quite apart from taking photographs, he was a master-forger. He could produce French identity papers and driving licences that were indistinguishable from the real thing. But for the most part his skills were used to produce passports. The organisation possessed a stock of well over four hundred blank passports stolen from various consulates around the world. The master-forger used his special talents to produce the embossing tools and stamps of authentication required. He enjoyed his job very much. Duteil saw to it that the job also paid well.

'What passport are you giving the English girl?' Duteil asked.

'Dutch.'

'You don't have a British one for her?'

'Not at the moment.'

Duteil thought for a moment. He didn't like the idea of the girl using the Dutch passport in France. She might well be arrested for a second time. The police would then discover she wasn't really Dutch. Worse still, they might match her face to that of the missing British girl. Either way, they would know the passport was a fake. And then they would want to know where it had come from.

Duteil decided his first duty was to cover himself. He had already broken his rules by helping someone who had been 'subverting' the French state. The only thing in his favour was that she was not a French citizen; that really would have been asking for it.

He didn't regret helping her. Her speech at the Mutualité, though rather flippant, had been different – funny, impressive. It had stayed in the mind. Just like the girl herself.

Also she was British. There were two reasons why this made a difference. The first was that there were no hardliners active in Britain at that time, and he rather liked the notion of encouraging one. The second – and more important – reason was that, though a Jew, he had been born and brought up in Egypt, and there were few educated Egyptians of his age who hadn't despised the British occupation of their country.

No: he didn't regret helping her. But his first duty was to himself.

'I think we must be careful,' he said. 'I think we must only provide her with the passport as she is about to leave the country.'

'I said she could have it tomorrow,' the photographer replied.

'Well, you'll have to say it is no longer possible.'

'If she stays in Paris she'll need papers of some sort,' the priest pointed out.

'We'll have to persuade her not to stay in Paris.'

There was a rapping at the outer door. Unhurriedly Duteil went to answer it. He wasn't expecting anyone, but there was nothing unusual about casual callers from among the many refugees living in the city under the organisation's wing.

Duteil turned the latch and swung open the outer door.

It was the girl.

He took a deep breath. 'Good evening,' he said eventually. 'What can I do for you?'

'The gentleman from the Studio Vincenne. Is he here?'

So that was how she had found the place. He stood back. 'You had better come in.'

He closed the door behind her and led the way down the passage into the main office. The girl entered the room and, seeing the priest, looked surprised. Then she smiled slightly as if his presence confirmed something.

'We were just talking about you,' Duteil began immediately. 'I'm afraid we think it unwise for you to remain in France.'

'Why?'

'Because the authorities know all about you. They have your passport. If they arrest you again, they will soon realise your new passport is not genuine. It would get us into a great deal of trouble. We – are reluctant to let that happen.'

She nodded. 'I understand.' She did not look too unhappy at the thought of leaving.

Duteil asked softly, 'Why did you follow us here?'

'I wanted to talk to you.'

'Yes?'

She chose her words carefully. 'I was hoping you could help me. In the long term.'

There was a silence.

'Ah.' Duteil nodded slowly. He turned to the other two men. 'We will meet another day.'

When the priest and the photographer had gone Duteil sat down opposite her and lit a cigarette. 'What sort of help did you have in mind?'

'Papers. Passports. Contacts . . . You see, I don't know how to go about – organising myself.'

'What exactly are you hoping to achieve?'

She gathered her thoughts. 'I want to – activate groups in England. Freedom groups. To operate against organised repression. To – *expose* the repressiveness of the Establishment. To show people what the system is *really* doing. The anger is there,' she added, 'the injustice, the repression. People just can't *see* it. The situation needs to be polarised – *crystallised*.'

'You follow Petrini.'

A flicker of surprise crossed her face.

Duteil smiled. 'Petrini is an old friend of mine.' He asked thoughtfully, 'You have no training?'

She stared at him. She obviously wasn't certain of what he meant. She said uncertainly, 'No.'

He considered for a moment. Her philosophy was raw and undigested. She had little idea of what was involved in being an activist. Yet she had qualities that impressed him: determination and straightforwardness.

'Then may I suggest something?' he said eventually. 'Why don't you join an existing group – a group who share your ideals – and learn from them?'

'There are none in England.'

'Quite so. I was thinking of Italy.'

'I speak hardly any Italian.'

He shrugged. 'That may be an advantage. You can always pass as a tourist.'

She blinked. 'What would they teach me?'

'A great deal, I think.'

'Who are these people?'

'Well . . . They have a name of sorts. Lotta – "struggle". But the name is not important. What is important is that they have been active for some time – a year or more. They have experience.'

She thought hard. 'I have no money.'

'I will give you some travelling expenses.'

'Oh – and when I'm there?'

'The group will look after you. They have – er – benefactors.'

She nodded, slowly absorbing the idea. 'Then – when I come back – you'll help me?' she asked.

'As far as I can. But you must understand there'll be no money. You will have to do your own fund-raising.' He could see that she hadn't thought that far ahead.

Nodding briskly, she said, 'That's fine.'

It was a firm rule of Duteil's – one he never broke – that, apart from small amounts of cash handed out to refugees, he provided no money, and certainly not to hard political groups. He was happy to provide logistical support and training free of charge, and weapons at very reasonable prices. But large quantities of cash were out of the question. For one thing, there would be no end to the financial demands of the groups. For another, the money would be traced back to him sooner or later and eventually – God forbid – to its source. There would be an almighty international row. He would be closed down and considerable embarrassment would be caused to Moscow.

But as long as these new groups financed operations by robbing banks in their own countries, then he could not be accused of direct interference.

Indicating the poorly furnished room, he said, 'As you see, we are not a wealthy organisation. We rely on our friends for financial support.' It was true up to a point – voluntary subscriptions were always welcome. However they covered only a small amount of the running costs.

Duteil decided that further discussion was best avoided: the less the girl knew about Aide et Solidarité at this stage the better. He stood up. Catching the hint, she got to her feet and they shook hands.

She said, 'You won't help any other British group, will you? I mean, before me?'

Duteil shook his head.

They walked to the door. He said, 'You will get some travelling money, an air ticket and an address in Milan from the priest.'

At the door she turned and faced him. She was a very striking woman. She said, 'I want to do it properly, you understand that?'

'I understand. That's why I have agreed to help you. That's why I think you should go to Italy first.'

She paused. 'I don't know your name.'

'I'm known as Raymond.'

She shook his hand again. 'Goodbye, Raymond. I'll be back.'

He nodded. 'Yes, I have no doubt of that.'

When she had gone Duteil considered what he had promised, and was satisfied. He would not offer help to any other British activists because apart from a single group of unpredictable anarchists there *were* none. Even if a new group did spring up he doubted any leader would be quite as ambitious or determined as this girl. When she returned he would give her all the help he could.

She might not return, of course, but then she would not have been worth the trouble anyway.

But he had a feeling about her. She would return. He gave her six months.

Five

'You were injured in the fighting?'

Henry Northcliff said with emphasis, 'Only slightly.' He didn't want any false heroics creeping into the article.

'And where was that?'

'At Jarama, during the battle for Madrid. In February '36.'

'How old were you?'

'Just eighteen.'

The young journalist scribbled on the pad and referred to his list of questions. They were sitting outside, under the copper beech tree. Henry turned his face to the sun and thought how nice the garden was looking. Caroline had worked very hard on it. The borders were a bright mass of colour and the lawn had lost its patchy uneven look.

It was July. The summer recess was only a week away. Then at long last he and Caroline would have a holiday.

The journalist cleared his throat. 'What influenced you to go to Spain? Was it entirely your own idea, or were you one of a group?'

Henry made the effort to think back. It was such a long time ago that he could barely remember all the reasons for his decision. Eventually he replied, 'I came from a family who were very politically aware – *involved*. My parents felt very passionately about it.'

'For the Republicans?'

'Oh, yes!' Henry laughed. It was impossible to imagine his parents being for anyone but the people.

'So were you a communist at that time?'

'Now let's get this quite clear,' Henry said firmly. 'I was a fervent *socialist* at that time – as indeed I am now. The International Brigade included all sorts of people with all sorts of beliefs – including communists. But just because we fought together didn't mean we shared identical beliefs. So, let's not be confused about *that*.'

The journalist didn't like being talked down to, but he'd got the message, which was just what Henry intended.

The young man asked, 'So was it your family's idea for you to go?'

'Oh no, the idea was mine. I went entirely on my own initiative. Because I felt that one must follow things through and put one's beliefs into action.'

'Do you still believe that?'

Henry drew a deep breath. Journalists always tried to push you into a trite, quotable remark. He wasn't going to fall into that trap, he'd been in the game far too long. But at the same time he must produce a good reply and today it was rather an effort. It had been a long hard week.

'I believe you must do all you can to bring about the system that you believe is just—'

'Not by *any* means surely—'

'*No*. By political means.'

'But how do you define political means?'

He was fishing, Henry decided. Looking for a statement that he could apply to a specific issue. Henry wondered which one. He replied, 'Political means are the means of political expression which are permitted by the law of the land.'

The journalist came in quickly, 'Does that include demonstrations?'

Henry thought: Ah, so that's it. The Paris uprising. He hedged, 'Peaceful demonstrations are perfectly legal, therefore they are valid political means.'

'But demonstrators using violence are to be punished excessively?'

'I really cannot speak for what's been happening in France.'

'France? Oh no, I meant closer to home.'

Henry suddenly realised where all this had been leading. 'You are referring to the Linden House convictions, I take it?'

The journalist exclaimed, 'Of course. A three-year sentence for a first offence is excessive by anyone's standards. And you must admit that the convictions have been highly unpopular.'

He was right about that: the outcry had been considerable. There had been questions in the House, leading articles in most of the newspapers and hot debates in the correspondence columns of *The Times*. He remembered the final paragraph of one leader: 'These sentences are, presumably, designed to deter future demonstrators from the use of excessive violence. However, where the punishment is seen to exceed the crime, the effects may be quite the reverse, and serve to inflame the very young people whom it is intended to deter.'

Privately Henry thought the sentences were excessive too, but it was out of the question for him to say so.

'As you are aware,' he said firmly, 'I can only comment on the prosecution of the case, not on the sentences. But as the judge commented, it is immaterial whether violence stems from gang warfare or from political motives.'

'Do you agree with that?'

The aggressive young man was getting on Henry's nerves, but he said calmly, 'Yes, of course I do.'

'Although you yourself fought for your beliefs in an illegal manner?'

Full circle. And not a very subtle circle at that.

'If you want to be pedantic about this, wars usually *are* legal.' Suddenly he was impatient with this intense rather unlikeable young man. 'But *really* – is this worth debating?' He rose to his feet. Realising the interview was over, the journalist closed his notebook with a snap.

Caroline met them coming across the lawn and, grasping the atmosphere immediately, took charge of the journalist to show him out. Henry returned to the chair under the tree, annoyed with himself for agreeing to give an interview on a Saturday afternoon. He liked to keep his home as separate from his work as possible, and now the loveliness of the garden seemed a little spoilt by the aggressive young man.

Spain. The memories, sharp yet vague, echoed in his mind. He'd been desperate for action, he remembered. Burning with righteousness. And bitterly disappointed when he'd been wounded after a scant two weeks in the Brigade. It had all been very intense. He'd never felt quite so passionately about anything since.

He supposed the young people who'd terrified the diners at the Linden House Hotel felt passionate too. But their actions had been provocative and wantonly dangerous. And that was the difference.

Caroline re-emerged from the house and he got up to meet her. She said, 'The young man left looking less than happy with his interview.'

'Well, I was less than happy with it too. I'm used to getting stick in court and the House, but I object to smart-alec questions from a young man who's merely trying to prove a point.' He gave a short laugh. 'Actually, his principal mistake was to catch me on a Saturday when all I wanted to do was sit in the sun with you.' He squeezed her arm. 'Why don't we sit out here and have tea? Just us.'

'Ah . . .' Caroline looked a little sheepish. 'We've got a visitor.'

Henry groaned. He hated it when people dropped in. 'My God – who?' he asked peevishly.

'Victoria. She swears she's only staying a minute.'

It could have been worse, Henry decided. It could have been Victoria's mother.

They found Victoria in the kitchen. Henry blinked at her. The Indian outfit of a few months ago had been replaced by a floral yokel costume of quite astonishing design. There were enormous baggy trousers in vivid yellow, a loose top in white embroidered with large flowers whose colours took your breath away, and a battered old straw hat on top of the mass of fair hair. Just in case you failed to notice all that, she also had flowers painted on her cheeks.

'Cor,' said Henry. 'Don't you look rural.'

Victoria grinned and kissed him on the cheek. 'I'm only popping in because I *know* how busy you are – but I just had to bring you *this*.' She delved deep into her shoulder bag and brought out a jar which she waved triumphantly in the air. 'Honey!'

'Good Lord! Where did this come from?' Henry asked, already knowing the answer.

'From the farm! Isn't it wonderful?' She threw her head back and laughed and Henry was struck by the intensity of her happiness. He found himself smiling too.

'Don't tell me you got hold of some bees and persuaded them to produce in four weeks flat.'

'No. *silly*.' She creased up her nose, taking the teasing in good heart. 'We found them in an old hive at the far end of the upper meadow and the honey was already *there* . . . But we got it out! Isn't that amazing!'

Knowing the experience that Victoria and her friends had of farming and bee-keeping, Henry thought it probably was.

'And we've got two cows producing milk,' continued Victoria. 'And a goat. Oh *and* we've bought a pig. We've named her Bella. She's absolutely gorgeous!'

Henry guessed that the animals on the farm were going to live long and happy lives without fear of the slaughterhouse. 'How's all the work going?' he asked cautiously. 'The renovations and so on?'

'Oh, we're all working like mad,' breathed Victoria. 'From dawn till dusk. We've done two roofs and cleared out the yard and got the kitchen scrubbed and *planted* things and . . .' She shook her head. 'Honestly, it's *terrific*.'

Henry couldn't resist asking, 'And how's the communal decision-making going? Do you have solemn pow-wows at the end of each day?'

Caroline shot him a warning glance but he avoided her eye.

Victoria giggled. 'No-o-o. We just discuss things round the kitchen table. There are only six of us, after all.'

'I thought it was going to be ten.'

'Well, the others weren't really committed, so . . .' Suddenly she was kissing Caroline. 'Must fly. I only came up to see my stockbroker.'

To sell more shares, no doubt. Henry wondered how much the whole exercise was costing and if anyone else in the commune was chipping in. But he was afraid he knew the answer to that.

'By the way,' Victoria said on the doorstep, 'perhaps you'd better know . . . Mother's not best pleased, so I'm keeping clear of her for the moment.'

A wise move at the best of times, Henry wanted to say.

When the Mini had disappeared up the road, Caroline turned

and said, 'Oh dear, I do hope it's going to work out. She's so desperately keen to be happy.'

'If only that were enough.'

He closed the door and, leading Caroline through the house into the dappled sunlight of the garden, gratefully pushed all unwelcome thoughts from his mind.

The briefing meeting was already under way when Ryder arrived. An officer of the Security Service was speaking. The Security Service – known in the Met as Box 500 after its internal mailing address, and never by its more famous name of MI5 – regularly briefed Special Branch. The officer today was Reece-Jones from the 'F' Branch of Box 500, which covered extreme political parties on both right and left. Nick knew him well: Reece-Jones specialised in the Left. That didn't mean to say that the two men got on. On the contrary, Nick sometimes wondered if Reece-Jones didn't come from another planet. Or perhaps all Box 500 men were secretive and obscure.

'According to the latest reports,' Reece-Jones was saying, 'bar a few minor strikes, the workers have all returned to work. De Gaulle's government is firmly back in the driver's seat and the revolt has well and truly collapsed.'

The eight Special Branch men fidgeted in their seats. It was very hot and there was a fault in the air conditioning. Detective Chief Superintendent Straughan, Ryder's boss, sat sprawled in his chair, his shirt sleeves rolled up over his heavy forearms, beads of sweat running down his cheeks into the plump folds of his neck. The DCS roused himself and asked, 'So what's happened to all the French troublemakers? Any coming our way?'

'Not as far as we know,' replied Reece-Jones. 'But obviously we are interested in any political group who might try to start trouble of the same kind here. Specifically, it has now been decided that we would like you to keep a closer watch on certain Leftist groups. You're already familiar with these organisations, but now we've got to take an even closer look at them.' He handed out a duplicated list. 'We want to know about their leadership, about their links with known communists and subversives. It is quite a task, we realise.'

Nick read the list. All the organisations were well established, and some quite large. There were eight of them, ranging from the International Marxists to the Vietnam United Front and the

Campaign for Nuclear Disarmament. Nick raised his eyebrows. 'Why are the peace campaigners included?'

Reece-Jones replied in a tone that suggested the answer was obvious. 'They are communist based, and they've got strong links with the World Peace Council.' It was well known that the World Peace Council was Soviet-backed and had been manoeuvring behind the scenes for years. None the less, Nick felt that Box 500 were on the wrong track.

He said, 'Surely these people aren't about to start a revolt in the Paris style?'

'No, maybe not,' said Reece-Jones defensively. 'But their aims are still subversive, and it has been decided to keep a much firmer eye on potential troublemakers.'

Straughan gave Nick a look that suggested it might be best for him to shut up. But Nick continued, 'Well, if we're looking for real troublemakers shouldn't we be looking at the latest splinter groups?'

Reece-Jones took a deep breath. Nick sensed that the intelligence officer wished he was back among his colleagues in Box 500 where the atmosphere was more co-operative. Reece-Jones said patiently, 'Well, I think we have to concentrate on the main groups, the ones on this list, because they're the ones *known* to be communist-controlled. They're also the most *organised*.'

Nick frowned. Reece-Jones – and the rest of Box 500 for that matter – had tunnel vision when it came to looking for Soviet and orthodox communist links. That was virtually all they were trained for. Which was all very fine when there were spies and fully-fledged Soviet-trained subverters around. But the students weren't like that. Most of them had rejected conventional communism. But he was on to a loser here, he could see that. The policy had been decided somewhere in the Ministry of Defence and it wasn't going to be changed on his say-so. He decided to shut up.

Reece-Jones brought the briefing to a close with a resumé of the information Box 500 itself would be providing.

'We're putting taps and mail intercepts on all the leaders of these organisations who have communist contacts or sympathies. This information will be available to you as necessary.'

Nick thought: Like hell. Box 500 were notoriously mean with their intelligence. Their attitude was guarded and, if not actually obstructive, then distinctly unhelpful. Nick suspected this was partly because they were all public school and Oxford and stuck together, and partly because they regarded Special Branch as a force which existed solely for their convenience – to do all the dog's work and to make arrests for them.

Reece-Jones was summing up. 'So what we need is a record of these people's movements and who they associate with, the things they write and for which publications' – he smiled ingratiatingly – 'but then I don't have to tell you what we need, gentlemen. You've done it all before.'

Nick winced slightly. The flattery was unnecessary and more than a little patronising. He resented it. He glanced at Conway and saw that he did too, but then, like Ryder, Conway had spent some time out in the big wide world of regional CID. Which was more than ninety per cent of Special Branch ever had. In fact, Ryder and Conway were something of an experiment. Men with outside experience. And, Ryder sometimes thought, the only people used to getting things done.

When Reece-Jones had gone Straughan continued the meeting. 'Right, we're going to go into the mechanics of all this tomorrow, when the commander has okayed the deployments. In the meantime, let's tidy up some loose ends.'

He darted a look at Nick. 'Ryder, what about your lot? The students seem to have been reasonably quiet, thank God.'

'Well – maybe. But Paris has certainly given them ideas.'

The DCS looked displeased. 'Oh?'

'In Italy the disturbances are spreading like wildfire—'

'But *Italy* . . .' The DCS made it sound as if it were a faraway country reachable only by mule. 'What goes for Italy and France doesn't necessarily go for here. I mean, our students aren't as bolshie or as well organised, are they? *Also*,' the DCS added emphatically, 'the defeat of the French students is bound to make them think twice, isn't it?'

'On the contrary. I think it might *encourage* them.'

There was a heavy silence. The DCS frowned. Eventually he murmured, 'Well . . . We'll see, we'll see.'

Nick thought: I'm wasting my time.

'What about the students expelled from France?' asked Straughan. 'What news of them?'

The French had expelled twenty-four British students at the height of the troubles. Nick looked at his notes. 'Most of them have resurfaced in their usual haunts,' he reported. 'Two have made fairly inflammatory speeches, but that's nothing new for them. Oh, and three are still astray. Two went to Belgium and haven't chosen to return to the UK yet. The whereabouts of the third, a girl name of Wilson, aren't known. She was on the expulsion list but gave them the slip.'

'Any other loose ends?'

'Only a student leader who spoke at one of the big Paris rallies back in May. The DST report that her name was Schroeder and that she was British. But we can't find any trace of her, either in Passports or Naturalisation. Nor can French immigration – no one entered the country under that name. Bit of a mystery.'

Straughan grunted. Things like that were always happening. He looked at his agenda. 'Okay. So, what have we got coming up in the next few months?'

Nick went through the list of events being planned by Trotskyists and allied extremists, from a large anti-Vietnam rally in Trafalgar Square to recruitment drives in the universities. He brought up a final point. 'There's still a lot of aggravation over the sentences in the Linden House Hotel affair. There was another minor demonstration in Oxford only yesterday.'

The DCS said, 'Yes, well, that was bound to happen, wasn't it? Thought they were special, didn't they? Well, now they realise that they go to prison like everyone else. But the aggravation will die away in time,' he said with an air of absolute confidence. 'They're just letting off steam.'

He sat back in his chair. 'So, nothing to suggest that our Trots are up to anything in particular?'

Nick resisted the impulse to ask if the DCS wanted them to make a declaration in writing. Reluctantly he shook his head.

'Good,' said the DCS, 'let's get on to rent-a-crowd. I'll bet that's where the next bout of aggravation is going to come from.'

Nick sighed inwardly. It was back to the professional industrial agitators, Straughan's favourite bogey men.

Later, when they filed out of the meeting, Nick muttered to Conway, 'Should have saved my breath.'

As Nick threw the papers on his desk he reflected that the DCS's ideas were like the Ten Commandments: etched in granite.

The files on the expelled students lay on the desk. He glanced through them. Most of the information was painfully thin. Photocopies of passport applications and photographs. In ten cases a bit more: known membership of political parties or groups; an address. In two instances, arrests at demonstrations.

Not a lot.

He picked up the files on the three students who had failed to return to England and took another look. He wanted to be sure he had memorised the names. Cook, Appleyard, Wilson. He peered at the photographs one by one. They were typical passport pictures, that is, pretty awful. The one of the girl was particularly bad. Her face was a white blur with black dots for eyes, like a couple of currants in a rice pudding. She looked terribly young. The picture must have been taken when she was still at school. It was almost impossible to tell what she really looked like.

Roll on the day when the British had photographs on their identity cards or driving licences, then there'd be more to go on.

He had another fleeting memory of the Wilson girl's body at the house in Kentish Town, and reflected that if he'd been a better copper he would have paid some attention to her face.

As it was he had no decent picture. That was because someone had boobed. Though the girl had been held after the Linden House Hotel affair, no mug shots had found their way on to the file. When a charge against someone was dropped there was a strict rule that the negatives and prints were destroyed. That was, *officially*. But in practice Special Branch usually managed to 'acquire' a few copies on the quiet. However on this occasion someone somewhere had been excessively stupid – or stuck rigidly to the rules – and none had got on to the files.

He put the file into the tray to return to Records.

Cook. Appleyard. Wilson. At least he had the names. The ports had been posted. They'd turn up sooner or later.

It was late September, during the last hot gasp of summer.

The warmth of the day lingered in the stillness of the night. Gabriele could feel the heat rising from the dry dusty earth, drifting up through the pines towards the transparent blue-black sky. Beneath her, the hillside fell away in a series of slopes and ridges down to a wide valley. In the far distance another spur of hills, ink-black against the sky, reached away towards the higher ranges of the Apennines to the north.

It was very beautiful.

She raised the binoculars to her eyes and focused on the hills opposite. She watched for a long time, occasionally lowering the glasses to rest her eyes.

Then at last it came. A slight flicker of light.

She never heard the *woomph*! of the explosion itself; the distance was too great. Nor, unfortunately, was she near enough to see the brand new Mercedes enveloped in a ball of fire.

The tiny flutter of light died away, then rose up again, flickering gently. Suddenly a bright bolt of white flame leapt into the air, much higher than the first, and a distinct *crack*! floated across the valley.

Soft footsteps sounded behind her, and Giorgio laughed, 'An oil tank, eh? Or bottled gas.'

The new flame was voracious and spread steadily, forming an oblong block of fire that illuminated the surrounding hills. Soon the whole house was burning.

Gabriele watched impassively. It was no more than the owner of the house deserved. The man, an army general, was a fascist and a murderer. The fascist secret society of which he was a leading member extended into every branch of the Italian establishment, including the police and judiciary.

The general had ordered the bombing of a Bologna bank. Ten innocent men, women and children had died. With suspicious rapidity the authorities had arrested a group of harmless anarchists, and announced that the case was closed. The fascists looked after their own. The general would never be brought to justice.

The firing of his car and house was scant punishment. To Gabriele's mind he should have been executed.

She turned and led the way back through the woods. Suddenly there was a loud screech above their heads. Instantly Gabriele swung the Kalashnikov up into her hand, and sighted up the barrel.

'It's only an owl,' Giorgio murmured.

She slid the catch on to automatic and listened. The screech came again. She adjusted her aim and squeezed the trigger. The rifle rattled deafeningly at a hundred rounds a minute.

She stopped firing and listened. It was very quiet. 'I must have got it,' she said with pleasure.

They continued through the woods. Gabriele cradled the Kalashnikov under her arm. At over eleven pounds loaded weight the rifle was heavy for a woman – so she had been warned – which was one reason why she'd been determined to master it. It also had the disadvantage of being almost three feet long, which made it difficult to carry around unobtrusively. But she didn't care. The

Russian-made rifle was the king of weapons; she liked the weight and security of it in her hands.

She'd learnt to use other weapons too: the small ultra-light Skorpion automatic machine pistol, a short-range weapon, easily concealed and therefore ideal for urban missions, and the Makarov pistol, a handgun that each of the group used as a personal weapon.

But she liked the Kalashnikov the best. This one belonged to a leader of the Lotta; it was on loan for the evening. One day very soon she would have one of her own.

They came to the rough road where they had left the car. Leaning against the bonnet, Gabriele paused and lit a cigarette.

Giorgio hovered impatiently by the driver's door. 'We should go. Someone might have heard.'

She shook her head in the darkness. 'No, they couldn't have heard. We were too far away. We will wait here a while. It's safer.'

Giorgio acquiesced, as she knew he would, and settled down to wait. She had long since discovered the key to Giorgio's character. It was quite simple. He had a terror of being bored. And he got bored very easily. Indeed, left to his own devices, he was incapable of escaping it. He needed someone to take the initiative, to create the situations that stimulated him. As long as the promise of excitement was dangled in front of him, he would follow. And the person he followed was Gabriele. She enjoyed her power over him, just as she enjoyed the power of the rifle.

After half an hour they got into the car and drove towards Bologna and the Milan *autostrada*. Gabriele kept the Kalashnikov across her lap the whole way, but they saw only one police car, and it showed no interest in them.

They arrived in Milan at dawn. Giorgio was about to turn the car into the street where they lived when Gabriele gestured him to continue past and park some way beyond. Gabriele walked slowly back, turned into the street, and sauntered up to the apartment building. Making a show of searching for her keys, she took a good look round.

Nothing.

She went up to the apartment and checked it. When she was satisfied that everything was quiet, she went back to the car and unloaded the weapons into a large suitcase.

'You worry too much,' Giorgio said.

'It's impossible to worry too much.'

Once in the apartment Gabriele made some coffee and sat at the window, watching the street. It was unlikely that the police would suspect her or Giorgio directly – they'd been too careful for that – but suspicion could easily fall on them through the others. The others were often less than cautious. The man who had actually made the incendiary was known to the police. So were at least two of those who had planted the device. Yet they made little effort to be careful: like good Italians, they still visited their families and friends regularly. Also everyone in the group knew everyone else, if not by name, then by face. Security was appalling. No one thought of operating in small cells. They liked the camaraderie of large and frequent meetings.

Gabriele didn't want to be caught for someone else's carelessness. In Italy they put you in jail and threw away the key. You were lucky if your case came to trial within three years.

The more active the group became, the more nervous Gabriele felt. She had an intense dislike of being at the mercy of other people's decisions.

Eventually she left the window and joined Giorgio in bed, sleeping uneasily with the Kalashnikov beside her on the floor. She awoke at three in the afternoon and, still restless, went for a walk. She shopped for food and, for the first time in weeks, bought an English newspaper. She also went to the poste restante section of the main post office in Piazza Affari and, using her Dutch name of Anneke van Duren, asked for mail. Unusually, there was a letter. She recognised Max's handwriting.

Taking the envelope to a quiet corner of the post office, she opened it.

She reread the first part of the letter twice, to make sure she had understood.

Stephie's appeal had been refused.

The full three and a half years would have to be served.

Gabriele's first thought was: Thank God it wasn't me.

Three and a half years. She tried to imagine it. Holloway: dark, depressing. The other women: lesbian, ill-educated, cruel, scornful. The cell: cream-painted, tiny, *claustrophobic*. Three years. *God* – for *ever*.

She suppressed a shiver; she couldn't have taken it. Even though she might have become a famous martyr in the process.

She allowed herself a moment of satisfaction: avoiding that charge had been the smartest thing she'd ever done.

She read on. Max's scrawl was almost illegible. He must have been almost hysterical when he wrote it. The situation was desperate, he said. He had tried everything – he'd organised petitions and protest marches, written to MPs. It had done no good. He begged her to think of other tactics he might try. Did anyone over there have any ideas? He felt that everyone who'd been on the demo had a responsibility to Stephie, to help her, to get her free. Gabriele *must* help! The situation, he repeated, was desperate.

Gabriele thought: It's not my problem.

She owed Stephie nothing. They'd all run risks that day. The difference was that Stephie had been stupid enough to lob that brick. *And* get caught.

Gabriele tucked the letter into her bag and put it out of her mind.

On the way back to the apartment she stopped for a coffee and read through the British newspaper. The news reflected the usual preoccupations of a capitalist society: the bank rate, growing inflation, the number of strikes. The strikes, she noted, were not reported as a sign of workers' desperation, but as a bad omen for world trade and the profits of the fat capitalists.

And yet the stories interested her – very much, in fact. She discerned a strong current of pessimism. The newspaper seemed to think that everything was going to get much worse – strikes, inflation, trade. Reading between the lines, they seemed to be worried about a possible recession and widespread social unrest.

As she walked back to the apartment Gabriele reflected that social unrest would give rise to all sorts of opportunities – opportunities that shouldn't be missed. But how long would it take for the situation to deteriorate? She would have to study the British news regularly to make sure she kept in touch.

Giorgio was watching television when she got back. He was obviously morose and bad-tempered. He would be better later, when he'd had a few drinks. In the meantime she left him well alone.

At six a news bulletin was announced. With pleasant anticipation, Gabriele settled down to watch. She imagined the newcaster's opening words: *Last night the home of the distinguished soldier, Generale Fausto Lamberti, was gutted by fire* . . .

The newscaster appeared. He began to speak.

The smile vanished from Gabriele's face. She listened incredulously.

'. . . Generale Lamberti was shot in the knees as he left a restaurant in Milan last night . . .'

She stared at the screen, speechless.

It was nothing short of betrayal.

The others had kept their main plan a secret. They had purposely not told her. They had not trusted her. She had been excluded. It was a bitter humiliation.

Angrily she stood up and switched off the television.

She thought suddenly: This is the end.

'We'll leave tomorrow.'

Giorgio shot her an angry look. She touched his cheek. 'Will you come with me?'

'Where to?'

She said carefully, 'To Britain. Eventually.'

Giorgio asked resentfully, 'But what is there to do in Britain?'

'What there is to do,' Gabriele said, 'is to operate on our own. And to drive in the first splinter.'

PART TWO
October 1969

Six

Nick Ryder turned into the grim dark street near King's Cross and thought: It's places like this that make people give up hope.

The Barley Mow was half-way along, its tattered red and white façade the only splash of colour in the unremitting grey of the largely derelict buildings. Above the pub hung a sign depicting an incongruous sunlit harvest scene complete with joyful farmers.

Nick pushed open the ornate glass doors of the public bar and paused while his eyes adjusted to the darkness. It was already one-fifteen but Nugent wasn't there. He wasn't surprised; he'd been dealing with Nugent for eighteen months now, and the man was never on time. Buying himself half of bitter, he sat down in a place where he could watch the door.

The other occupants of the bar were students, railwaymen on their midday break, travellers who frequented the numerous cheap hotels in the area. Nick could only guess at their occupations, of course, but he was rarely wrong. He'd made a habit of watching people ever since he was a kid in Barrow, hanging around outside the Crown, waiting for his dad to come out.

It seemed a long time ago. It seemed a long time since he'd joined Special Branch. Almost three years in fact. It was eighteen months since the Paris uprising.

Nugent eventually turned up at two-fifteen, dirty, dishevelled, and jumpy as a rabbit. One look at his sunken eyes and white glistening skin and Nick knew that Nugent was in a bad way.

'Hi,' Nugent began in an urgent whisper, 'got things for you.' He reached awkwardly into a trouser pocket and, with a shaking hand, pulled out some much-folded papers. 'Latest stuff. Hasn't been around before.'

'Let's have a look then.'

Nugent held on to the papers, his eyes darting nervously up and down. 'It's good stuff. Er . . . Ten quid maybe?'

'Price of horse gone up, has it?'

Nugent exhaled through his teeth. 'Yeah. Prices are high — *high*.'

'I'll see what I can do. But I've got to look at the stuff.'

Nugent hesitated and Nick could see that he was reluctant to part with the papers before firming up on the deal. But defeated by his own desperation he suddenly handed them over. Nick glanced through the material. Three different broadsheets. Nothing amazing . . .

And a pamphlet.

He stared at the cover. This was different all right. Trying not to show too much interest, he flicked slowly through it and almost gasped.

Nugent leant forward in his seat. 'Something, isn't it?'

Nick thought: You can say that again. During his time in Special Branch he'd never seen anything like this.

Aware of Nugent watching him he made an effort to hide his excitement. 'It's *okay*,' he conceded. 'Though I've seen quite a bit of it before.'

'*Can't* have,' Nugent said sharply, 'It's new.'

'Maybe,' Nick admitted quickly. 'Where d'you find it?'

Nugent looked away and muttered evasively, 'Dunno . . .'

Nick handed him twenty pounds in fivers. 'Here. But I can't promise that much every time. It always depends on how good the stuff is. Understand?'

Nugent's hands clutched the money as if it were about to save his life. 'Gotta go now.'

Nick said quickly, 'If you find any more like this, you'll let me know?'

Nugent started to get up. Suddenly he paused, his face taut with indecision. 'There's something—'

'Yes?'

'A split.'

'Where?'

'In the SSL. And in other groups. Maybe.'

'What other groups?'

Nugent fidgeted nervously. 'Dunno. Not sure. Just know there's a group off on their own . . .'

He rose abruptly and was gone.

Nick followed in time to see Nugent disappearing in the direction of Camden Town. Within five minutes the twenty quid would be in the hands of a pusher and Nugent would be happy again. For a while.

Nick took the Tube back to Victoria, resisting the urge to look at the pamphlet tucked in his pocket.

He hurried into the office. The seventh floor was almost empty. There was a lot on at the moment: a top IRA man in the country and a visiting delegation from Bulgaria. Conway was in, however, lounging in his chair, looking half-heartedly at some papers. As Nick made for his desk, Conway looked up and brightened visibly. He was obviously in the mood for a chat.

'Blimey,' he said, eyeing Nick with amusement. 'You look more like a Trot every day.'

Nick sat down at his desk. 'Thanks.'

'Well, enjoy it while you can.'

Conway obviously had a gem of information to impart. Nick leafed through the pile of neglected paperwork in the in-tray until Conway could bear it no longer. 'We're on a big surveillance job next week, up in Neasden, you and me included.'

'Damn!' Nick said automatically. He loathed jobs like that at the best of times.

'Thought you'd be pleased. It's the strike at the photographic processing place.'

Conway finally achieved his reaction. Nick exclaimed, 'But that's purely *industrial*. Why aren't Munro's section handling it?'

'Rent-a-mob have been seen on the picket lines. They want us to have a look see. Also they're a bit overstretched.'

'So are we!'

'Trouble is, our students have been a bit quiet of late,' Conway pointed out. 'Whereas quiet is the last word for what's happening on the industrial front.'

It was true. On the surface anyway. Since Paris the students had been reasonably quiet. The last Vietnam rally, though large, had passed off without incident. Now, with galloping inflation and a wage freeze, all the trouble was on the workers' front.

Nick shook his head wearily and, putting an elbow on the desk, shielded his eyes with a hand to show that the conversation was over. Conway prattled on for a few minutes about duty allocations and finally gave up. 'You know, Ryder, sometimes I think Box 500 would be more your line. I've heard say they never even talk among *themselves* . . .'

Nick let the remark pass.

Conway wandered off and Nick pulled out the crumpled papers that Nugent had given him. With great self-control he looked at the broadsheets first. He had recognised two immediately and was certain he already had them on file. They were, he knew, printed by an extremist intellectual group called the Federation for Workers' Control. Their publications were always in the same vein

– workers must unite . . . form rank-and-file committees . . . take the offensive in every strike. The print style of the third sheet was different from the other two and it probably came off another press. He would try to find out which. He put the sheets on one side to look at again later.

The pamphlet.

He picked it up and began to read.

It was about twenty pages long and entitled *Strike Back!* The first few pages dealt with the basic philosophy of an urban guerrilla. It was strong reading. 'Kill as a matter of course – it is the guerrilla's sole reason for being. Do not kill in anger or haste. Kill carefully, coldly . . .' He recognised the ideas; they were very similar to those in the *Mini Handbook* written by the Brazilian revolutionary Marighella – a book which had just been openly published in Germany, Italy and Britain, although, to Nick's mind, such writings counted as blatant incitement, and should be banned.

But this pamphlet went further, much further. He read on grimly. There were detailed instructions on how to incite violence on picket lines and in demonstrations. Then half-way through there was a section headed 'Meet Violence With Violence!' One page was devoted to a drawing of a Molotov cocktail. The next to written instructions and a detailed recipe for what was called 'Easy Brew' – an explosive mixture of garden chemicals and diesel fuel – plus instructions on how to detonate it with a common wristwatch. There were specifications of incendiary devices, more sophisticated detonators, and letter bombs. Then at the end there was the really grown-up stuff. Plastics – the military RDX type was recommended 'if available' – and, in enormous detail, how to parcel and detonate the stuff, and where to place it in cars and buildings for maximum effect.

There was a final page of exhortations to ruthless direct action. 'Activate – Pulverise, Energise, Polarise! Fabricate crystal splinters!'

Nick stared at the explosives section for several minutes. He'd never seen anything so cool and detailed. A complete idiot's guide to killing.

It would have to be checked for accuracy. He phoned the Home Office Branch of the Royal Armament Research Establishment at Woolwich and asked them to check the copy he'd be sending over.

He made five photocopies of the pamphlet, collated and stapled them, and sent one by messenger to the armaments people. Then he went along to see the boss.

Straughan was in. He eyed Nick sharply, making an obvious effort to suppress his distrust of jeans and long hair. 'Yes, Ryder. What can I do for you?'

'I thought you might like to see this, sir.'

Straughan glanced through the pamphlet, frowning as he came to the explosives section. Eventually he murmured, 'Bloody hell – that's all we need. Everything in writing. Any ideas on this yet?'

'No. Only just got hold of it.'

'Source?'

'A student – or rather an ex-student. An addict.'

'And where did he get it?'

'Don't know. And he wouldn't say. But he used to be heavily involved with the left at the LSE – mainly the Socialist Students' League.'

The DCS pulled at his face as if it were india-rubber. 'This doesn't look like student stuff to me. It's far too – advanced. I'd have thought they picked this up from the Spanish Anarchists or the IRA or people like that. They're the only ones with this sort of knowledge—'

'*Lots* of people have this sort of knowledge,' Nick insisted.

The DCS looked unconvinced. 'Well—'

'We know that the IRA have connections with the Palestinians. And that there's a Swiss arms connection between the Basque Separatists and some of the Italian groups . . .'

The DCS stabbed a finger at him. 'Exactly! The professional terrorists. Not the *students*.'

'But I'm not saying the students *produced* this thing. I'm saying they might *use* it. We should find out exactly who's handing out these things and who's receiving them.'

'Look . . .' The DCS's voice assumed a tone of long-suffering tolerance. 'If any of the pros want to go on a bombing rampage they're going to use their own people, aren't they? I mean they're not going to use a bunch of wild kids, not unless they've gone out of their minds, are they?'

Nick tightened his lips and thought: Here we go again. 'Yes, but the students have their *own* causes, their own targets—'

'Such as?'

'Oh, unemployment, bad housing – the capitalist system in general.'

'But they're not organised,' the DCS said slowly and patiently, as if explaining something to a small child. 'Who's going to give them the explosives? Who's going to provide the back-up? Where's the money to come from? The foreign groups aren't going to help and the Soviets sure as hell won't be interested in the lunatic fringe—'

'But they're in contact with several groups who *are* Soviet backed. Indirectly.'

'No. No. I just don't see it. Students are all hot air and demos and shouting. Always have been. No, these kids have just picked up this pamphlet because they think it's smart. *Clever*. They picked it up abroad, no doubt.'

'But printed and produced here, or at least intended to be used here. The spelling's definitely English rather than American, and the grammar and style is – well, perfect.'

'It is, is it?'

Nick let the sarcasm diffuse into the air before saying, 'I'm sure I could find the source given time—'

'Well, let's try the Irish Section first. And Box 500. They'll probably know where it comes from straight away.'

Nick tried not to let his exasperation show. 'But – shouldn't we at least follow it up. I could ask around.'

Straughan nodded slowly. 'All right. But . . .' he paused thoughtfully. 'Just be careful about your methods, I have the feeling that you've been getting perilously close to infiltration recently and we all know what that can lead to.' Some months before a Branch man had passed himself off as a docker at a union meeting and got half murdered. There'd been questions in high places. Everyone paid lip-service to the policy of non-infiltration, but if you wanted to get really good results you went your own way and shut up about it.

The DCS sat up in his chair. 'You'll get this circulated, will you? To the Irish and Anarchist Sections. And the original to Technical Support.'

'Look, I'm lined up for the Neasden surveillance. Could you square it for me?'

'Eh?' Straughan made a disapproving face, then looked at the pamphlet again. 'Well, *maybe* I'll see if I can get someone else to fill in for the first few days – but no promises.' He threw Nick a hard unforgiving stare. 'But just keep me informed, will you? No waltzing off on your own with no one knowing where the hell you've got to. Okay?'

*

As Nick opened the flat door a flood of warm light and safe domestic sounds swept towards him. He was glad to be home. Then the clatter of china in the kitchen reminded him – it'd been his turn to shop and cook, and he had forgotten. But Anne would forgive him – from the cooking sounds she already had. He realised he was extremely hungry and went hopefully into the kitchen.

'Hi,' she said sharply without looking up.

He stared, surprised. She was packing plates into a box.

'I'm leaving in case you're wondering.' She spoke harshly, her face taut and unyielding. Nick's heart sank. He leant back against the doorframe.

The silence stretched out. Eventually she said sadly, 'I wouldn't have thought you were capable of such a thing.'

Normally he'd do anything to avoid a row, especially on an empty stomach, but he parried, 'What does that mean?'

'All that gentle concern!'

'Oh—?'

She stared at him resentfully. 'Well, you're a sham, aren't you? A phoney!'

'Anne, what on earth is this about?'

'Your people came and spied on us!'

'*Spied?*'

'Came to our meeting and took notes.'

He asked incredulously, 'Your *social* workers' meeting?'

'Our Women Against Vietnam meeting!'

'I would have thought you'd be flattered.' Immediately he wished he'd left the words unsaid.

'My God!' she gasped.

'Anne, look – I knew nothing about it. Believe me.'

'Have you got a file on us? *Have you?*'

'I can't answer that.'

She shook her head. 'You leave me no choice.'

'If you're going it's because you want to.'

'Because I *have* to! I can't live with a' – she struggled to find the word – 'with a rotten *informer*!' She paused to find more ammunition. 'Besides, you're a chauvinist. It took a bit of time to come to the fore. But it's there, isn't it? *Who* ended up with all the chores, eh? Me! You're a sham, Nick!'

He thought: Ouch! and wondered why women always had to apportion blame, had to analyse and dissect until the last spasm of pain had been extracted. He shrugged and said evenly, 'Fine. Let's just call it a day then.'

Before she could make a retort he walked into the living-room and sat down with a magazine. There was a silence and he could almost feel the strength of her anger. Finally there were sounds of heavy suitcases being dragged into the hall.

She put her head round the door and, without looking him in the eye, said a stiff, 'Goodbye then.' A few moments later the front door slammed and she was gone.

Nick sat in silence, wondering what on earth had gone wrong. They'd lived together reasonably happily for – what was it? – eight months, and now suddenly she had gone. He'd never made a secret of the fact that he worked for Special Branch, and she'd known – or *guessed* – what it had involved. None the less it was unfortunate about the Vietnam meeting. He could have told her the truth – that many of the committee members were known communists – but she wouldn't have believed him. People only believed what they wanted to.

It was a pity she'd gone. They'd had good times, bed had been wonderful and he still thought her exceptionally pretty. But since getting involved in peace movements and women's rights her wonderful softness and vulnerability had given way to an increasingly strident and dogmatic harshness, and the magic had gone. As for the domestic front, he thought he'd behaved rather well there. Certainly he'd made an effort about cooking and going to the launderette – well, when he could. As for being a chauvinist, that was just unfair. He actually liked women which was more than a lot of men did. No, he couldn't see that he'd been unreasonable.

His stomach rumbled and he remembered that he was hungry. In the kitchen there was a stack of washing-up in the sink, a pile of dirty laundry on the floor and almost nothing in the fridge. So much for meeting each other half-way. Eventually he settled for a stale Ryvita and a tin of sardines. He looked for some beer but remembered that they'd run out some days ago.

He went to put on a record. He decided against opera – in his present mood it would make him maudlin – and chose Desmond Dekker instead. He flopped back in a chair to the soothing sounds of 'Oh-Oh-S-e-v-e-n . . .'

The problem with women like Anne, he finally decided, was that they were made to feel inadequate if they didn't take up causes and follow them through to the bitter end. In the early sixties causes had been a mere fashion, now, in 1969, they were compulsory.

He thought immediately of the pamphlet. A cause taken to the limit. With relief he put Anne out of his mind and, finding the photocopy he'd brought home with him, began to study it. In the last year his library of political writings had grown considerably and, to simplify the impossible task of making sense of it all, he'd made detailed notes of all the various extremist philosophies and card-indexed them by doctrine, structure and actions.

Now he looked through the pamphlet for clues as to the writer's origins and affiliations. The philosophy *might* fall into one of several general categories – Marxist-Leninist, Trotskyist, anarchist, nationalist. Then again it might just as easily *not*. Each category consisted of dozens of splinter groups, each preaching the true and only philosophy. Furthermore, the New Left were inclined to pinch ideas from all over the place, regardless of origin, and stick them together in whichever way suited them, so that you couldn't categorise their ideas in the old way at all. They were an elusive bunch, constantly merging and splitting and reforming.

If it was an organised group at all . . .

Then he looked at the jargon they had used. Most of it, as he'd thought, was borrowed from the urban guerrilla leader, Marighella. Then there was this sign-off, about pulverising and polarising and fabricating crystal splinters, whatever that may mean.

No: he couldn't narrow the field at all.

Where would they have got the explosives info? Cuba? North Korea? The IRA? But the IRA weren't in need of education on the making of bombs nor so philanthropic as to be printing pamphlets for the benefit of other people.

Suddenly he realised he was looking at the problem from entirely the wrong angle.

He should be looking at the *why*.

Why would anyone want to produce such a document?

Only people dedicated to spreading the word.

It had to be a group with missionary zeal, prepared to spend the money on what was undoubtedly an expensive piece of printing, happy to hand it out to whoever might use it, and not at all fussy about which cause the information was put to.

Anarchists? Unlikely. As one might expect, they were usually very disorganised.

A subversive group with funds behind it, then.

He sighed. It was pointing to a Soviet-backed organisation. And that was most definitely Box 500's sphere of interest.

Perhaps Straughan had been right after all.

By midnight he was feeling thoroughly discouraged and decided to pack it in for the night.

Before going to bed he checked his diary. According to *Red Notes*, the periodic guide to revolutionary meetings published by the New Left, there was to be a major meeting of the Socialist Students' League at the LSE next week. Nugent had mentioned a possible split. It might be worth going along, just to see if any of the usual faces were missing.

Another splinter group, another faction, another entry on the card index.

He switched off the living-room lights and stood in the hall, absorbing the quiet calmness of the little flat. In some ways it would be enjoyable to be on his own for a while. But not for too long. He'd got used to having someone else around. He'd enjoyed the domesticity and the companionship.

Yes. He would find someone else. Quite soon.

Six days later, on the dot of seven, Nick turned off the Aldwych into Houghton Street, a narrow lane overshadowed by the numerous grey buildings of the London School of Economics. He automatically assumed the preoccupied, tense look of a student, his eyes down, a frown on his forehead. He walked briskly up the steps of the main building and into the Old Theatre, pausing only to read the notice-board.

The audience was smaller than he'd expected for such an important meeting – there were no more than eighty. Perhaps the Socialist Students' League was going out of fashion. He slid into a seat and pretended to read the latest issue of the Red Mole, a student publication of impeccable Marxist dogma. Only when the meeting finally started ten minutes late did he begin to study the group of young men and women on the platform: the Central Committee of the Socialist Students' League.

He recognised three of them immediately – postgraduates who'd been in the league since it was founded in '67. Their names came to him from the files which he'd examined earlier in the afternoon. Another two were familiar; he memorised their faces so that when he went back to the office he could identify them from photographs taken at marches and demonstrations.

There were a couple of others. They looked pretty young – probably new recruits. He studied their faces too so that he would know them again.

Who was missing?

The red-haired one called Reardon. He'd got two months for the Linden House Hotel affair. He'd always been an angry one, just the type to walk out in disgust at any lack of action.

And there was someone else missing, another who'd been heavily involved since '67. An undergraduate with a sullen intense look. One of those who'd been booted out of France. What *was* his name?

The meeting was starting to warm up. There was some disagreement about joining yet another protest march to the American Embassy. Someone from the floor was arguing that the march would be a complete waste of time because they wouldn't be allowed near Grosvenor Square. Too right, thought Nick: there'd be no repetition of that first large demo when a breakaway group had got within yards of the Embassy.

In patronising terms one of the comrades on the platform started lecturing the floor about the importance of attracting media attention. The floor replied that the media was capitalist-controlled trivia and wasn't worth attracting in the first place.

Nick wondered if he could slip away. The thought of sitting through another hour of this stuff bored him rigid.

But he decided against leaving – it would attract attention. Instead he tried to think of the name that went with that missing face . . . It was earthy, he remembered . . . Rural? No, agricultural. Mower, reaper, farmer . . . Suddenly he had it. Wheat. *Wheatfield*. First name Max. *Max Wheatfield*.

He sat through the meeting for another half an hour until a couple of nearby students got up to leave and he was able to slip out behind them. He went back to his office and found the files marked Wheatfield, M. and Reardon, A. In both he pencilled the comment: 'Not present at 15th March meeting of SSL at the London School of Economics. Possibly forming splinter group?'

It was almost nine. Time to go home. Then with a sigh he remembered that he hadn't filled in his daily diary for almost a week. He loathed the bureaucratic side of police work, but if anyone like Straughan chose to notice the incomplete diary, it could get him into trouble. He went back to his desk and half-heartedly began to write.

Seven

Once an outlying hamlet, the village had long since become a suburb of the ancient walled city of Chester. None the less it retained its identity in a comfortable almost complacent way. The houses were well maintained, the gardens tidy, unemployment was low. The local industries – Morgan's, the brewery, and Bradbury's, a plant assembling electrical appliances – were busy. There were rumours that, even allowing for the traditional caution of the management and the gloomy economic outlook, both would soon be taking on more workers.

Fridays were always difficult for parking in the centre of town, and Mrs Ackroyd peered anxiously through the windscreen as she manoeuvred the Morris into the car park. But it was all right. There was a space and quite near the entrance too. She turned off the ignition and looked at the time. One minute to ten. Perfect. She did like to be punctual on these occasions.

There were butterflies in her stomach. But she was quite used to that. Her boss, Mr Wilson, the financial director of Bradbury's, always apologised for asking her to make these trips, but in truth she rather enjoyed them. It gave her a thrill to carry so much money. And it wasn't as if she had to do it every week. Four of them, all trusted employees, took it in turns. They also tried to vary the timing as much as possible, but with two hundred wage packets to prepare – and a hundred and twenty of those before the end of the day shift at four – one couldn't leave it too late.

She patted the grey curls to her head and, picking up a voluminous shopping bag, got out of the car. The bank was only just across the High Street. As she went in Mr Chesil, the assistant manager, looked up and nodded to her. He met her at the last window and they exchanged greetings through the glass screen. She handed over the withdrawal cheque. As always, the bank had been notified of the exact amount by telephone the previous day, so the money would already be prepared in tidy parcels.

As she folded up the shopping bag and pushed it under the screen, Mrs Ackroyd said, 'How's the football going, Mr Chesil?' She knew that the assistant manager was very keen on the game and played for the bank's regional team.

'Very well, thank you,' he replied. 'We won last Saturday.' He disappeared into an inner sanctum where he always put the money into the bag.

Five minutes later he reappeared and, taking a cursory glance around the bank, went to the door which connected the banking and public sections. He emerged and handed the bag to Mrs Ackroyd, saying, 'Yes, we're playing Barclays tomorrow. Should be a good match.'

'Hope you win,' she said cheerily. 'According to the weather people you should have a good day for it.' She waited expectantly for a suitably light response that would mark the end of the conversation.

But the poor man suddenly looked quite ill. His face had gone deathly white and his eyes seemed to be popping out of their sockets.

His gaze was fixed on something over her shoulder. Feeling the first flutter of anxiety Mrs Ackroyd began to turn.

She cried out in alarm.

Something cold and hard was jabbing into her neck, preventing her from looking round.

She cried out. Another jab and she found herself staggering sideways.

Shocked, she turned at last, and gasped.

A figure stood before her, dressed entirely in black. A devil-mask hid the face, except for the eyes which glinted darkly through the slits. The figure moved, and Mrs Ackroyd suddenly realised what had jabbed her. An enormous great gun.

Her knees went weak and she had to lean against the wall. As she told the policeman later, everything after that was a complete blur. Although she *did* remember to grasp the shopping bag.

The assistant manager knew what he should do. He should get to the alarm button. But the black figure was advancing on him and he froze. The long thin neck of the gun met his ribs and he gave a small cry.

The figure was holding up something in front of his eyes. A message. He blinked rapidly and read it. Nodding, he stepped slowly into the banking section and, with the black figure a short pace behind him, went into the manager's office. A few moments later, he and the manager were standing helplessly beside the safe.

Out of the corner of his eye Chesil saw that all four of the tellers were in their seats. He felt a glimmer of hope. By now one of them was bound to have pressed a foot alarm. Almost immediately he realised he was mistaken. The tellers were sitting well back from the tills, out of reach of the alarms. He saw why. The barrel of a second gun was visible above the glass screen, pointing down at them. Even as he watched, the tellers were leaving their seats to lie face down on the floor. Only one remained in her seat. Keeping a cautious eye on the gun, she began to open the tills and stack the cash neatly on to the counter.

The manager showed no hesitation in opening the safe which, everyone later agreed, was the most sensible thing to do. As the manager piled the money into a large sack the assistant manager made an unhappy mental calculation. Fifteen thousand-odd in the safe plus seven in the tills: twenty-two thousand. Then he remembered Mrs Ackroyd's bagful and thanked God they hadn't got hold of that. It contained over ten thousand pounds.

But a minute later he realised that this hope, like the first, was premature. He heard Mrs Ackroyd's voice crying hysterically, 'Take it! Take it!'

The first gunman appeared with the shopping bag and threw it on the floor next to the two sacks of money beside the safe.

Suddenly there was a commotion and, almost sick with fright, Chesil craned his neck to see what was happening. Framed in the main doorway was a customer whom he recognised as a cantankerous ex-colonel. The old man was haranguing the second gunman, shouting, 'Put that thing down *immediately*!'

Dear God, thought the assistant manager, this is no time for British heroics.

Suddenly a voice rang out. 'Shut up or I kill you!'

There was a dull thud and a shower of glass. The assistant manager jumped with fright. He looked up, terrified, but the colonel was still standing there, alive but shocked. The old man lay down on the floor beside the other customers.

The first gunman, hovering nervously at the connecting door, spun back to face the manager. He held up another written message. The manager nodded furiously. With a thud of fear, Chesil realised the gunman was motioning to *him*. He was to pick up the money and take it towards the back of the bank. They knew about the rear door then. Of course.

With shaking fingers he unlocked the heavily secured back door and carried the sacks out into the alleyway. There was a delivery van waiting there. He got a brief glimpse of someone in the driver's seat before the gunmen hurried him round to the rear doors, which were ready open.

Just before he was forced to climb into the back of the van he made a mental note of the registration number. But it didn't do any good. The van was found abandoned two hours later, not half a mile from the lay-by where the assistant manager himself was discovered, trussed hand and foot, his trousers unceremoniously tied round his ankles.

Gabriele pushed her foot down and watched the speed of the Vitesse climb to over a hundred. But there was no exhilaration in it and, with an effort, she reconciled herself to a long boring drive to London. She felt unexpectedly depressed. The tension of the last few hours had vanished, leaving her drained and strangely dissatisfied.

Max sat silently beside her, shaking his head now and then at some confusing inner thoughts. In the back Giorgio was cleaning the Skorpion, clicking the magazine in and out, whistling contentedly.

Gabriele tried to concentrate her thoughts. She was feeling a letdown after the action, certainly, but there were other, more concrete doubts nagging at the back of her mind. Had they made any mistakes? She went through the raid, detail by detail, looking for deviations from the plan.

There was the shot Giorgio had fired. But no one had been hurt.

And – what?

Giorgio had said something.

She looked at him in the driving mirror. 'What did you say – in the bank?' she demanded.

'What – to the old man?' He laughed. 'I don't remember.'

'Try.'

He sighed loudly and there was a long pause. Eventually he replied, 'I said, "Shut up or I kill you".'

Gabriele thought: I *knew* there was something. She tried to control her anger. '*Exactly* like that?'

She saw Giorgio shrug. He said heavily, 'Yes, like that. So?

'You could have spoken proper English. You sound – like an Italian waiter!'

Giorgio let out an exclamation of disgust and lay back. Max shifted uneasily in his seat.

Gabriele turned the problem of the words over and over in her mind. One moment they seemed like a horrendous mistake, the next she convinced herself they meant nothing. In all the confusion, no one would have noticed the precise words. Anyway, what if they had? Where would it lead? No, she was worrying too much.

All things considered, her meticulous planning had paid off. She allowed herself some satisfaction. It was the first raid. There would be many more, and each would be just as successful.

They hit the M1 at last, and she accelerated again. She smiled, her optimism returning, and said, 'We'll go out and have a good meal tonight.'

Max eyed her uncertainly. Good food was wasted on him. Not that she'd planned to include him anyway. 'You'll go back to your new place,' she said. 'I'll give you some money. We'll speak on the phone in a few days.'

Max nodded. Ever since her return he had been dog-like in his devotion. He was riddled with guilt about Stephie and pathetically grateful for any opportunity to do something to strike back.

Giorgio was a different matter. He was more difficult to please. But money would make him happy. For a while. Then she would dangle the plan of the next action in front of him, and he too would follow her unquestioningly.

She glanced in the mirror and stiffened. There was a white Rover some distance behind, approaching fast. She slowed down until the Vitesse was doing a safe seventy and moved into the middle lane.

The police car approached and slowly overtook. The men inside did not even glance at her.

'All right,' said Inspector Morrow wearily, 'let's go through it again, shall we?'

The bank manager and his assistant shifted in their seats and waited obediently.

The inspector tapped his fingers on the interview-room table. 'An exceptional amount of cash in the bank. The accounts lady from Bradbury's with ten thousand in a shopping bag. And no security guards.'

There was a silence. Put like that it didn't reflect too well on anyone, especially the bank.

'Tell me,' the inspector continued, 'do Bradbury's always get little grey-haired ladies to carry large amounts of cash for them?'

'They have always used their staff,' said the manager defensively.

Morrow shook his head. He'd been in Cheshire CID for fifteen years and it never failed to amaze him how stupid people were with their money. He said, 'Bradbury's tell me they use four different people and vary the times when they collect. Is that true?'

The manager nodded.

'You didn't actually *see* the gunman take the bag from Mrs Ackroyd?'

'No,' the manager said firmly. 'We were by the safe. The customers lying on the floor had the best view . . .'

'Quite. Now – this is very important. Mr Chesil—' The assistant manager sat up. 'When you handed the bag of money to Mrs Ackroyd were the gunmen already in the bank?'

The assistant manager thought desperately. 'I don't know. One moment everything was normal then . . . I'm afraid I didn't see them until they were *there*.'

'What I'm trying to discover,' said the inspector patiently, 'is whether the villains *spotted* you handing the cash to Mrs Ackroyd. D'you see what I mean?'

They saw, but couldn't help. Morrow drew a deep breath and moved on. 'Right. Now what about the guns? You've had a chance to look through our little gallery of photographs, but I gather you're not quite agreed about the type.'

'Well, *I'm* quite sure,' declared the manager. 'I pointed the gun out to your sergeant. I'm positive it was the one.'

The assistant manager shook his head. 'I'm afraid – I don't think the gun was there in your collection. There were *similar* ones, but . . .' He trailed off and shrugged.

The inspector wondered what else the numerous witnesses could disagree about. He supposed he should be grateful for what he'd got: that the two weapons appeared to be sub-machine-guns, and probably identical. Although the thought of sub-machine-guns did not make him happy, not at all. No one had used those kind of weapons on his manor before. The local villains and the ones from Liverpool and Manchester who did him the honour of committing armed robbery on his patch used sawn-off shotguns.

Ballistics had not been as helpful as he'd hoped. The bullet fired at the wall of the bank had spread, and it was impossible to establish the calibre. Neither could the interim report establish *why* the bullet had spread: it might have been a consequence of using a silencer – all the witnesses were agreed on the lack of a loud explosion – or it could have been a result of using a soft-nosed bullet. Or both.

Inspector Morrow drew a deep breath. 'Any more thoughts on the gunman's voice?'

Both men shook their heads. The manager said firmly, 'I only remember his words. "Shut up or I'll kill you!" he said.'

'And what about the van driver, Mr Chesil. You've no more to offer us in the way of a description?'

The assistant manager shook his head. 'It was only the briefest glimpse. Like I said, he had dark hair. And a white face. But as to what he *looked* like, well, it was all rather a *blur*.'

There was a pause. The inspector reflected that you couldn't get blood out of a stone. He tried to end on an optimistic note. 'But we do have some serial numbers, I gather.'

The manager looked pleased. 'We do indeed. We had an unusual amount of new notes in the bank. We have numbers for notes totalling almost six thousand pounds.'

Almost a fifth of the money. Better than nothing.

The inspector then interviewed Mrs Ackroyd. The sergeant had told him what to expect: an earful. And that was what he got. Mrs Ackroyd had decided she was in some way to blame for what had happened and was determined to share the burden.

The inspector interrupted her, 'Mrs Ackroyd, I need to establish one fact. But it's very important.'

She blinked. 'Yes?'

'Did the gunman come *straight* up to you and take the bag of money?'

'What do you mean?'

'Did he seem to *know* you had it?'

'Oh . . . I see what you're getting at. Well, yes, I *think* so. But – I can't be sure.'

'No?'

'Well, you see, I was lying down like the others. And – I didn't *see* a lot. In fact,' she said miserably, 'I had my eyes shut.'

When she'd gone, the inspector pondered. This one had more than a whiff of inside knowledge. And yet there was nothing *conclusive* . . .

He was wondering if he'd ever know for sure when his assistant, a particularly bright WPC, came in and said that in her opinion one of the witnesses – another bank customer – would most definitely be worth talking to.

The witness, Miss Izzard, was about twenty-five and very precise. She answered questions with a calm composure. The

102

inspector wished that more witnesses were like her.

'So Miss Izzard. You are positive about the gun.'

'Yes, I looked at it very carefully to be sure I would be able to identify it when the time came.'

He looked at the sheet the WPC had put in front of him. *Skorpion VZ 61 machine pistol; .32 cartridge; 840 rounds a minute automatic, 40 rounds a minute single shot; made in Czechoslovakia* . . . He ran down the specifications and noticed that a silencer was among the optional extras. His eye fixed on one of the notes at the bottom. *Use of the silencer has the effect of spreading the shot.*

He looked warmly at Miss Izzard. 'And did you notice if both guns were of the same type?'

She nodded. 'Definitely.'

'Did you see the gunmen enter the bank?'

'Yes. I was standing waiting my turn and I saw them come in. They already had their masks on. One jumped on to the counter, the other went straight to where Mr Chesil and the woman – Mrs Ackroyd – were talking.'

'Talking?'

'Yes, I saw Mr Chesil hand her the shopping bag and then start talking.'

'*Before* the gunmen came in.'

She nodded.

'So the gunmen couldn't have seen the money change hands?'

'No, but they knew it was there.'

The inspector started slightly. 'How's that, Miss Izzard?'

'After they'd got everyone lying down and quiet they went straight to the bag and took it out of her hand. They didn't search her – or *anyone*. They obviously knew.'

He could have kissed her. 'Yes, Miss Izzard. That's what I think too.' It was too much to hope that there'd be more, but he asked, 'Anything else you think I should know?'

She thought for a moment. 'Yes, two things.'

The inspector felt a stab of excitement. 'Yes—?'

'The one who spoke . . . Well, he talked like a *gangster*. He said, "Shut up or I kill you." Not I'll kill you but *I* kill you. Like in a gangster film.'

He tried to hide his disappointment. 'I see . . .'

'And the other thing,' Miss Izzard continued. 'The gunman who went into the banking section . . . was, I am absolutely certain, a woman.'

'A *woman*!'

'Yes. I only saw her for a moment when she walked through the bank, and then again briefly when she grabbed the money from Mrs Ackroyd. But I'm sure.'

He shook his head in amazement. No one else had spotted this, there hadn't been so much as a *suggestion* . . . He asked incredulously. 'Why are you so sure?'

'The way she moved. She was wearing very loose clothing – a sort of boiler suit. In black. She was tall and at first sight she could've passed as a man. But she moved like a woman. In the hips, you understand.' She added hastily, 'Oh, and she had small hands and feet. Far too small for a man.'

A few days later the inspector found himself wishing Miss Izzard hadn't been quite such a wonderful witness. The information about the shopping bag had been first class – it pointed firmly to someone having inside information or, at least, a great deal of local knowledge.

But the rest . . .

There had been no fingerprints. Neither had Scotland Yard been able to match the *modus operandi* – and particularly the machine pistol – to any known criminals.

For a while he'd pinned his hopes on an Irish connection. But Special Branch in Liverpool were doubtful. The IRA used a variety of arms – their favourite was the Armalite sub-machine-gun – but they weren't fond of Skorpions which were essentially close-range weapons. Also they preferred to rob banks on their home ground in the Republic where they stood the best chance of going to earth and evading capture.

It didn't leave him with very much: a local job which had none of the hallmarks of the local talent; and two villains, one of whom appeared to be a gangster film enthusiast, and the other a woman.

He would just have to hope that some of the numbered notes turned up soon.

All in all the case had a bad feel to it. And the more he went into it the more he suspected it was going to drag on to a less than satisfactory conclusion.

The flat was on the third floor, overlooking Montagu Square. It fulfilled all the requirements: it was in a block of fifteen similarly anonymous flats, it was just the right size, and it came fully furnished. But there was one problem: Gabriele hated it on sight.

The furniture was appalling: a brown Dralon three-piece suite with black screw-on legs and brass feet, miniature chandeliers and too much gilt. In itself the overblown look wouldn't have mattered if it hadn't reminded her so forcefully of her childhood.

She said to the agent, 'No. It won't do. Haven't you anything else?'

'Nothing similar in this area,' said the young man. 'Although if you were prepared to change your mind about having a *flat*, I do have a lovely mews house. Just behind here.'

She hesitated. A mews would be too quiet and one's movements too easily observed. Also the neighbours were likely to be nosy. She shouldn't even consider it. At the same time she was getting tired of looking. She agreed to go and see it.

Montagu Mews was even worse than quiet: it was a dead end. Number 42 was half-way down on the right. It had been fully converted into a house, the old stables on the ground floor having been replaced by a gaily painted brick façade with large windows. Two small fir trees in wooden tubs stood either side of the front door.

Full of misgivings, Gabriele followed the agent inside. She had to admit that the place was rather nice. The house was a snug arrangement of small rooms, each brightly decorated in sun colours and floral prints. The living-room, which ran the depth of the house, had a sitting area at one end and a small dining table at the other. A plant had been trained up the wrought-iron banisters of the spiral staircase which rose from one corner. In the bathroom the loo had been painted bright yellow with a ring of green and red flowers inside the bowl.

She looked thoughtfully out of the window. There was parking immediately outside which would be handy . . . And perhaps the quietness would be an advantage.

It was much too expensive, of course, and she quibbled with the agent. But she could see that he wasn't going to budge on the price; she looked too well dressed.

Eventually she said grudgingly, 'I'll take it.'

In the agent's office she gave her name as Gabriella Carelli and produced an Italian passport as proof of identity. She stated her occupation as freelance photo-journalist, and gave the magazine *La Posta* of Milan as a reference. She paid a deposit and two months' rent in advance.

Gabriele drove straight to another house agent behind Marble

Arch. This time there was no problem about getting exactly the right thing: the agency specialised in service flats for visiting foreigners. She was shown several in the area north of Oxford Street, and settled on a fifth floor three-roomed flat in a block on Weymouth Street. It was furnished in a modern characterless style and had a well-equipped kitchen. She took it for four weeks in the name of Mr and Mrs L. C. Hoerst of Bern, Switzerland. She paid the deposit and rent in cash on the spot. The agent looked pleased.

On her way back she drove past the end of Montagu Mews and noted that it was only two minutes away from Weymouth Street, which would be most convenient. Then she headed the car down Park Lane towards Knightsbridge and Chelsea. The Vitesse had gone back to the rental firm three days ago, and she was now driving a small Fiat which she had bought through *Exchange and Mart*. The Fiat was better suited to her new occupation.

She parked off the King's Road and, going into a couple of the better boutiques, bought a pair of high boots and a trouser suit in white cotton. In the last three weeks she'd spent over two hundred pounds on clothes. The camera equipment had cost even more – there were two Olympus OM1 camera bodies, three lenses from 28mm to 50mm, a zoom, and a powerful telephoto.

She took her purchases back to the flat in Chelsea Manor Street, where she and Giorgio had been living since their arrival nearly four weeks before.

Giorgio was not at home. Systematically, she began to sort everything out, ready for the move to the mews house. She would keep this flat on, but only as a safe house to be used in the last resort. Certain things would need to be left here: a little money well hidden, a change of clothes, a list of telephone numbers, a passport.

She took a briefcase containing the money from under the bed. There had been just over thirty-two thousand when they'd first counted it. Now there was twenty-four. It seemed to go surprisingly quickly. And she would need a great deal to pay for supplies from Paris. Nevertheless it should last some weeks. Although there was one complication.

The money was divided into two piles, carefully separated. On the left, the slightly dog-eared used notes which they had been using for their expenses. On the right, the clean crisp new notes, virgin and untouched: six thousand-odd, sequentially numbered. She eyed the wads of notes uneasily.

It was far too risky to use the new stuff, either here or in Paris, and yet without it they'd be short.

Something would have to be done about those notes. And at the moment she couldn't think what.

She removed two thousand pounds from the pile of old notes and put it on one side. From her old clothes she selected a pair of trousers, a blouse, a jacket, and some flat shoes, which she put with the two thousand.

Taking a list of numbers from the lining of her handbag, she copied the numbers on to another slip of paper, replaced the original, and tucked the copy into an Argentinian passport, which she slipped into the pile of clothes.

Finally, she took a copy of *Strike Back!* from her bag of books and papers and put in on top of the clothes. She couldn't think why she should need it if she was on the run, but one never knew.

Now to find a hiding place. The kitchen units were built in, the base units raised above the floor by a recessed plinth. The cooker, however, was free standing. She pulled it out and, kneeling down, tried to lever out the plinth that ran alongside the cooker. She broke two knives before she thought of going down to the car and getting the wheel-changing kit. The small wrench used to remove the hub caps was strong enough to lever the plinth out and, wrapping the clothes, papers and money in a bag, she slid the bundle under the unit, knocked home the plinth and replaced the cooker.

She peered down. Apart from a slight splintering of the wood on the corner of the plinth, there wasn't a sign.

Now to pack. She put her considerable number of new clothes into a couple of holdalls, and put them by the front door. Closing the case of money, she placed this too in the hall.

There was one last job to be done.

Going to the fridge, she removed a thick plastic container, the size of a large shoebox, from the bottom shelf. Opening the lid very carefully, she peered at the contents. Then, slowly, she put her nose to them and sniffed.

Satisfied, she closed the container again and placed it in one of the holdalls, well protected by clothes.

There was nothing to do now but wait for Giorgio.

Whenever she was on her own and had a free moment she liked to look at her list. With anticipation she sat in a chair and pulled the slip of paper out of the handbag lining again. The telephone numbers which she had copied were on one side, numbers which she had jumbled slightly to hide their true sequence. On the other side was a list of abbreviations of names.

The chief targets. The capitalist oppressors.

The list of names was not complete. But she was working on it.

Eight

Victoria braked hard and spun the wheel. In a hail of loose stones the Mini careered off the road and, skidding sideways, shot on to the farm track, missing the ditch by a whisker.

The car ground to a halt. The radio was blaring '. . . the age of Aquarius, A-quar-ius . . .' Victoria sat shivering in a hot sweat. It had been a near thing, that ditch. The tiredness had ruined her judgement. She just wasn't used to staying up late, not after all this time. But then it wasn't every day your sister had a party in London. She shouldn't have gone, though. She hadn't enjoyed it.

Shakily she started off again. The bottom of the car hit the lip of a pot-hole with a loud grinding noise. The holes needed fixing – like everything else.

Ahead the chestnuts arched upwards, their summer magnificence quickly fading in a flurry of dry yellow leaves. Soon she would get her first glimpse of the house. During the early months at Hunter's Wood she'd always looked forward to this moment, even if she'd been away a short time. But today . . . Today she remembered the work list, and how very long it was and how behind they were.

She drove on and pulled up in front of the house. The camper van, the only other vehicle in sight, was parked carelessly in the middle of the yard. Victoria looked at the house and frowned. Although it was noon and the day fine the living-room windows were tightly shut and the curtains drawn.

She stiffened, listening hard. Away past the tractor shed Bella, the sow, was grunting, not in her familiar snuffly contented way, but in long sorrowful snorts. And the chickens – there was no sound from them at all.

Apprehensive, Victoria hurried round the corner of the house and across the yard. The door of the tractor shed was open and the engine of the ancient Massey Ferguson lay strewn in small pieces over the floor. She sighed inwardly; there would be no ploughing today then.

In the sty a distressed Bella pushed an anxious snout over the wall. Her trough was quite empty. Victoria realised with growing despair that it had probably been so for some time. She gave the wildly grunting pig some water then went to the reed store. That too was empty. She exclaimed aloud, 'God! It isn't much to ask. Not *much*!' Who was it – yes, Martin – who was meant to have picked up the monthly supplies? How *could* he have forgotten?

Angry now, she marched across to the chicken shed. She stopped short and caught her breath. The door was wide open and there wasn't a bird to be seen. Only feathers and remains scattered widely over the ground. Foxes' leftovers.

Muttering bitterly to herself, she strode into the farmhouse kitchen. The remains of a meal were spread over the table and draining board. Victoria went straight to the slop pail, topped up the sparse plate-scrapings with porridge oats and stale muesli, pulled up a whole fresh cabbage from the vegetable patch, and gave the mixture to a grateful Bella.

Crying now, she returned to the kitchen and stared dejectedly at the mess. A note was propped conspicuously against a bowl on the dresser. She recognised Ned's tidy handwriting. Victoria reached out hesitantly, uncomfortably sure of what it would say. She unfolded it. 'We hereby resign. We feel that the original spirit and intentions of the commune have been lost. We have taken a few vegetables, but nothing else. Ned and Kate.' There was a forwarding address.

She leant hard against the dresser, thinking: They're right, the heart has gone out of this place. She felt a black despair.

She went into the hall, the slap of her sandals echoing loudly across the stone floor. The living-room was empty and dark, the air close and stale. The other ground-floor rooms were lifeless too. She climbed wearily up the stairs and stopped outside Martin and Janey's room. Gentle snores were audible through the closed door. She thought bitterly: How *could* they? She opened the door and looked in. The room was dark but she could see the two figures sprawled across the mattress. Martin muttered angrily in his sleep. Janey was very still. Victoria went up to the mattress and touched her hand, then shook her firmly and shouted her name a couple of times. Janey responded with a loud moan and turned over.

On the floor beside the mattress were the leftovers of the party: home-made elderberry wine, a couple of half-smoked joints, some pink tablets – speed – and a plate.

Victoria stared at the plate and her heart moved painfully. On it were the remains of a brashly coloured cake, marbled with veins of vivid yellow and green and purple. Crouching, she picked up a piece and, lifting it to her nose, sniffed it.

She should have known. Mel had joked about it often enough. Rainbow cake – psychedelic and mind-blowing. Full of junk.

In the passage she took a long deep breath and started towards the room she shared with Mel. Even as she approached, she caught the whiff of booze and grass and overflowing ashtrays.

Suddenly she had a horrible yet tantalising thought: that there'd be someone else in the bed with him. Another girl – the blonde art student, the one who often arrived uninvited and walked naked in the back meadow; the one he sometimes disappeared with. She hesitated at the door, miserable in case her suspicions were correct, yet desperate to know.

She walked in. He was alone. She exhaled, half with relief, half with a curious sense of disappointment.

He was lying on the bed, face up, his mouth wide open. He was out cold, like Janey. The room was a mess and the smell unpleasant. With despair she realised that at one point Mel must have been sick.

She screwed up her face and muttered, '*Honestly* . . .'

After a few moments she went closer, drawn by a need to see the full extent of his dissipation.

Suddenly she held perfectly still, her senses reaching out like an animal scenting the wind.

With disbelief yet perfect certainty, she knew.

He was dead.

She remained still, as if the moment could be frozen or undone. But gradually she became aware of her own breathing, of infinitesimal fractions of time flickering past. Slowly she began to absorb the details of the sight before her: the eyelids which were not quite shut, the whites of the eyes which gleamed dully through the lashes, the bluish, almost transparent skin. Slowly she reached forward and touched his arm. It was cold. Cold and dead.

She felt nothing. Not then. The day took on a curious dreamlike quality. It wasn't until much later when a policeman asked her what her relationship had been to the dead man that her detachment peeled away like a bandage from a wound.

And then she cried, not just for Mel but for herself. He'd never loved her very much, she realised that; but he was the only man who'd ever accepted her just as she was; the only man who'd made her feel at all desirable. Now he was dead and she felt ugly and fat again.

It was dawn the next day before the police drove them back to the farm. Martin and Janey, drowsy and shocked, went to bed. Victoria climbed slowly up to the top meadow and sat in the dewy stillness, watching the thin light creep into the secret valley.

She thought: This is the last time I'll sit in this meadow.

There was no point in going on. It was the end. And she didn't even understand why . . .

The sun rose. The valley filled with a strong yellow light which illuminated the lush fullness of the dying summer. It was still the most beautiful place she had ever seen.

Defeated, she walked down the hill and wandered round the farm buildings, seeing as if for the first time the dilapidated fences, the rusty gutters, the patchy repairs, the roofs that had started leaking again.

Eventually she slept for a few hours. At ten she woke the others and by midday most of the arrangements had been made. A neighbouring farmer agreed to buy Bella and arranged to fetch her at two. The three cows and one heifer were going to be collected for market on Tuesday. That left only the goats grazing up in the meadow and the fruit and vegetables unpicked in the field. Martin and Janey could deal with all that. They were staying on, for a while at least.

Victoria packed her belongings. She left Mel's things – she couldn't bring herself to touch them – except for the embroidered Tibetan jacket and collar of bells she'd bought him last Christmas. These she put in her bag.

At some point arrangements would have to be made to sell the few modest pieces of furniture, the farm equipment, the vehicles – the tractor – such as it was – and the camper. Finally the farm itself. But she couldn't face that just yet.

She left without saying goodbye to Martin and Janey who

were meditating in the living-room, softly chanting their mantras. As she drove away up the hill towards the vaulted chestnuts she didn't look back.

A week later Henry Northcliff sat in his study at home, holding the telephone slightly away from his ear, and wishing the conversation would end.

But Mrs Danby's voice continued to travel relentlessly down the wire. 'It's just so *dreadful*, the whole thing. *Drugs* – I mean, I had no idea Victoria was mixed up in such things – all those drop-outs and drug-addicts. Honestly, Henry, I'm really *hurt* . . .'

He made a few pacifying noises then pointed out, 'She's not actually being charged with any offence, Mrs – er – Elizabeth.' She had insisted on the use of her first name.

'Maybe not. But the *inquest*. It's all going to come out. It's going to be dreadful – for *Victoria*.' A distinct whine had come into Mrs Danby's voice and Henry found himself thinking that her concern didn't extend to Victoria at all.

'And what's even worse,' Mrs Danby continued, 'is that she should drag *you* into this! I'm so embarrassed I don't know what to say.

'She didn't drag me into anything,' Henry corrected her. 'She phoned me and asked me for the name of a good solicitor, which I was delighted to give her. She didn't ask anything more.'

'No? She hasn't come round to see you then?'

'No,' Henry lied.

'Oh . . . well. That's *something* at least . . .'

She rang off at last and Henry sat at his desk for a moment, wondering if he was wise to get embroiled in all this. He was doing it partly for Caroline, of course, but also because there was a vulnerability and innocence in Victoria which appealed to the protective side of his nature. At the same time he would have to be careful not to let things get out of hand. Unhappy people could be leech-like in their consumption of other people's time.

He found the women sitting either side of the kitchen table, Caroline composedly in her chair, Victoria slumped over a cup of coffee.

The moment Victoria saw him she jumped to her feet. 'I must go. I only meant to stay a minute—'

'No, don't go yet,' Henry found himself saying, and hoped he wouldn't regret it. When she was back in her seat he added, 'That was your mother on the phone. I didn't tell her you were here.'

Victoria closed her eyes and shook her head as if the news were the final straw in an already heavy burden.

Henry sat down and said patiently, 'Now – let's look at the positive side of things. Everything's been sorted out on the legal front. There's absolutely nothing more to be done about what happened last week. What you must consider now is your future.'

Victoria looked at him blankly. 'I – haven't a clue. The commune was what I wanted .. Or what I thought I wanted.'

'Isn't there anything else you could do?'

She shook her head miserably. 'That's the trouble. I'm not *trained* to do anything. I was brought up to be jolly company at hunt balls and make a terrific quiche lorraine and avoid serious subjects. And I'm not very successful at *that*!'

Henry couldn't help smiling. 'Well, there's nothing wrong with tackling serious subjects.'

'Oh! You wouldn't say that if you'd met my county friends!' she exclaimed passionately. 'They think it's bad form to discuss politics or Vietnam or the Third World. And if anyone *does* mention anything like that, they just make a ghastly *joke* of it.'

'The British disease,' said Caroline. 'Making jokes.'

Henry watched Victoria and realised what else he liked about her. She had a delightful ingenuousness. She was incapable of guile or subterfuge. Everything came spilling out, straight from the heart.

He said gently, 'Look at it another way. Can you afford to go without a job for a while?' She nodded. 'Well then,' he went on, 'why don't you do voluntary work? For some charity or another. Something you really care about.'

She thought for a moment. 'Well – I do feel strongly about poverty. And bad housing. And Vietnam. And the Third World. And oppression. And injustice—'

'That should do for a start.'

She caught the gentle mockery in his tone and shot him a self-deprecating smile. 'Well, perhaps I'd choose *one* thing to start with ... Perhaps Vietnam. I do feel very strongly about that.'

'And how exactly would you serve this cause?'

Her round freckled face puckered into a frown of concentration. 'I think – by helping raise awareness of the atrocities committed against the people ... And collecting money to help the victims of American bombing ... And combating American imperialism generally – that sort of thing.'

The speech had more than a hint of propaganda to it, but Henry let it pass.

She said abruptly, 'I suppose you don't approve? The British government always supports US imperialism, whether it's Labour or Tory.'

Henry didn't want to argue the point. Remembering his own commitment to Spain when he was young, he said, 'If that's what you really believe, far be it from me . . .' He got to his feet and, taking her cue, Victoria picked up her bag and followed Henry and Caroline towards the door.

'Thank you *both*,' Victoria said. 'And I'll think very hard about what you've said.'

Henry paused thoughtfully. 'Only one thing, Victoria. I'm all for the free expression of opinion, whatever that opinion might be. But if you do get involved in any of these movements, take care, won't you?'

'What do you mean?'

'Well' – he tried not to sound like an old woman – 'keep a sense of proportion. There's always an element who like to take things too far, to – use an issue to provoke discontent rather than to make a point.'

'Oh, you mean at demos and things? Don't worry, I wouldn't get involved in any of *that*. It frightens me rigid.'

'Was I too pompous?'

'No,' said Caroline. 'I thought you were – just right.'

'She probably won't take a blind bit of notice of what I said anyway.'

They walked slowly towards his study. 'I've still got a pile of work to do. I'm sorry.'

Sensing that he still wanted to talk she followed him in and sat on the edge of the desk.

She said, 'You're tired.'

He sat down and ran a hand across his forehead. 'No more than usual. It's just that' – he thought for a moment, trying to analyse his mood – 'I've lost my optimism, I suppose.'

'Any particular reason?'

He exhaled slowly, a long pensive sigh. 'For the first time I feel that, as a government, we've failed – in a number of important areas. We've been evading some vital issues and now we're paying the price – the highest strike record of any government, wages out of control, prices going mad. And it's going to get worse. I feel it.'

'Why do you think so?'

'There's a new discontent – a real anger. People are in a militant mood . . .' He looked up at her. 'It'll lose us the election, you realise that?'

'I see.'

He patted her hand thoughtfully. 'For myself, I won't be that sorry.' He examined her face. 'In fact, I thought of stepping down anyway. Even as Shadow Attorney-General. I've been meaning to talk to you about it—'

'Whatever you think is best—'

'Would you mind very much?'

She laughed a little. 'Mind? No, of course not. You work too hard and if it's what you *want* . . .'

Having voiced his decision, Henry knew it was the right one, and felt the beginnings of an immeasurable relief.

Nine

The rain beat furiously against the showroom windows, cascading down the glass and blurring the outlines of the buildings opposite. Manchester at its wettest. Not a good afternoon for selling cars, even the expensive ones that filled the showroom. In monsoon conditions, well-heeled people liked to stay at home just like everyone else. Bisley, the joint proprietor, sales director, chief – and only – salesman, got out his paper and had another look at the clue for twenty-five across. 'Illegitimate form of history (7).'

Bastard something? he wondered. No, that didn't sound right. What else were illegitimate children called . . .? Another word was just easing its way into his mind when the showroom door opened with a bang. He looked up and saw a young woman shaking out an umbrella.

She was well dressed in a modern casual sort of way. Comfortable middle class, he decided, with artistic tendencies. Not the buying type – Bisley could tell these things at a glance – but very striking. Worth a pleasant chat anyway.

He put on a smile and went to meet her. 'Good afternoon,' he began warmly, running an admiring look over her. 'And what can I do for you on this *lovely* day?'

She looked at him as if he were slightly mad. 'I want the blue Aston Martin, please. Assuming there's nothing wrong with it, of course.'

Knock me down with a feather, thought Bisley. You never can tell.

'Ah, now that's a very fine car – one owner, regularly serviced. And of course, less than a year old. I think you'll—'

'Let's cut all the talk, shall we?' she said briskly. 'Just tell me what you're prepared to offer?'

'Offer? Do you want a part-exchange?'

'No, no,' she said with a touch of impatience. 'I want a price reduction for cash – and I mean notes, not a cheque.'

The car was an expensive model – a DBS – and was priced at five thousand four hundred. Bisley thought quickly. The cash would certainly be useful; he could easily falsify the books. At the same time he was a little annoyed at this young woman's peremptory tone. He wasn't sure he was prepared to play her game.

'It's already a fair price,' he said firmly. 'In fact, we price *all* our cars fairly. There really isn't a lot of room for manoeuvre.'

She gave him a hard stare and he could see the anger behind the dark eyes. 'I was offering you a straightforward deal,' she said sharply. 'And all *you* want to do is go through the boring old rituals just to satisfy your ego. Don't you think it's rather a juvenile waste of time?'

Bisley blinked. For northern bluntness she beat any Mancunian into the shade. Although, from her accent, he'd bet she was a southerner.

Trying to recover the advantage, he joked weakly, 'My ego's perfectly satisfied. I have it serviced regularly. How's yours?'

They settled on five thousand one hundred – a drop of three hundred on the asking price. It was much further than he would normally have gone, but he'd bought the car at a good price and the sight of the tax-free wads of crisp new notes was too much to resist.

She produced an insurance cover note and announced she was going to take the car with her.

'For yourself, is it?' asked Bisley, wondering where she'd got the money for such an expensive machine.

'No. For my employer. He's a wealthy businessman.'

That explained a lot. When she'd gone Bisley wondered if she wasn't *more* than just a rich businessman's employee. She was very – *animal*, that one. Definitely one of the permissive Society.

It was 4.00 p.m. and Friday. He would take the money home for the weekend and bank a small part of it in his business account on Monday – some, after all, had to go through the books. The rest he would keep in cash. He might even buy a new lawn mower tomorrow, and a bicycle for his daughter.

Flush with well-being, he went back to the crossword. A moment later he grinned with satisfaction. He had it at last: illegitimate form of history – *natural* history.

He decided that, despite the rain, it had turned out to be a most satisfactory day.

Gabriele chose Hendon to dispose of the car because it was a prosperous area of London and the garage forecourts were already thick with used Jaguars and Mercedes. The first garage offered her a cheque, which she turned down, but the second promised cash by 11.00 a.m. on Monday. She decided it was safe to accept. There was no way that the hot money could be spotted in the Manchester banking system, traced back to the car and every garage in the country alerted in that time. Even assuming the police were bright enough to realise the point of the whole exercise.

Nevertheless when she returned on the Monday morning she watched the garage for an hour before driving on to the forecourt. By noon she was back in the mews house with four thousand seven hundred pounds in used notes. Enough to pay rents, bills and major expenses for some months.

That left only nine hundred of the difficult money to dispose of. It should be safe to use it for small transactions, as long as it was spent in crowded places well away from the area of the mews house.

Things were beginning to look a little tidier.

She had several more jobs to do that day. First she went to a small printer's nearby and picked up some business cards. These gave her name as Gabriella Carelli and her occupation as photo-journalist accredited to *La Posta*. The address and phone number of the mews house were printed at the bottom.

Next she telephoned several photographic processing laboratories, and went to visit one in Covent Garden which specialised in fast developing and machine duplication. It was run by three energetic young men who were perfectly happy at the idea of doing rush jobs at odd hours. She left them one of her new cards.

At three she went to a firm called Inter-News, off Fleet Street. This was a photo-news agency which, for a modest fee of fifteen to twenty per cent, took freelancers' pictures and tried to sell them to newspapers and magazines worldwide. The firm had a staff of five, including the tea boy, and was headed by Stan Geddes, a former picture editor on a national newspaper. Like most newspapermen, he liked to think he'd seen it all.

Putting his head out of his office door he spotted the girl waiting. Quite a looker. He decided to see her personally.

He glanced at her card. '*La Posta* – but we can't handle their stuff.'

'No, no. I'm freelance,' she said firmly. '*La Posta* commissions me to do occasional jobs. Otherwise I'm on my own. Will you handle my pictures?'

'I'd have to see some of your work. We don't take on people just like that.' He thought: Even when they're as tasty as you.

She eyed him firmly. 'Look – if I walked in here with some hot news pictures, what would you do with them?'

Ah, he thought, a smart dolly, this one. He gave in gracefully. 'We'd flog 'em.'

'Quite.' She got to her feet and shook his hand. 'You'll be hearing from me then.'

After she'd gone, Stan Geddes smiled to himself. Then, taking her card, asked Beryl, his secretary, to enter her name and address on the file.

On her way home, Gabriele made a detour to the Marylebone Public Library and spent an hour in the reference section, taking notes from such diverse publications as *Who's Who*, *Encyclopaedia Britannica*, the *Legal Gazette* and the London Telephone Directory. It was amazingly easy to discover who did what in Britain, and, more important, their private addresses.

It was six when she finally got back to the mews. Giorgio and Max were already waiting. She didn't like Max coming to the house, but since they were going to meet so rarely in the future the risk was really quite small.

'Well, what have we got then?' she asked Max.

He fished a copy of *Red Notes* out of his pocket and, opening it at the right page, passed it to her.

The item was listed under Forthcoming Events for October, and was printed in bold type and capital letters, to give it emphasis. The item read: '25th: DEMONSTRATION AGAINST NATIONAL FRONT. Meet 12 p.m. Speakers' Corner. March to Russell Square. All welcome. Organisers: Third World Liberation Council.'

Max also passed her a leaflet, giving the objectives of the march:

– To show our abhorrence of the racist, fascist National Front and all they stand for.
– To demonstrate to these fascists that the people of this country will NOT tolerate anything to do with their vile aims. The stated aims of the National Front are 1) to protest against the presence of *all* coloured people in Britain, 2) to demand repatriation of all coloured people to their country of origin and 3), as an immediate aim, to ban all further immigration by coloured people to Britain.

These aims are obnoxious and abhorrent to all free thinking people!

On 25th October the National Front are holding a rally in Holford Hall, Russell Square. We must counter-demonstrate to show our repugnance.

COME AND JOIN US! DEMONSTRATE AGAINST FASCISM!

Gabriele read it a second time. Yes, it would do very well. The National Front always provoked strong feelings. This counter-march should produce an explosive situation. A popular journalistic phrase came into her mind: emotions are likely to run high.

She said, 'It looks as though it'll be quite an event. How many people are likely to turn up, Max?'

'Several thousand.'

'I think we'd better find out exactly who's going to be there. We need to be sure that the crowd will be – the right sort.' She added, 'What about your group. How many people can we rely on?'

'Twelve or so. Including Reardon, of course.'

Gabriele pondered. It would mean depending to a certain extent on people over whom she had no direct control. Her instincts were against it. And yet an opportunity like this might not turn up again for months.

She looked sharply at Max. 'And you're prepared to' – she didn't know quite how to put it – 'to be the *star*?'

Max looked at the floor, frowning. 'Yeah. It's okay. I don't mind.'

Gabriele guessed that he was thinking of Stephie, and how the event would cheer her up. She warned, 'We're going to keep a low profile on this, you know. There can't be a communiqué.'

'No, I understand.'

Giorgio roused himself from his silence. 'But some time?'

'Maybe. When it's necessary.'

'Then we should have a name,' Giorgio said. 'The Fifteenth of May Group!'

'Too – complicated,' Gabriele said. And, though she didn't voice it aloud, far too similar to the names of other groups in Europe. It was important to have their own quite separate identity. She suggested quietly, 'The Crystal Faction. I prefer that.'

Giorgio frowned. 'What does that *mean*?'

Gabriele sighed inwardly. Sometimes Giorgio could be very awkward. 'Crystal, as in clarify – *harden* – and faction, as in *splinter group*.'

She fetched her bag and took out the notes she had made in the library. 'Now, I've been making a list. A sort of strategy. It's only provisional. But I think it'll make a good start.'

It takes four hours in an unheated warehouse early on a cold October morning to seize up one's bones, Ryder discovered. It takes less than an hour to become bored rigid.

The gates of the factory opposite were deserted. Very sensibly, the pickets were having a nice warm breakfast elsewhere. He thought: What a waste of bloody time.

Conway turned up late, at ten past eight, muttering, 'Don't complain, mate. You've only done *one* morning of this. We've done *four*.'

Nick went straight to the office, shuffled through the pile of bumf on his desk for an hour, then joined the rest of the squad in the briefing-room.

'Okay, let's get going then,' said Straughan. 'The National Front march and counter-demonstration. One, A8 has given permission for both marches. You'll find details of the planned routes and stops on the operation order. Two, there are going to be about fifteen hundred on the National Front side. No surprises likely there – all the usual faces. Three, the leftist march is being organised by the Third World Liberation Council. Now, this lot have always been reasonably peaceable in the past. Mainly lobbying and propaganda. *However* –' he paused to add weight to his remark '– this time they're obviously out to provoke. Choosing to rally in Russell Square at the same time as the Front.'

Straughan clasped his hands together to make a precise arch. 'Now, what I want is the following – I want to know who's in with this Third World Liberation lot. Normally they've only a few dozen members at the most. Now, all of a sudden, they're expecting a thousand supporters. Where do they come from? My bet is that they've been busy phoning round their friends.'

The DCS looked at Nick. 'I want to know exactly who those friends are, Ryder. Then we'll know who to be looking out for on the day. Right? Any questions?'

The room was silent. Nick scribbled on the information sheet: *CPGB, IMG, IS, VUF*. They'd all be there, he'd bet his life on it – the Communist Party of Great Britain, the International Marxist Group, the International Socialists, the Vietnam United Front.

He thought for a moment then added *SSL* – The Socialist Students' League.

The briefing turned to other matters. The DCS held up a copy of the *Strike Back!* pamphlet. 'We're still on the look-out for this, all right? If you see something like it, I want to know where it came from and how it got there.' The DCS shot a glance at Nick. 'Although I gather we do have something from Technical Branch, Ryder?'

'They seem to think it might have been printed on the Continent.'

'Right!' Straughan's eyes gleamed triumphantly. 'Probably a foreign group then. As we thought. Still, we've got to keep a sharp look-out. In the wrong hands this could be dynamite.'

The pun was awful. Nick gave a short derisory laugh. Straughan shot him a hard look and Nick realised the joke had been strictly unintentional.

As soon as the meeting broke up, Nick went to Records to see what they had on the Third World Liberation Council.

The Council appeared to have a staff of one, a part-time secretary who worked in a borrowed office in Camden Town. Originally it had been formed by the 'broad left', including some members of the Labour Party and the Communist Party of Great Britain. It still had a Labour peer as its president. The organisation was run on a shoe-string and had at one point almost faded into obscurity.

Recently, however, it had come to life again, becoming increasingly vocal on the subject of immigration and the rights of millions of citizens in former British colonies to full British citizenship.

Nick wondered how best to tackle this one. Sometimes there was nothing like the direct approach. He closed the office door and dialled the number of the one-roomed headquarters in Camden Town. It seemed to be permanently engaged but finally he got through on the sixth try.

A crisp female voice answered. 'Yes?'

'I'd like to know about the march . . .'

'Twelve noon. Meet at Speakers' Corner.'

'What about banners. Are we co-ordinating?'

There was a slight pause and the voice asked cautiously, 'Who is this calling?'

'Manchester branch of the SSL. The name's Randall.' The name was perfectly accurate. He just hoped the secretary didn't know Randall.

'Oh, nice to talk to you.' The voice was trusting, friendly. 'We've been lent a place, in fact. Belonging to the Vietnam United Front. 2a Berners Road, off the Holloway Road. We're getting together there most evenings. Bring some materials, won't you? We don't have much money. Paint and stuff. You know. Are you in London now?'

'Er, not yet. On the Thursday, I hope.'

'Right. Well, we look forward to seeing you. You'll be bringing a group down, will you?'

'Yes.'

'Oh, good. How many?'

'Not sure yet. But at least fifty. We *hope*. Look forward to seeing you.' He cut the conversation short. He didn't want it to get too detailed.

He picked up the jottings he'd made in the inspector's office and ticked off the Vietnam United Front. No prizes for getting that one – the Vietnam protesters were into everything.

2a Berners Road. That was new. He checked his pocket notebook which he used for quick reference. The Vietnam people had been using a place in Tufnell Park up till now. He went back to the main files. Yes: just the Tufnell Park address.

He made a call to his friend Barbara at the GPO and within five minutes had three phone numbers in use at 2a Berners Road. One he immediately discounted: a tailor's on the ground floor. The other two, on the first floor, were in the name of the Holloway Workers' Council.

Another name, another organisation. It was like a jigsaw puzzle which was impossible to complete because the pieces were constantly changing shape. Yet the connections would be there, in the people. The same faces turned up time and time again.

The direct approach had got him this far. He decided to keep going, and dialled first one then the other number serving the first floor of 2a Berners Road.

No reply.

What next? It might be worth trying Nugent. If he could find him.

He phoned the flat where Nugent sometimes stayed. Eventually a sleepy masculine voice answered and told him that Nugent had 'split, man'. The voice had no idea where he'd gone and, no, they didn't know when he'd be back, if at all.

Nick wasn't surprised. Nor was he disappointed. Nugent had more or less dropped out and, apart from the pamphlets, the information he'd been passing recently hadn't been worth very much.

There were two other possibilities; good contacts Nick had built up in the previous year. But he wouldn't be able to find either of them until the evening, and he was impatient.

It had to be 2a Berners Road then.

He took the Tube to Islington and walked up the Holloway Road, not yet certain of what he was going to do. Number 2a was at the beginning of Berners Road, an undistinguished two-storey building, its façade once painted but now streaked in grime. The tailor's window was covered in heavy reinforced grilles. Those of the upper floor were blank and uncurtained. There was no access to the first floor from the front of the building; however there was an alleyway running down the side.

It was two in the afternoon. The sensible thing would be to come back later and watch for the evening arrivals – the organisers and banner painters. But to do it properly he'd need the van and the full camera set-up. Too much aggravation.

Besides, he was feeling lucky.

He walked purposefully into the alley. It led to a courtyard and an unexpectedly large two-storey storehouse which abutted the main building. There were two doors. On one of them was a

123

sign: *Holloway Workers' Council*, and beside it in chalk: *Vietnam United Front*.

The door was unlocked. At the top of the stairs were two doors, one of them open. The open door led to a large airy room which was empty except for four trestle tables, several piles of boxes and, spread over the floor, wooden poles and sections of white fabric.

On the nearest table was a pile of broadsheets; on the next posters. Mostly Vietnam United Front, but some for the Third World Liberation Council, advertising the march.

'Hello.'

The voice startled him, but he made the effort to turn slowly.

It was a girl in her mid to late twenties. Plump. Long frizzy fair hair decorated with beads. Ethnic clothes. Sandals. No make-up. Freckles. Nice smile.

He replied, 'Hi,' and waited.

She came forward, looking friendly. '*Sorry*. I just popped out . . . Can I help? Did you want some literature? There's quite a bit here. And more in the office . . .' She indicated the closed door across the landing. 'Gosh, I've been here all morning and the moment I pop out somebody *comes*. Honestly, *typical*!' She laughed awkwardly, waiting for him to respond and ease the moment along.

'Just wanted some details of the march on the 25th.'

She brightened visibly. 'Oh, right! *No* problem. Gosh – do you want a poster or would a broadsheet be okay? And, let's see – what *else* do we have? Mustn't let you go away without *everything*, must I!'

Nick thought: God, what *have* we here. The accent – straight out of Cheltenham Ladies' College. Upper-class Belgravia gone native.

She handed him a broadsheet and a leaflet. 'That's all there is, actually. Sorry. Will that be enough? We're only helping out on this one. It's not really a Vietnam Front thing, although of course we all support it. God, wouldn't *anyone*? I mean, really, when you see the blatant racism it' – she shook her head as if it were impossible to find the right words – 'it makes you *sick*, doesn't it?'

'Ya. Makes you sick.' Nick agreed. He strolled towards the closed office and paused by the door. She got the hint and, opening it, let him in. He wandered casually around. There were two desks, two telephones, and a clutter of papers piled haphazardly on the floor.

She came up behind him and asked, 'Who are you with?' The question was conversational rather than probing.

'Oh. Er – various groups. But mainly the SSL.'

'Ah.' A moment of complete blankness, then she nodded doubtfully.

She obviously hadn't a clue. Nick almost smiled. With growing confidence he asked, 'Er ... D'you know what the order of marching is ... You know, who's going to be there and who'll be leading the thing up ... That sort of thing?'

She frowned. 'Oooh. Got me there. You see, I'm a bit new and, well, I man the desk and do what I can. To be honest, I'm just a volunteer and ...'

He amended his opinion: naïve upper-class Belgravia do-gooder with a social conscience – perfect left-wing fodder. He nodded understandingly. 'Know where I can find out?'

'Oh yes! Tomorrow evening. There's a meeting here at seven. I expect they'll be discussing all that ...'

Nick thought: As simple as that. He said easily, 'Thanks. You've been really helpful.'

Her face lit up at the compliment. 'Not at all! That's what I'm here for!'

He paused at the top of the stairs. 'Bye. Er – sorry, what was your name?'

'Oh, Victoria. Victoria Danby.'

The moment he'd gone Victoria realised she'd forgotten the name of his organisation – SOL, was it? And she hadn't even asked for his name. She *should* have – the committee were very keen on that.

She muttered 'Blast!' and made a mental note to get everyone's name in future.

Still, it was only her second day here and, all things considered, she wasn't doing too badly. She'd read all the information sheets, articles and pamphlets issued by the VUF, and quickly realised how little she really knew about the Vietnam conflict. It made her ashamed to think how ignorant and ostrich-like she'd been in the past.

All that was going to change now. She was determined to be useful, and that meant knowing her stuff.

Taking a doughnut out of the desk drawer, she began to read a pile of news clippings. The doughnut disappeared very quickly and she found herself eating another. Weak and sinful. But she was *definitely* starting a new diet next week.

The telephone rang a couple of times. One caller wanted to join the VUF, the other wanted details of the anti-Front march. At first she'd been confused at the VUF's involvement in the march. But as one of the committee had pointed out to her, the coloured immigration issue and the Vietnam anti-colonial struggle were two sides of the same coin. She'd never thought of it like that, but of course it was absolutely true. Blindingly obvious, in fact.

The Workers' Council phone rang on the other desk and she took a message. There'd be someone in later. People were always coming and going.

The time began to pass more slowly; she had nothing more to read and by three she'd finished sticking down the last batch of envelopes she'd been given. By four she was wishing she'd brought a book with her.

There was a sound. She gave a slight start and looked up.

A man was standing in the doorway. She smiled. 'Hello, can I help you?'

He came in. He was very dark, with rich black hair that came down to his collar, and a thick but well-trimmed beard. He wore jeans – good ones, she noticed – and the sweater was pale blue cashmere.

He looked slowly round the room then fixed his eyes on her. They were dark brown and penetrating.

Victoria thought: Absolutely gorgeous. The kind you could die for.

She reminded herself that dozens of women probably had.

She laughed nervously. 'Did you want some information?'

He gave her a small rather mechanical smile. 'I want information about the march . . .'

An accent. Very attractive. Latin? She replied, 'Yes, of course. I've got a leaflet or a poster or—'

'Yes . . . But we wanted details –' He came up to the edge of the desk and looked down at her. He was even better close up. She caught a scent of eau de cologne.

He went on: 'We want to know who will be there, and how many . . . We want to bring many, many friends, but we want to know what is happening . . . You understand?'

'Yes, of course. There's a meeting. Tomorrow at seven. For all the organisers.' She looked away hurriedly, aware that she had

126

spoken in a silly girlish voice, and thought: Get a grip. This one is *way* out of reach.

She suddenly remembered to ask, 'Who are you? Which organisation do you come from?'

For a moment she thought he wasn't going to answer, but then he replied a little grudgingly, 'We are foreign students. We want to show our solidarity against fascism.' He pronounced 'fascism' in a totally foreign way – Italian or Spanish, she decided.

He was wandering back towards the door. 'Thank you,' he said, looking back at her with a sudden warm smile. 'You have been most kind.'

She smiled to herself until long after he'd gone.

Then she remembered that she was large and whale-like and unattractive, and he wouldn't have smiled so much if he'd seen her standing up.

Completely beyond her reach. But there was no harm in imagining.

Ten

At six it would be twilight. Nick took a look through the lens of the Nikon and focused on the alleyway. On the other side of the van, Wicker, a young detective constable who specialised in photography, was tightening the clamp on one of his two Canons, which were loaded with high-speed 400 ASA film. Nick checked that the spare film and battery cartridges were to hand, so that he'd be able to pass them to Wicker when necessary.

They settled back to wait. They had managed to park in a good position, a few yards beyond the alleyway, so that people coming from the Holloway Road were facing the van's one-way back windows.

Nick said, 'You just keep firing the shutter until I tell you to stop, okay? Even if it's a housewife with shopping bags.'

'Okay.'

It was only ten to six. Plenty of time.

Then, suddenly, there were two of them. The first arrivals.

Looking at street numbers, searching for the alleyway.

Nick urged, 'Go!' and heard the Canon's motor-drive fire off half a dozen shots. He took a couple of frames himself, just in case. But it wasn't vital because he knew the faces anyway. He scribbled their names in his notebook.

After ten minutes there were more. Committee members of the Third World Liberation Council. He knew their names too.

By six-forty they were coming thick and fast, and, with only seconds to spare, Wicker had to switch from camera to camera while Nick hastily loaded new film.

Then it grew dark and the dim streetlights cast deep shadows. Nick put his camera aside and left the photography to Wicker.

At seven-ten there were a couple of latecomers, and five minutes after, one more. Then nobody for a long time. Nick began to relax. There'd been a few he hadn't recognised, but those would soon be identified from Wicker's shots. There were no surprises: all the usual trendy-lefties – the smooth articulate revolutionaries loved by the media; the university lecturers living in intellectual cuckoo land; the well-paid actors assuaging some deep-rooted personal guilt by assuming it for the world as a whole; the self-important clerics with their messages for mankind; and the proud self educated worker activists.

Nick didn't hate them or anything like that. In a curious sort of way he actually admired them – the clever ones at least – for the way they stuck at it. The problem was, they weren't to be trusted. They advocated lunatic policies and, like all zealots, turned a blind eye to the means. Not that they themselves cared to get involved in any dirty tricks. They left that to the followers, the ones who worshipped at the shrines of wealth-for-all and revenge-on-the-rich; people so eaten up by envy that they were incapable of clear thinking; the ones whose anger, having no rational outlet, became bottled-up and explosive. They were the really dangerous ones. And they had to be stopped.

That was why Nick did the job – because they had to be stopped and he was the best person to do it.

Nearly eight. Suddenly Nick sat up. Two men. Nearly an hour late. He said 'Go!' to Wicker, and peered at the fast-approaching figures.

He exclaimed softly, a gentle 'Hah!' of satisfaction. One of the men was Wheatfield. Max. Late of the Socialist Students' League.

But the other—?

His satisfaction evaporated. The head was down, the features hard to distinguish. But foreign-looking. Black hair, beard, dark complexion - or was that a trick of the light?

Damn it, put your head up. How can I get a good shot if you don't show me your *face*?

But even as the man came into the dim glow of a streetlight he turned his head away, looking back towards the Holloway Road, as if checking on his retreat.

Then they were gone, disappearing into the darkness of the alley, and Nick sat back with a sigh of exasperation. 'Dammit!'

Wicker decided to state the obvious. 'Impossible to get a full face on that one.' After a moment he added unhelpfully, 'Was he important?'

Nick gave a wry laugh and murmured sarcastically, 'Sure. Very important. Wasn't it obvious from the back of his head?'

Victoria sat by the door and counted thirty-five people crowded into the storeroom. They sat on the trestle tables and the available chairs or leant against the walls. She had managed to account for almost all of them by name or by organisation. Athena, one of the VUF committee, was very keen on security. Because of the bloody spies in Special Branch, she had explained, though sometimes she suspected it was MI5. Victoria had laughed until she'd realised that no one else thought it a joke. Somewhat chastened she had then kept quiet.

Now Victoria tried to concentrate on the meeting, but it seemed to have developed into a rather woolly discussion about long-term objectives.

Suddenly there were footsteps on the stairs and Victoria quickly got up to open the door. Two men appeared: the first a thin, intense-looking man with long straggly hair and wire-rimmed glasses; the second, she suddenly realised, was the gorgeous foreign man from yesterday. She brightened. Then, remembering her task for the evening, politely asked which organisation they came from. The first man glared at her with sudden and vicious hostility and, without answering, pushed rudely past.

Victoria stared after him, feeling well and truly snubbed. The foreigner was still by the door, leaning unconcernedly against the frame, casting his eyes slowly round the room, looking bored. She said a little peevishly, 'Anyone would think I'd asked him how often he kicked his *dog*.'

His eyes swivelled round to her, deeply puzzled. 'Kicked his *dog*?'

She laughed nervously. 'Er – old English expression.' She regarded him hopefully. 'Don't suppose there's any chance of knowing your name—'

'My name?' For a moment he didn't answer, then a flicker of amusement passed over his face, and he gave a slight shrug. 'Vespucci. "A" for Amerigo.'

The name was vaguely familiar but she couldn't quite place it. Definitely Italian though, just as she'd thought. She added the name to the list.

She looked up to find him smiling, and she noticed how white his teeth were against the darkness of his beard and skin. He leaned down and put his lips to her ear. 'You like it?'

'I – what?'

'You like my name?'

She stared at him. 'Yes. Yes, very nice.' She suddenly realised he was making fun of her. Looking as businesslike as possible, she went back to her seat and sat down again. She thought a little resentfully: This is the last time I do *this* job.

The meeting droned on, with a lot of talk about support and press coverage.

At the mention of the press the Italian stood up a little straighter. She stole a look at him. A small frown of concentration had appeared on his forehead.

She wondered why he was interested. Then she wondered all sorts of other things about him, none of them to do with the meeting ... Like the sort of women he went for – beautiful, inevitably. And how many he knew – without doubt, a depressingly large number. She could imagine him with a woman, sensual, confident in his approach, very practised, yet caring, wanting to give a woman pleasure.

Lucky women.

Unlucky *her*.

She sighed inwardly. Thinking about unobtainable men wasn't any help when there was an empty flat to be faced again tonight. A place of her own had seemed a good idea, but she hadn't allowed for the loneliness. The decision to break with Mel's crowd had been right, she was sure of that. Yet she had no wish to see her county friends from the old days either. And, though the people in the VUF were friendly in a brisk no-nonsense sort of way, they weren't likely to become real chums. It was all very difficult.

The meeting was coming to an end. People were standing up and talking in groups. The Italian went to join his companion. Because she couldn't think of anything else to do, Victoria took her list across to Athena who was busy talking. Athena stared at it vaguely and was about to tuck it under her arm when she took another look and gave a short laugh. 'What on earth is *this*!' she exclaimed, pointing at the Italian's name. 'A joke? Amerigo Vespucci – *really*!'

Cold fingers of embarrassment crept up Victoria's spine. It came to her now that, according to the history books she had paid such scant attention to at school, Amerigo Vespucci had at some time or another been associated with the discovery of America.

The committee woman demanded, 'Who gave you this name?'

Victoria indicated the Italian. The woman seemed mollified. 'He came in with Max Wheatfield. He should be all right then . . .' She gave Victoria a hard look. 'Still, it was hardly worth writing it down, was it?'

Victoria turned away. As she made her way back towards the door she eyed the Italian resentfully and thought: You aren't very nice at all.

Suddenly, on a whim, she veered across and tapped him on the back. Smiling pleasantly, she said, 'It's remarkable. You don't look a day over three hundred.'

His face flashed with suspicion then, suddenly understanding the joke, he said. 'Thank you. Nor do you.' His tone was friendly and she softened a little.

She explained, 'I was only doing as the organisers asked, you know.'

'Sure.' With deliberate effect, he fixed his eyes on her and, putting his hand lightly on her shoulder, moved his fingers across it in a soft caress. 'It was their mistake then, to ask it of you.'

Ah, the treatment, Victoria thought. She tried to show that it wasn't going to work on her, and almost succeeded.

'What *is* your name?' she asked, for something to say.

He gave a slight bow. 'Emilio.'

'Nicer than Amerigo,' she replied. 'Not so continental.' She giggled slightly at the joke.

The thin straggly-haired man called Max came up and glared at her again. She said a fleeting goodbye to Emilio and retreated.

As she made her way down to the street, she reflected that

Emilio was the type of man that good girls were warned against. Yet she had a sneaking suspicion that it was merely sour grapes; that people only said that because they were jealous of the fun and excitement that surrounded people like him.

If she ever had the choice she knew what she'd go for. The fun and excitement.

That she should be so lucky . . .

When she got outside she paused for a moment and breathed in the cool autumn air and wished that, instead of heading back to an empty flat, she was looking at the vast dome of glittering stars above the calm stillness of Hunter's Wood.

Nick watched the girl staring at the sky and recognised the Belgravia-type volunteer from the previous day. While Wicker took a couple of snaps he wrote in his notebook: Victoria Danby, VUF.

Then she was on her way, walking rather listlessly towards the Holloway Road.

He barely had time to look back towards the alleyway when they were there: Wheatfield and his foreign friend. He said sharply to Wicker, 'Quick, those two!'

The camera motor whirred away, firing the shutter at staccato speed. Nick squirmed with frustration. Although Wheatfield's profile was visible for a brief moment, the dark-haired man kept his back firmly to the camera and was even now disappearing briskly down the street.

'Damn,' Nick said simply.

He left it a moment then, stretching his arms wearily, said, 'Okay, let's call it a day.'

'Already?' asked Wicker. 'There're still quite a few to come out.'

In the dim light Nick gave him the benefit of a hard stare. 'Yes – *already*. You may want to sit through another performance, but I've seen enough of the actors, thanks very much, and I'd like to get home.'

Only eight days to the demonstration.

Gabriele beckoned to Giorgio and, taking out a large sheet of plain paper, spread it out on the floor of the mews house. Using a thick pen she drew a large square in the centre, and marked all four sides with small counter-strokes. 'Railings,' she explained. In the middle of the square she drew a few trees. With one eye on the street plan of London, she added an outer square, with approach roads at all four corners.

'Russell Square.'

Using a red pen she drew a dotted line down the northern approach road to Woburn Place, into the square at the north-eastern corner, and along the northern side. 'Is this right for the National Front?' she demanded.

Max indicated a point about half-way along the northern side. 'The hall's about there.'

She brought the dotted line up to the approximate position of the hall. Then, starting from the opposite south-western approach road of Montague Street she traced another line up into the square, along the south side and out again towards the south, like an inverted U.

'That's the route of our march, right? Now, we can be absolutely sure that the police won't want us anywhere near the fascists on the northern side. So, to keep us firmly to the south side, they'll have to seal off the right- and left-hand sides of the square.' She drew two lines where she imagined the police would be.

'Now, after the column has entered the square, we've got to get it to slow down. Jam up a bit. That's where your friends come in, Max. Right?'

He nodded thoughtfully. 'Yeah. They'll just make some noise or something . . .'

'Then – you and Giorgio and Reardon and the other three, you must end up here.' She marked a cross on the demonstrators' side of the first police line.

'And I'll be just behind the police . . . Here.' She added a red blob in the no-man's land between the two demonstrations.

Giorgio said, 'But they will not let you arrive with a car . . .'

I'm going to park it there on Friday night. There's no reason for them to move it.' She looked up at Max. 'Reardon – how much have you told him?'

Max shrugged slightly. 'He had to know everything, otherwise he'd be no good. Don't worry. Reardon's okay.'

She nodded. She'd have to believe him.

They went through the whole operation again, trying to foresee the snags. Then she destroyed the map.

When Max had gone Gabriele made some calls. First she phoned

Stan Geddes at the Inter-News Agency and told him she'd be covering the demonstration. His tone was polite, but uninterested. He confirmed that the office would be staffed until at least five on the Saturday afternoon.

Then she called the processing laboratory and told them she'd need some rolls printed up very quickly the same day.

That covered the picture side of the operation. Except for the quality of the photographs themselves. That was up to her. She'd taken several test rolls of people walking in Hyde Park, to get familiar with the Olympus equipment. The results had been reasonably good.

There was nothing else left to do so far as the demonstration was concerned. She turned her mind to the longer term.

She needed supplies.

Taking the slip of paper from her handbag lining, she checked the dialling code for Paris and then called the third number on her list. The connection took some moments but eventually it rang. Gabriele was aware of being nervous and gripped the receiver more tightly.

A woman answered. Gabriele asked for Acheme. There was a pause and a male voice asked for her name. When she had given it, he told her, 'Your consignment will be ready for Wednesday, the 29th. When you get to Paris telephone between ten and noon. You will be told where to go. You will need to bring the money.' He added, 'The consignment will be bulky. You understand?'

'All right for a car, though?'

'All right for a car.'

Gabriele put down the receiver and immediately considered the problems. Only twelve days away and a bare four days after the demonstration. She would have to get organised. She would have to find a suitable vehicle, something in which the consignment could be safely hidden. None the less, passing through Customs would be very risky. Perhaps they should use a circuitous route?

No, there had to be a better way, one which involved less risk. Or best of all, one which involved no risk at all.

Eleven

Ryder wondered if he was in the right place. The groups of marchers had got fairly muddled, but as far as he could see the bunch around him was Vietnam United Front. They were young, most of them, and noisy, their chants echoing loudly across Great Russell Street towards the dark dignified mass of the British Museum. Nick kept step with them, mouthing the chants, merging into the group.

Futher back were the Marxists, the International Socialists and various other factions; ahead the organisers – the Third World people – with whom he'd mingled at Speakers' Corner. A few known agitators in each group. But no indication as to which lot – if any – were planning trouble.

Ahead was Montague Street which led directly into Russell Square. Somewhere in a building on the corner was Conway with an array of cameras hidden behind a curtained window. There would be other Branch members in the square itself, some behind the uniformed police lines, others on rooftops.

As the procession turned into Montague Street Nick decided to move up towards the leaders who were in clear view about twenty yards ahead. He made up ground gradually, picking up the chant of the forward group, swinging his legs and pumping his arms to the rhythm of 'Fascists *out*, fascists *out*'.

Trees became visible over the sea of heads – the square. And ahead, a line of helmets – the mass of uniformed men blocking the marchers from the western perimeter.

He followed the leaders into the square, and made the swing right, past the cordon and along the south side. The crowd was bunching up now as the leaders slowed down and the back-markers, anxious to get into the square, pushed forward. Movement slowed to a shuffle. The chants became louder, the waving of the banners more agitated as the leaders shouted their message in the general direction of the National Front somewhere on the far side of the square and, more particularly, Nick guessed, to the inevitable band of mediamen, hungry for some colourful pictures.

He took a quick look round. No pushing or shoving nearby.

Craning his neck, he gazed back over the mass of heads towards the entrance to the square. The middle of the column seemed to have come to a halt and a thick concentration of demonstrators was pressing up against the police line.

A nasty feeling crept into Nick's stomach; he suddenly had the suspicion that he was in the wrong place.

He took a last look at the head of the column, and then, turning against the tide, tried to make his way back. It was hard work. The crowd was closing in tighter. Why the hell weren't the uniformed boys keeping the front of the column moving? People panicked when they got claustrophobic.

Almost on cue a banner jerked into the air ahead, somewhere near the police line, then jerked rapidly down again, as if being dragged to the ground. Anxiously Nick stood on tiptoe and peered over the throng.

A person turned. A quarter-profile. Tantalisingly familiar. Long straggly hair . . .

Wheatfield.

Where on earth had *he* sprung from?

And beside him – dark hair, beard. Wheatfield's foreign friend. The one who was camera-shy.

And then another, with bright red hair. Reardon.

Suddenly Nick was certain of where the trouble was going to be and with a hard shove, forced his shoulder into the crush of bodies and began to fight his way through.

The police line was thick, about five men deep. Gabriele hadn't bargained on that. From her vantage point on the car bonnet she could hardly see over them.

Clutching her cameras, she scrabbled up on to the car roof, and hastily reset the tripod.

That was better. She could now see the demonstrators well bunched up against the rows of uniforms. Almost immediately she spotted Giorgio, his dark head clearly distinguishable in the crowd. Max would be close by. They were right in position.

She braced her legs well apart and, focusing the camera, took a couple of shots.

Just in time. A roar came up from the crowd, there was a surge, and the middle of the police line began to sag.

Any moment now . . .

A voice yelled from close by, '*You! Down!*'

She ignored it. A hand grabbed her by the ankle. She looked down angrily. A senior policeman in a peaked cap was motioning her off the car. 'Come on! We're moving everyone back!'

She shrugged as if she didn't understand, and pointed to the press pass strung around her neck.

'I don't care,' he yelled. '*Everyone* back!'

Gabriele looked desperately towards the crowd. It would be any moment now! She stalled again, shrugging her shoulders.

Another roar went up and the crowd surged. The police line showed signs of breaking completely.

The senior officer hesitated, then, abandoning his attempt to move Gabriele, ran towards the straining line.

The roar died down, the line held and for an awful moment Gabriele thought the momentum of the demonstrators had been lost.

Then from behind her came a clattering sound and a drumming of heavy boots on the roads. She spun round and saw a stream of reinforcements running from a side street. They ran towards the bulging line and, at a shouted order, the line opened up to let them through.

Immediately a bitter throaty howl of anger went up from the demonstrators. Gabriele saw Max jostling for position, Giorgio beside him.

It was going to happen. Tense with excitement, Gabriele settled back behind the camera and, carefully framing the picture, placed her finger on the shutter.

Victoria yelped as someone stood on her foot. She turned, intending to smile and show she didn't take it personally, but an elbow came out of nowhere and hit her on the side of the head.

'Oh, please mind out. *Please.*'

She began to feel uneasy. Everything was changing. The unified, friendly, chanting faces had gone. The voices were ugly now, the shouts and cries jarring in her ears. Tall bodies were pushing in on her, jostling roughly.

It wouldn't last, she felt sure. Everyone was bound to sort themselves out in a minute.

Suddenly voices rose angrily and the crowd surged. The movement pushed Victoria sideways. She cried, 'I say!'

But the mass moved on, crushing in on her, carrying her relentlessly forward. Victoria was appalled at her own helplessness. She stifled the urge to panic.

A leaden weight came down on her foot. Stumbling, she fought to regain her balance, but couldn't disentangle her foot from the weight. With terrible certainty she suddenly realised what was happening, and panic shot through her like a wedge of ice. Everything moved into slow motion. She was being dragged down, slowly, inexorably. The bodies were closing in over her and the patch of light that had been the sky slowly receded . . .

She shrieked and grabbed at whatever she could find – hands, clothes, legs . . .

A kick, a foot in her back, a sharp pain. Her head hit the ground and she flung up her arms to protect it. But the feet kept coming – hard, brutal, kicking, stumbling, crushing.

They'd realise in a minute, then they'd stop. *Surely* . . .

But they didn't stop and through her pain, all Victoria could feel was an immense and profound surprise.

Nick ducked as an arm swung wildly over his head. He came up, trying to get his bearings. He knew Wheatfield and company must be very close, but they were maddeningly invisible due to a large belligerent bull of a man who was bellowing and roaring in front of him.

All of a sudden the crowd heaved to one side, throwing some people to their knees, and a gap opened up. Nick forced his way through.

He was close to the police line now. Dimly he took in the fact that the line had been reinforced by the Special Patrol Group. And then, right in front of him, almost at the front of the crowd, he spotted Wheatfield. Next to him was red-haired Reardon carrying a banner pole and yelling a chant that sounded like 'Go! go! go!' Even as Nick struggled to reach them, he saw Reardon lower the pole and thrust it forward, stabbing viciously into the mass of police.

Immediately all hell broke loose and the crowd became a fighting screaming mass.

Wheatfield was close. Nick went for his arms but withdrew with a yelp of pain as the full force of a truncheon landed on his elbow. Fleetingly he thought: Christ, that's all I need. He regained his balance and in the maelstrom reached for Wheatfield again, a Wheatfield who was jabbing and kicking furiously at a sack on the ground, except it wasn't a sack it was a policeman. Nick thought: You bastard. He almost had him, but one of the SPG was already there, yanking Wheatfield out of the crowd, raining blows on his head.

138

Nick elbowed through to the front and, fending off the shoves and pushes of the crowd, saw the SPG man deliver a couple more blows to a strangely apathetic Wheatfield, inert on the ground. Nick wished the stupid idiot of an SPG man would stop. This sort of thing looked bloody bad.

At last the SPG man reached for Wheatfield's arm and, bending it up his back, pulled him to his feet, ready to haul him off into custody. Nick thought: One safely out of the way at least.

Even as he was thinking it, five or six people pushed out of the crowd and closed around the two men. The next moment they retreated and Nick felt a small tremor of shock. The SPG man was on his knees looking dazed.

And Wheatfield had disappeared.

It had all happened so *quickly*.

Nick thought: *Oh no you don't*! and cast quickly around.

Got you! There was Wheatfield. Back in the crowd, just away to the left. Black Beard and red-haired Reardon on either side of him.

Nick went for him again, but fell foul of two sprawled bodies on the ground. He got clear, then let out a sudden yelp of surprise as someone grabbed his arm and tried to wrench it out of its socket. He yanked his head round and glimpsed a black uniform.

Nick yelled, 'No you great . . .' but no one was listening and the truncheon was whistling down through the air and Nick reacted in the only way he knew. He dodged the blow and, with only passing regret, flung a hand up and simultaneously twisted and shoved at the face under the helmet. The SPG man staggered back, clasping a bloody nose, and Nick dived away.

Damn it, where are you, Wheatfield?

He craned his neck.

Black Beard. Reardon. Very close but in the thick of the crowd.

They were leaning over something.

Nick ducked down to see. It was Wheatfield lying on the ground.

Injured? Not *that* badly. Then *why*?

Nick gasped. Something black thudded into Wheatfield's head and snapped it viciously to one side.

What the hell?

A *kick*?

But who from?

The foot appeared again, coming in with a vengeance, landing full in Wheatfield's face.

The foot belonged to Black Beard.

Fighting among *themselves*? No. *No*.

This was something else, something that stank to high heaven.

Curious, Nick held back and watched.

Black Beard and Reardon were lifting a slumped Wheatfield to his feet and, supporting him by the arms, beginning to elbow their way through the crowd. They were heading towards the remains of the police line.

A flicker of a suspicion lodged itself in Nick's mind.

And then, suddenly, he knew.

He exclaimed, '*Shit!*' and rushed forward.

Almost immediately he realised he was too late. The wounded man and his two bearers had already passed between the groups of uniformed men, and through the line of mounted men now advancing on the crowd. The strange group was out into the open. Already, a photographer on a car top had her camera trained on them.

Nick followed, dodging through the line. He was stopped by a mounted man but, having identified himself, managed to squeeze between two horses without getting a truncheon on his head.

He was far, far too late.

Ahead, Black Beard and Reardon were setting Wheatfield down on the pavement and leaning him back against the railings, revealing a face bright scarlet with blood. The girl photographer had come down from the car and was taking shots from a variety of angles.

Nick groaned. He couldn't possibly grab Wheatfield now: it would look even worse than it undoubtedly looked already. Also, he would get his face in the paper, and that would be horribly public.

But the others were a different matter. However he would need help. Panting, he ran up to a group of three coppers and, showing his warrant card, led them back to where Wheatfield lay.

As they approached, Nick felt his heart sink. Reardon and Black Beard had disappeared. He looked everywhere, but there was no sign of them.

As for Wheatfield, he was the centre of a veritable circus of attention. Five or six photographers and a TV news crew were all vying for the best shot of the blood pouring down Wheatfield's smashed and agonised face.

Terrific theatre. Wonderful television.

Bitterly, Nick watched as the newsmen carefully recorded Wheatfield being lifted gently on to a stretcher, Wheatfield moaning loudly, Wheatfield being attended by a doctor who looked sufficiently worried to suggest that Wheatfield was somewhere between the critical list and death.

Someone should have provided hankies.

As Wheatfield's stretcher disappeared into an ambulance, Nick cast around again desperately. Where *had* the other two gone?

Suddenly he had a glimpse. A head of red hair in the distance, down a side street, walking jauntily past a police van.

Reardon.

Nick yelled to the coppers, 'There! The red hair!' And they pounded off at the run.

Nick ran up the steps of a house and, hoisting himself up on the railings, searched the crowd.

The police line had dissolved into a series of violent skirmishes, with horses pressing hard into the remains of the crowd. At the rear, many of the demonstrators were trying to escape down Montague Street, back the way they had come.

No sign of Black Beard . . . And yet he *must* have gone that way.

Nick dropped to the ground and loped towards the police line. A gap opened up and he dived through it. Dodging past a group of fighting police and students, he forced himself back through the crowd until he came to the beginning of Montague Street.

He paused on the corner of the street and hoisted himself up on the railings again. He watched the demonstrators leaving the square. Nothing. He examined the last few groups still facing the police. No sign.

He'd lost him.

What a hell of a day.

Out of habit, he kept an eye on the crowd, looking for other faces, but saw none he recognised.

The crowd was quietening down at last, the police were pressing forward and forcing more and more demonstrators out of the square.

Across the street there were groups of demonstrators who had retreated into doorways or, like Nick, had climbed up on railings and steps to watch the action. Nick cast his eyes over them for perhaps the fifth time. And nearly fell off his perch.

He stared in disbelief.

Black Beard.

Moving out of a doorway.

He must have been there all the time, but hidden from view.

Right, thought Nick. This time I've got you.

He jumped to the ground and pushed his way through the crowd, tense with excitement, keeping his bearings, working out the right angle to cut Black Beard off . . .

He caught a glimpse of the black hair. Further ahead than he'd thought.

He quickened his pace to close the distance. A last group of people were in his way. He pushed violently past them.

Almost there.

A couple more strides.

Yes! *Got you now.*

Triumphantly, he reached for Black Beard's arm.

Then, in a split second of incredulity, Nick realised everything was going dreadfully wrong.

An enormous weight was driving into him from behind and crashing him to the ground. He kicked out and, wriggling violently, managed to stagger to his knees. But his arm was suddenly forced half-way up his back in a text book arm lock. Nick twisted his head and dimly took in the sight of an SPG man with a bloody nose . . .

Nick began to yell 'Special Branch –' when something with the solidity of a sledge-hammer smashed into his head and sent his cheek grinding into the road.

As the world faded in a nauseating storm of blinding lights, Nick thought hazily: What a bloody shambles.

Victoria sat on the doorstep and had a good cry. After a while she felt better and dried her eyes on her sleeve. Still trembling she lifted her skirt to examine the red blotches and grazes that covered her legs. Some patches were swollen and very tender. She moved her shoulder and winced – something strained. A bruise on the ribs, too. And then her eye – a bump above and a big swelling below.

It could have been worse. She might have broken something. She could have been dead. She gave a laugh half-way between a giggle and a sob, then, realising she was getting mildly hysterical, forced herself to calm down.

Someone – she didn't know who – had brought her to this side street. In the midst of the terrible crush the feet had suddenly stopped bumping and kicking, and somehow a space had opened up and some kind people had reached down to pull her to her feet. A man – she hadn't even seen his face – had got an arm round her waist and led her clear. He'd left her here in this doorway, when – ten minutes ago? She'd lost all track of time.

'You okay? Do you need an ambulance or something?'

She looked up. Curious faces stared at her, standing a little back, concerned but distant.

She said quickly, 'I'm fine, I'm fine,' and they left, hurrying on. Many people were walking quickly past, escaping the pandemonium in the square. Perhaps she should get away too.

Shakily she gathered herself together. She brushed some of the dirt off her skirt and tried unsuccessfully to tie up a broken strap on her sandal.

Then she put her hand to her waist.

Her bag. It had gone. It had been tied round her waist.

Not much money. Two pounds. But her *keys*. Then she remembered that the caretaker would probably be able to let her into the flat.

Just no money then. No way of getting anywhere.

A taxi and write an IOU? Hardly: no cabbie would trust her looking like this. Her sister? No, Diana was away for the weekend.

She got to her feet, almost in tears again.

People were still streaming past, moving fast, talking angrily, not looking her way. She moved tentatively forward, plucking up courage to ask someone for a lift, when she stopped dead, unable to believe her luck.

'Emilio!'

He was quite close, walking purposefully down the centre of the street with his head down. She called again, louder, but he didn't hear. She was sure it was him.

She went after him, running painfully, almost tripping over her loose sandal. Eventually she caught up with him and touched his shoulder. 'Emilio!'

He spun round, looking defensive and angry.

She said quickly, 'It's me. From the meeting. Please – I've lost my money. I was wondering – could you lend me some . . .' She trailed off under the blank incomprehension of his gaze.

His eyes flicked past her, back towards the square, and then he seemed to focus on her for the first time and, seeing the state of her, raised his eyebrows. He started to walk on, simultaneously reaching into his pocket, and handed her a five-pound note. She limped along beside him, and exclaimed, 'This is too much. Really. Two pounds – one – would be plenty.'

He didn't reply. Putting in a couple of extra steps to keep up, she gasped, 'How can I repay you? Is there somewhere I can find you?'

He gave a minute shake of the head and strode on. After a few moments he stopped abruptly. 'I must go now. Sorry.' He repeated, '*Sorry*,' in a tone somewhere between impatience and regret.

She insisted, 'Please – I must repay you. If I can't contact you, then will *you* find me, Victoria Danby, 53 Moscow Road.'

'Danby. Moscow Road,' he repeated vaguely, then turned on his heel and was gone.

Victoria walked slowly away. The effects of the shock were beginning to wear off, leaving her exhausted and horribly empty.

The young man in the processing lab was very quick and Gabriele had the contacts in front of her in forty minutes. She spread them out on the viewing table and peered at them with a magnifying glass. Occasionally she marked the promising shots with the Chinagraph pencil. Then she went over them again.

The shots of Max sitting on the pavement had come out well – lots of blood and agony and tragedy. But good as they were, these shots weren't vital – there had been enough photographers around to ensure that similar pictures would appear in every newspaper.

It was the earlier shots from the car roof that were essential. The picture had to contain a policeman with his baton raised over a clearly identifiable Max. She had got one of a raised baton all right, the policeman in a wonderfully aggressive stance over a cowering Max. But maddeningly, Max's face was blurred. Obviously the shutter speed had been too slow.

She drew a ring round the face and, taking the contacts through to the young technician, asked him to blow up all the pictures she had marked and to see if he could get more out of the ringed face.

It was four. The Sundays would be setting up their front pages. Time to get things moving. She telephoned Stan Geddes at the photo-news agency. Someone offered to take a message, but she insisted on talking to Stan. When he eventually came to the phone he sounded harassed.

She said briefly, 'I got some good shots of the demonstration this afternoon. I think a lot of people will be interested—'

'Love, there's only one problem,' interjected Stan's voice, 'the whole of Fleet Street was there and I think you'll find they're all running their own pics.'

'But they don't have what I have,' said Gabriele confidently. 'There was a demonstrator seriously injured, and I've got a picture of him being beaten up by the police.'

'Actually being beaten?' Stan's voice was suddenly loaded with interest. 'Where are you?' She gave him the name of the photo lab and he promised to call right back.

The young technician came out of the darkroom with the first batch of eight-by-tens. 'Just to be going on with,' he explained. Gabriele looked rapidly through them. *Much* better now they were blown up. She spread them out in sequence: Max being pulled from the crowd, Max falling to the ground, Max with the raised baton high above his head, and finally a terrific shot of the riot policeman bringing the baton down on to either Max's back or head – it was difficult to tell just which. And Max's face, though blurred, was clearly identifiable.

Gabriele clenched her fists in a small gesture of triumph. The young technician smiled.

A door opened and she glanced round to see Giorgio coming in. '*There* you are!' she exclaimed angrily. 'God, I could –' Aware of the young technician, she prevented herself from saying what was on her mind. Instead she asked harshly, 'Have you got the car right outside? We'll have to get these over to the papers right now.'

Giorgio regarded her sullenly and didn't reply. She was about to demand an answer when she was called to the phone. It was Geddes. 'The *Sunday Times* is interested in an exclusive,' he began.

'No exclusives.'

'Why the hell not!' Geddes exclaimed. 'It's worth *money*, for Christ's sake.'

'No exclusive,' Gabriele insisted. 'I want you to offer the pictures to everyone.'

Geddes sighed. 'Blimey. If you insist. Though the total fees won't add up to an exclusive . . . But anyway, the *Sunday Times is* interested, although it may not be front-page stuff.'

A *frisson* of anger shot up Gabriele's spine. 'Why not?'

'Well, they've got to see the pics, of course.'

She relaxed. 'They'll put them on the front page, don't worry.'

She put the phone down, and seeing that the young man had gone back into the darkroom, advanced on Giorgio. She could hardly contain her anger. 'You nearly *killed* Max, you bloody idiot! What did you think you were doing? What came over you? All that was necessary was a little *blood*. And you go and mangle his face up! You—'

'He is not badly hurt.'

'Did you *see* him? He was badly hurt all right! You must have really hit him hard. No control. You've got no *conrol*, you bastard!'

Almost immediately she realised she had gone too far. Giorgio's face had gone pale with rage. He said very quietly, 'You cannot have it both ways.'

Then, abruptly, he turned on his heel and was gone. Thinking fleetingly of the car and the importance of getting the pictures to the agency quickly, she nearly called him back. But she was damned if she was going to chase after him and apologise. She would rather take a cab.

Victoria knocked back another whisky and felt much better. Slowly and rather stiffly she stripped off her clothes and examined her body. She was going to have some terrific bruises. Who needed body paint when your body was a work of art?

She wrapped herself in a bathrobe and went into the bathroom which led directly off the bedroom. Carefully avoiding her reflection in the mirror – she didn't want to make herself cry – she turned on the hot tap. The gas geyser hissed and popped and refused to light. She bashed it with her hand to no effect and realised the pilot light had gone out. She went in search of a match and, while passing the bottle, took another small nip of whisky. Marvellously warming.

The doorbell rang and she jumped.

The caretaker?

She wrapped the robe more tightly round her waist and cautiously opened the door.

She blinked in disbelief.

Emilio.

She began ineffectually, 'I – er – gosh, come in, won't you?'

He entered and wandered through the flat, peering into the rooms, picking up a couple of her Indian ornaments. 'Nice.'

She recovered slightly. 'Well, it's small, but it suits me.'

He wandered up to her and regarded her gravely. She was

suddenly aware of how very dreadful she must look.

He remarked, 'You're shivering.'

'Yes, I feel very cold. I was about to have a bath.'

'Please . . .' He gestured to show that she should go ahead.

'But you've come for your money. I'll give you a cheque.'

He shrugged. 'No, I didn't come for the money.' His eyes slid away. 'I come to see if you are okay.'

'Oh –' It was such a simple kindness that she was overwhelmed. She stood stupidly, trying to think of something to say.

He insisted, 'Please – take your bath.'

'I can't light the geyser.'

It took him only a moment to relight the pilot with a match. As the bath began to fill, she followed him back to the main room.

He remarked matter-of-factly, 'Your eye – it will be very black tomorrow.'

'Oh dear, will it? Oh dear!' Victoria ran exploratory fingers round the eye and suddenly felt very ugly and dispirited. 'You're right,' she sighed. 'I've never had a black eye before.'

He stood by the window, looking out, restless, she sensed; thinking of other things. In an effort to pull back his attention she said brightly, 'Would you like some whisky, Emilio? or wine? I have some in the fridge.'

His eyes slid round to hers. 'Giorgio. My name. Not Emilio. And wine, please.'

'Oh.' So *that* name hadn't been true either. But she was so glad to have his company that she took it in good heart and smiled. 'Giorgio then. A nice name. I'll get the wine.'

She went into the kitchen and, taking out the wine, made a fumbling attempt to open it and broke the cork. She took the corkscrew and the bottle in to him and shrugged apologetically. 'Not very good at this, I'm afraid.'

He leant over the bottle, drew out the cork first time and looked up at her, smiling a little. Chameleon-like, the indifference and remoteness had vanished from his face. Instead, the eyes were focused, interested, amused.

She looked away, only too aware of her dirty face and swollen eye. 'I think I'll go and have that bath then . . .'

'Leave the door open,' he said, 'then we can talk.'

'Er – yes.' Another kind thought. Victoria was pleased and rather flattered. Perhaps she had misjudged him; he seemed very considerate. She just wished she felt more relaxed in his company.

147

She went into the bathroom and closed the door almost to the jamb, so that only a small crack remained.

The water was so hot it made her shiver as she got in. But the heat was glorious, like a balm, soothing her, creeping slowly through her body, easing the pain. She shouted, 'This is wonderful!'

He muttered a vague response. She guessed that for the moment he was preoccupied.

When the delicious warmth had penetrated every inch of her blood, she dropped her head back into the water and wet her hair. Sitting up, she let the water drain off her head, and reached for the shampoo.

There was a movement in front of her.

She jumped and let out an involuntary cry.

It was Giorgio. Sitting on the closed loo, leaning forward, offering her a glass of wine. 'I thought you would like your wine, so – I brought it. You don't mind?'

He said it as if only someone exceptionally stupid and unworldly would mind. She gaped, horribly aware of her beastly unattractive white body billowing massively out of the water. He must be horrified.

She thought: I'm not going to show a thing. Not a *thing*.

Trying to look calm and sophisticated she drew her knees carefully up in front of her and managed a thin smile. 'You gave me a bit of a shock.' She took the wine and drank a great gulp of it.

Completely unembarrassed, Giorgio inspected her colourful legs and asked her how she'd got the bruises. When she had told him, he remarked, 'These things – they happen. It is a necessary part of the struggle against oppression. Always, people will be hurt when fascists try to exercise their power.'

She had half a mind to point out that it had been the crowd who had crushed her. 'You feel very strongly about it?' she ventured.

'In Italy it is part of our lives, always a danger. Fascism did not die with Mussolini. In Italy the rich are very rich, the poor very poor. The rich exploit the poor completely. You understand? Completely. Politically, economically . . . In every way. And, to stay rich, they use force. The police. The law.'

He sounded very sure, very knowledgeable. Discussing such things with him made her feel very responsible and wise. She asked, 'Do you think there's a danger of it happening *here*, though?'

He gave an infinitesimal shrug and she sensed he was suddenly bored with the conversation. 'Of course.'

He reached down and, picking the bottle up from the floor, poured himself some more wine. Victoria sat still, feeling awkward. She wished she was liberated enough to sink back into the bath and finish washing her hair.

She stole a look at him. He was watching her again, his eyes sharp and gleaming. She averted her gaze and pretended to soap her feet.

'Why do you hide your breasts?'

She almost choked. 'What?'

'You shouldn't. They are very beautiful.'

'No. No, they're . . .' She reached wildly for the shampoo and poured some into her hand.

'Here, let me help you.' He knelt beside the bath and lathered her hair. Then he pushed her firmly back until her head was in the water and her hair rinsed. As he guided her up again he caressed her shoulder, then her arm, and finally her breast, murmuring, 'Very beautiful.'

Victoria sat quite motionless, unable to speak.

He got up and, taking a towel, waited beside the bath. Reluctantly she half stood up and reached for the towel.

'No, stand up. Let me see you.'

'No!' She remained crouched sideways, horribly aware of what gravity did to her body.

'You don't like it? You don't like being as you are?' He laughed. 'You must learn to be proud of your body. It is *important* to love your own body. In Italy we like many kinds of woman. And many men, they *prefer* women like you. Here.' He wrapped the towel round her and pulled her upright. 'You must love your body,' he repeated and, leaning forward, kissed her slowly on the lips.

His hand reached under her towel. She froze, not daring to move, in case the moment should somehow evaporate. She gulped as he found her breast again, and, taking it firmly in his hand, kneaded it gently. The towel dropped away and then he was kissing her body, infinitely slowly, travelling each inch as if it were precious and beautiful. She closed her eyes and decided that she didn't care what he really thought as long as he didn't under any circumstances stop.

Abruptly he moved away from her and she opened her eyes in alarm. But everything was going to be all right – he was holding his hand out, motioning her to take hold of it and follow him. He led her to the bed and, as she lay down, began to take off his clothes with a deliberate almost teasing slowness.

As last he bent down and began to kiss her again, going over every part of her body with his mouth until she pulled him to her, desperate for him, wanting him with such a powerful longing that even after his weight had sunk, motionless and spent, on top of her she kept him inside her, hugging him, covering his head with kisses, weeping gently, wondering what on earth she had done to deserve a man like this.

Twelve

The doors opened and a stream of Sunday visitors entered the ward bearing flowers, bags of fruit, and children. The noise level rose to a babble.

Nick turned his head and winced.

'Serves you right for not taking your pills,' said the nurse mercilessly as she straightened his bedclothes.

Nick had already got the message: taking your own decisions was a criminal offence in this hospital. For what must have been the tenth time, he explained, 'I'd rather have a headache than feel half alive.'

The nurse retreated, shaking her head. Nick closed his eyes for a few moments only to reopen them and find Chief Superintendent Straughan standing beside the bed.

'They say you're going to live,' said Straughan, without enthusiasm. 'No thanks to what went on in that mob yesterday.' He sat down on a chair by the bed and, glancing at the nearest visitors, lowered his voice. 'Assuming you're feeling up to it, I'd rather like to have your version of events, if you don't mind.'

'My version of the whole demonstration?'

Indicating Nick's bandaged head, Straughan said angrily, 'Your version of this bloody fracas.'

From the sound of it, the DCS already knew quite a bit about it. Nick prompted, 'You've been hearing about it, have you, sir?'

The DCS gave him a hard stare. 'Yes, of course I have! The Special Patrol Group have an officer who says you mashed his face up, then ran off into the crowd without identifying yourself.'

'And what did he have to say about crushing my head in?'

'He says he was only trying to arrest you but you put up a fight.'

Nick rubbed a hand over his aching eyes. 'The first bit's true, except he was walloping me hard with a truncheon when I twisted his nose. The second bit isn't true. He got me from behind and I never raised a finger. Wish I had.' There was no love lost between the elitist Special Patrol Group and the other branches of the Met.

'God save me from small boys who belong in playgrounds,' Straughan remarked heavily. 'I won't even ask what the hell you were doing in the middle of the crowd when you were meant to be observing from the sidelines.' He sighed. 'As if it wasn't enough of a fiasco.'

Nick felt a ripple of alarm. 'Oh?'

The inspector's mouth was a thin line of disgust. 'It could have been worse, but I can't imagine how.' He chucked a newspaper on to the bed. On the front page were two large photographs, one of a person being beaten by a member of the Special Patrol Group, the second of the same person propped against some railings, covered in blood and looking half dead.

Wheatfield.

On page three there was more: a sequence of six pictures, obviously taken with a motor-drive camera, which showed Wheatfield being hauled out of the crowd and cowering under a hail of blows from a truncheon.

The photographs were excellent; the point of the story inescapable. And the journalists had made the most of it. Nick knew that he had been thoroughly outmanoeuvred. It made him feel slightly sick.

'All the other papers have got at least one picture,' said Straughan wearily. 'On the front page, of course.'

Nick tapped the pictures. 'This is why I asked to see you.'

'Yes, so they told me.'

'It was a put-up job. They set it up. This bloke – Wheatfield – was beaten by his friends, *in* the crowd, and *after* the SPG man had hauled him out. I saw them doing it. They kicked him in the face . . .'

151

Straughan exhaled slowly. 'Let me understand this – you are telling me that this customer was injured by his friends to make things look bad for us?'

'Right.'

The DCS paused, then shook his head. 'Well, they've bloody succeeded, haven't they? I mean in making things look bad.'

Nick argued. 'But I *saw* them do it.'

'Yes, so you did.' He didn't look happy about it.

A suspicion began to harden in Nick's mind. He asked, 'This is going to be taken further, isn't it?'

'Of course.'

'But?'

'But it's your word against these pictures,' said Straughan briskly. 'You'll be believed in the Force – that goes without saying. But outside – they'll think we're making up stories to cover our thuggery, won't they? And they'll argue that the kick you claim to have seen was in all likelihood accidental, won't they? They'll say you were seeing what you wanted to see. Get my point?'

Nick settled his pounding head back on the pillow. He got the point all right, and it was the one he'd suspected he would have to accept all along.

'Well, at least this sod Wheatfield's not going to die on us,' said Straughan, getting to his feet. 'Apart from a broken nose and an ugly face he's not badly hurt. They say he'll be out in three or four days. That's something at least.'

Nick said a little too quickly, 'Where is he?'

The DCS gave him a sidelong glance. 'Never mind that. The best thing you can do is to forget about the whole business for the moment, okay? I don't want to see you back until you're fully recovered. Two weeks, three weeks – whatever. You're no use to me with a sore head. Right?'

As soon as he'd gone Nick rang for a nurse. Eventually the disapproving girl arrived. He asked, 'Is there someone called Max Wheatfield here?'

She replied waspishly, 'Did you bring me all the way here just to ask me *that*?'

He gave her what he hoped was an open and appealing look. 'Yes.'

'You've got a nerve,' she said with half-hearted annoyance. 'Well – the answer's yes. He's in a room up the corridor. Your colleagues have been in there most of the morning.'

Absorbing the information greedily, Nick muttered vaguely, 'My colleagues?'

'You *are* a policeman, aren't you?'

He asked suddenly, 'Does everyone know that?'

She shrugged. 'I wouldn't think so. I've only just found out this minute.'

'Well, keep it a secret, will you, love? There's a good girl.'

She winked at him. 'Mum's the word, eh?'

After she'd gone, Nick thought for a long time, until, irritatingly, his eyelids began to droop. But even as he fell asleep, the image of Wheatfield remained tantalisingly in his mind.

Gabriele cut out the front page of the *Sunday Times* and taped it to the kitchen wall beside the other cuttings. The collection was impressive. Altogether, four newspapers had featured one or more of her pictures, and a fifth had published their own less spectacular pictures, showing Max against the railings. One far-right paper had published hardly anything, but then that was to be expected.

Later there would be more, in weeklies, monthlies, and political publications. Inter-News expected good foreign sales. Stan Geddes had even mentioned the possibility of *Newsweek* and *Time*.

It had gone remarkably well.

But, best of all, there might be *more*.

Max's injuries had been awful, certainly. When she'd seen his face she'd almost forgotten to take any more pictures. But then, later, she'd begun to see the possibilities . . .

With Max seriously hurt, the affair could become a major issue, a focus for student discontent, a *cause célèbre*. All it needed was a long stay in hospital, some uncertainty about whether he would ever fully recover, a lost memory, an inability to concentrate. A ruined life. That should be easy enough to arrange. He could fake most of it.

She regarded the cuttings again with satisfaction.

The phone rang.

She jumped slightly then relaxed. It would be Giorgio, of course. Announcing his intention of coming home.

Pips sounded down the line. She waited for him to get the money in, then said a very cool 'Hello'.

The reply came back and she gulped. *Max*.

She listened, gripping the receiver in disbelief. 'It's just a broken nose . . . And my face looks pretty bad. But there's nothing serious. I'm going to discharge myself tomorrow. Can't stand this place . . .'

She said, 'Can't you stay in for a while?'

'No . . . They're driving me mad. And the filth are here, giving me aggravation . . .'

'They're not going to charge you with anything, are they?'

'Haven't said so.'

She sighed heavily. 'Well, sit tight for the moment. I'll be in touch.' She rang off quickly.

The vision of Max the martyr evaporated before her eyes. Now the media would print a couple more articles, letters would appear in the correspondence columns, there'd be a question in the House – and then nothing. The story would die a death.

She sighed heavily and said, 'Shit!'

She strode into the kitchen and searched for a cigarette. At last she found one and lit it angrily. She felt cheated.

What was she going to do now?

It would have been a help to discuss it with someone, but without Giorgio . . .

Damn him, where had he got to? He'd been off before, of course. In Italy he'd disappeared quite often, usually on one-night stands. But she'd always ignored it for the simple reason that she didn't care. That, of course, was why he always came back. Because she never gave him any hassle.

But this time was different. She didn't want to be alone.

She paced restlessly around the house. Then, suddenly, she stopped. There was still a way . . . Still a possibility of getting more out of Max's situation. It wasn't much, but it was better than sitting around doing nothing. There was an element of risk, of course, but she rather liked that. Besides, it would give her someone to talk to.

She scribbled a note in case Giorgio returned.

Grabbing her camera bag, she checked that she had enough film, and hurried out into the mews. As she turned the corner the phone began to ring inside the empty house.

Victoria forced a piece of bread and marmalade into her mouth and realised it was the first food she'd had for nearly twenty-four hours. She didn't feel a bit hungry.

She wrapped the dressing-gown more tightly round her waist and peered at her face in the bathroom mirror. Not a pretty sight.

The black eye was a stunner, covering the whole of her eye and half her cheek. It was psychedelic purple and black, with tinges of dark green and red.

The bruises on her arms and legs had also developed well. In an odd way, she felt rather proud of these scars of war, as if they gave her an entry into the exclusive group to which Giorgio belonged, a group, she vaguely realised, in which action was everything.

In the long night hours he had told her more about Italy and the corruption and injustice of the system there, and of the need to fight fascism and the repression of the poor. She was very impressed by his commitment. She was also flattered and pleased that he should have taken the trouble to explain it to her.

Then they'd made love again.

She brushed her hair and ran her hands thoughtfully over her body. She still found it extraordinary that someone should like her just as she was.

The door opened and Giorgio stood there.

'Did you manage to get through?' Victoria asked with a smile.

He shook his head briefly, with irritation. She saw that his mood had become dark and ominous. She felt a twinge of alarm. 'Why not try again in a few minutes?' she suggested.

There was a long pause, then he sighed angrily. 'I have to go away. Abroad. And I must organise . . .'

Her heart sank. She should have known. It had been too good to last. She said lightly. 'Perhaps I can help . . . with the arrangements.' She thought: What a brave face I'm putting on it.

He was hardly listening. Instead he sighed again and murmured petulantly, 'Idiotic arrangements . . . It is left to me to do it all.' Suddenly he shot her a glance. 'Have you any wine?'

'No, but I can go and get some.'

'And food. And newspapers, all of them.'

'Yes, of course.'

Hurriedly she got dressed. At the door she called, 'I'll be about fifteen minutes,' but there was no reply.

The newspapers were easy, but it took her twenty minutes to find a food shop that was open on a Sunday and, because she couldn't remember where the nearest off-licence was, she had to go into a pub to buy the wine. The landlord stared at her black eye with frank curiosity.

When she returned she had an appalling suspicion that he would be gone. She fumbled nervously with the key.

The living-room was empty. She felt sick. She called, 'Giorgio?'
'Mmmm?'

She let out a sigh of relief. The sound came from the bathroom.

She took a glass of wine to him in the bath and kissed his head and touched his cheek.

His mood had not improved. 'The newspapers,' he demanded impatiently.

'Sorry!' She hurried to get them.

'Hah!' He flicked the *Sunday Times* with his fingers. 'Hah!' It was a small cry of triumph.

She looked over his shoulder at the front page. There were two photographs, one of a battered demonstrator. She stared more closely. Underneath the blood the face looked familiar. She gasped, 'Oh – *oh!* Isn't that – isn't that your *friend?*'

He didn't reply but opened the paper to the next page and laughed out loud.

It was hard to see anything funny in the appalling sequence of pictures. She was shocked by the viciousness with which the policeman had obviously struck his victim. The man looked as though he was in agony.

Then Giorgio exclaimed, 'This shows what *really* happened, yes?' and she finally understood. He was pleased because the police had been caught in the act, red-handed. It had never occurred to her to look at it from that point of view.

The newspapers and the wine seemed to have improved Giorgio's mood, and he began to talk with animation about his days in Paris during the student uprising, about the viciousness of the police there, and the way the students had fought back.

As she sat on the closed loo watching him, she thought: It's no good, I love you already, and it's going to break my heart.

'They were good days,' he said finally.

'It sounds very exciting.'

He sat up suddenly, sending water slopping over the edge of the bath. His face had clouded and she could see he was irritated again. He sighed peevishly, 'Tomorrow I have to find a van to go to Paris. How can I know how to rent a van in London?' He asked the question rhetorically, gesturing with upturned hands.

'But I can arrange that for you,' she replied quickly. 'First thing in the morning.'

He stared at her then, coming to a decision, nodded slowly. She felt a surge of happiness.

'What kind of a van?' she asked.

His eyes slid away. 'Something – where it is possible to conceal things. I want to return with certain' – he thought for a moment – '*publications* that must not be discovered.'

It took a moment for everything to sink in – that he was returning. She couldn't help visions of the future leaping into her mind: visions of the two of them together, loving each other . . .

'Publications,' she repeated vaguely, to keep the conversation going. Then the meaning of the other words became clear. He was talking about an important, perhaps even dangerous, journey. Yet he had not hesitated to trust her, to confide in her. She felt very proud. She thought: He won't regret it.

In a businesslike way she repeated, 'A van. Where things can be hidden. It'll take a while to find one, but I'll start first thing in the morning.'

He nodded briefly, obviously relieved at having handed the job over to her. She could see that his mind was already on other things. He said pointedly, 'I'm very hungry.'

'I'm *so* sorry! What *was* I thinking of.' She hurried into the kitchen and started peeling potatoes, wondering feverishly how she was going to find precisely the right van. Suddenly she stopped dead.

Of course.

When she got back, he was standing naked beside the bath, drying himself. She panted, 'Stupid of me, but I've *got* a van! A camper van, in fact. It's got cupboards and bunks and plenty of places to hide things!'

He threw the towel over the edge of the bath and was silent. His body was very beautiful. With an effort she continued, 'You could borrow it for as long as you want.'

He went to the mirror and began to brush his hair. She murmured, 'Well, why don't you think about it,' and returned to the kitchen.

She tried to make the meal a success. She laid the table with care and, though it was the middle of the day, placed candles on it. She put out a fresh bottle of wine and crisp French bread and served thick steaks with sauté potatoes, and tomato and olive salad. Later, she produced Brie and fruit and freshly ground coffee.

While they ate she tried to be light and amusing but he hardly spoke except to ask her about her family. She showed him a couple of photographs, one of the family having a formal tea on the lawn.

He remarked on the house and how large it was. But then he fell silent again and the conversation trailed off. Dejected, she thought: He's not interested in me at all. I was a fool to think he was.

Then without warning he focused on her and smiled a small intimate smile. 'This – er – van, it will get to Paris all right?'

Surprised, she stumbled, 'Yes . . . Yes. Some friends have been using it, so it should be working okay. When did you want it?'

'Tuesday.'

Only two days away. She thought rapidly. 'I'll have to go and fetch it. Tomorrow. It's in the country, you see. I'll have to get someone to drive me down there. It's a bit out of the way . . .'

He eyed her thoughtfully, weighing her up. Eventually he said, 'If I had business in Paris, could you bring the van back for me – into England?'

'Of course!' she exclaimed, laughing.

Paris. With him. She could hardly believe it.

'Even though the – publications – would be inside?'

She met his gaze and shrugged, as if such a risk was something she dealt with every day. 'It's no problem.'

'Good.' He was smiling, obviously pleased with her. She grinned back at him, and, in a burst of bravado, said, 'You'll stay tonight, won't you? And then we could drive down to the country together! In the morning. To collect the van.'

His expression changed subtly, and a thin but impenetrable barrier dropped over his eyes. She could have kicked herself. She'd obviously pushed him too far. In an attempt to retrieve the situation, she said mildly, 'Well, think about it.'

She cleared the table and did the washing-up. When the last dish had been put away she stood uncertainly by the sink. How could she persuade him to stay? How could she make it as wonderful as it had been the night before? What on earth was the *right* approach? Discretion? Indifference? Blatant interest?

She took a large gulp of wine and considered the options. Eventually she decided that, whatever the situation called for, it probably wasn't discretion.

After swigging more wine direct from the bottle, she walked into the living-room. Shaking slightly, she went straight up to Giorgio and knelt in front of him. With what she hoped appeared like calm confidence she began to undo his shirt. His expression was impassive. She had a moment's doubt. But it was too late now.

158

She pulled the shirt off his shoulders and, kissing his arm, worked her way slowly across his body, just as he had done to her the previous night. Then she pulled him gently to his feet and began all over again.

Still he stared at her, his face emotionless.

Then, finally, he moved. His fingers grasped her hair and she looked up to see the glint of desire in his eyes, and she knew that she had won him. For the moment at least.

Despite all his years of legal training, Henry Northcliff was a great believer in instinct. One still had to keep one's mind open to new possibilities, of course, to different interpretations of the evidence, to shifts of emphasis. But, having studied all the facts and heard the various arguments, that first intuitive conclusion – what the Americans called gut-feeling – was, in Henry's experience, rarely wrong.

He'd got a very strong feeling about this one an hour ago and since then the other two had said nothing to make him change his mind.

They were sitting in Henry's office at the House. The Sunday stillness, devoid of traffic noise and secretaries' chatter, clung to the room, creating an air of unreality.

Opposite Henry sat the Commissioner of Police, Peter McCabe, looking slightly uncomfortable in golfing clothes, and David Garner, the DPP, immaculate in blazer and flannels.

'The fact remains,' said Peter McCabe, 'that if no prosecution is brought against this Wheatfield they'll háve made monkeys of us. And that'll be bad for morale.'

'But we *will* be prosecuting – what – about thirty, people,' pointed out David Garner. 'In fact, nearly all those arrested. I'd have thought that would keep morale high enough.'

The Commissioner indicated the Sunday newspapers. 'But not the person responsible for *this*. I realise that we're not blameless and that the officer in the photograph went a little too far perhaps. But, according to the Special Branch evidence, we were set up. The lads know that and they want to see justice done. So do *I*, for that matter.'

Henry sat up in his chair. They were repeating themselves. It was time to bring the discussion to an end. 'Let's just be clear about the facts,' he began. 'There is absolutely no doubt that this Wheatfield *was* assaulted by a police officer. The newspaper pictures are, I'm afraid, irrefutable. Now, whether that officer used reasonable or *excessive* force can never be established. Neither can we ever know how many of Wheatfield's injuries were sustained at the hands of the police officer and how many as the result of the attack by his companions.'

He chose his next words carefully. 'There is also the problem of pinning the whole case on the evidence of one man, albeit a Special Branch officer, who was in the centre of a heaving, jostling crowd, where, as I understand it, there were a large number of skirmishes going on. Can he be certain of what he saw? Can we establish that the kicks Wheatfield received to the face were delivered *deliberately*? For all we know the men who kicked Wheatfield might have been perfect strangers to him, or, if we believe that they were indeed friends of Wheatfield, then there is nothing to say they didn't kick him for some purely personal motives, without the slightest intention of conspiring to prevent the course of justice.'

There was a silence. The Commissioner looked unhappily out of the window. Henry thought: He knows he's lost.

Time for the concluding shot. Henry added, 'As David has said, it would be best to go for what we can be reasonably sure of getting – affray. Even then – well, we might have trouble getting good witnesses. As for assaulting a police officer . . .' He shook his head. 'In view of the rather damning evidence of the newspaper photographs, that may be difficult to prove, particularly if it goes to a jury. In which case Wheatfield could become something of a martyr and the image of the police suffer accordingly.'

The Commissioner shook his head. 'So they get away with it almost scot-free?'

Henry sympathised with the Commissioner's point of view. To his own mind there had undoubtedly been a plot to make the police look like bully-boys, but his instinct told him that no case of conspiracy could ever be won on the existing evidence.

He offered a few crumbs of hope. 'But I think it's certainly worth proceeding against this fellow Reardon on assault charges. He was seen carrying the sharpened banner pole and he was seen wielding it against a police officer. I know it's not as much as one would have hoped for. However . . .' He paused, hoping he was not about to make a rash promise. 'I'm sure the Home Secretary will examine the facts of the apparent conspiracy very carefully. He may even choose to make a statement . . .' Henry left it at that, hoping that he had judged the situation correctly.

Later he spoke to the Home Secretary. It was their third conversation that day. Predictably, the Home Secretary was worried about the risk of martyrdom inherent in bringing the charges, but finally accepted Henry's recommendation to proceed.

Remembering the Commissioner's concern, Henry mentioned that, to his own mind, a conspiracy *had* almost certainly taken place, although it was impossible to prove. The Home Secretary agreed. 'In fact, I was thinking of making a statement in the house to that effect . . . But it would have to be suitably vague.'

'Even so, it would be very effective in improving police morale,' Henry suggested gently.

It was impossible to keep everyone happy, but as Henry got into his car to drive back to Hampstead and a late and probably ruined lunch, he felt he had done his best.

Nick waited until the ward was quiet, then slowly sat up in bed. Not a pleasant experience. A hammer tried to pound its way out of his head. He felt a moment's hatred for the truncheon-happy SPG man, then concentrated on exerting mind over matter.

After a minute, he felt better and got gingerly to his feet. Yes: not too bad at all. It just went to show how over-protective these hospitals were. The doctor had talked about a week in bed. He had to be joking.

The hospital-issue dressing-gown was not exactly what he would have chosen – faded plaid with a pink collar which had been washed almost to destruction – and the slippers were fluffy and rather feminine, but he put them on all the same, to make it look as though he had permission to be wandering around.

He padded up to the doors at the end of the ward and peered through the windows. No fierce nurses in sight. He went out into the corridor and, going in what he hoped was the right direction, started reading the labels on the various doors.

No private rooms that way. He retraced his steps past the ward and along the opposite corridor.

It was the third door along. Wheatfield.

The window was blocked by a curtain on the other side.

A nurse appeared at the far end of the corridor. Without any further hesitation, Nick pushed the door and went in.

He had a brief impression of a figure with a heavily bandaged face lying on the bed before he realised with a slight shock that there was someone else in the room.

A girl. Back to the window. Dark hair lit by the sunlight. Attractive face. Camera in hand.

Strangely familiar.

Then he had it.

Of course – the *photographer*. Standing on the car. *The taker of those damned pictures.*

'Hi,' he murmured.

She regarded him coolly. 'Hello.'

'I came to see my – er friend.' He indicated Wheatfield whose bleary eyes gazed black and bruised from beneath the stark whiteness of his turban of bandages.

'Your friend?' she asked, tilting her head to one side.

'Well, in a way.' He went up to the bedside and said to Wheatfield. 'I heard you were bashed around yesterday, like me. A truncheon, was it?'

Wheatfield was silent. Nick gave a short ironical laugh. 'They came for me when my back was turned. Bloody marvellous.'

'Going the opposite way, were you?' There was a hint of scorn in the girl's voice and Nick looked at her sharply, thinking: Charming!

He said, 'Just getting my breath back. Ready to go for another.'

'Another?'

'Cop. I'd already got one. Mashed nose. Bled like a pig.'

She dropped her gaze. 'I see.' When she met his eyes again her expression was softer, less critical. 'Pity I didn't get pictures of that.'

'You were there?'

'Yes. I'm a freelance journalist.' Briskly, she moved to the bedside. 'Well, Mr Wheatfield, thanks for the pictures. I hope they didn't tire you too much. Get well soon. Goodbye.'

She moved towards the door.

Nick said, 'Did you take those pictures in the paper?'

She paused beside him, so close that he could see the flecks of gold in her eyes, and the slight break in the line of one eyebrow. 'It depends which paper. But yes, most of them had my pictures.'

'Congratulations. They were very good.'

Something seemed to amuse her and she smiled suddenly. It transformed her face and Nick couldn't help noticing that she was rather attractive. Pity she was a journalist.

Wheatfield or no Wheatfield, he suddenly wanted to provoke this self-confident lady who'd caused all the trouble. He repeated his thoughts out loud: 'Pity you're a journalist.'

'Why?'

He wanted to say, because you're biased as hell and only show one side of things. Instead he said drily, 'Journalists are the most promiscuous people I know.'

She stared at him, uncertain and defensive.

He said, 'They're only faithful to a cause or a story as long as it gives them what they want. Then they abandon it. They're anybody's for a night.'

She scoffed, 'At least we give satisfaction while we're around. I'd rather do some good for a short while than stand on the sidelines and do fuck all. Anyway – I haven't abandoned *him*, have I?' She indicated Wheatfield.

'You will when you've finished with him.'

'But he'll have had all the publicity he needs by that time, won't he?'

Nick conceded the point with a shrug of the shoulders. 'What about me though?'

'You?'

'I get a bash on the head and no publicity at all.'

She hesitated and he was aware that she wanted to end the conversation. She said vaguely, 'I didn't get any pictures of you . . . It's different.'

'Always the bridesmaid.'

'Tough.'

Suddenly everything went a bit strange. Nick leant back against the wall, feeling very ill. The girl looked at him curiously. 'You okay?'

He didn't reply. A hot sweat was spreading over his body and his legs had gone weak. He sat down on a chair and put his head in his hands.

He was aware of the door opening and closing then the bossy nurse stormed in and demanded to know what on earth he thought he was doing. As they put him in a wheelchair to take him back to the ward he caught sight of Wheatfield staring at him impassively from the bed.

The girl, however, had gone.

Thirteen

The wind swept down from the hills, gusting against the blank farmhouse windows, sending an army of dry leaves scritch-scratching across the drive. The place looked desolate and neglected, as if nobody had ever cared for it.

Saddened, Victoria led the way round the corner into the yard. At least the camper was there, as Janey had promised. It sat in front of the tractor shed which still contained the shell and entrails of the Massey Ferguson, now brown with rust. She noticed that the fencing round the kitchen garden, which they had repaired during the early days of the commune, was down again, and that the garden itself had already become a wild tangle of weeds and overgrown vegetables. She was surprised at how detached she felt. It was as if her time here belonged to a dream long in the past.

But Giorgio. He belonged to the present. And she didn't want him to see her depressed. Indicating the house, she said brightly, 'I'll have to go in and find the keys to the van.'

She unlocked the back door and he followed her into the kitchen. The auctioneers had taken away some of the better furniture – the scrubbed table and a pine dresser – and the room was bare and cold. 'It used to be lovely . . .' she said wistfully.

The keys of the camper were in their place on the mantelpiece. She picked them up and, having no desire to prolong the visit, turned to go. There was no sign of Giorgio. She found him wandering through the living-rooms, glancing incuriously at the faded curtains and brightly-painted walls that now seemed garish and out of place.

Giorgio stooped to pick up a leaflet from a window-sill. Victoria recognised the estate agent's brochure. He flicked through it and, pausing at one page, shot her a glance.

'A lot of money . . .' he said.

'What?' She looked over his shoulder. He was pointing at the estimated price for the forthcoming auction. 'It's the land that makes the price so high,' she explained. 'But I'll be lucky to get it. Quite honestly, I'll be very happy just to get my money back. The place is a bit run down, you see . . .'

They strolled back into the hall. Idly, Giorgio opened the door to the cellar and peered down the steps. He turned back and said casually, 'So you're rich.'

Was he mocking her? She said a little defensively, 'No, not really. I don't have money to *burn*, if that's what you mean.' Then, because she wanted him to enjoy her company, she made a little joke of it. 'Anyway, I wouldn't complain. If you're good I'll buy you an outrageously expensive dinner in Paris.' She grinned up at him, with a look that she hoped was full of fun and the promise of good times to come.

He accepted the remark with a slight nod. She turned away to hide her pleasure.

'Is this working?' He was indicating the telephone.

'I think so. I paid the bill.'

He put the phone to his ear to check. Satisfied, he held the receiver against his chest and stared at her. She realised he was waiting for her to leave.

She smiled. 'I'll go and try to get the camper started. See you outside!'

She closed the back door loudly behind her, so that he would hear it and know that she respected his privacy. There was a very secret side to him, she had to admit, and it took some getting used to. But she was determined not to resent it. This phone call, for instance: it would be very easy to imagine that he was calling another woman. But that would be childish. It was much more likely that he had a meeting to arrange or important matters to discuss with some of his friends. In which case he was merely being discreet and trustworthy, which was admirable.

She jumped into the van, full of optimism. She was certain that this was the start of a wonderful new phase in her life, and that the key to making it a success was to think positive. Even when the starter produced a low strangulated moan and lapsed into deathly silence, she wasn't disheartened.

Whistling cheerfully, she went in search of some jump leads which, if she remembered correctly, should be under a pile of junk in the tractor shed.

Gabriele could hardly believe her ears. 'Who *is* this girl?'

There was a pause and Gabriele could almost feel Giorgio making a face at the other end of the line. 'Don't worry,' he said, 'she's fat, stupid and rich.'

'So? What the hell are you doing there?'

'I tell you. She has a van.'

'But I told you to hire one.'

He sighed heavily. 'But this way there is no connection. She drives the van – a nice little English girl – *innocent*, you understand? And she is not stopped by the Customs. I go through later. More safe, more simple.'

Gabriele thought for a moment. She hated to admit it, but he was right. 'Maybe it's a good idea,' she conceded reluctantly. 'But for God's sake be careful. She mustn't know anything.' She added coldly, 'And when she's done the job, drop her completely.'

'Yes, no problem,' he said immediately, and she could hear the scorn in his voice. He was bored then. He didn't like this girl. She was glad.

When he'd rung off, she thought for a while. She hated the idea of having someone new involved. Especially this kind of girl. She could imagine the type only too well. British upper class. Not a brain in her head, not a seriously-considered thought in her repertoire of upper-class trivia, effortlessly patronising to the rather quaint but not to be mixed with lower classes. How on earth had Giorgio got involved with her?

Yet it was worth the risk of using her. Giorgio was right.

Going into the kitchen she turned on the radio for the one o'clock news in case there was anything more about the demonstration. The newsreader began to drone through the first item about a wildcat strike at Ford's. She put on the kettle for some coffee and paused to admire the latest additions to her cuttings display. Two newspapers had printed shots of the heavily bandaged Max swaddled in the hospital bed, and three had sent reporters to get a story.

Not great, but a lot more mileage than she'd expected.

Suddenly she stiffened.

The newsreader's voice was saying, 'In a statement to the House of Commons this morning, the Home Secretary said that Saturday's demonstration in Russell Square had been the scene of unprecedented violence in which the police were subjected to deliberate and vicious provocation. The Home Secretary went on to state that there was some evidence of a conspiracy to blacken the reputation and good name of the Metropolitan Police. He added that such attempts to undermine public order would not be tolerated, and those responsible would be dealt with most severely.'

Gabriele went cold. She thought: They *know*.

Then she decided it was impossible. They *couldn't*. It was just a suspicion. It *must* be.

Suddenly she listened again.

'In answer to a question the Attorney-General, Sir Henry Northcliff, stated that, as a result of the Russell Square demonstration, a total of thirty-five people had been charged. He confirmed that the most serious charge brought so far was that of causing an affray.'

She turned off the radio and sat, thinking rapidly. They *couldn't* be sure about the conspiracy – they didn't even know about Giorgio. And they hadn't charged Max.

Or had they?

Uneasy, she went out and bought an early edition of the *Evening Standard*. She leafed quickly through it.

'The following appeared at Bow Street Magistrates' Court this morning charged with causing a breach of the peace . . .' There was a long list, then: 'Paul John Reardon of no fixed abode was remanded in custody on a charge of causing an affray.'

She walked thoughtfully up the mews.

They must have spotted Reardon stirring up trouble, that was all. There could be no proof of a conspiracy. Reardon knew nothing damaging. So even if he talked, no real harm would be done.

No. These accusations in Parliament were a great big guess. A shot in the dark to make up for the Establishment's humiliation. What else could they be?

There was no need to worry. It was going to be all right.

All the same, it was time to move on to the next event. Time to let this one go.

As she let herself into the house, the feeling of unease persisted and, before stepping inside, she looked over her shoulder.

Nick wondered if conversations with Wheatfield were always onesided. Probably.

Ignoring the other man's silence, he continued with the story of his life. 'I went to work in the foundry, like my father,' Nick said. 'Then I organised a stoppage and got fired. Of course, the bastards were out to get me from the beginning. The union didn't protect me either. Just as bad as the bloody employers.'

None of the facts was true, except for Nick's father working in the foundry. But they *could* have been.

Wheatfield said nothing. Most of the bandages had come off to reveal a bloated purple face. Beneath the bruises his expression was impenetrable.

Nick said, 'Now I'm a mature student.' And then he thought: That's a mistake. Wheatfield would have contacts at all the universities and polytechnics and could check. He thought rapidly. 'I mean, I'm *meant* to have started at Newcastle this term. But I want to transfer down here, to the North London Poly.' Nick added, 'There's more happening down here, isn't there? By way of action, I mean.'

Wheatfield murmured something like, 'Sure', and seemed pre-occupied.

'Something the matter?'

Wheatfield seemed to be struggling with a decision. Finally he said, 'They've charged a friend of mine with affray. D'you know if that's serious?'

Nick frowned, as if thinking hard. 'Wait, let me think . . . Um, there was a mate of mine who – what *was* it? Yes, yes . . . It *was* that charge. It's serious, I think. Goes before a Crown Court rather than a magistrate. Could carry a couple of years.'

A look of bitter hatred crossed Wheatfield's face. He hissed, 'God, the bloody bastards.'

Nick said casually, 'Mind you, they've still got to prove it, haven't they? And it's a difficult one to prove.'

Wheatfield shot him a suspicious glance from his bloodshot eyes. 'How d'you know?'

Nick decided to go the whole hog and paint himself black. 'Oh, I'm – well acquainted with the ways of the law. From *this* side, you understand.'

Wheatfield waited for him to continue.

Nick shrugged. 'I took a car once. No – twice, I suppose. But the owners were rich. They didn't miss them. And then there was a bit of trouble about going into a house uninvited. I only wanted to stay the night.' Nick hoped he'd got it right. He didn't want to appear like a common criminal, but as someone who considered himself above the law.

Wheatfield nodded slowly. 'And you think he might get two years?'

'Or he might get off altogether. You never can tell.'

Wheatfield got out of bed and taking off his pyjama top, pulled on a shirt.

With alarm, Nick realised he was planning to leave. 'You off?' he asked.

There was a slight nod.

It was now or never. Nick said smoothly, 'I'm running a bit short . . . You don't know where I could doss down for a while, do you?' He paused. 'I mean, you wouldn't have a few feet of floor to spare?'

Wheatfield was reaching into the bedside cupboard and taking out a sweater. Eventually he replied, 'I've no room.'

'Oh.'

A pause. 'There are places . . . Try 43 Tulip Street. In North Kensington.'

'Thanks.'

Wheatfield was pulling on the sweater.

'They're letting you out, are they?' asked Nick.

Wheatfield snorted, 'How should I know? Who cares. I'm off anyway.'

'Yeah. Not a bad idea.' Nick got to his feet. 'Well, see you again some time. These are friends of yours in Tulip Street?'

Wheatfield nodded briefly.

'See you around then.'

Nick sauntered back to his bed, then hurriedly threw on his clothes. Sister came pounding up to him. 'Where do you think you're going?' she demanded. 'You've got a fractured skull!'

'Home, Sister. And it's only a hairline fracture.'

'Now, don't be ridiculous!'

He didn't have time to argue and pushed firmly past her. When he got to the corridor he saw a nurse come striding purposefully out of Wheatfield's room. He intercepted her. 'Is he there, nurse?'

'No!' she exclaimed indignantly. 'I think he's just walked out!'

Nick ran along the corridor and pounded down the stairs. A sharp pain shot through his head and he felt a moment of nausea.

He came to the last flight. The main hall of the hospital was visible below. He ground to a halt.

Wheatfield was emerging from the lift.

Nick stayed still, ready to dart back out of sight if Wheatfield should look round. But Wheatfield walked straight towards the main doors and went out.

As Nick emerged into the street and picked up Wheatfield twenty yards ahead, he wondered if the man would be watcher-conscious. If so, he hadn't a hope in hell of keeping on his tail. Not on his own, not without any back-up. But Wheatfield was no professional. With a bit of luck he'd never know.

Wheatfield turned into Tottenham Court Road. Nick guessed he was heading for Warren Street Tube station. In which case he would have to close the gap. Risky.

He quickened his step a little. So far so good. Wheatfield hadn't looked back once.

But now Wheatfield was stopping at a crossing and glancing back. Nick looked into a shop window.

Suddenly a small warning bell sounded in his mind. A nasty nagging little feeling that made him uneasy.

He looked behind him.

There.

On the other side of the road.

He groaned inwardly and thought: I should have known.

A watcher.

He looked back. There was another, further behind, walking faster, coming up to overtake. Nick recognised him. The man was from his own section.

Nick thought furiously. But he knew it was no good. There'd be a hornets' nest if he went on.

He stopped and leant against the shop window. The one on his side was coming up fast. As he approached he gave Nick a long look and, passing close to him, said out of the corner of his mouth, 'Conway wants a word with you.'

Nick thought: I bet he does.

Wheatfield had reached the station and disappeared into the darkness of the ticket hall followed by the first watcher and then the second.

Nick waited. After a few moments an unmarked car slid to a halt by the kerb. Nick went over.

Conway wound down the window. 'Why aren't you in bed like a good boy?'

'Couldn't sleep. Look, do me a favour. Don't tell Straughan.'

Conway looked doubtful. 'Well, all right. But piss off home, will you? I can do without the extra aggravation.'

'How long's the watch on for?' Nick asked quickly.

'Until we know where our friend lives.'

'That's all?'

'Yeah, for the moment.'

'Another favour. Give me the info when you've got it. I'll phone later.'

Conway groaned, 'Now what would you want to know that for?'

'Come *on*.'

'All right,' Conway agreed reluctantly. 'But don't go and get into trouble, for Pete's sake. Oh, and as far as I'm concerned, we never even saw each other, right?'

The headache was a stinker, the sort that makes you feel heavy, bad-tempered and sick. Nick regarded his bed longingly. It looked very tempting. But it would be a mistake to lie down. He'd only sleep for hours. Instead he found some aspirin in the kitchen and washed three tablets down with a cup of bitter strong coffee.

He put on a record of *Carmen* and, massaging his temples, wished the aspirins would take effect. He felt so damned *fuzzy* . . .

He risked sitting down for a moment. He wondered if Conway had found Wheatfield's abode yet. Even if he had, it wouldn't achieve very much. It wouldn't establish who his friends were . . . Only a proper surveillance would do that . . .

Nick considered phoning the boss and making a request for a proper observation, but immediately discounted it. He'd only get bawled out for not taking sick leave. Of course, if he was really stupid he could watch Wheatfield on his own, but it would be impossible to do a good job.

What else was there?

His eyes were trying their best to close. He fought them open and, turning up the music, walked backwards and forwards across the floor.

Photographs.

Damn. He'd forgotten to ask Conway what 'makes' – positive identifications – he'd got from his shots at the demo. Perhaps there was something on Black Beard.

He suddenly remembered the pictures taken by the girl journalist. They had been very good. He wondered if any of the lads had checked the rest of her shots, the ones that hadn't actually been published.

He thought for a moment. It would give him something to do . . .

He called the *Sunday Times* and asked for the picture editor. He got an assistant who gave him the information he wanted without even asking for his name.

Miss Gabriella Carelli. Care of Inter-News.

An Italian? He was puzzled. She'd had no accent that he'd noticed.

171

A brisk woman answered the Inter-News number. She said firmly that all enquiries for Miss Carelli could be channelled through her and that, no, it was impossible to give him Miss Carelli's private number. She'd specifically asked them not to give it out.

Nick thought of saying it was a police matter, but decided against it. If it got back to Miss Carelli she would refuse to see him. Being an avid left-wing journalist, she would be no lover of the police.

He hung up and called his friend Barbara at the exchange. He chatted her up for a minute, then asked for a fix on any telephone number in the name of Carelli, Gabriella.

There was a long pause. Nick began to feel pessimistic. Barbara usually prided herself on producing numbers in two minutes flat.

Then she was back.

727 8674. 42 Montagu Mews, W1. A new number. Ex-directory. Hence the delay.

After Nick rang off, he thought for a while. Strange for a journalist to be ex-directory. Perhaps she had an ex-boyfriend who'd been bothering her. Perhaps she just liked her privacy.

It created a problem though. How was he to explain finding her address and number?

Through Wheatfield? No.

Then he had it. Not perfect, but good enough. However it would be best to go straight round without phoning first.

The headache was showing no signs of responding to the aspirin so, on his way out, he took another two tablets and, after a moment's thought, thrust the packet into the pocket of his jeans.

It was five by the time he walked up Montagu Mews. Number 42 was a typical mews house, expensively converted, though in need of a fresh coat of paint. The miniature firs on either side of the front door were looking neglected and some flowers hung brown and shrivelled over the edges of the tubs and hanging baskets.

He pushed the bell. The sound echoed inside the house. He had the feeling the place was empty. If so, he would come back later.

There was a tiny sound from inside. He waited patiently. A moment later a latch turned and the door swung open.

It was the girl.

He smiled. 'Hi.'

She glared at him. 'What on earth?'

Not at all friendly. Nick dropped the smile; he wasn't going to beg for anything from this lady. He said coolly, 'Look, I was wondering if I could see all the pictures you took at the demo. Just in case there was one of me being bashed. The civil liberties people are interested in my case, you see. But we're a bit short of evidence . . .'

She demanded, 'How did you get my address?'

'Well . . .' He hesitated, as if not wanting to betray a confidence. 'There's a journalist on one of the Sundays who's helping me out a bit. He got it from – would it be your agent?'

She exhaled loudly to show her annoyance, then paused, eyeing him thoughtfully. Eventually she murmured with ill grace, 'All right. But you'll have to be quick. I haven't got a lot of time.' She stepped back to allow him in.

He went into the centre of the living-room and took a quick look round. 'You're busy then?'

'Busy enough.' She walked quickly to the far end of the room and bent down to pick up a large brown envelope from a pile of magazines and papers on the floor. Returning, she said abruptly, 'What was your name?'

'Nick. Nick Riley.' Close enough.

'And which group were you marching with?'

'Well, I suppose with the VUF mainly.'

'Mainly?'

She was interrogating him. Typical journalist. He replied a little impatiently, 'I'm involved in several groups. The VUF, the IMG, the SSL . . . I couldn't march with them all.'

'You're a student?'

'Yeah.'

'Where?'

'Look, is this an interview?' Nick demanded. 'If so, then I'd like to know how and when you're going to use it.' The last thing he wanted was to have Nick 'Riley' spread across the newspapers like Wheatfield.

'No . . . it's not an interview,' she said, retreating slightly. 'I just wanted to know who I was dealing with.'

But I bet it gets stored away for future use, thought Nick. Nevertheless, she would have to be given something.

He told her the same story he'd told Wheatfield, about being accepted for Newcastle but wanting to get into the North London Polytechnic. She appeared satisfied.

She turned on some lights then, kneeling on the carpet, took some enlargements out of the envelope and sorted through them.

She passed him a batch. 'Might be something there . . .'

There was one in which Nick himself was clearly identifiable in the crowd. He pretended to show an interest, then searched quickly for Wheatfield. Yes, *there*. But half hidden.

He went on to another and another print. Several showed Wheatfield, but not, unfortunately, doing anything provocative.

Ah, but even more interesting . . .

Black Beard.

Hiding his excitement, Nick examined each shot, looking for a full face. He checked them all again.

Maddening. *Strange*. There wasn't a single one.

He laid the enlargements out in sequence and realised there was a large time gap between the first batch of pictures, taken well before the trouble started, and the second batch which showed Wheatfield being dragged from the crowd by the SPG man. There was nothing of Reardon thrusting the lance into the police or of Wheatfield kicking the copper when he was down. He supposed those events might have been hidden from the camera. But, just as disappointing, there was nothing of Wheatfield being dragged back into the crowd by his friends.

It was odd. He asked, 'Is this it?'

She nodded.

'No contact prints?'

Her eyes hardened. 'No, they're with Inter-News. Anyway, I got everything blown up. It's all here.' She scooped them up and put them back in the envelope. 'How do you know about things like contact prints?'

Damn her, Nick thought, why the hell's she so suspicious? 'The newspaper guy,' he explained. 'He let me look through all the stuff their photographer took.'

He threw the last picture back on the pile, and regarded her thoughtfully. 'Carelli. An Italian name.'

'I'm half and half. Italian father.' She raised her eyebrows. 'Am *I* being interviewed now?'

He nodded. 'Where were you brought up?'

'In both countries.' She was more relaxed now. She seemed to want to talk about herself. 'I went to school in Italy, then came here as a student, then went back to Italy to train as a journalist.

My father's dead. He was a war hero. He fought with the communists.' She said it with pride.

'And your mother?'

'She was English. But she was never interested in coming back. She hated Britain.'

'You've hardly any accent.'

'I spoke nothing but English until I was five. Then my father started to take me everywhere with him, and I became a real Italian and forgot all my English for a while. Then my father died.' She looked wistful. 'And I came here to relearn my English.'

They stood up. He made a mental note to check up on this lady, just as a matter of routine. He asked, 'So are you going to stay in this country for a while?' She was standing close to him. He was aware of those eyes again, extraordinarily clear and steady. And the lovely dark hair. And the arched eyebrows against the pale skin.

She shrugged in an exaggerated way, making the movement unexpectedly sensual. 'For a year or so, I expect. It depends on how interesting it is.'

'The work?'

'Yes. *And* all the rest.'

He examined her face, looking for her meaning. 'The rest?'

'Life in general.'

'Quite.'

'The British are cold and dull.'

'You're probably right.'

'Which is a great pity.'

Had he misunderstood her again? But there was no doubt about it. There was a slight but unmistakably provocative smile on her lips.

'Well, I trust that you'll get a pleasant surprise.'

She was enjoying the tease. 'I doubt it.'

'Really? Well, you've obviously been mixing with the wrong people.'

'Yes.' She held his gaze. It was an open expression of interest.

He should leave, of course; go home and rest his head, call Conway . . .

Yet there was something about this lady.

He heard himself saying, 'I have exactly five quid in the world. How about fish and chips?'

*

It had started to rain heavily. Gabriele ran round the Fiat to the driver's side and got in. She unlocked the passenger door and watched Nick Riley ease himself into the opposite seat. He was very attractive. A nice body, strong face. And amazingly self-assured, sophisticated even. She liked that. That and the fact that he'd stood up to her.

Besides, she was bored with being alone.

She enjoyed playing the part of the sophisticated Italian photo-journalist. She felt the role suited her very well. It was much closer to the real her than Linda Wilson had ever been. Anyway, the story of her parents hadn't been that far from the truth.

She drove towards Chelsea. She noticed Nick tearing at a packet and putting some tablets in his mouth. 'Aspirins,' he explained. 'For my thundering head.'

'I'm surprised they let you out.'

'They didn't. I discharged myself. Like Wheatfield.'

Her foot slipped on the throttle and the car lurched. He looked at her sharply. 'You didn't know?'

She gripped the wheel and thought: Damn bloody Max. Why the *hell* did he do that. After a moment she said easily, 'No, I didn't know. But I'm surprised, I must say. I thought he was meant to be seriously hurt.'

'Only skin deep,' Nick murmured.

Realising what he had said, she made an effort to recover herself. 'What do you mean?'

There was a short silence. 'Nothing. The nurse just told me that his head looked worse than it was.' He added in an undertone, 'Unlike mine.'

'Is yours bad?'

'Split up the back apparently. Mind you, it might be an improvement.'

They drove up the King's Road and Gabriele pointed to a restaurant she'd never been to. 'Let's try that one.'

'My fiver should buy the first course and the wine.'

'I'll stand the coffee,' she said archly, 'and we'll negotiate over the main course.'

The rain was coming down in a solid wall, drumming against the car windows and bouncing noisily off the roof. Eventually they found a parking place some way beyond the restaurant. Passing cars were sending up sheets of spray. Gabriele locked her door and slid across to the passenger side. She got out on to the pavement, locked the door and slammed it. Nick offered her a newspaper to put over her head. The gallantry of the gesture took her by surprise. She thought: What a strange man you are.

Suddenly she groaned, 'Oh *shit!*'

'What is it?'

'I've left the bloody *keys* inside.' She could have kicked herself. God, what a thing to do. She *hated* making stupid mistakes. She searched through her bag, but she knew she didn't have any spares. 'Shit!' she repeated.

There was no sound from Nick and she looked round.

He was leaning over the door handle as if trying the lock.

'It's no good,' she sighed. 'I damn well locked it.'

He took no notice, intent on his task.

'Come on. Let's get out of the rain at least,' she said irritably. 'I'm getting soaked.'

The next moment she stared in amazement.

The door of the car was open. Leaning down, Nick disappeared inside. The next moment he was holding the keys in his fingers.

'How on earth did you do that?'

He took her elbow and hurried her along the street. 'Old Indian trick.'

She stared at him, wondered what other talents this man possessed.

She was good, Nick had to admit. As one would expect, she knew her stuff about the Italian student and communist movements, but she also had a good understanding of the philosophies of the New Left throughout Western Europe.

He found himself thinking that she might be quite useful. If handled with care. There was no doubt where her personal politics lay – well over to the left.

Nevertheless, she would have good contacts. Yes, useful – as long as she never discovered who he was.

The aspirins had clouded his mind, and he was feeling horribly tired again, but he made the effort to keep the conversation going and to draw her out as much as possible.

While discussing politics she was reserved, almost formal. But when he asked her about Italy, she became animated and relaxed. She described the many places she knew in Piedmont and Tuscany, and talked knowledgeably about the cultural life of Milan. She added, 'The Italian way of life beats Britain hands down. And the Italians themselves – well, they are culturally far less inhibited. That's why I like them.'

'They're certainly less inhibited. But I wouldn't know about the cultural side.'

She raised her eyebows. 'I suppose like all the British you disapprove of Latin emotion?'

'Not at all. I think it's great. It's good and wholesome and refreshing.'

She pulled at the tablecloth. 'But your family weren't open with their emotions, were they?'

He remembered his mam. She clouted him when he was cheeky and looked surprised if he was good. She hadn't been open exactly, but he'd always known she was on his side. His father – that was different. There had been a lot of affection there, shown as often as possible, but, being northerners, expressed by nothing more than a pat on the shoulder.

He answered, 'Not open by Italian standards, no wild hugs and tears, but it was pretty good really. And you?'

Her eyes dropped and he felt her withdraw slightly. 'Great on the Italian side, rotten on the British.'

'I'm sorry.'

She looked at him sharply, as if she wasn't certain of his sincerity. 'It wasn't that bad.'

A touchy point. He tried to smooth it over. 'But the Italian part of you has come to the fore. I mean, you're obviously more Italian than British. So . . . it's all right.'

She was pleased. 'Yes. It feels good to know what you are and where you're going.' She smiled. It made her face look quite different.

They talked about the problems of choosing the right path in life, and whether you should stick to it, and the importance of commitment. He was aware that some barrier had been passed. The reserve, the careful choice of words, had gone. He had the feeling that she was being direct, even trusting, for the first time.

Eventually she said, 'You know, I was wrong about you.'

'Yes?'

'I thought you were one of those sheep – the blind followers of the nearest tame philosophy, the ones who *call* themselves political thinkers but actually haven't an idea.'

'But?'

'You're all right.'

'Thanks.'

He had a sudden feeling that there was a purpose behind the appraisal, as if she had something serious in mind for him, some involvement.

It suddenly occurred to him that the involvement she might have in mind was an affair. He hoped not. He didn't mind the idea itself – on the contrary, now she'd decided to be open and friendly, he found her extremely attractive in a dark, brittle sort of way. What worried him was his ability to deliver the goods, tonight at least. The wine had made him dizzy and tired, and he knew he was slurring his words, which was unusual for him. Something to do with all those aspirins or the head or both. Whatever, it didn't bode well for a night of passion. He drew a deep breath. Better to get these things sorted out sooner rather than later. He said, 'Look, I'm not feeling too well. It's something to do with this head . . .'

A spark of disappointment – or was it annoyance – passed across her face; she'd got his meaning all right. But then her face cleared and she was nodding understandingly. 'That's all right. I'll get the bill and drive you home.'

He said with relief, 'The complete liberated woman.'

'God, you're not a goddam reactionary, are you?'

'No. I like independent women.'

She tapped his hand. 'Good. Because you've certainly found one here.' She laughed, suddenly gay and happy.

God, he was feeling really awful now. He glanced at his watch. Ten. With a jolt he suddenly remembered Conway.

Getting to his feet he said, 'Completely forgot to make a call. It's' – he tried to think, to be consistent in his new story 'about some floor space at a friend's.'

There was a phone by the kitchens. Reaching it, he had to lean hard against the wall. A cold sweat hit him. When the worst had passed he called Conway.

Conway didn't sound glad to hear him.

Nick said, 'Well where does Wheatfield hang out then?'

'Wish we knew.'

Nick's stomach did a nasty turn. 'You bloody *lost* him?'

'Showed no signs of having spotted us, not one. Then he did a disappearing act as neat as any I've seen. Into a shop and straight out an emergency exit.'

'Bloody marvellous.'

'You would have done better on your own, I suppose?'

Nick let it pass. 'All right. What about "makes" on Wheatfield's friends?'

'Only Reardon, who's up for assault anyway. Nothing on your bearded friend. No good snaps, I'm afraid.'

Nick put the phone down in disgust and leaned his head against the wall. To hell with Conway, to hell with Wheatfield. The only thing he cared about now was getting his head down on a nice warm pillow.

The mews house was dark. No Giorgio then.

She said, 'You can stay here.'

He didn't argue. His head was resting on the back of the seat, his face ashen.

She opened up the house and led him upstairs.

Before she could decide where to put him he had stumbled into the main bedroom and sunk on to the bed. She began, 'Why don't you get *into* bed?'

But he didn't reply. He had the look of someone who wasn't going to move again that night.

Gabriele regarded him critically. Even if she wanted to share a bed with a half-conscious man, which she didn't, it would be very uncomfortable with him on top of the bed and her inside it.

She went to the linen cupboard, got out an eiderdown, and placed it over him. Then she found some sheets and took them into the spare bedroom.

PART THREE

Fourteen

The lights changed and the four lanes of traffic roared away up the wide boulevard, like racing cars from a starting grid. Victoria gripped the wheel and accelerated. Driving in Paris was certainly different.

'Here!' Giorgio pointed sharp right, up a side street.

They were almost past it. Victoria flicked on the indicator and braked hard. There was an angry blaring of horns and a car wove violently past, the driver gesticulating rudely.

'*Excusez* – so sorry,' Victoria muttered, and, hoping there wasn't something coming up behind, turned right across the traffic.

Safely into the side street, she stopped and put her hand to her chest. 'Well, French drivers certainly have something,' she said breathlessly. 'If only a short fuse.'

Giorgio was already getting out. He said, 'You wait here.' He walked off and, half-way up the street, disappeared into a doorway.

A horn sounded: the camper was blocking the road. She drove on a little and, where the street widened, pulled up on to the kerb and turned off the engine.

She looked across the road. It was somewhere near here that Giorgio had disappeared. There was a linen shop, a boutique selling mini-skirts and jeans, an antique shop, and, in between, doors leading to the upper floors.

But what did it matter where he had gone? The important thing was, everything was going well.

The journey had gone very smoothly. She'd left London at seven that morning, caught the ten o'clock ferry and been at Orly to pick up Giorgio by three. She hadn't got lost once. Well – just for a moment, coming into the city, when she'd misunderstood Giorgio's directions.

She wasn't sure where they were now – she didn't know Paris that well – but the Seine was close by, and Giorgio had mentioned the Left Bank.

She closed her eyes for a while, then checked her face in the mirror. The black eye was fading fast and she'd managed to cover the greeny-blue shadow with make-up so that it barely noticed. Her skin was much clearer, too, and she had lost quite a bit of weight in the last few days. Definitely an improvement. It was Giorgio's doing. When he was around she forgot all about food. She forgot about everything. She sighed deeply. That was the problem. She was in love with him. And not just a little, either. She could hardly think about anything else. His presence obsessed her; she related everything she did to him. The thought of displeasing him was agony. She vaguely realised that the relationship was unbalanced, that there was too much pain with the pleasure. But it merely made her more determined to please him, to become indispensable to him, so that he would get used to having her around, and maybe even come to care for her.

She thought: It's all right for beautiful women. They can pick and choose. But for people like her – well, one had to grab at whatever one could. Better to feel alive for a short time than to drift along waiting – *imagining* – for ever.

It was getting dark. She looked at her watch. He'd been gone nearly an hour.

A movement caught her eye.

At last. There he was. Coming from beside the antique shop. Striding across the street.

He jumped in and said immediately, 'We must go to one more place.' He motioned her to drive off.

As she negotiated the streets she noticed that he was agitated and restless. She kept quiet.

They turned into a wide tree-lined street. At some lights Victoria managed to read a sign: Boulevard St Germain. Then they were into another network of narrow streets. Using gestures and the occasional word Giorgio directed her to the next address. Again, he left her waiting in the van. This time she watched to see where he went. It was a doorway beside a newsagent's. She examined the windows above. Nothing to indicate what went on there. But she'd noticed the street name: Rue St Médard.

It was six now. She wondered what sort of an evening they would have. A meal on the Left Bank, a stroll along a boulevard, a coffee in a pavement café? Yes, she'd wear that long black midi-length skirt and pull her hair back in a knot and look smart.

Five minutes later he was back. 'Okay, we go and find a hotel now. Then we eat.'

She smiled and started the van.

'But I have not much time,' he added. 'I have a meeting later.'

Count to five. 'When?'

'At nine. It will last until late.'

'I thought we'd have the evening together at least.' She could hear the peevishness in her voice and hated it.

He gave her a sharp look. 'I have to do my business,' he replied. 'That is why we are here.'

With an effort, she said quietly, 'Of course.' And, doing her best to drive smoothly, negotiated the camper into the thick of the rush-hour traffic.

As the van moved away, its registration number was noted.

The DST man was sitting in a car a few doors away from the newsagent's. He sat in this spot quite often, sometimes several days running, at other times not for several weeks, watching the doorway to the right of the bookshop, noting who came and left. It was rather a farce really. The people at Aide et Solidarité knew he was there, and he knew that they knew.

But the purpose of the surveillance was merely to let them know that they *were* being watched. A reminder that they and the numerous other political organisations encamped in Paris were tolerated but not condoned.

The number of the van would be logged in the central records and that would be that.

It was getting on. He'd been there four hours. Quite long enough to ensure that his presence had been noted. Starting the engine, he drove quickly away.

Nick had seen worse places than 43 Tulip Street. It was on the border of Kensal Green and North Kensington, off the Harrow Road. The house was shabby on the outside, but reasonably neat and well kept on the inside, with ethnic rugs thrown over the ancient furniture and posters on the white-painted walls.

'There's a mattress somewhere,' the girl said. She looked half-heartedly round the living-room and then gave up. She drew heavily on her cigarette. 'Or there's the settee . . .'

'Don't worry. Anything'll be great.'

Her name was Bet – short for Elizabeth presumably, though he hadn't asked. She appeared to be one of the permanent residents of the house, which, as far as he could tell, was occupied by six people. She was about twenty-five, he guessed, and fashionably dressed in a trendy off-beat way.

She asked abruptly, 'Where's Max living, d'you know?'

It was exactly what he'd been hoping to find out himself. 'Not sure,' he replied. 'He split.'

She nodded, unsurprised.

'You've got no gear?' she asked.

'No. Travelling light.'

'Going to stay long?'

'Dunno.'

'That's okay,' she said. 'A friend of Max's . . . But it might be difficult after a week. I mean, staying without contributing.'

'I understand.'

They strolled into the hall. She said, 'I'm going to the pub to meet some friends. Want to come?'

What he really wanted was to go home to bed. He'd slept until eight that morning, when Gabriella had woken him and offered him a hasty breakfast, but he had got up dog-tired and stayed that way all day. He decided the sleep would have to wait a while longer. The Bet connection might be tenuous, but it was all he had.

He said, 'Yeah, that'd be great.'

The Red Lion was crowded. Bet's friends, five of them, were at the bar. Two of them were teachers, Nick gathered, and one worked for a big charity. The remaining two were not forthcoming about their occupations.

He was disappointed. Neither the names nor the faces were familiar. If they were on file, it must be as ordinary members of relatively harmless organisations. Not likely to be bosom pals of Wheatfield.

Nevertheless he asked casually, 'I'm trying to get hold of Max. Know where he might be?'

One of them answered, 'He's got a new place, but nobody knows where. You might find him at the Duchess of Teck. Up in Camden Town. He used to go there a lot . . .'

Nick wondered if he could face going straight away, tonight. It was a good half-hour away and he was still feeling pretty rough. He put off the decision by having another beer.

Fifteen minutes later two girls joined the group. He recognised neither. Then he realised there was a third arrival, standing at his shoulder just outside the circle. A man.

Nick's interest quickened.

This one he knew.

It took him half a minute to place him, working backwards from the face to the organisation, then to the occasion and the year, and finally to the name.

London School of Economics. SSL. Linden House Hotel affair, 1968. Wally Bishop.

Definitely a friend of Wheatfield.

He left it for twenty minutes then, just as he was wondering how to introduce the subject, Bet did it for him.

She said to Bishop, 'Nick wants to find Max.'

Bishop nodded, a flicker of defensiveness in his eyes. 'He's around . . .'

'It was about the demo on Saturday,' Nick said easily. 'We both got walloped. I'm trying to get the civil liberties people interested in my case, and I wondered if Max was taking the matter further . . .'

'You got beaten up, did you?' Bishop asked, looking at the slight graze on Nick's cheek.

'Fractured skull.' Nick drew an imaginary line from the back of his collar upwards. 'Right up the back.' He laughed and took another swig of beer.

Bishop looked impressed. While the others were talking he said, 'Tell you what. Max'll probably be around later. Up the Portobello, in the Castle.'

Nick asked doubtfully, 'Er – much later?'

'Ten.'

Nick pursed his lips. 'Well, to tell the truth, I'm dead beat. I'll have to give it a miss. But give him the message, will you? And tell him I'll catch him later. Okay?'

It was eight when Nick left the pub. It was raining again and there was a cold wind blowing. Pulling up the collar on his jacket, he walked briskly to keep warm. He bought some fish and chips on the corner, and ate them as he walked down Ladbroke Grove to the Portobello Road. The Castle was a small pub sandwiched into a terrace of shops at the northern end of the road, on the unfashionable side of the elevated motorway, and well away from the tourists and the antique markets.

There was no obvious place to wait. He chose a doorway with a deep recess, diagonally opposite the pub. His head was aching again.

At quarter to ten he recognised Bishop coming along the street and turning into the pub.

Ten came and went. No Wheatfield. Ten-fifteen. Ten-thirty. For some reason he was unbelievably cold. He shivered violently and stamped his feet in an effort to keep warm.

Only half an hour until closing time.

Then at ten-forty, suddenly, there he was.

There was no mistaking the long hair, the black donkey jacket he always wore, and, as he came into a patch of light, the narrow bruised face with the wire-rimmed glasses.

Nick felt a surge of triumph. Then calmed himself. *Don't count on anything. Not yet.*

At chucking-out time Bishop and Wheatfield emerged together. They paused on the pavement, exchanged a few words, and left separately, Bishop heading north, Wheatfield south.

Nick gave Wheatfield thirty yards then followed, staying on the opposite side of the road.

Wheatfield walked under the Westway elevated motorway then, pausing to look over his shoulder, crossed the street and headed down Lancaster Road, parallel to the Westway. The glance had been cursory, checking for traffic. Wheatfield was not worried about being watched.

That made all the difference. Nick relaxed a little.

Wheatfield paused at the next junction and turned left into a small residential street, quiet except for the drone of the traffic on the elevated road.

Wheatfield paused outside the front door of a house and, reaching into his pocket, produced a key and let himself in. Half a minute later a light went on in a top second-floor window.

Number eleven. And the street was called St Mark's Villas.

Nick allowed himself a moment of satisfaction. Nailed Wheatfield all on his own. Wait until he told Conway.

But now it was decision time. He could stay for a while and see if anyone else went in. Or he could go home and return early in the morning in the hope of tailing Wheatfield to his friends – specifically to Black Beard. But he was feeling horribly tired again – the head seemed to make him permanently sleepy – and to make matters worse he seemed to be getting a cold. The sensible thing would be to go home.

He started back along the street, but hesitated on the corner.

Damn it, he couldn't bear to let Wheatfield slip through his fingers again.

There was a telephone box in the next street. Out of order. He swore vehemently. Eventually he found a working box in Westbourne Grove.

Conway wasn't at home. He tried the office. He wasn't there either.

He returned to St Mark's Villas and waited for over an hour.

When he tried Conway's number again, he was in. He was not happy to be disturbed. 'What the hell, Nick. It's one in the bloody morning!'

Nick said, 'You won't be so cross with me in a moment, Conway. I have something for you. But it's going to cost you, old lad.'

Victoria didn't need to ask Giorgio how he felt: it was only too obvious. He had all the signs of a terrible hangover. She'd heard him stumble in at four that morning, the smell of drink on his breath. The meeting must have gone on a long time. She conjured up the scene in her mind: the political discussions, the bottle of brandy, the smoky room. Men together, sharing ideas, scornful of outsiders. She was envious.

Now it was eleven and she was driving south-east out of the city, towards the suburbs. Giorgio sat beside her, his head against the seat, his eyes closed. Victoria resolved not to say anything unless it was absolutely necessary.

When they reached Ivry she finally stopped and, dreading the moment, whispered, 'We're here. Do you have directions?'

He groaned slightly and, pulling a screwed-up paper from his pocket, handed it to her. It was a street name and number in Ivry, but she had no idea where. She showed the paper to a passer-by who gave her directions and, after a couple of false turns, she found herself in a small backstreet. It was a poor area, near a main railway line. The houses, which fronted straight on to the street, were shabby and colourless. Half-way along there was a car repair works, but otherwise there were few signs of life.

The house numbers were difficult to read but finally she identified the address on the paper, and stopped outside. It was a house, shuttered and quiet. She turned off the engine. Giorgio opened an eye and frowned. He said, 'Down the side.'

She started up again and, after reversing, began to manoeuvre the van forwards into the gap between the house and its neighbour.

'No, backwards!' Giorgio hissed impatiently.

Victoria gripped the wheel and stopped. She backed out, did a three-point turn, and slowly reversed the van down the alley to a courtyard at the end.

Giorgio said, 'You go for a walk now, for one hour.'

She opened her mouth to object, but he added impatiently, 'I should not have brought you at all. I was not meant to – you understand?'

As she walked away she made the effort to accept the snub. But it was difficult. They were only leaflets, after all. Why she couldn't be trusted to see them being loaded was beyond her.

She sat on a wall and watched the trains thundering past on the main line. She thought the matter through again. Perhaps she was being ungenerous; perhaps Giorgio was only trying to protect her.

She returned in a more cheerful frame of mind to find Giorgio waiting by the van. As she approached he got in and they drove off in silence. 'Everything all right?' she asked.

He nodded matter-of-factly. 'Yes. Okay.' But she noticed that he was wide awake now, his eyes gleaming, his manner restless.

When they reached the main road Victoria couldn't at first identify what was different about the van. Then she realised that it was slower, more sluggish. There must be a lot of leaflets. She said, 'You managed to get everything in?'

He gave her a black look, but she went on, 'The load's very heavy. I can feel it.' Suddenly she wasn't in the mood to be put off. She demanded, 'Tell me, what are the leaflets for? You never told me exactly.'

He was silent for a moment and she could feel his eyes on her. Eventually he said, 'They are to be sent out, given away . . . To working people. To' – he was searching for the English words – 'to make them realise they are being exploited.'

'I see. Can I have a look at one?'

'No, not possible.'

'Why not?'

'They are in boxes, hidden away . . .'

He was looking at her differently now, appraising her. He slid his hand across the back of the seat and began to stroke her neck. 'Don't worry. It is just better that you do not see them.'

She kept silent, but she wasn't happy and she let it show on her face.

Giorgio said pleasantly, 'We will have a good lunch – do you like seafood?'

'Yes.'

'Then – later, perhaps dinner too. Would you like that?'

'Will you be going to another meeting afterwards?'

He shook his head.

She softened a little. 'What about getting back?'

'The morning will be all right. If you leave early.'

'And you?'

'I will fly tomorrow afternoon. You can meet me at the airport.'

She pictured the evening: a long leisurely dinner, candles, no rush, no meetings. And then back to the hotel to make love. One perfect evening. An opportunity that might never come again.

Her resistance vanished. One had to grab these moments – why not? Everyone else did.

Suddenly gay she said cheerfully, 'I promised to take you out for a meal in Paris, remember? Well, dinner will be *my* treat! We'll go somewhere really good. Do you accept?'

He shrugged. 'If you wish.'

She glanced across at him, but he had turned to stare out of the window and she could not see his face.

Nick dreamed that he was in the wreckage of a road accident, sitting in a car which had been crushed by a lorry. Something heavy was pressing on his head. Helpers were trying to cut him out. Faces bent over him, discussing his condition. 'It's no good,' someone said. 'He's had it.'

Then his mother was leaning over him, saying, 'I told you this would happen.' It wasn't a car that he'd crashed now, but his go-cart which he'd built out of plywood and old pram wheels, his pride and joy and the envy of all his schoolmates. There was only one good slope in the area, at an old tip, and he'd raced down it for a bet, and hit a ridge and crashed into a metal refrigerator. His mam had said, 'I told you so, but you wouldn't listen.' Which was true enough, because he never did listen. And now his head was hurting like hell and the ambulance bell was ringing loudly in his ears.

It jangled on and on. He woke resentfully and reached out for the alarm clock. He opened his eyes and screwed up his face. The cracking headache wasn't a dream, nor was the raging sore throat and stuffed up nose. He thought: Terrific.

Before he had second thoughts about getting up, he swung his legs to the floor and sat up. He may have felt worse in his life, but he couldn't remember when.

Ten-thirty. He'd had three hours' sleep. And now he must hurry. He'd promised to relieve Conway at eleven.

Finding a piece of stale bread in the kitchen, he covered it with jam and made his way out. He saw a cruising cab and, taking it as divine intervention, hailed it and sank gratefully back against the seat. Extravagant, but today he didn't care a damn.

He left the cab in a road adjacent to St Mark's Villas and wondered if he'd find Conway on station or not. By now Wheatfield – and therefore Conway – could be anywhere in the Greater London area, which made it difficult for Nick to relieve him – a point Nick had carefully glossed over, both on the phone the previous night, and at seven that morning, when Conway had stood in for him.

But when he turned into St Mark's Villas Conway was still there, sitting in his car, looking fed up. 'Not a dicky bird,' he reported as Nick climbed in. 'No one remotely like Wheatfield.' He gave Nick a hard stare. 'Now look, me old mate, this is lunatic. You can't stake this place on your own. Why don't I go back and persuade the boss to do it properly, eh?'

Nick shrugged. 'If he agrees, great. But I doubt he will.' A full-scale surveillance was costly in men and resources, and was mounted far less often than people imagined. Nick added, 'Just don't mention my name, that's all. He'll go bananas.' He hunted through his pockets for a handkerchief and sneezed.

'And I'm to say I got this address from a snout, am I?'

'Well, don't complain, for God's sake,' Nick retorted. 'It'll be a gold star for you, won't it?'

'I'm not *complaining*. I'm just trying to get it right.' He eyed Nick harshly. 'You look bloody terrible, did you know that?'

'Piss off. And without the car, if you don't mind.'

When Conway had gone, Nick slid across to the driver's side and, sinking deeper into the seat, settled down to wait. A heavy sneeze shook him. An aspirin would have been a good idea, but it was too late now.

He closed his eyes and dozed off for a second. Waking, he sat upright with a guilty start and turned on the radio. He listened to the news, then retuned the station. There was a symphony on Radio 3. He tried to identify it. Brahms? No, more like Mahler. Yes . . . lovely.

It was nice and warm in the car. The sun streamed in through the windscreen. His head fell forward. He dozed.

Wonderful dreams. On a warm beach. The sound of people in the distance. The whole afternoon ahead of him. But no. There was something wrong. The dream was disturbed. There was some reason why he mustn't sleep and he couldn't remember what it was . . .

Waking with a jolt, he rubbed his eyes and peered at his watch. Hell! How long had he been asleep?

He really *must* make an effort.

He looked up.

Christ!

Wheatfield.

Crossing the road. Heading this way. Coming towards the car.

Quickly, Nick opened the driver's door and, sticking his feet out, spread his body across the front seats and pushed his head under the dashboard. He made a show of hunting for some imaginary electrical trouble.

Count to ten. *Slowly.*

He looked up tentatively. No Wheatfield in front.

He swivelled round. There! Behind – and disappearing fast round the corner.

The car would be a nuisance. He abandoned it and followed on foot.

Wheatfield was moving more cautiously today. Like a cat. Glancing from side to side. *Much* more alert.

Nick felt a twinge of excitement. *Whatever you're up to, Wheatfield, I'll get you.*

Twenty minutes later Nick was trying hard not to feel disappointed. After visiting a chemist, Wheatfield had gone into a stationery shop in the Bishop's Bridge Road and emerged with a small parcel.

Now he was in an old-fashioned hardware store. It was all horribly domestic. Nick looked through a newsagent's rack in disgust.

Wheatfield remained in the store for some time. Nick waited impatiently. Eventually Wheatfield emerged with a large packet of some product or another under his arm: a white packet brashly printed with what looked like a manufacturer's name in bright red; with a gaudy green picture underneath. It was impossible to see exactly what it was.

Next Wheatfield went into an electrical shop. Then a small supermarket. Nick took the risk of peering in through the numerous cut-price posters stuck on the window. He spotted Wheatfield at the far end of an aisle, putting a large packet of washing powder into his basket. At the next aisle he appeared to have trouble finding what he was after, but after much searching finally picked up several packets of what could have been either sugar or flour, and came towards the check-out.

Nick moved away and waited up the street.

Wheatfield came out and, despite the obvious weight of the

various packages, moved off fast, away from home, in the direction of Paddington. After a while the weight of the shopping slowed him down and, pausing to redistribute the bags, he carried on at a slower pace.

Suddenly Wheatfield stopped and took a long look round. Nick side-stepped into a doorway and peered out cautiously.

He swore under his breath.

Wheatfield had hailed a taxi and was climbing in.

Not another in sight. As Wheatfield's cab drew away Nick ran to the next corner. Still no cabs. Only one, cruising round a corner two streets to the south. Nick put two fingers in his mouth and whistled hard. The cab braked and he sprinted towards it.

His lungs aching, he jumped in and shouted, 'U-turn, right at the top and then go like hell. I'm trying to catch someone.'

The cabby held his tongue with difficulty and, executing the turn, went for the lights, which were red.

'Jump them. I'm a police officer.'

Muttering hard, the cabby found a gap in the cross-traffic and swerved right into the Bishop's Bridge Road. He shouted over his shoulder, 'I've been waiting for this for twenty years.'

They roared across the next two lights, which were green, and came to the roundabout under the Westway. There was only one other cab in sight, heading east out of the roundabout towards Marylebone.

Nick realised that in his panic he'd forgotten to take the number of Wheatfield's cab. Now he couldn't be sure he had the right one.

They closed on the cab ahead. A single passenger was visible through the back window. They followed past the Planetarium and Madame Tussaud's, then the cab slowed and turned right into Marylebone High Street. Half-way down it turned left into Weymouth Street and came to a halt in front of a small block of flats.

Nick told the cabby to stop a little further on. He looked back. It was Wheatfield all right. Paying off the cab.

Exhaling with relief, Nick reached in his pocket for some money. 'You're joking, mate,' said the cabby, gesturing his refusal. 'Worth a guinea a minute. I wouldn't have missed it for the world.'

Wheatfield was going up the steps, taking a good look round before disappearing into the building. There appeared to be only the one entrance. It looked the sort of place to have a porter.

Nick gave it three mintues, then approached cautiously. The main doors were open, revealing an empty entrance hall. Nick strode in purposefully, looked around as if searching for someone, and said to the porter, 'Just saw a friend of mine come in. Does he live here?'

The porter stared at him blankly and shrugged.

Nick demanded, 'D'you know which flat he went to?'

'Probably fifth floor, I would say. That's where the lift stopped at any rate.'

'You don't know which number?'

The porter put on the air of having to deal with an idiot. 'These are service flats. People come and go all the time. Always changing. How should *I* know?'

Nick found a phone box and called the office. He told Conway to get hold of the letting agent and discover who'd rented the flats on the fifth floor. Conway cut him short, quietly triumphant. 'The boss has agreed to a proper job. Didn't I say he would? Give me ten minutes and someone'll be over.'

As he waited, Nick made an effort to keep a watch on the front entrance. He tried to memorise the description of each person passing in or out of the block. There were ten people in five minutes. By the time his relief arrived he couldn't remember anything about the first eight.

He briefed the new man then set off wearily for home. For some reason he began to feel very hot. Within minutes was sweating like a pig. It must be the flu. The thirty-minute Tube journey with a longish walk and nothing but an empty cold flat at the end suddenly seemed very unattractive.

He paused. Montagu Mews wasn't far away. Ten minutes at the most. Would she mind? Surely not. They'd made a tentative arrangement to meet that evening. So he'd be a bit early. She wouldn't turn him away; most women had some maternal instinct tucked away somewhere. He could do with a bit of tender loving care.

He was feeling distinctly shivery now. The walk was longer than he thought. By the time he reached the mews he was ready to drop.

He rang the bell. She wasn't in. He considered going home after all, but the prospect was very depressing.

He checked the wall of the house for an alarm. No sign. The door had a single Yale lock: a fifteen-second job. He reached into his wallet and took out one of the four 'loids' – strips of celluloid – he kept there.

As the door yielded he listened for a hidden alarm, but there was

195

none. He went in. Pausing only long enough to find a scrap of paper and leave a note on the stairs, he went straight up to the bedroom and undressed. Vastly weary, he climbed into the double bed and was instantly asleep.

Fifteen

Considering what she was about to do, Gabriele felt very calm.

She checked the contents of the parcels which Max had spread out on the table. Six batteries, two lengths of thin single-strand electrical wire – one in red, one in black – a pair of cutters, a soldering iron, a stick of solder, electrical tape, Sellotape, a roll of corrugated cardboard, six sheets of stiff white card, brown paper, small white plastic bags, string, six padded envelopes measuring ten by seven, a packet of wooden clothes pegs and a box of drawing-pins. Also a quantity of common garden weedkiller containing a high proportion of sodium chlorate, five bags of sugar, and one large packet of Surf soap powder. She rearranged everything in the right order, so that she could put her hands on the items as she needed them.

She said, 'Go and empty the Surf packet.'

While Max was gone she went to a holdall and removed the plastic container which she had been keeping in the fridge at the mews house. She opened it and took out six detonators. These she laid on the table.

With care she then removed the contents of a second box: two tubes, about ten inches long, each marked 'Nitramite 19C' and stamped with the French manufacturer's date and identification codes. The mixture consisted of TNT and ammonium nitrate, extremely powerful when detonated, but safe to handle under normal conditions.

She put the sticks of explosive on the far side of the table, next to the batteries and wires, but well away from the detonators.

Almost ready now. As a final preparation she tore two pages out of *Strike Back!* and taped them to the table where she could read them easily.

Max returned with the empty Surf packet which Gabriele placed on the floor. Handing Max the sugar and weedkiller, she motioned him towards the kitchen. She followed with a piece of paper and taped it on to the wall just above the work surface. On the paper were written the quantities of weedkiller and sugar to be weighed and mixed together in five separate batches, four small and one large. She pushed five plastic mixing bowls and the kitchen scales towards him. 'Take your time, mix the stuff well, and leave it in the bowls. And when you come in, don't speak to me or disturb me in any way.'

She returned to the main room and began work.

The important thing was not to rush it. With five devices to make it would be tempting to cut corn rs. That was the way to blast herself to pieces.

She decided to start with the simplest job. The four small packets.

First she made the initiators – the triggers that would fire the explosive. She took a wooden clothes peg and cut two lengths of red wire ten inches long. She made a small hole in each of the two jaws of the clothes peg, and pushed a wire through the hole from the outside. She stripped the end of each wire and wrapped it round the pin of a drawing-pin which she pushed firmly into the wood. When the clothes peg was clamped shut the two drawing-pins touched and contact was made between the two lengths of wire. She sprang the peg open and shut several times to make sure the drawing-pins always made good contact.

She made three more of these devices, then slid each inside a padded envelope and fixed them firmly in place with strong tape. Next she cut four rectangles of heavy card to fit inside the envelopes. As she put each card into the envelope she slid it between the jaws of the clothes peg. In this way, the card prevented contact between the two wires.

She got up and went into the kitchen. She found Max bent over the scales, spooning minute amounts of sugar back into a packet. She was pleased to see that he was doing the job with care.

He had completed three batches of the sugar-weedkiller mixture and these she took back to the table. She poured each batch into a white plastic bag and thrust a detonator into the centre of the crystals. With the wires from the detonator trailing out, she then sealed the bag with Sellotape, and slid it into the padded envelope on top of the card, being careful to keep the wires to one side.

Now, all that remained was to connect the various components to a battery.

She paused. She'd watched one of the Lotta make a similar letter bomb in Turin, and she'd practised it without explosives, but this was the first time she had done it for real.

She wired up the device until, if it weren't for the card, she would have a complete electrical circuit: one wire of the detonator to positive terminal on battery; negative terminal to clothes peg via red wire; clothes peg (second red wire) to second wire of detonator.

Max brought the last batch of sugar and weedkiller and she completed the last envelope.

There were now four small bombs in front of her, consisting of trigger, detonator and explosive. She sealed the envelopes.

When an envelope was opened and the card pulled out the circuit would be completed, the charge from the battery would fire the detonator – which would make a suitably frightening *bang*! – and the sugar mixture would go up in a sheet of flame complete with smoke.

Under normal circumstances it shouldn't kill anyone, but then it wasn't designed to.

She put the completed envelopes into the holdall, along with the things she no longer needed – the spare envelopes, cards and clothes pegs. The empty mixing bowls went back to the kitchen.

She relaxed for a moment.

So far so good.

Now the large parcel. This was different. This would very definitely kill.

She moved some of the items on the table nearer to her. Then after reading the instructions carefully, she began work.

First she taped the two HP2 batteries together and wired them together in series. Next she soldered a short length of red wire to the spare positive terminal, and a longer length of black wire to the negative.

Using insulating tape she strapped the two sticks of Nitramite together, and then strapped the batteries on to the sticks. From now on it was essential that the two wires leading from the batteries never touched one another, so she taped them on to the explosive, but as far apart as possible, the red running up to the top of one stick, the black to the bottom of the other.

So far it had been easy. Now the tricky part. She took a detonator and connected one of its wires to the red wire leading from the battery.

She now had half a circuit. The two loose wires must on no account come into contact with each other, otherwise the electrical charge from the batteries would fire the detonator, and that would be that.

She stretched the wires well apart and, to be doubly safe, wrapped some insulating tape round the one from the detonator which she would remove only at the last moment.

She paused. The operation had become oddly unreal. She had imagined having to make an enormous effort to create something like this. But it was incredibly easy. Apart from an odd feeling in the pit of her stomach, she had no fear. Instead she felt a curious detachment, as if this device would have come to exist anyway, without her help.

Max appeared from the kitchen, carrying a large bowl of the weedkiller and sugar crystals.

At that moment the telephone rang. Max gave a visible start. The bowl jerked in his hand and some of the mixture spilled on to the carpet.

Gabriele hissed, 'For Christ's sake!' and, getting up, took the bowl from his hands. She said impatiently, 'Answer the phone!'

Max picked it up. He turned to her. 'It's Giorgio.'

Gabriele let out a sigh of irritation. She had spoken to him the previous night and again that morning. He'd told her everything was going to plan. So why the hell was he calling again? And *now*.

Putting the bowl carefully on the table, she took the receiver from Max and snapped, 'Do you realise what you nearly *did*!'

'You told me to call if there was a change of plan.'

'But not *now*!' She forced her anger back. 'So what is it?'

'The girl. I can't do things too fast.'

'What do you mean?'

With obvious irritation Giorgio explained. 'She wants to take me out to dinner. She expects it. I have to go.'

Gabriele tried to think calmly. The girl had to be played along. She said harshly, 'Okay. But make her start for England first thing in the morning.'

'It's arranged. And I will fly at midday. I'll call you—'

'Don't call me *here* again!'

'The number's on the list,' Giorgio replied angrily. 'How was I to know?'

She put the phone down and spent several minutes sitting at the table, composing herself again. Then she went back to work.

Pouring most of the weedkiller–sugar mixture into the bottom of the empty Surf packet, she bedded first the detonator, then the

Nitramite sticks well down into it, and poured more of the sugar mixture on top, until it was flowing over the sides. Leaving the two loose wires trailing out of the top of the packet – one from each side – she taped the hinged lid of the Surf packet well down.

Now the trigger. She used a spring-loaded mechanism, rather like a mousetrap. It had to be rigged so that it would be activated by the opening of the parcel.

She took some corrugated cardboard and, wrapping it round the Surf box, cut it to size and taped it very tightly around the box. Then she took the mousetrap device and, without attaching it to the wires, cocked it and slipped it under the corrugated cardboard at the side of the box. She chose the side of the box because the pressure of the outer wrapping was greater there and would keep the trigger firmly cocked, and because people generally lay parcels flat when opening them, so leaving the side unimpeded and the mechanism free to operate.

She took a careful look at the trigger. There was no way it could operate accidentally while the corrugated cardboard was in place. But as soon as it was removed . . .

To test it, she tore the cardboard away, as if opening the parcel, and heard the mechanism give a satisfying snap.

She took another section of corrugated cardboard and fastened it tightly round the box.

Her mouth was dry. Fear at last. She was aware of Max close by, breathing down her neck. To get rid of him she said, 'Get me a coffee, would you?'

While he was in the kitchen, she took the red wire, removed the safety tape, and soldered the exposed end to the contact on the mousetrap mechanism. Next she pulled back the spring and pushed the mechanism between the layers of cardboard until it was held firmly in place, properly cocked, but with the base of the trigger still visible.

Now. The worst moment. The black wire had to be soldered to the terminal on the base of the fuse itself. Her heart thumped in her ears. She swallowed hard. It was one thing to know that the two contacts couldn't meet, and quite another to be aware of them being so close, separated by only a few inches.

Shaking slightly, she put the wire on the terminal and, holding the stick of solder, put the hot iron against it. The solder dripped on to the wire and cooled.

The bomb was now live.

Gently, she pushed the trigger mechanism further down the side of the box until it was out of sight. She exhaled deeply and sat back.

Max brought the coffee. She allowed herself a moment of satisfaction. A workman-like job. And a good explosive chain. The electrical circuit would heat the hot wire inside the detonator which would explode the extremely volatile fulminate of mercury. This in turn would explode the sugar–sodium chlorate mixture, which would finally explode the more stable TNT and ammonium nitrate of the main charge.

For a moment she imagined the explosion, the man being blown apart and plastered over the walls and ceiling in the split second before the house collapsed around him.

When she had finished her coffee she wrapped the parcel in brown paper and string, and then addressed it in bold block lettering, using a thick black felt-tip pen. Finally she placed it carefully in the holdall.

'What now?' asked Max.

'Keep the cutters and the spare wire. Put everything else into a rubbish bag and put it downstairs, in one of the communal dustbins.' They weren't coming back here, but she disliked the idea of leaving even the smallest amount of evidence behind.

As Max collected the empty containers, the wrapping, the off-cuts of red and black wire, Gabriele wiped the table, hoovered the weedkiller and sugar from the carpet and checked the kitchen. Max had been rather messy here too, and it took her a good ten minutes to clean the work surface and the floor. But she found the cleaning therapeutic; it seemed to tidy her mind. When she'd finished she was in high spirits.

Max was waiting at the flat door with the rubbish. She said, 'You've got the communiqués?'

He nodded.

'Remember to give the cabbies plenty of money, so they don't hesitate to take them. If you argue about it they'll remember your face.' She opened the door. 'You go first. I'll follow in a minute.'

In fact it was ten minutes before she was ready to leave. She put on a long blonde dolly-bird wig, some dark glasses, and a nondescript coat, which she normally wouldn't have been seen dead in. She was rather amused by her disguise, and stood in front of the mirror for a couple of minutes. It was really very simple to look completely different.

Down in the street she loaded the holdall and the large parcel into the boot of her car. Then, like dozens of young office girls all over London that afternoon, she took her batch of envelopes to the nearest post office to catch the last post of the day.

There was no one to see her go. The watchers had spotted Wheatfield leaving ten minutes earlier and, pleased to have identified him safely, were tailing him westwards, back towards North Kensington.

Gabriele parked outside the mews house and went to the boot. She decided to leave the parcel in there overnight – the car wasn't worth stealing, and there was no reason why anyone should be interested in it. However, she removed the spare detonators, to be on the safe side. There must be no accidents.

The holdall itself could stay in the boot until she found another service flat some time the following week.

She locked the boot. Letting herself into the house, she went to the kitchen and put the detonator into the fridge. Then she removed the wig and sunglasses and shook out her hair.

Now what?

Restlessly, she paced the kitchen. She was still exhilarated from the bomb-making. She wanted company. She wanted to talk. But now Giorgio wouldn't be back until the next day. And it wouldn't be wise to go calling on Max.

There was Nick Riley, of course. In fact if she was being honest he was the first person she'd thought of. But he hadn't phoned since he'd left the previous morning. And she didn't know where to find him. *Damn.*

Coffee mug in hand, she wandered into the living-room.

She stopped in her tracks.

A white blob of paper stared up at her from the staircase.

Her stomach twisted unpleasantly. *Who?*

She grabbed the paper and read fast.

Nick Riley.

For a second she went very cold, thinking of what he might have discovered.

Then she calmed herself. There was nothing in the house, nothing to suggest she was anything but a journalist. *Even* if he'd been snooping around, which he probably hadn't.

But how the hell had he got in?

She thought: How *dare* he!

But mingling with her annoyance was a tinge of grudging

admiration: he certainly had a nerve. As she climbed the stairs she rehearsed what she'd say to him.

The door of the bedroom was ajar. She pushed it wide open. Clothes were littered over the floor.

He was in her bed, breathing quietly, fast asleep. His top was bare. She suspected he was naked.

She shook him by the shoulder. 'Hey, wake up, you!'

He turned over and, opening half an eye, groaned, 'Hello.' He stretched and rubbed his hand mercilessly over his face. 'What time is it?' His voice was a thin croak.

She retreated slightly and said accusingly, 'You've got a cold.'

He opened the other eye and pulled himself up on to one elbow. 'I didn't actually *ask* to have it . . .'

'It was uninvited, was it – like *you*?'

'Quite.' His tone was unrepentant.

She demanded, 'May I ask how the hell you got in?'

'Ah.' For a long moment he looked at her through half-closed eyes, and she thought he wasn't going to answer. But eventually he said, 'There was a window open.'

She thought: Ah no, you don't get me that easily. She said firmly, 'Oh no, there wasn't.'

He made a face to show he'd been caught out. 'Well, you remember the car door? I used a trick like that.'

'Show me what you used. To get in.'

He looked at her for a few moments then slowly reached down to his jacket on the floor. From a packet he brought out what was known in the trade as a jiggler, a thin dagger-like steel spike. He said, 'What I used for the car. Nothing to it.'

'That wouldn't do it.'

He stared at her, suddenly wary. 'No?'

'You can't open locks like Yales with *that*.'

There was a silence. Suddenly he grinned. 'Well, you're absolutely right. Now how did you know that?'

She'd learnt a few basics from a former housebreaker in the Lotta. She persisted, 'So how did you get in?'

His smile vanished. Taking out his wallet, he removed a strip of celluloid and held it in the air. 'Takes fifteen seconds.'

'But only when you know how.'

He slipped the plastic and the spike back into his jacket. 'I can see that you're thinking bad things about me.'

She decided to go on giving him a hard time. She got a curious pleasure from it; also she wanted to know more. She said, 'Yes, I am.'

He reached out and, without a word, took the cup of coffee from her hand and began to drink from it. The bedcovers moved and she saw the side of his hip. Naked.

She said, 'You're a thief.'

He looked at her over the cup. 'No.' It was a bald statement.

'Then you break and enter for amusement?'

'Useful for getting into friends' flats. It's just a trick I learnt in my misspent youth and – I like to keep it up.' He shrugged, draining the last of the coffee. 'Strange though it sounds, it's the truth.'

She didn't believe a word of it. He was a thief, no doubt about it. But she wasn't angry. On the contrary, she was seeing Nick Riley in a new and very interesting light.

But she decided not to pursue the subject for the moment. All in good time. Instead she said caustically, 'So – do you usually sleep in the afternoons?'

'Only when I'm feeling bloody awful.'

'The cold? Or is it still the head?'

'Both. And lack of care and attention.'

'Well, well, that won't do, will it?' she replied archly. 'Can I get you something – apart from *my* coffee, that is?'

'Aspirin and hot lemon.' He added a hasty 'Please', and gave her a big smile.

'I'll get some from the chemist.' It was a long time since she'd gone on an errand for a man. But this was different.

As she moved to the door, he said, 'Any chance of a bath?'

'I should think so. The bathroom's next door.' She added facetiously, 'You're sure you'll be able to manage the lock?'

He grinned appreciatively, his expression warm and unguarded. Very attractive. For a common thief.

On the way back from the chemist, she began to realise that her snap judgement was probably mistaken. If he was just an ordinary thief then he was an extremely bad one – he had nothing to show for it in the way of a car or a place to live – and she couldn't believe that he was bad at anything he did.

No, going by his part in the demonstration and their conversation at dinner, he was undoubtedly committed politically and therefore above such things as common thieving. As such, he would keep his housebreaking and car stealing talents for special occasions: *political* occasions. The chances were he was *already* an activist.

204

If so, what a stroke of luck. It couldn't have worked out better if she'd planned it.

Back at the house she made a hot lemon drink and took it up the stairs. Sounds of splashing came from the bathroom. She paused and, leaving the drink on a shelf, looked into the empty bedroom. Most of his clothes had disappeared, but his jacket was still there, hanging up on a chair.

Silently she crossed the floor and, feeling through the pockets, pulled out the wallet. Money. The piece of plastic – no, *three* pieces of plastic. A train ticket. In the pockets, a comb, the steel spike, some paper handkerchiefs.

And a full set of keys. Skeleton keys.

But nothing else.

She frowned. Strange. No bus pass or student union card. Nothing to identify him.

His voice said: 'I hope it's interesting enough.'

She spun round.

He was standing in the doorway, wrapped in a towel. He walked casually up to her and, feeling through the jacket, pulled out the comb. He met her gaze and said mildly. 'If you want to know more about me you only have to ask.'

'Just checking. After all, it's not every day I find a housebreaker in my bed.' She asked lightly, 'What's your real name?'

'Nick Riley. Just like I said.'

She stared up into his face. Even if it wasn't his real name, did it really matter?

This man was exactly what she wanted. In every way.

The trouble with telling a lie, Nick thought unhappily, was that it led you into deeper and deeper water. The original lie – pretending to be a student – had been harmless enough, but now he'd had to tell a dozen more to cover himself.

Of course he could always tell her the truth, but that would be the end of that. Once she realised he was one of what she so charmingly called the filth, she'd never give him any information. In fact she'd chuck him straight out.

Also – and by no means least – there was the lady herself. Today she was radiating a nervous energy, an excitement that was overtly sexual. There was the firm promise of an affair, he was certain. And why not? Besides, the cold was making him feel sorry for himself and he wanted to be spoilt a little.

She handed him the hot lemon, asking, 'Would you like something to eat as well?'

He'd forgotten when he'd last had a meal. 'Yes, I'm starving.'

'Chicken, pasta, salad okay?'

'That's very good of you.'

She gave a little smile of triumph. 'Not of *me*. But of the Italian restaurant on the corner. I'll ask them to send it over.'

He thought: No chinks in her armour.

He went back to the bathroom and, finding a razor in the wall cabinet had a shave. It was a woman's razor. It may have been great for legs but it was blunt as hell on his face.

He examined the other contents of the cabinet. A stick deodorant. A bottle of eau de cologne. Brand: Rocco. Made in Italy, purchased in Italy. Packaging: masculine. Wording: *per uomini*. For men.

Ah. Masculine tastes.

Or a lover.

Back in the bedroom he looked in the wardrobe. Male clothing. Definitely a lover, then. Some of the shirts had Italian labels. He had a quick look through a jacket and some jeans. Nothing.

Presumably this lover was away. He wondered how long for. She didn't seem worried about an imminent return.

Feeling better for the bath, he got dressed and checked that his ID was safely tucked into the lining of his shoe. Gabriella had been quick off the mark searching his jacket. But then she was a journalist and they were always nosy.

As he went downstairs he thought of phoning Conway. It was seven: there might be something on the Wheatfield observation by now. But Gabriella was already putting plates of food on the table and he realised he was ravenous. The meal was delicious and he wolfed it down. His headache had disappeared. She produced a bottle of Chianti and he drank several glasses. They talked quietly, reflectively. The atmosphere was mellow, almost dreamlike.

Gabriella turned on Radio 3. There was a symphony. He recognised Brahms' Fourth. They listened for a while in silence. The music worked its usual spell on Nick. Everything became accentuated: the warmth and comfort of the room, the taste of the wine, the loveliness and desirability of Gabriella.

She met his eyes and smiled. There was still a reserve there, he noticed, a guard she was determined not to let down. He said quietly, 'Thanks for looking after me.'

She bristled immediately. 'Don't start being polite. That's

bourgeois crap.' She hesitated. 'Besides I wanted someone around. I didn't want to be on my own tonight.'

'I wouldn't have thought you'd be on your own very often.'

She regarded him over the rim of her glass. 'I hope you make love better than you talk, otherwise we're in for a disappointing night.'

The directness of the approach gave him a slight shock. Then he laughed, 'Well, there's only one way to find out, isn't there?'

He's just another man, she told herself. Another man like any other. To be enjoyed on her own terms.

And yet . . . Even now, he still had his arms round her, was still caressing her gently, making small sounds of pleasure. Unafraid of affection.

She wasn't sure she understood men like this.

He murmured, 'Your skin is incredibly soft.'

She turned her head, trying to examine his face in the darkness. He began to cover her cheeks with small kisses. Then, aware of her reserve, he pulled back. 'Was it all right for you?' His voice was soft, concerned.

'Yes.' It should have been – he had been very generous, over-whelmingly so – and yet she had felt nervous, unrelaxed.

'I – had the feeling – that it wasn't.'

'No. It was – great.'

He sank back on the pillow, drawing back from her. She wanted to explain. She said awkwardly, 'I've just got a lot on my mind, that's all.'

He said wryly, 'Thanks.'

'I meant . . .' What had she meant? That he made her feel vulnerable, and she didn't like that. 'I meant that I'm very bound up in my work at the moment.'

'Tell me about it.'

She hesitated. 'I'm working towards an important goal. Some-thing I feel very strongly about. And – it takes all my energy.'

He was silent for a moment. 'What is this goal?'

'I'm trying to – make people see the world for what it is. A twisted, rotten place. I'm trying to make them see how meaningless and empty their lives are. Living in boxes, working like ants – and for nothing. For crap like television sets and washing machines – things that they *think* will make them happy. They don't realise that they're just being bought off, made to live the roles that society has allotted to them . . . .' She paused. 'I want to change all that.'

'Why? I mean, why d'you feel so strongly?'

'Because nobody counts for anything. Not in the system as it is now. The system crushes you if it can. It doesn't care a shit about the individual. I know. I've *been* there.'

Nick could feel the shudder of rage pass through her. Her vehemence vaguely worried him, nagging at an idea in the back of his mind. But then he remembered the early life in Italy, the dead father and the cold mother, and he saw that there was a lot of the hurt child in her; a child full of anger and resentment who still didn't understand why things had gone wrong for her.

He pulled her gently towards him. 'It's all right, it's all right . . .'

She was still fretting and he could feel the tension in her body. But finally she calmed down and her body relaxed against his. She turned her face to him and he could feel the warmth of her breath. Raising her head off the pillow, she stared at him in the darkness and seemed to come to a decision. She lowered her mouth on to his and kissed him, slowly at first, and then hungrily. This time there was no reserve.

Much later, after the last sigh of pleasure had come from deep within her, she held him close to her for a long time.

Sixteen

Henry Northcliff glanced at his watch. Seven fifty-five. His driver was already outside the house. He should leave in five minutes if he wasn't to be late for his early meeting.

He finished his coffee and went into the hall. He wondered why Caroline hadn't appeared yet. Then saw her, just coming downstairs. He noticed she was still in her dressing-gown, which was unusual for her. As they met at the foot of the stairs the telephone rang.

Caroline said, 'I'll take it,' and went across the hall into the study.

Henry picked up his coat and briefcase, checked that he hadn't forgotten anything and stuck his head round the study door. Caroline was perched on the desk, listening hard, muttering the occasional 'No, I'm afraid not.' She saw Henry and beckoned him over. Henry was about to shake his head and point at his watch, when she beckoned again, more urgently. He put down his things and, going to the desk, looked at her questioningly. She thrust the receiver into his hand and panted, 'Elizabeth Danby.'

The horror showed in his face.

Caroline shook her head briefly. 'Sorry! Got to go – sorry!' She rushed past him and out of the room. Henry thought: What on earth?

Crossly, he put the receiver to his ear. Interrupting Mrs Danby's abject apologies, he managed to establish that she had heard some disquieting news about Victoria; a rumour that she had been injured.

'Injured?' he asked.

'In this awful demonstration, apparently. I mean, *really* – I thought I'd better check up on her, but her phone doesn't answer. For all I know she might be in some *hospital* . . . I just wondered if you'd *heard*.'

He cut her short with assurances that they hadn't heard anything, but would let her know the moment they did.

The instant he'd got rid of the woman, he went in search of Caroline. He called out but there was no reply. He was about to look upstairs when he heard a sound from the downstairs cloakroom. He strode across the hall and pushed open the door.

Caroline was draped over the basin, swilling out her mouth with water. He suddenly realised that she had been sick.

She looked at him sheepishly. 'I was going to tell you, but I wasn't really sure until today.'

He stared at her, shocked, trying to take it in.

She said unhappily, 'I know we hadn't exactly planned a baby . . . And it's a bit of a surprise for me too . . .' She caught the expression on his face and trailed off.

Henry's first reaction was one of sharp disappointment and – yes – resentment. The two of them had been perfectly happy. He'd been looking forward to their having time together, to travel and explore Florence and Venice . . . To enjoy *each other*. And now *this* . . .

A baby would intrude into their relationship, steal from it, diminish it. The extra dimension their happiness had possessed would be suffocated by the sheer weight of dreary day-to-day trivia; nappies, feeds and sleepless nights. And by the time they were free again – God, he would be an old man . . .

In a wave of self-pity he looked at her and thought: All I ever needed was *you*.

She dropped her eyes and turned away to pat her face with a towel. She was putting a brave front on it, but he could see that she was upset. He realised he was being very selfish. He should look at it from her point of view. She would enjoy being a mother. He mustn't deny her that.

He grasped her shoulders and leant his head against hers.

She said in a low voice, 'You're not happy about it.'

He stroked her hair and said finally, 'Of course I'm happy about it. It was rather a shock, that's all. Really.' He managed a thin smile. 'It's wonderful.'

For all its faults the British postal service is more efficient than most. In 1969, in the days before it was split into a two-tier system of first- and second-class mail, eighty-seven per cent of all letters were delivered the next day, a figure which rose to well over ninety per cent for letters sent within the London area or to other large cities such as Manchester or Birmingham.

The first padded envelope was delivered at seven-fifteen to an address in Bradford. It was not opened immediately for the simple reason that there was no one there. The place was the one-roomed office of an organisation called the Anglo-Asian Society, one of the many groups and societies that had sprung up in the area since the large influx of Asians in the fifties and sixties. Although the organisation's title suggested that it embraced all Asian immigrants, in practice the membership did not include Pakistanis, who as Muslims liked to keep themselves to themselves, but consisted almost entirely of Indian Hindus.

The organisation was a peaceful one which prided itself on furthering understanding between the British and Indian communities. This was not always easy because, like most immigrants, the Indians liked to stick together and Bradford's Asian population had now got to the point where, in many streets, it was rare to see a white face. To the consternation of the society's president and secretary, Mr Binodh Gopalji, this fact was somewhat resented by the shrinking white community. However, he worked hard to smooth out what he called 'the minor little hiccups' that interrupted the smoothness of his community's absorption into the British way of life. It was a source of some satisfaction to him that, by and large, his modest efforts appeared to be successful.

The next envelope was delivered at seven thirty-nine, to an address in the North 8 district of London. This was the location of the West Indian Action Group, which, as its name suggested, was fairly forceful in pursuing the interests of its West Indian members, though even its critics could hardly describe it as militant. The members, who were mainly younger second-generation black immigrants from the islands of the Caribbean, were vociferous, educated, and angry. They wanted jobs, houses, and an end to discrimination. Despite the provocative suggestions of certain right-wing politicians that they should be encouraged to return to Trinidad or Barbados, they regarded Britain as their home, which was not surprising since most of them had spent the greater part of their lives there.

For much of the time the office was run by a slim twenty-two-year-old law student called Leonie Brown, whose family had emigrated from the island of Antigua in 1949. But, being a girl who liked to go out dancing almost as much as she liked going to bed with her lusty new boyfriend, she didn't often get to sleep before two, and was rarely in the office before nine-thirty.

This envelope, too, remained unopened on the floor.

The third envelope was delivered later, at eight-twenty. Here, at an office in the City, there was someone to receive it. David Levene often arrived early. He found he got a lot of work done in the quiet time between eight and eight-thirty. Although he was a journalist and it wasn't really his job to do so, he picked up the mail and sifted through it.

He noticed the buff-coloured padded envelope straight away. The six staff at the *Red Star* kept a wary eye open for unusual packages. As an official publication of the Communist Party they were used to receiving the occasional hate mail. People had been known to send dog turds, bad eggs, and other such subtle indications of resentment.

But *was* this package unusual?

No clue to who the sender might be. Post mark: W1.

He flexed it in his fingers. A hard object half-way down. The rest crunchy – as if it contained granules of some kind. He sniffed at the flap. Slightly acrid. Could be a chemical that let off a bad smell.

He thought for a moment. Always better to be on the safe side. He put the envelope in his desk. As soon as the others got in he'd discuss it with them.

At two minutes to nine Binodh Gopalji unlocked the door of the

Anglo-Asian Society's office in Bradford and, as was his habit, carefully hung his coat and hat on the hook behind the door. Then he stopped to pick up the mail off the mat. He recognised an electricity bill, which was not at all welcome since the society was always short of funds; two circulars; a batch of Indian publications; fifteen letters and a padded envelope.

He sat down at his desk and looked out of the window for a moment. A nice day, and getting better. The sun was making an effort to break through. It didn't happen very often in the British winters. But he didn't mind that. He loved Britain: it was tolerant, ordered, and comfortable. He thought with pride: Simply the best country in the world.

He began to open the mail, carefully and methodically, as was his way. Leaving the bills and circulars until last, he began with the letters. Requests for news of relatives, requests from India for an introduction to a possible bride – the only quick way of getting into Britain nowadays – requests for help. Requests, always requests, which was just how it should be.

He came to the padded envelope. It was taped down at one end. By opening it carefully, it could be reused. Since this type of envelope was expensive, it was a consideration not to be sniffed at.

Patiently, he stripped off the Sellotape and was pleased to see it had not brought away any of the paper.

Then, angling the envelope so that he could see inside it, he unfolded the end. A piece of card. He pulled it out.

Although he remembered nothing about that afterwards.

The force of the explosion, though relatively small, was sufficient to knock him backwards off his chair on to the floor, leaving him stunned. However, it was the sheet of flame that blasted outwards in a three-foot arc that did the damage. It scorched away all the hair and much of the skin from his face and hands. And, though the eyelids can close faster than the shutter of a camera, Binodh Gopalji's reacted a fraction of a second too late, and the blast hit his eyes.

He was found almost immediately, by another tenant, and fifteen minutes later was in the emergency room of the nearest hospital. His condition was not critical, but severe enough – skin grafts would be required to repair the burnt skin; and his eyes would never quite recover from their blasting. However, for Binodh Gopalji the blast to his body was nothing compared to the shock to his moral sensibilities. Life could never ever be viewed in quite the same way again. The exploding envelope had blasted more than his face; it had destroyed the tolerant comfortable Britain he had loved like a true son. Moreover, he was totally mystified as to the reason why.

The fourth envelope was delivered at nine-ten to the Council for Civil Liberties, a fiercely independent organisation which fought for and defended individual rights. Although it examined all manner of threats against personal liberty, it had inevitably concentrated its efforts on protecting the interests of the underprivileged, and was regarded as firmly left-wing.

The envelope was opened by the secretary-receptionist, a girl of twenty-three. She was extremely lucky. For one thing, she was standing up when she opened it on the desk, so that it was some distance from her face. For another, she was talking to someone else at the time, so that her chin was up and her face at an obtuse angle to the blast. Finally – and luckiest of all – the weedkiller – sugar mixture did not ignite properly. As a result, she was stunned but not seriously hurt.

Leonie Brown was not so lucky. She arrived at the office of the West Indian Action Group at nine-forty, having had far too little sleep. She made some coffee, took a couple of phone calls, and yawned. At ten she looked at the mail, such as it was. Nothing very interesting. Except for the padded envelope. Sitting at her desk, she ripped off the Sellotape and pulled out the card inside.

The blast itself would not have hurt her seriously, but for the fragment of metal from the detonator case which, sharp as a knife, flew into her chest and pierced a lung. Unfortunately there was no one about and it was some ten minutes before she was discovered, choking on her own blood and hardly breathing. She was taken to hospital where they poured ten pints of blood into her and, against all the odds, just managed to save her. It was four weeks before she left hospital.

In the offices of the *Red Star* David Levene was working hard on an article which had to be finished by that afternoon, and completely forgot the envelope in his desk. Then at noon a fellow journalist, coming in late, mentioned the news story he had just heard on the radio.

Then, with something of a shock, David Levene remembered the envelope. Very quietly he locked his desk, and told the others not under any circumstances to approach it. Then he telephoned Scotland Yard.

At about the same time a communiqué was delivered to *The Times* and the *Daily Express*. It was titled: 'Britain for the British', and contained a vitriolic tirade against immigration and subversives. It purported to come from an organisation called the National Coalition.

'Who the hell are the National Coalition?' demanded Chief Superintendent Straughan.

Everyone stared at Mason, the Branch man who covered right-wing organisations. He shook his head. 'Nothing on file, sir. Never been heard of before.'

Ryder sneezed and blew his nose. He'd just arrived, having phoned in earlier and heard the news. He was rather glad he wasn't in Mason's shoes, having to admit he knew nothing.

'Right,' said Straughan, 'Commander Kershaw, late of the Serious Crime Squad, is in charge of the investigation. Mason and Smith are being seconded to assist. For the rest of you – I want ears to the ground. I want to be reassured that no one on the left is going to get agitated and start thinking about reprisals.'

As they got up to leave Straughan frowned at Nick. 'No one told me you were back with us, Nick. Got clearance from the CMO, I trust?'

'Sir. Should come through tomorrow.'

As they returned to the office Conway murmured, 'Careful, he'll check up on it.'

With bad grace, Nick phoned the Central Medical Officer's office and made an appointment for later that afternoon.

Then he went down to the incident room, which had the air of frenetic activity that marked the early stages of a new case.

Nick found a face he vaguely recognised, a sergeant he'd worked with a few months back, and reintroduced himself. After chatting for a bit, Nick let it be known that he'd like to hear when any info came back from the explosives people at Woolwich. There was no reason why the sergeant should keep him in touch, except it was asked as a favour, and a lot of business around Scotland Yard was done by favours.

Nick went back to his office and, tempting some hot water out of the coffee machine, made himself an aspirin and hot lemon drink from a sachet that he had taken from Gabriella's supply.

He thought back to the morning. What a strange lady she was. On waking she'd been cool and distant, almost resentful. She'd watched him covertly, as if assessing him afresh. Then, abruptly, she seemed to break out of whatever constrained her, and to regain a little of her confidence. Some of the previous evening's mood had returned, and she became sharp and funny again.

He wondered if there was any future in the affair. Probably not. And in some ways he was sorry. She was good company when she made up her mind to it. He liked her smartness, her clever mind, the tough exterior which hid the vulnerability underneath. But at the same time she was uncertain, evasive, and volatile, as if, underlying all the toughness, there was a deep lack of self-confidence. She didn't seem to know who she was, and that was a pity.

In the end she'd be trouble, he sensed it. And yet – there was something about her that intrigued him.

Also – he couldn't help remembering – she might be useful.

The sergeant from downstairs phoned up with the preliminary report from Woolwich – the Home Office Branch of the Royal Armament Research and Development Establishment. The device found at the offices of the *Red Star* consisted of a continental-style detonator, a home-made initiator and a mixture consisting of a weedkiller containing sodium chlorate, and sugar.

'No trace on the source of the explosive?' Nick asked.

'Dunno. Nothing reported anyway.'

Nick rang off, wondering how a right-wing group had suddenly got so proficient in the making of explosives. One somehow expected trouble of this sort to come from the Left, who had a traditional fondness for drawing attention to their cause with violence and loud bangs. He remembered *Strike Back!*

God! He had a sudden thought. Perhaps, by a perverse stroke of chance this National Coalition or whoever they were had got hold of a copy. That would be an ironical twist: the Left hoist by its own petard.

He took a copy of *Strike Back!* out of the drawer and looked through the explosives section. Here it was . . . under the heading 'Easy Brew'. Sugar and weedkiller. Flashes up with searing, yellow flame. Not most powerful explosive . . . but ingredients easy to buy and easy to make. *Required*: sugar – any type; and sodium chlorate – principal ingredient of certain weedkillers (it listed the best brands).

The detonation – it went on to explain – could be effected in any number of ways. But, if limited to easily available means, then the methods on page 12 or 13 were recommended.

Nick looked at page 12. Glowing element of a broken light bulb powered by battery. Page 13. Drip acid on to a contraceptive, until it leaked through on to the mixture and explodes it.

But the letter bomb had contained a proper detonator. Things hardly available from a mundane shopping expedition. No. These right-wingers had contacts, sources, *sophistication*.

And yet – it was no good: something about all this bothered him deeply. It just didn't ring true. The right-wingers were stirrers, agitators. They liked to march in black uniforms through immigrant neighbourhoods shouting loud slogans. And they were young, ill-educated and unsophisticated for the most part. Somehow these letter bombs just didn't *fit*.

He would have believed it of Wheatfield's sort. Every time. If the recipients of the letter bombs had been *right*-wing he'd have put Wheatfield near the top of his list straight away.

It was ironical that Wheatfield, of all people, *had* been on quite a shopping expedition the previous day.

Somewhere in the back of Nick's mind a small alarm sounded.

That large bag bought from the hardware shop. It had looked just like a garden product. And the purchases in the supermarket – he had thought he had seen Wheatfield buy flour. But it could just as well have been *sugar*.

It was ridiculous of course. There was no motive.

It didn't make sense.

And *yet*.

He racked his brains to remember the name of the shop in Westbourne Grove. His mind was a blank. He called the local Notting Hill nick.

After a long wait while someone asked around, he finally got it.

Westbury's.

He called them.

Yes, said the sleepy assistant, they stocked all sorts of weedkiller. Nick sat a little more upright in his chair.

Containing sodium chlorate? the assistant repeated back to him. He hadn't a clue, he'd have to ask the boss. After a long time the boss came to the phone. Weedkiller with sodium chlorate? Well – he'd have a look. There was a long pause. He came back to the phone and, obviously reading off the packaging, listed various chemical-sounding names. Then Nick realised that they probably *were* only names: manufacturers' registered names for the concoction of chemicals in that particular product.

'Is there a brand in a white bag with red lettering on it?' Nick asked.

216

The shopkeeper answered without hesitation. He named a well-known brand. He described the red lettering, and said it had a picture of a garden underneath. And, yes, the picture of the garden *was* mainly green. Nick could almost hear him thinking, well, it would be, wouldn't it, being a garden.

'How big is this bag?' Nick asked.

'We've got it in bags of five, ten or twenty pounds.'

'And the manufacturer – what's their address?'

The shopkeeper gave it to him. Nick rang off, his mind racing.

Conway wandered into the office and opened his mouth to speak. Nick waved him to shut up and got on to the telephone exchange to find the number of the weedkiller manufacturer. Within five minutes he was talking to their chief chemist. Two minutes later he was replacing the phone, shaking his head with disbelief.

Mainly sodium chlorate.

Conway, who'd been listening avidly, demanded, 'You on to something, Ryder?'

'God only knows.' He jumped up and grabbed his jacket. 'Where's Wheatfield, Conway?'

'*Wheatfield?* Why?' Then, catching the full implication of the question, he exclaimed, 'But he's left of *Marx*, for Christsake!'

'Where *is* he?'

Conway suddenly looked crestfallen. 'At this precise moment no one knows. The watch was called off an hour ago.'

Nick tried to contain his disbelief. '*Why in hell?*'

'Because we *know* where he lives. And because a lot of people were needed for *this*.'

Nick closed his eyes and said, 'Oh shit.'

It took half an hour to get hold of Commander Kershaw, to stop briefly at the shop in Westbourne Grove and pick up a packet of the weedkiller, and meet him at St Mark's Villas with a raiding party. Even before they had stationed two men at the back, obtained confirmation that a search warrant had been granted, and run panting up the stairs to the room on the second floor, Nick knew what they would find.

Nothing.

Wheatfield had done a bunk. They spent ten minutes establishing that no trace of the shopping expedition remained, and sped across town to the service flat in Weymouth Street, where they met up with Conway. Faced by five policemen the porter was suddenly more forthcoming about the occupants of the fifth floor. He thought that flat number 502 was most likely to be the one they were after. Conway referred to the list of residents he'd obtained from the letting agents. Four of the flats on the fifth floor were let, either to companies or American visitors. However, flat 502 had been let to a Mr and Mrs Hoerst of Switzerland.

They knocked on the door of the flat. There was no reply. The porter let them in with a pass key.

It was quite empty. There were no signs of a hurried departure. Conway phoned the letting agents again. The rent was paid up for another two weeks. No, references had not been requested because the tenants had paid the rent in advance and left a £150 deposit. And no, the deposit had not been reclaimed.

Everything was very neat and tidy. The porter explained that the maid would have been in that morning. She would have cleared out the wastepaper baskets and the kitchen rubbish.

Nick walked round the flat with an empty feeling in the pit of his stomach.

An expensive service flat, money to burn, smooth organisation. The letter bombs were Wheatfield, all right, but *this* set-up? No. Not on his *own* anyway. This sort of lifestyle was quite out of his league.

He sat disconsolately in an armchair, ignoring the angry glare of one of the two forensic men who were bent over tables and carpets, busy with small brushes and scrapers, like a couple of fastidious housewives.

Kershaw came in and sat in the opposite chair. He was a tall, thoughtful, softly-spoken man, although Nick had the feeling the calm manner was deceptive. 'Okay, Ryder,' he said. 'Tell me about Wheatfield.'

Making an effort to remember all the details on the file, Nick listed the catalogue of Wheatfield's political activities.

Kershaw drew a deep breath. 'Any ideas as to why a well-known left-wing activist might be trying to score against his own side?'

Nick drew a deep breath. 'Trying to stir it up. That's all I can think of.'

'Well – I'm not saying you're wrong, but according to the surveillance reports, Wheatfield did not go near a post box yesterday.'

'No. But then there were others involved. I'm sure of it.'

'An organisation?'

'A group. Trained, possibly abroad.'

Kershaw stroked his chin thoughtfully. 'Okay, Ryder. I'll buy that. But I can't say I'm happy with the motive. If you can come up with some more answers, that would be appreciated.'

'Excuse me –' It was one of the forensic men. He was holding a number of small plastic bags. 'I think you might find this interesting . . .' The bags all contained granules of what looked like sugar. 'I found these crystals down several cracks on the kitchen work surface. Also on the kitchen floor. And quite a quantity in the carpet, just here. Also a few were caught in the bristles of the floor brush. They'll have to be analysed, of course. But taking a preliminary look, there appear to be two types of crystal here. At least one is granular, like sugar, the other more powdery, like salt . . .'

At that moment the telephone rang.

Giorgio held the telephone to his ear and counted the rings with growing impatience.

Suddenly it answered.

There was a pause, then a man's voice said, 'Hello?'

Giorgio hesitated then slowly replaced the receiver. It wasn't Max's voice. Gabriele must have given up the flat. Why hadn't she told him? And would it be relet already? He sighed with annoyance. How could he be expected to understand the British way of doing things?

He looked at the last number on his list. He'd already tried the mews house. There was only the flat in Chelsea. It was strictly for emergency use, so it was unlikely she'd be there, but he tried the number anyway.

As he'd expected, no reply.

He stared out of the window of Victoria's flat until a movement distracted him. She was offering him a glass of wine. She had already laid the table for a meal. Her efforts to please were almost painful.

He sipped the wine and regarded her. She was pliable, naïve, impressionable. And of course she was madly in love with him to the point where she would do anything for him. It was rather amusing to see how far he could make her go. Sometimes her submissiveness annoyed him, sometimes it pleased him. At this moment it was just about tolerable.

'Do you want to unload the van?' she asked.

Immediately his good humour evaporated. Women were unbelievable. They could never leave you alone; they always had to try to manipulate you, to try to make you as small-minded and obsessed with trivia as they were. He was overwhelmed with irritation and didn't answer.

'Well then,' she was saying. 'I'll start to get the meal, shall I?'

Suddenly he felt bored. And resentful. This girl had nothing to say. He rather missed Gabriele. She was tough on him, but she knew what he wanted.

He drained the glass of wine and decided that, as soon as the van was unloaded, he would drop this girl. She had served her purpose. He had put up with her for quite long enough.

The telephone rang and Victoria answered. From her manner it was obviously a good friend. He wasn't in the slightest interested; her friends would be dull and unimportant.

He flicked idly through a magazine, only half-listening.

'. . . Oh, I just got caught up in the crowd . . . No, no, honestly, I'm fine now . . . Just a little bruised . . . Promise . . . Yes, I *will* call mother. Yes . . . Yes, Caro, I *promise* . . .'

Giorgio fidgeted and wished she would get off the phone. Her high-pitched chatter was annoying.

'. . . How's Henry? . . . Really? But I've got it here. Hang on . . .'

Victoria pulled one of the newspapers up off the floor and spread it out. 'Got it . . . Yes, *what* a good picture.'

Giorgio let the magazine fall to his lap and stared out of the window.

'. . . Is he very busy? . . . Yes, I'm sure . . . No, I quite understand. Perhaps in the next holidays – what do you call them? Yes, the *recess* . . .'

Giorgio picked up the magazine again. Finally Victoria rang off and said brightly, 'Sorry about that. Family – sort of.'

She disappeared into the kitchen. After a moment Giorgio reached out and slowly slid the newspaper towards him. The paper was open at the centre page. There were two news pictures, one of some visiting foreign politicians, and one of a man in a preposterous white wig.

The caption under the man with the wig read: The Attorney-General, Sir Henry Northcliff.

Henry. The name on the telephone.

He refolded the newspaper and, getting up, wandered into the kitchen and leaned against the door frame. Victoria was at the stove, adjusting the gas under a pan.

She turned and jumped. 'Oh! You gave me a fright.'

He was still for a moment then, reaching out, he caressed her cheek. She looked at him uncertainly, not sure of what he wanted.

220

He smiled to show that he was pleased with her. She stepped forward and, putting her arms around him, leant her head against his chest.

He said gently, 'Tell me about your friends.'

Gabriele found the address and, driving on a little, turned a corner and parked the Fiat on a double yellow line. She looked at herself in the driver's mirror. The blonde wig was uncomfortable. She readjusted it and checked her make-up, which was heavy, with thick black eyeliner and several layers of mascara. She added a preposterously large pair of sunglasses. A real dolly bird.

She got out and went round to the boot.

The parcel sat lodged against the side of the car where she had positioned it the previous day. She picked it up and put it on the pavement while she slammed the boot shut.

Picking it up again, she crossed the pavement and went into the office of Cardinal Couriers Limited, a company who specialised in fast reliable deliveries.

She put the parcel down on the front desk.

A young man in overalls appeared. 'Where's it to go to?'

'Putney.'

'When do you want it delivered?' He looked at the clock on the wall. 'It's a bit late for today—'

'First thing tomorrow morning would be ideal.'

Taking the address from the top of the parcel, he made out the chit, asked her for two pounds ten shillings, and began to make out a receipt. 'What company?'

She hesitated for a moment. 'Crystal Designs. 3 Margaret Street.'

He entered the details on the receipt, and passed it to her.

'We do collect, you know. You only have to ring.'

She nodded. 'I know, but I was passing. I thought it might be easier.'

She returned to the car. No warden, no ticket. Her luck was good today.

She turned the ignition and, revving hard, let the clutch in with a jerk. The Fiat shot off down the street, barely missing a slow-moving pedestrian.

Gabriele hardly noticed. She was thinking: Wait until they read about this one in Italy.

Seventeen

Helen McCabe stared at herself in the bathroom mirror and sighed. There seemed to be a dozen more wrinkles on her face since she had last looked. She was getting old, and she couldn't think where all the years had gone.

The house was lovely, of course. Four bedrooms, double garage, standing in a third of an acre in a very pleasant part of Putney; quiet yet only five minutes from the river and twenty minutes from Peter's office. For years all she had ever wanted was a nice home. Now she'd got it and . . . And she felt empty and dissatisfied and she didn't understand why.

She walked through into the bedroom and thought vaguely about what to wear. It was eleven and time she got out of her dressing-gown.

The doorbell rang. She muttered, 'Oh dear!' Pulling on a sweater she hastily stepped into a skirt and, still shoeless, went breathlessly down the stairs to the front door.

A rather startling figure stood in the porch. He was dressed entirely in black leather with a shiny black crash helmet on his head. He looked like one of those Hell's Angels she'd read about. Then she saw that he was holding a parcel. Of course: a delivery boy. What else would he have been. Silly of her.

She signed for the parcel and took it into the kitchen. It was addressed to Peter. She wondered what it could be. Had he ordered anything? Unlikely. He usually left all the household purchases to her. Something to do with the garden perhaps. Even then, he would have told her.

She went back upstairs to find some shoes. She brushed her hair and half-heartedly patted a little powder on her nose.

Back in the kitchen, she made herself a cup of coffee and, sitting at the table, considered what to do with her day. She should write a note to her daughter.

She got up to put the cup in the sink and noticed the parcel again. Quite large – something interesting, certainly. A present? She wondered if Peter had got her a surprise. But it wasn't her birthday and – well, he wasn't that sort of husband. He was considerate, but not *imaginative*. That was because he was so busy and didn't have time to think about domestic things. She was pleased at his success, of course, and didn't resent the long hours he worked. At the same time she felt left out, excluded. *Useless*.

She found a scrap of paper and tried to start a shopping list for the weekend. She should make the effort to find a new dress as well. There was an official dinner coming up in two weeks and she had nothing suitable. She dreaded occasions like that. She didn't feel at home among crowds of important people. And she had never got used to being Lady McCabe, although it was four years now since Peter had become Commissioner and been knighted.

She watched a pigeon pecking at the lawn, then, aware that her list was still blank, wandered over to the fridge to see what was needed. On the way she fingered the parcel, and picked it up again. Quite heavy and solid. What *could* it be?

Suddenly it seemed rather a treat, this parcel. Something unexpected and exciting in what was otherwise a dreary day. It *would* be nice to open it.

She mustn't, of course. It was addressed to Peter. She looked at her watch. Twelve. Perhaps she might just give him a ring . . . She didn't often, so he wouldn't mind. Yes, why not? It would be nice to hear his voice, if only for a minute.

She dialled and waited a little nervously. The line went direct to his secretary, who answered immediately. They exchanged greetings, then the secretary said she wasn't sure if he was free, but she'd just find out.

A few seconds later Peter came on the line. Helen's heart sank. She could tell from his tone that he was busy. Although she already knew the answer because he'd told her that morning, she asked what time he expected to be home. He was abrupt; she'd obviously chosen a really bad time. Quickly she mentioned the parcel. Was he expecting anything? Did he want her to open it? There was silence for a moment. No, he wasn't expecting anything. Unless it was something to do with his wine club. Or maybe it was that golfing book Harry Sidley had promised to send him. Yes, why didn't she open it. He asked after her, as he always did, and rang off.

He was a good husband, Helen decided. She really mustn't complain.

With a sense of pleasant anticipation, she got the kitchen scissors out of the drawer and approached the parcel.

What a treat. Not a book. Too big. Wine perhaps.

She snipped the string and pulled at the Sellotape fastening one end. She removed the brown paper with care so that it could be reused. The parcel was certainly well wrapped. There was a thick layer of corrugated cardboard and under that another piece of brown paper.

Wine, almost certainly.

Impatient now, she cut quickly into the corrugated cardboad.

Alison Miller shouted at her son, Matthew, to come back immediately. But the three-year-old had no intention of being denied a run and scampered off across the lawn. Alison put her load of shopping down by the front door and ran after him. She caught him and, unlocking the door, carried him into the kitchen. She popped him down beside the sink while she undid his windcheater.

As she pulled off one arm of the jacket, there was an enormously loud noise.

She felt herself lifted up and thrown backwards through the air. She opened her mouth to cry out, but the wind had been knocked out of her.

She found herself lying on the floor with a small weight against her chest. Matthew. *Safe*. She thought: Thank God! She grasped him to her.

Panting, she regained her breath. Matthew started to scream and, sitting up, she saw that the back of his head was bleeding. She had a moment of utter panic, then saw that the cuts to his head were superficial. Glass. It was everywhere.

Still holding the child, she stood up and staggered uncertainly to the window, which had been completely shattered. Finding a tea-towel she put it to Matthew's head. Then, realising the towel would be covered in glass, she looked for another in the cupboard.

As she wrapped it round the child's head she looked out of the shattered window. She stared blankly at the McCabes' next door, trying to comprehend what she was seeing. There was a great empty space in the side of the house where the kitchen had been.

For a moment she gaped. Then she reached for the wall phone and, shaking so much she could hardly get her finger in the dial, called 999.

She tried to speak slowly and clearly, and she managed very well until she happened to look back towards the McCabes' garden and saw a piece of meat-red flesh with a hand attached to it hanging from a tree.

Then she screamed.

Two minutes later the first police car arrived.

By chance the newsmen got their first whiff of the story almost immediately and before Scotland Yard could even think of putting an embargo on it, an item went out on the radio news at one o'clock, saying that there had been an explosion at a house in Putney.

Half an hour after that a taxi drew up outside the offices of *The Times* in Gray's Inn Road, and the cabby delivered a letter to the reception desk.

There was a stunned hush in the incident room. Nobody could think of the appropriate thing to say. Kershaw and his team had rushed off to Putney and those who remained were manning the telephones.

Nick paused only long enough to discover that there was no fresh news before dashing up to his own office. Conway was already there, looking ashen-faced.

'Christ,' he said. '*Who?*'

Nick shook his head. But he had a feeling. It was Wheatfield's friends. It had to be.

He went to Records and, collecting the files on all Wheatfield's known associates, took them down to the incident room.

The phone call from *The Times* came through five minutes later. A sergeant took the message down in longhand. Then the room burst into activity. A car was sent to *The Times* for the original communiqué, a message was transmitted to Kershaw in Putney, and the sergeant's handwritten jottings were photocopied.

Everyone read the communiqué. Then they looked at Nick. They were expecting him to have an answer.

He read it fast, then again more slowly:

THE PSEUDO CHIEF OF PIGS WAS SENTENCED TO DEATH BY THE REVOLUTIONARY TRIBUNAL FOR:

1. THE CRIME OF ENCOURAGING AND PROTECTING THE FASCIST BOMBERS.

2. THE CRIME OF GROSS OPPRESSION AGAINST THOSE WHO OPPOSE THE CAPITALIST SYSTEM WHICH HE AND HIS KIND SUPPORT.

SIGNED: THE CRYSTAL FACTION.

The Crystal Faction. Nick had never heard the name before, he was sure of that. He shook his head so that those watching would realise that he didn't have any quick and easy answers.

Then he sat with his head in his hands, thinking his way through it.

Faction equalled dissenting group equalled splinter group – equalled *new* group? New group.

Crystal. Glass? Yes, but . . . what did the word actually *mean*. A substance that was hard and clear. Clear. This group was seeking to clarify things? Or to harden existing attitudes.

It all added up to – nothing. A new revolutionary group.

Crystal . . . Crystal . . .

It rang no bells.

Start again.

He thought for a long time, jotting words down as they came into his head. He put the word crystal in the centre of the page with a sunburst of connecting words round it. Crystal – hard – clear – transparent – glass – crystalline – sweet – crystallise . . .

He paused. A tiny memory nagged at his mind.

But which word had prompted it?

He went through them again. Crystalline . . . *crystallise* . . .

He closed his eyes, trying to see the word in his memory.

Then at long last he had it. Yes.

Jumping up, he raced back to his office and grabbed the facsimile *Strike Back!* pamphlet from his tray. On the last page: 'Pulverise, Energise, Polarise! Fabricate crystal splinters!'

He walked back down to the incident room, trying to work out what if anything he'd gained. A connection.

Between a single word and a bomb-making guide.

A connection. Which led nowhere.

It was possible that the authors of the pamphlet had direct connections with the makers of the bomb; it was possible that the authors were themselves the bomb-makers.

But it was equally possible that Wheatfield's friends had no direct connection with the people behind the pamphlet. Influenced by the call to action, they might simply have set themselves up in isolation.

The incident room was busy now. Someone had seen a motor-cyclist call at the Commissioner's house about an hour before the explosion. The witness thought it might have been a delivery boy. All the phones were manned as every delivery firm in London was checked.

Half an hour later, just as Commander Kershaw returned from Putney, they got the lead. A company by the name of Cardinal Couriers had delivered a parcel to the McCabe address that morning. The receipt had the sender's name: Crystal Designs, 3 Margaret Street. It took only fifteen minutes to establish that there was no company of that name in Margaret Street nor at any other address. Companies with similar names were checked but, not surprisingly, had no knowledge of any parcel. Two men were sent round to the courier company to get a description of the person who had left the parcel.

Apparently it was a woman. Long blonde hair. Dark glasses. Tallish. Attractive. But the description of the woman's face was vague, due to the dark glasses.

A grim-faced Kershaw summoned Nick. Straughan was there, looking grey and worried.

'Well?' Kershaw said in his quiet voice. 'Do we have anything?'

'Nothing concrete,' Nick said truthfully. 'Only a possible link between the communiqué and this *Strike Back!* pamphlet.' He explained the crystal connection. 'But I think we could waste a lot of time and energy trying to go into that link, sir. We've a better chance if we go straight for the motive.'

'Yes?'

'Now, this first "crime" mentioned in the communiqué – the crime of "encouraging and protecting the fascist bombers" – it suggests that the bomb this morning was in direct retaliation for the letter bombs yesterday. Well – that's rubbish, sir. First, we know that the supposed "fascists" who sent the letter bombs were in fact Far-Lefters trying to stir it up. Second, it's highly unlikely that any group would have had time to hear about the letter bombs, get hold of the explosives, make the bomb and leave it with the delivery firm, all in the space of a few hours.'

'So?'

'So it was all pre-planned.'

'By the one group?'

'Yes. Wheatfield's friends.'

Kershaw nodded and said slowly, 'Yes, that's the way I see it too.' He picked up the communiqué again. 'What about the second "crime"? Of gross oppression against the opponents of capitalism?'

'That's what they're really about. Bringing the system down. Revenge.'

'For what?'

Nick drew a deep breath. 'There could be a link back to the Linden House Hotel affair. Through Reardon – the one charged with assault at the Russell Square demonstration. Now he did six months last year for the Linden House affair. He was probably a friend of Stephie Kitson, who's still serving time for assault and

227

actual bodily. Now *both* of them wcrc – *are* – friends of Wheatfield.'

Kershaw rubbed a hand over his face. 'So we're saying Wheatfield's behind all this?'

'No . . . I think there must be others who . . .' He paused, trying to clarify the suspicions in his mind. 'Who are trained, *practised*.'

'Good God!' exclaimed Kershaw, glancing at Straughan. 'Are you suggesting a red *plot*?'

Nick shook his head. 'Not exactly. Just that . . . They're so *good*, so *polished*, they must have had experience elsewhere.'

Looking unhappy, Kershaw nodded his agreement. There was a strained silence.

Eventually Straughan said, 'Have we got anything else, Ryder?' But he knew the answer even before Nick shook his head.

Kershaw said grimly, 'So, where do we go from here? The explosives report is still to come, of course. But – what we don't have is a lead on Wheatfield, and *that*'s what we want.'

Straughan looked as if he could shoot himself. It was he who had called the watch off Wheatfield.

Kershaw mused, 'We *could* issue a warrant and plaster his face all over the papers . . . But it might just send him to earth. At the moment he probably doesn't realise we're on to him. That might be the only advantage we have.'

'Give me a few days,' Nick said.

The two men looked at him with sudden interest.

'It may lead absolutely nowhere,' Nick added hastily. He didn't want false hopes raised. 'But it's just possible I might be able to find him again.'

Kershaw said immediately, 'Do it.'

'I might not be in touch for some time.'

'Agreed.'

'I might have to go right under cover.'

'Agreed.'

'It'll only work if Wheatfield has no idea we're looking for him.'

Kershaw nodded. 'Agreed. Do whatever you have to do. I don't care what it is. Just *do* it.'

Henry Northcliff had thirty seconds to get from the House of Commons to Number Ten for a meeting with the Prime Minister. It was impossible, of course, but with a bit of luck he would be no more than three minutes late.

Picking up his briefcase, he went into the outer office with the idea of rushing straight through and downstairs to his car. But his secretary had a look on her face that suggested he wasn't going to get away that easily. She said, 'Sir Henry, there's an officer from Special Branch here . . .'

The officer, who looked quite senior, stood waiting with that air of stubborn patience that all policemen seemed to possess. Henry could see there would be no escape. He said, 'Join me in the car, would you, and we'll talk there.'

Henry's car was waiting at the Members' Entrance and they got in. As the driver nosed into the traffic around Parliament Square the officer identified himself as Inspector Smith of Special Branch Protection Group. Henry knew this group: they guarded the Prime Minister.

The inspector said, 'Following the tragic bombing of the Commissioner's home today, sir, we are extending police protection to all those members of the government directly concerned with law and order.'

'Oh?' Henry had a nasty suspicion of what was coming.

'That will include yourself, of course, sir, as well as the Home Secretary and certain other Cabinet Ministers.'

Henry frowned. 'This protection – will it be full-time?'

'Most certainly, sir. Round the clock.'

Henry considered the implications. It would be comforting to have a policeman outside the house at night, he had to admit, but the thought of having someone hanging around the whole time – on Sundays and on private evenings out – was rather odious.

'It's absolutely necessary, is it?' he asked.

'We think so, sir,' said the inspector with an air of finality.

Henry thought: Well, there's no arguing with *that*.

The car completed the near-circuit of Parliament Square and turned into Whitehall. The entrance to Downing Street was just ahead.

Henry said, 'Very well, inspector. I'll try to make your men's job as easy as possible. When do they start?'

'Immediately, sir. You'll find a Constable Hunter waiting for you after your meeting. He will be with you until midnight.'

The car drew up outside Number Ten and they both got out: Henry shook hands with the inspector and went in through the famous black door. The protection would be a temporary measure, he was certain. After all, violence had never been a part of the British way of life. He couldn't see why it should suddenly become so now.

Gabriele pushed the curtain aside and looked out into the night. The mews was empty. No one. Nothing.

Restless, she turned away. The newspaper stared up at her from the sofa. She turned it over, so that the screeching words of the headline were hidden face down.

Stupid woman. Why had she opened the parcel? What sort of a marriage was it when the wife opened something addressed to the husband? Extraordinary.

Stupid woman. It was all her own fault.

But the bomb had worked. Very well. Gabriele permitted herself some satisfaction. It was a professional job. That was the way to think of it. Professional.

She must close her mind to negative thoughts, close her mind to thoughts of the woman. Already one part of her mind was becoming separated and frozen, the part that thought of the woman, blown to pieces. The suppression of the mind must be complete, just as her training had taught her. It was a matter of determination, that was all.

There was a sound and Gabriele stiffened. A key turned in the front door. Giorgio and Max came in at last.

She said immediately, 'Were you followed? Did you check?'

Max replied, 'There's no one. It's all right.'

'And where are you living? Is it safe?'

He nodded. 'A bedsitter in Paddington. People come and go. They don't notice me.'

They sat down. Max picked up the newspaper and stared doggedly at the front page. Gabriele could see that he was unhappy.

To pre-empt any discussion she demanded, 'Well, Max? Did you find out about Reardon?'

'He's coming up at Bow Street on Monday. For remand.'

'That's it, then. That's what we'll go for.' She turned to Giorgio. 'Where's the stuff?'

'In the van.' He indicated that it was outside in the mews.

The van mustn't stay there. She probably shouldn't have let Giorgio bring it at all. But events were moving so fast and she hadn't had time to find another service flat.

'We'll take out what we need now,' she said. 'And keep the rest in the van. Until we find another place. Then we'll empty the van and get rid of it.' She gave Giorgio a sharp look. 'And then you can finish with that girl.'

Giorgio picked at his fingers with deliberate indifference. Then he grinned, 'Maybe. But she has special friends, this girl.'

Gabriele didn't like guessing games. She said impatiently, 'Yes?'

'She is a special friend of a government minister. His name is Northcliff. He is the Attorney, the Attorney of the government.'

Gabriele frowned. 'What do you mean she's a *special* friend?'

'A family friend. She speaks to the wife on the telephone.'

Gabriele absorbed the information greedily. Northcliff. Attorney. The Attorney-General. He was on her list. He was one of the names. The one directly responsible for Stephie's prosecution. The information was bound to be useful, though she wasn't yet sure how.

She smiled at Giorgio. 'Well, aren't you a clever one?' She went across and sat beside him. She stroked his hair, aware that she felt nothing for him but a dull worn-out familiarity. 'That's different, then, isn't it? You must stay with the girl.'

Giorgio sighed. 'It's hard. She is boring. And not pretty.'

Gabriele thought: But I bet that didn't stop you. She prompted, 'But you can keep her interested.'

He shrugged.

'You must. Just for a while longer. Just for a while.'

He looked doubtful, but she knew he would do it, because she had asked him to and because he knew it was important.

She stood up. 'I have some more money for you.' She picked up two piles of notes off a side table and handed the men one each.

'But there're some new notes here,' Max said.

'This time, yes.'

'I won't use them—'

'It'll be perfectly safe as long as you use them in different places, where nobody knows you.'

He stared at the money for a while then, shaking his head, repeated, 'I won't use them.'

Gabriele suppressed the urge to argue with him and said calmly, 'Okay. But hang on to it, just in case.'

He nodded and, separating the money, slipped the old notes into his wallet and the new ones into an inner pocket.

They went to the van and, prising up the floor with a crowbar, removed a number of containers and took them into the house. Then Gabriele settled down to make the device. It took an hour. She used an acid delay fuse. The timing was not as accurate as a clock and battery, but it was simpler. Sulphuric acid was placed in a small serum bottle and a contraceptive stretched over its neck. When the bottle was upturned the acid burnt through the rubber on to a mixture of sugar and potassium permanganate, which exploded with a sheet of hot flame. The hot flame then ignited the detonator and thence the main explosive.

The nice thing about using an acid fuse was that there was less chance of it going off accidentally. Even if you were stupid enough to upturn the bottle of acid at the wrong moment there was plenty of time to reverse it. To keep the finished bomb inactive you merely kept it the right way up and upturned it once you arrived at the target, knowing you had plenty of time to get away – roughly forty minutes per contraceptive.

When she was finished, she put the bomb in a holdall, packed plenty of newspaper round it, then gave it to Max to take back to his room in Paddington.

'Now, there's one last thing,' Gabriele said. 'We need a car. In time for Sunday night.'

'We could hire one,' said Max.

Gabriele shook her head. 'Too much trouble. And too risky. No – there's a much better way. And it won't involve any risk at all.'

Eighteen

Nick woke early, cold and stiff. He tried to stretch his legs, but his feet came up against a chair arm. Then he remembered where he was: on a lumpy sofa at the house in Tulip Street. He listened hard, but the house was silent. Nobody was up yet. But then it was a Saturday morning and people would sleep in.

He had arrived at eight the previous night. Bet had been out, but another girl living at the house had let him in. He'd gone to the Castle in the Portobello Road and waited until ten-thirty, but Wheatfield hadn't been there. He wasn't entirely surprised: it would have been too much to hope for.

At eleven he'd returned to the house and waited for the others to drift in. He'd chatted to those in the mood to talk – only two – then he'd gone to bed. If Bet had returned he hadn't heard her.

Now he got up and, pulling on a sweater, padded through into the kitchen and made himself a cup of coffee. There was still no sound from upstairs. Time for a quick look round. He started in the hall where various coats and bags were slung over an old table, and went swiftly through them. Nothing. The living-room was full of books, magazines and piles of papers and looked more promising, but after half an hour it too had yielded nothing apart from a few copies of *Time Out* and *Black Dwarf*, a library of political writings, and some Ban the Bomb literature.

Later, if he had the chance, he might try some of the bedrooms. But it would be more out of habit than expectation. The lead to Wheatfield would not come from the house itself but from Bet or one of her friends. And that lead was flimsy enough, God only knew. It could be a complete dead end – he might hang around this place for weeks without hearing a whisper of Wheatfield. The thought was exceedingly depressing.

In the meantime he could search. He'd scooped up a few of the more fashionable New Left books from his flat the previous evening. Now he picked one up and, lying on the sofa, began to read. What was he looking for? He wasn't sure. But a clue, anyway, something to do with crystal perhaps. It was all very tenuous. But it was *something* at least.

Half an hour later he heard a door opening upstairs, then another. One by one the occupants of the house began to clatter downstairs. Nick strolled into the kitchen and chatted with them over coffee. Two hours later he had drunk a lot of coffee and discovered that Bet was at her boyfriend's and wouldn't be back until Sunday. At one point he mentioned that he was looking for Max Wheatfield. One of the girls knew him all right, but hadn't a clue where he was living. Nick didn't dare force it, and the conversation moved on. Gradually the occupants drifted off on various errands until he was alone in the house.

Keeping an ear open for the front door, he went quickly through the bedrooms. The search revealed nothing.

At midday he went off to visit a few pubs in the area. He returned at two-thirty to find the house empty. He thought: This is a complete waste of time.

He had two options: to wait and hope something would turn up, or to make the rounds of his contacts. But would people like Nugent know anything? He doubted it, or they'd have told him before now. No: this place was still his best bet.

Depressed, he settled down to read some Vaneigem. But he couldn't concentrate on the obtuse and convoluted thinking, and found he had read the same page three times without understanding it. He put the book down. Was there a better way than ploughing through books? Who might be able to throw light on the crystal connection? Conway was already trying a tame professor at the LSE, and inquiries were being made abroad through the intelligence services.

Part of the conversation floated into his mind. He tried to remember the circumstances.

Of course.

Gabriella. Yes. He should have thought of her before. She certainly knew her theory. It would definitely be worth a try. But *when*, that was the question. He couldn't spend a whole evening, let alone a night, away from Tulip Street. Perhaps he could meet her for a drink. Yes: he would phone her a little later and suggest it.

The afternoon dragged on. At five Nick was so restless that he went for a short walk. He made a plan for the evening. If Bet's friends couldn't suggest where he might find Wheatfield, then he would make one more round of the pubs which Wheatfield was known to visit. At some point he would meet Gabriella if she was free.

At five-thirty he let himself back into the house. He called out, 'Hi!' in case anyone had returned.

There was silence.

He went into the kitchen and put on a kettle. Taking a spoon out of a drawer, he scooped some coffee into a mug. There was a battered transistor radio standing on the side and he turned it on. It was dead. He picked it up and fiddled with the knobs.

Suddenly a floorboard creaked.

There was someone else in the room.

Surprised, he turned, ready to say a casual hello.

He stared, unbelieving.

Wheatfield.

Nick recovered as best he could, keeping his face in a mask of indifference. 'Well, hi. How goes it?'

Wheatfield's expression was unreadable under the still-bruised face. He advanced into the room and leaned against a cupboard.

With an effort, Nick turned back to the boiling kettle and poured his coffee. He asked, 'Want one?'

Wheatfield gave the briefest of nods.

'Well, how's the face?' Nick continued, pouring another cup.

'Okay.' He shrugged as if it were totally unimportant.

Nick handed him the coffee. 'My head's mended,' he said

conversationally. 'At least it doesn't ache any more.'

Wheatfield grunted a response. Nick thought rapidly. Wheatfield wasn't exactly the warm outgoing type, yet Nick had to establish some sort of friendship with him. But *how*?

He sat on a chair and said, 'You're–er–not being hassled by the cops any more?'

Wheatfield shot him a sharp glance and for a moment Nick thought: That was a mistake.

Then Wheatfield relaxed. 'No. After those pictures in all the papers, they wouldn't dare.'

'That girl photographer certainly did you a favour.'

'Ya, lucky she was there.'

There was a silence. Wheatfield was certainly heavy going. Nick racked his brains for something to say.

'A pity she didn't get a shot of *me* being bashed. Still . . .'

He was aware of Wheatfield watching him critically, and thought: He suspects something. But then Wheatfield was pulling out a chair and sitting down at the table beside him and saying, 'Look, I was wondering if you could do me a favour . . .'

Nick gave it a second. He mustn't seem too keen. 'Ya?'

'I need a car – er – borrowed.'

'Mmm.' He looked a little doubtful.

Wheatfield responded, 'For Sunday night. Something ordinary, a Ford or Vauxhall or something.'

Nick pretended to consider the idea. 'What's it for?'

'A demonstration. A big one. Against the fascists.'

'Ah. So a good cause?

'Absolutely.'

As if making up his mind, Nick nodded. 'Sure. Be glad to do it.'

'It'll be easy, will it? I mean, there won't be a problem?'

Nick remembered what he'd told Wheatfield in the hospital, about having got into trouble for pinching cars. He said quickly, 'No, no. It only takes a minute. I've done it many times before. There's never a problem.'

Wheatfield was getting up to go.

'You off?' Nick asked in surprise. 'What about a drink?'

'No. Gotta go.'

Nick followed him towards the door. 'Tomorrow then? I was going to go to the Castle at one.'

'No.'

Nick gave up. He'd already pushed as hard as he dared.

'What about the car? When d'you want it?'

'Tomorrow night. By ten.'

'Where shall I take it?'

'Here. I'll meet you here.'

Wheatfield opened the front door and, with a brief wave, was gone. Nick went to the kitchen window and watched him stride up the street. His instinct was to follow, but it would be too risky. Wheatfield would see him and realise immediately, and then there'd be no hope of finding his friends.

Nick watched Wheatfield disappear round the corner and hoped he wasn't making a terrible mistake.

After ten minutes he left the house and went to the nearest phone box. He called Kershaw and spoke to him personally. They arranged to meet half an hour later in Notting Hill.

Nick left the booth and paused. Gabriella. Was it worth calling her now? The crystal information could surely wait.

But no, it was best to leave no stone unturned. He went back into the booth and dialled her number. She answered straight away. He suggested meeting for a drink at ten that night.

There was a pause. She said, 'Can't you make it earlier, for dinner?' There was a hint of resentment in her voice.

'I'm tied up at the moment.'

'Tied up?'

'Trying to fix up a new place to stay,' he lied.

'All right then,' she conceded. 'But come over here, will you? We'll have a late dinner. I don't want to go out.'

He thought: Damn it, she's trapping me. He said evenly, 'I don't know if I'll have time for more than a drink . . .'

There was a deathly pause. 'I see.' Her voice was like ice.

He suddenly gave in. She had outmanoeuvred him. 'Okay, we'll have dinner. I'll try to make it before ten. But I could be late.'

He put down the phone, angry with himself. Damn. He should never have phoned. She was bound to expect him to stay the night.

The door closed behind Giorgio, and Victoria burst into tears. He was gone again, and as usual she had no idea when he'd be back. She could take almost everything else – the sudden changes of mood, the caustic remarks – but not this terrible uncertainty. She never knew where she was with him, and it was eating away at her.

And she'd been so good until now. When he'd disappeared on Thursday she'd put a brave face on it. When he'd come back again yesterday to collect the van, she'd been calm and smiling. But when he'd returned this morning and settled down to a meal and read the papers and treated the place like his own, she'd been silly enough to let her hopes rise. That had been her mistake. To think he'd stay. What a *fool*.

And now he was gone and she felt very empty and it was Saturday night and she was on her own.

She dried her tears. She must look on the bright side. He hadn't actually *said* he wouldn't be coming back. And then there was the van – he needed it some time in the week, so he'd said.

The van.

She went to the window and peered down into the dark street. It was there; he hadn't taken it. But it was parked very untidily on a corner with two wheels on the pavement. Typical. She found the spare keys and, putting on a coat, went down the two flights of stairs to the street.

As she approached the van she saw that a number of parking tickets were tucked under the windscreen wipers. She removed them and got into the van to repark it. She drove round the block and finally found a space.

She looked into the back. It was a bit of a mess. Putting on the interior light, she climbed over the driving seat and half-heartedly began to pick up bits of paper and cellophane off the ancient carpeting. As she walked over the floor, she noticed it was uneven, as if there was something between the metal floor and the carpet. She stooped down and, lifting a corner of the carpeting, examined the metal floor.

Of course. It was the lid of the spare wheel compartment; it wasn't quite closed.

She got out of the van by the front door and, going round to the back, opened the rear doors. She tried to force the lid of the wheel compartment down, but it wouldn't close. She rolled the carpet back and pushed up the hinged lid.

She saw immediately why it wouldn't close. Arranged around and inside the spare tyre were six or seven bundles wrapped in heavy cloth.

She hesitated for a moment then slowly picked up one of the bundles and unwrapped it. Inside the cloth were six tubes about ten inches long and an inch or so across, covered in a heavy oiled paper. Each tube had a printed label on it. She squinted at one of them. It read: Nitramite 19C, *Explosif Rocher, Société Française des*

Explosifs, Usine de Cugny. Underneath was a date: 20th March 1968.

She stared at the tubes for some time, thoughts chasing through her mind, clashing, failing to connect.

Then the realisation of what she was holding hit her like a punch in the stomach.

A moment later came the related thoughts, equally terrible; how had they *got* here? How *long* had they been here?

Slowly a dreadful scenario came into her mind: that she herself had brought this terrible load from France, brought it through Customs, that Giorgio had lied to her, that the leaflets had never existed.

Feeling sick, she replaced the tube in the bundle, wrapped the cloth round it, and put it inside the wheel. She rearranged the bundles so that the lid would close properly and unrolled the carpet over the top. She closed and locked the doors.

She went up to the flat and let herself in. She went into the living-room and sat in the darkness, trying to make sense of the thoughts ricocheting around her brain.

Whichever way she looked at it, the conclusions she reached were appalling. It was impossible to find a reasonable explanation. And yet – it was just possible there *might* be.

She must give Giorgio the chance to explain.

Just one chance.

Drawing her legs under her, she curled up in the chair and, sick at heart, settled down to wait.

Nick lay in the bed and thought: I should never have stayed.

He'd hardly slept at all. Neither had Gabriella – she'd tossed and turned all night. And the evening had not been a success. During the meal Gabriella had been brittle and tense. He'd tried to bring the conversation around to extremist groups, but she'd wanted to talk about other things. Then, when he'd got up to go, she'd snapped out of her mood and turned on that animal sexuality of hers. He had weakened. But for all her passion there had been something mechanical and heartless about their love-making. There was no sign of the warmth and vulnerability she'd shown a few days earlier. She w e two different people – and he didn't like this one at all. He'd been left feeling empty and cold.

The trouble was, he didn't really *know* her. He thought: I should never have stayed.

He heard Gabriella moving around downstairs and, getting up, went into the bathroom. He noticed that the male toiletries had gone. Perhaps she'd chucked the lover out. It might explain her mood.

He dressed and went down to find Gabriella sitting on the sofa reading the Sunday papers, a frown of concentration on her face.

Nick glanced at the headlines. Not surprisingly they were all about the bombing of the Commissioner's house and the death of Helen McCabe. He made himself a coffee and, sitting down beside Gabriella, said, 'Who d'you think did it?'

Without looking up, she said, 'Could be anyone, couldn't it?'

'Why d'you say that?'

'Well, there are so many people who've had a raw deal at the hands of the filth, aren't there?'

'But not many who can hit them with explosives.'

She shrugged. 'Explosives are easy enough to get.'

'But what political group is it? I mean, if it *is* political.'

She turned to him. 'Oh, of course it's political!' she exclaimed. 'This is a statement. A warning.'

'But who by? I mean, Trotskyists or what?'

'No, *no*,' she said impatiently. 'These people are way beyond that.'

He tried not to let his interest show.

'What philosophy do they follow then? Situationism?'

'Possibly.' She paused. 'But that's a bit general. Things have moved on since Paris, you know. These people will be way ahead, past Vaneigem and Debord and old stuff like that. They're probably into Petrini.'

He tried to remember. Petrini. Italian. Philosopher.

'Tell me, what's different about Petrini then?'

'Ah.' She began to talk with the fervour of a teacher lecturing a new pupil. 'He believes in the necessity of *action* to accentuate and polarise the divisions in society so that people *see* and *understand* the exploitation that's happening right in front of them. He says it's necessary to clarify things on their behalf; to crystallise their thinking.'

Crystallise.

She talked on but Nick was hardly listening. *Crystallise.* There it was! Good God, why hadn't he got on to this Petrini before? Why hadn't he realised that this new philosophy had been taken up by the young activists? *She* knew all about it. He'd obviously slipped up somewhere in his research. He could have kicked himself.

He asked, 'Are they a big group, these – what do you call them?'

She shrugged and said very carefully, 'They have no name, as far as I know. But they won't be a large group. The whole idea is to work in small cells, in isolation.'

'I see.' He did, only too clearly. He saw that the answer had been there all the time and he'd missed it. Thank God for Gabriella. He forgot his coldness towards her and smiled encouragingly.

She continued, her eyes gleaming. 'They're the beginning of a big movement, though. They'll succeed where all the others will fail. In a few years the movement will have spread all over Europe.'

He stared at her. 'How do you *know* about this?'

'I just know. I keep my ear to the ground.'

'Do you . . .' He hesitated. It was a difficult question. 'Do you have any idea of who these people are? Where they might come from?'

Immediately her face became a mask, and she said deliberately, 'No. Why do you ask?'

He shrugged. 'I just wondered, that was all. What sort of people they were.'

'You're interested? In their ideas?'

He must step carefully here. She was probing. 'Yes,' he said vaguely. 'It seems a good way to get things done.'

She said, 'Perhaps the *only* way.'

There was an awkward pause. The baldness of the statement had taken him by surprise. He said, 'If you believe in the Petrini philosophy that strongly, yes, I suppose it *is*.' He thought: She's no better than the rest. An intellectual revolutionary without the courage of her convictions. Spouting precious theory without the nasty consequences. All talk and dangerous hot air – from a safe distance.

'So what do you think of direct action?' she asked.

He had a good mind to tell her what he really thought of her half-baked ideas, but he didn't want to alienate her. The information had been pure gold, and there might be a lot more to come.

She was waiting for his reply; he sensed his answer was going to be important. 'I certainly believe strongly in changing the system,' he began. 'And I suppose I'd do almost anything that was necessary . . .'

She looked pleased. 'Of course you would.'

He stood up. 'Well, I've got to go now.'

To his surprise she didn't argue. It was almost as if she was expecting it.

'Will you come back later?' she asked.

'No. I've got a favour to do for a friend and I won't be finished till late.'

She nodded and led the way to the door. She turned abruptly and, putting her arms round his neck, kissed him for a long time. 'I'll miss you.'

Now she was all warmth and softness. A very confusing lady. He said, 'I'll see you again very soon.'

'Can I contact you? At your new place?'

'What?'

'You said you were moving.'

'Oh yes, but I don't know where to yet.'

'It was just that – there were some people I thought you might like to meet. People you'd find very – *useful*.'

What *did* she mean? Whatever, the opportunity was too good to miss. Without a word he wrote his Lambeth number on a piece of paper.

'Give me the address too, in case I'm passing.'

He hesitated. Normally he liked to keep a distance from informants. But this was different. He added his address. 'It's the flat of a friend,' he explained. 'He's letting me borrow it while he's away.'

Gabriele closed the door behind him and thought: He's going to be all right. At one point she'd had her doubts. But then he'd said he would do almost anything that was necessary. And that was just after they'd been talking about the bombing. Yes: he was going to be all right.

Stealing the car would be a start. If he made a good job of that then she would give him another more demanding task – driving on a robbery perhaps. Finally, when she was sure she could trust him she would bring him right into the group.

There would be problems, of course. With Giorgio. She hadn't worked out what she was going to do about that. She only knew that her relationship with Giorgio was going to have to change. He would have to find someone else.

She wanted Nick. The truth was, he had got under her skin. She shouldn't have let it happen, of course. Even more important, she shouldn't have let it show. She shuddered to remember how she had clung to him that first night . . .

It was a weakness, to show feelings like that, and he would only despise her for it. But it had been all right last night – she'd got herself under control. She would never let her feelings show again.

Everything was going to work out very well. Nick would come and live with her here and be a member of the cell. He was clever and cool and decisive; he would be a great help with the planning. Someone to share the load. She needed that. It was hard taking decisions on her own.

It was lonely at night too. She had nightmares all the time. They were often the same. A group of people sat in a circle and talked about her as if she wasn't there. 'She's *always* been difficult . . . Ungrateful and inconsiderate . . . We've done all we can . . . A strong will, of course. Uncontrollable.' Then someone took the decision to punish her, and she was locked up in her bedroom without books. The time crept by so slowly that she could have screamed. She felt her life slipping away, unfulfilled and hollow.

Then, instead of her bedroom, she was in a prison cell. She looked for Stephie, but there was no one else there, and she realised that she was on her own. And always would be.

Last night it had been worse. She had been making a bomb. Everything had gone fine until she connected the timing device. It started ticking and wouldn't stop. She tried to get out of the room, but the door was locked. She tore at the parcel, but she'd wrapped it too well and couldn't find the wires. In horror she'd watched the contacts closing on each other.

Then she'd woken, gasping for breath.

With a vast relief she'd realised that Nick was there beside her, breathing quietly. Gratefully, she'd moved over until her body lay close to his, and she was at peace.

–

The car was a two-year-old Ford Capri with thirty thousand miles on the clock. It was pale blue with wire wheels and a slight dent on the rear near-side wing. It was perfectly unremarkable.

'It was used in a robbery in March,' explained Kershaw. 'Mechanically sound. Oh, and we've put on some new plates, just in case someone somewhere thinks of checking against the stolen list.'

Nick went round the car and peered inside the wheel arches. Opening a door, he leant in and checked the interior.

'You won't find anything,' said Kershaw. 'It's all too well hidden.'

242

Nick nodded. Wherever they were, the listening devices and radio bleepers had been properly concealed.

'I might as well go then.'

He got in and Kershaw slammed the door.

Kershaw said through the open window, 'Well, we've done all we can.'

'Let's just hope he shows.'

Kershaw said a heartfelt, 'Yes.'

Nick could imagine the pressure Kershaw was under. The man must have everyone from his immediate boss to the Assistant Commissioner breathing down his neck.

The first car picked him up the moment he left the garage. It was a green Vauxhall Victor. As he came to Hyde Park Corner it peeled off and a white Morris took up station behind. A third car took over north of the park. They were using this trip to test the radio tracking device.

As he made the final turn into Tulip Street the last car, a dark blue Mini, left him and sped straight on. He parked immediately outside the house. The street was very quiet. One resident had the bonnet of his car open and was tinkering with the engine. Another was up a ladder repairing a window. It was a typical Sunday afternoon.

As Nick got out of the car he glanced up and down the street. Wherever the watchers were, he couldn't see them. Unless the man under the bonnet was part of the team. Or the one on the ladder.

Nick let himself into the house. Bet and a group of her friends were in the smoke-filled living-room, stuck into some red wine. He gave Bet ten pounds for rent and use of hot water and explained that he'd be moving out, probably that night. She said he was welcome any time.

The party went on into the evening. Nick managed to nurse a single glass of the rough red wine for two hours, then took it into the kitchen and poured it down the sink. Whatever happened he must keep a clear head. He remembered that he hadn't eaten since morning and, finding some cheese and bread, ate it hungrily.

At ten he listened for the front door and tried to suppress the awful suspicion that Wheatfield wasn't going to turn up.

At ten-thirty the party broke up and one by one the guests left the house. At eleven Bet and the other residents drifted upstairs to bed.

Nick sat on his own, feeling sick at heart. Wheatfield wasn't going to come. *Oh God.*

He tried to read but the words skipped in front of his eyes. Finally he lay on the sofa, staring at the ceiling, thinking of what other leads he had if this one failed. Gabriella, that was all. Gabriella and her friends, whoever they might be. It wasn't much. It was *damn all*.

Twenty to twelve.

Damn all.

A key sounded in a lock. Nick lay motionless.

A door was opening. The front door.

A floorboard creaked in the hall. A movement from the doorway. Someone was coming into the room.

Nick put his head up over the sofa. 'Hi,' he said casually.

It was Wheatfield. He could have shouted with relief.

Wheatfield came round the sofa and stared down at him.

'I got it,' Nick said calmly. 'It's just outside. A Ford Capri.'

'Okay.' Wheatfield looked relaxed, unworried. He obviously had no suspicions. 'It works all right, does it?'

'Should do. It's not very old.' Nick swung his feet to the floor and stood up. 'I'll show you how to start it.'

Wheatfield followed him out. Nick showed him how to start the car without an ignition key. Wheatfield practised connecting and disconnecting the necessary wires, which Nick had extended and led through from the bonnet to the interior.

Wheatfield was ready to go. 'Thanks. It's appreciated.'

'No problem. Can I ask what it's for? I mean, I wouldn't mind being in on the fun. You know.'

Wheatfield paused and looked at him thoughtfully. 'Perhaps next time. It's a bit late now, for this time . . . But you'll hear about what we're doing okay.'

'Great. Soon?'

'Yeah. Tomorrow.'

Wheatfield slammed the door shut. The engine fired. He fumbled with the switches on the dashboard and found the lights. The car moved forward and out into the street. Wheatfield did not look back.

Nick gave it a few seconds then, going into the house for his bag, let himself out again and ran to the corner of the street where Conway was waiting with the engine running.

Nineteen

The traffic was unexpectedly light for a Monday morning and Gabriele found herself driving north up Bow Street earlier than she'd intended, at a quarter to ten. On the left was the tall neo-classical façade of the Royal Opera House, incongruously grand for such a minor street. Opposite was Bow Street police station and just beyond it, the magistrates' court.

She took a careful look at the entrance to the court. There were no police in sight and no cars parked outside.

She drove on across Long Acre into Endell Street. She parked a few yards up, on the left-hand side, so that the Fiat was pointing north towards New Oxford Street.

She waited impatiently, her eye on the rear-view mirror. At five to ten a delivery van came bumping up the street and parked immediately behind her, blocking her view. She cursed and, looking at her watch, tried to work out if she had enough time to do a circuit and find a better parking place. The decision was made for her by the sight of an approaching traffic warden. She started the car and, turning right, drove round the block into Drury Lane and Long Acre. Coming to the junction with Bow Street she glanced sideways and gripped the wheel more tightly.

There he was.

A car was parked in front of the court. A Ford Capri. The unmistakable figure of Max was just getting out.

Right on time. Good dependable Max.

In a few minutes he would come looking for her.

To the right the delivery van was still parked at the beginning of Endell Street. It would be too awkward to stop behind it; she didn't like the idea of being boxed in. She continued down Long Acre for a few yards and stopped behind a row of cars parked on meters. The position was good. When Max came round the corner he would only have to look up the street to spot the Fiat.

She waited, keeping a careful watch in both directions.

She imagined Max putting the note on the windscreen – saying the car was broken down – opening the boot, turning the parcel upside down, walking away.

A horn sounded. A lorry was blocking the road near the junction with Bow Street. The traffic was slowing down to a crawl. She glanced at the cars slowly approaching from the opposite direction. One was indicating a left turn into Endell Street.

She stared.

No, it wasn't possible.

For one amazing moment—

She shook her head. She obviously had him on her mind. She was imagining things.

But for that one instant the front-seat passenger *had* looked amazingly like Nick. Ridiculous. The man, whoever he was, was in shadow now, bending his head down, holding something to his mouth. He looked as if he were eating.

Ridiculous, she repeated. She just had him on her mind.

She took a quick look in the mirror. No Max.

Then she glanced back at the traffic.

The car was almost opposite her now, moving very slowly. The passenger looked up and the light fell full on his face.

His face.

Gabriele gaped. The car passed by.

She twisted violently round in her seat. The car drew up beyond Endell Street and reversed back round the corner out of sight.

Nick. *What the hell?*

Nick. What was he *doing?*

She gaped.

Whatever was happening, something was wrong, appallingly wrong.

An idea shot into her mind and she grabbed at it. The pigs. It was the pigs. They'd got him! They'd forced him to tell. She said out loud, 'Oh Christ!'

But then in her mind's eye she saw his face again, sitting in the passenger seat, looking composed, the hand held to his mouth, holding something.

Something with a wire hanging from it.

Then she knew.

The shock hit her like a punch in the stomach.

For a split second her mind was frozen. Then she looked in the mirror. Max. He had just appeared round the corner. Max, whose every move was being watched. Max, who had spotted her in the Fiat and was even now quickening his pace.

With a shaking hand she turned on the ignition. She slipped the car into gear and, using her indicator, pulled firmly out into the road. A car braked suddenly to avoid her, but luckily did not sound its horn. She accelerated rapidly down Long Acre.

No car pulled out behind. No one followed.

Nothing.

Only Max standing stock still on the pavement, staring at her.

Nick said, 'Something's up.'

Wheatfield had paused, like an animal scenting the wind. Nick couldn't work it out. What had changed? One minute Wheatfield had been quite happy, now he obviously had the wind up. For an awful moment he thought Wheatfield might have spotted him, but he'd been very careful to keep his distance and Wheatfield had never once looked this way.

'I think he's going to bolt for it.'

Conway whispered, 'Yeah.'

Wheatfield was looking wildly about him. He was badly frightened. Suddenly he began to move. Fast.

Nick spoke into the mike and told Kershaw, 'He's off. West down Long Acre.'

The acknowledgement came back. Nick watched two of Kershaw's men fall in a safe distance behind Wheatfield; then, a few seconds later, Kershaw's car went by.

Simultaneously Kershaw's voice came over the radio. 'He's obviously abandoned the Capri. There could be a bomb in it. Proceed with bomb clearance procedure *now*. Get everyone away from that damned car!'

Nick nudged Conway. 'Come on, let's go.' Conway fired the engine and they shot forward into Long Acre. As they turned west to follow Kershaw, Nick saw the beginnings of all hell breaking loose in Bow Street as they cleared the area around the Capri.

Ahead, Kershaw's car had slowed right down so as not to overtake the men on foot. Nick could see Wheatfield in the distance. He was half walking, half running, and looking frequently over his shoulder.

Nick sighed heavily. He couldn't think what the hell had gone wrong.

Wheatfield reached the junction with St Martin's Lane and stopped, waiting for a break in the traffic. He turned and took a long look behind him. The two followers did their best to look inconspicuous as they closed on him.

Suddenly Wheatfield seemed to panic. One moment he was poised in a loose crouch, the next he was off, sprinting across the street, his long hair flying behind him. Nick gripped the seat. There was a loud hooting and a car braked as Wheatfield shot in front of it and ran for his life towards Leicester Square.

Nick said, 'Oh shit!' He could have wept. All that planning for nothing.

Kershaw's voice came over the air. 'Take him!'

With a screech of tyres Kershaw's car accelerated across the junction. Conway stepped on it and, hand on horn, jumped the lights. Ahead, Kershaw's car swerved on to the pavement beside two other squad cars. Men were already pouring down into the Underground.

Conway pulled in behind Kershaw's car and turned off the ignition.

There was a heavy silence, then Nick said wearily, 'What happened, Conway? What the hell went wrong?'

Conway shook his head. 'He just sussed us, that's all.'

'Balls. There was a bloody *reason*, I *know* there was. Something *happened*—'

'Or maybe didn't happen!' ventured Conway.

Nick looked at him and blinked. 'Yes. Maybe that was it.'

They brought Wheatfield out of the station ten minutes later, his face bloody, his arm twisted half-way up his back. Nick watched with mixed feelings. They may have caught themselves an Indian, but they'd probably lost all hope of finding the chiefs.

Victoria hoisted the shopping on to her left arm and pushed the key into the lock. As she opened the door she heard a sound from inside the flat. Giorgio was back.

Whatever happened she must stay calm. She went straight to the kitchen and, sorting through the shopping, put the milk and yogurt in the fridge. He came in as she was emptying the fruit into a bowl.

'Where were you?' she asked.

'I had to see a friend. It was easier to stay the night.'

She examined his face. He'd been drinking, she could tell; his eyes were red and his skin was pale and slightly mottled around the cheeks. He looked defenceless and lost, like a child who'd been sick from eating too many sweets. She suppressed the old urge to protect him, to make everything better for him.

'I was not clever,' he said. 'I drank too much and . . .' He looked at her ruefully and touched her arm. 'I would have been clever to come home. Yes?'

248

Her heart went out to him. When he was like this she could forgive him anything. *Almost.*

She pulled herself together. 'I have to talk to you.'

He dropped his eyes. 'Yes?'

'I went down to park the van last night and – I tidied it up.'

His eyes met hers, bright and wary.

'I found some – *things* – in the spare wheel.'

A flash of what could have been fear leapt across his face. There was a long pause. Then he nodded slowly. 'Ah. Yes, we must talk. Come . . .'

She followed him into the living-room and they sat down on the sofa. He took her hand and stroked it gently. 'You must believe me when I say I did not know these things were there – *before.*'

'Before?'

'When we were in France. The leaflets I put in the van myself. But that stuff – someone *else* put it in. I did not know. Not until yesterday. Believe me, Vittoria, it was terrible, *terrible*, to discover these things. Who could have *done* this to me? I am so upset. That is why I am out late last night. To try to discover who has done this terrible thing to me. Also, I must decide what to do.'

'What to do?'

'How to get *rid* of these things. Where to *leave* them. It is not easy.'

Victoria rubbed her forehead. It was so hard to make sense of it. She exclaimed, 'But Giorgio, those sticks are explosives. Whoever put them there must have – had a very good *reason.* They—'

'Yes. They were *using* us, Vittoria. They used us to carry this terrible stuff.'

'But who's *they?*'

'Extremists, Vittoria.' There was a pained expression on his face. 'We are both innocent *vittime.* You understand – victims. I have been used. You too. But I must tell you that they will try to collect the stuff, and this we must not let them do. We must stay hidden. They do not know you. They do not know where you live. As long as we stay here together, they will not find us.'

'But we must hand the stuff to the authorities. It's *far* too dangerous to have around.'

'Vittoria' – he gripped her hand – 'they will arrest us. They will never believe we did not *know* about it. They will think that *we* are terrorists. You understand?'

'Can't we just leave it somewhere? At a police station or something.'

'It's too dangerous,' he said quickly.

'Then what are we going to do with it?'

He made a wide gesture of despair. 'I am not sure. I am thinking all the time. Perhaps we take it somewhere and bury it. But we must be careful. We must think *very* hard before we do anything.' He looked at her fondly and took her face in his hands. 'I must tell you, I am glad that you know. It makes me feel better to share this knowledge. You make me feel strong. You make me feel we can escape from this thing. Will you be strong? For *me*?'

Her stomach twisted with pleasure. She thought: How I misjudged him. No wonder he'd been tense and difficult. No *wonder* he'd looked so worried. She breathed a long thankful sigh of relief. 'Oh, my love,' she whispered. 'You poor thing. Don't worry. Of course I'll help. We'll work it out together.'

She hugged him, and felt his arms close around her, warm and strong. And she was glad that this dreadful thing had happened, because it had brought them together. From now on she would be able to share in the other, secret, part of his life, and everything would be all right.

The phone rang. For a second Victoria ignored it. Then, kissing Giorgio hard on the lips, she got up to answer it.

A woman's voice said, 'I want to speak to Giorgio.'

Victoria felt a moment's surprise then without a word she handed Giorgio the receiver. She stayed to listen. Somehow she felt she had the right.

Giorgio grunted 'Yes' several times. Then his expression suddenly hardened. He closed his eyes and clenched his jaw, as if containing some deep fury. Victoria held her breath. It was obviously very bad news. Finally he said, 'I come . . . Yes. Right now.' And rang off.

For a moment he stared at the phone, deep in thought. Then he came and took her by the shoulders. She had never seen him look so grim.

He said, 'A friend, she' – he paused as if searching for the right words – 'she needs help. The extremists are coming for her. They have a crazy idea that *she* knows where to find the explosives. It is terrible. She must leave her house—'

'Who is this person?'

'Someone who is innocent, like us,' he said smoothly. 'I must help her. You understand?'

'I'll come too.'

'No! You stay here. It is better. We will talk later. About what we must do.'

Doubts fluttered about in Victoria's mind, doubts she couldn't put her finger on. All she knew was that she hated the thought of him going without her. But then she looked up into his eyes, and saw tenderness and concern. And she realised that he must have more than a little kindness to help his friends in this way.

It was some time after he'd gone that she began to wonder about the woman on the phone, and how she'd known where Giorgio would be.

Kershaw came out of the interview room at Cannon Row Police Station, looking grim. 'His mouth's shut tighter than a clam.'

Nick wasn't in the least surprised. Wheatfield was never going to be a great talker.

Kershaw said heavily, 'The only time he showed any interest was when I told him we'd defused the bomb. Then he raised his eyebrows.'

'If he'd spoken he'd only have said he was disappointed.'

'Quite.' Kershaw started off along the corridor. 'I'm just going to have another look at his belongings.'

Nick followed to the charge room. Spread out on the table were some keys, a battered old wallet, a ragged student union card, various scraps of paper, a wad of money and some coins. The scraps of paper looked interesting, but proved on closer examination to be nothing but bus tickets, receipts and other printed matter. There was only one piece of handwriting: an address in North London.

'We've checked that,' said Kershaw. 'It's Reardon's place. We went over it a week ago. We're taking it apart again now. Also the place in St Mark's Villas.'

Nick picked up the wad of notes and flicked through it. There was over three hundred pounds. 'A lot of money for a poor student.'

'And some of it brand new,' Kershaw pointed out. 'Just drawn. We're checking the banks and building societies to see if he had an account.'

'I doubt it. Wheatfield's not the sort. Banks are capitalist institutions.'

Kershaw rubbed his chin. 'Where did he get it from then?'

'It was given to him, I would think.'

'By the others in the group.'

'I would imagine so.'

'Then *they* must get their money fresh from the bank.'

Both men thought for a moment, then Kershaw said, 'We might

be able to trace the bank, but never the account against which the money was issued.' He sighed and shot Nick a glance. 'Any ideas, Ryder?'

'Only that this proves what we'd thought – that there's a high degree of organisation. That the Crystal Faction has backing.'

Kershaw said sharply, 'Yes. But where does that actually *get* us?'

It was a good question. Nick made a face to show he didn't have an answer. 'I'll see what I can dig up.'

He accepted a lift in Kershaw's car and the two men returned to the Yard in silence. Avoiding the incident room Nick went straight up to his office. He needed time to think. Kershaw's team would follow up the direct leads. What Nick must do was find the link between the crystal philosophy and Wheatfield. Somewhere in the middle might be a clue to the identity of Wheatfield's friends.

Conway was on the phone. He beckoned Nick over and, covering the mouthpiece, said, 'I've got the info on Petrini.'

Nick picked up Conway's notes and read: Antonio Petrini. Born 5th Aug 1929, Milan. Wealthy landowning family. Private schools, Milan and Switzerland. Graduated Rome University, philosophy 1952. Post-grad course Milan. Lecturer in philosophy and politics, Turin 1956–63. Publications inc. *The Revolutionary Society*, 1963; *The Tyranny of Modern Capitalism*, 1966; both pub. Gritti. Joined Italian Communist Party, 1956. Resigned 1963. Close links Far Left. Known associate of extremists.

Beneath, Conway had scribbled various notes about the Red Brigades, the Italian Communist Party, as well as some dates and places. At the bottom in a corner were the words: Gritti – *La Bandiera Rossa, La Posta*.

Nick stared. *La Posta.*

Gabriella's magazine.

Conway had rung off. Nick asked, 'What's this? The Gritti bit here?'

Conway peered at his notes. 'Ah, he's Petrini's publisher. Those are two of the magazines he owns. Leftist, of course.'

It figured. Gabriella would hardly work for a right-wing publication. It also explained why she knew so much about Petrini and his philosophy. Both she and Petrini had doubtless been part of the fashionable left in Milan – the radical chic who attended smart publishing parties and talked about revolution.

He remembered that he'd never got round to checking up on Gabriella. There just hadn't been time. As soon as he had a second he'd do it. But for the moment it would have to wait.

He brought his mind back to the immediate problem. Petrini's followers. 'Is there any more to come on Petrini?' he asked Conway.

'The SID in Rome are coming back to us. I also contacted the DST in Paris. Petrini was certainly there at the time of the troubles. Claude is digging out what he has. Oh, and Box 500 and the SIS are suddenly taking quite an interest.'

'Why?'

'Covering themselves, I expect. In case there's a KGB connection. Anyway, they're looking into Petrini too.'

Nick shook his head. It was all going to take too long, far too long. And they didn't have the time.

There was a call from the incident room: Nick was wanted downstairs. The lift was floors away so Nick ran down the four flights of stairs. One of Kershaw's team briefed him. The Bow Street bomb had been completely dismantled at Woolwich. The explosive was French. Manufactured by Explosif Rocher, Cugny, on 20th March 1968. Type: Nitramite 19C, a mixture of TNT and ammonium nitrate. Inquiries were being made through Interpol.

The stuff was bound to be stolen, of course. That would be no surprise. But it would be interesting to know if the French had unearthed any other explosives from the same batch and if so, where. It would be even more interesting if it had turned up in terrorist hands. It would be useful to talk to Desport. Nick picked up a phone and dialled the DST in Paris.

As the number began to ring Nick became aware of a hush in the incident room. Something was up. The senior detectives were getting to their feet and moving towards the door. Kershaw was standing there. Catching Nick's eye, he beckoned him over.

Abandoning the call, Nick hurried into Kershaw's office.

Kershaw waited until everyone had settled.

'The money found on Wheatfield is hot,' he said. 'It was stolen from a bank on the outskirts of Chester a month ago.'

Kershaw continued, 'This is not the first of the money to have shown up. They laundered several thousand by buying and selling an expensive car. Bought it in Manchester, sold it in London three days later. Small amounts have been surfacing regularly since then, and always in the London area. We have a list of shopkeepers and publicans who've inadvertently handled it. They've not been able to provide descriptions though. Not *yet*. But four of you will attempt to jog their memories.'

A thankless task if there ever was one, Nick thought. The witnesses would already have been interviewed and their statements taken; they wouldn't take kindly to a whole new round of questioning.

'There were two people involved in the robbery itself,' Kershaw went on. 'Both were masked. Both carried Skorpion machine pistols. A third drove the getaway car. Beyond that – not a lot. Cheshire CID have made no significant progress with the investigation, and have no suspects to date. Two of you will go up there and get a full briefing.' He named two officers.

'A couple more things,' Kershaw said. 'There's no firm evidence, just a *suspicion*, that it was an inside job.' He looked doubtful. 'But we'll see about that. And the other thing' – he paused for effect – 'it seems that one of the robbers might have been a woman.'

There was silence in the room. Nick shivered slightly. A *woman*. Like the one who had left the parcel bomb at Cardinal Couriers. He had several women agitators on file – it seemed that women were making up for their centuries of political inactivity with a bang. But bank robbery? That was a very different story.

Suddenly he made up his mind. Conway could stay on the end of the phone in the office and follow up all the leads from abroad. He wanted to take a few hours off and go to Chester.

Gabriele sat in the Fiat for a long time and watched the entrance to the block of flats in Chelsea Manor Street. Finally she was satisfied. She said to Giorgio, 'I'll be fifteen minutes.'

She took a bag from the luggage on the back seat and got out. She carried the bag up to the flat and let herself in. The place seemed to be just as she had left it. She went from room to room until she was satisfied that nothing had been disturbed. In the kitchen she moved the cooker slightly and examined the plinth. The wood showed no signs of having been forced.

She brought in the heavy bag and, opening it, pulled out five magazines of ammunition for the Kalashnikov and placed them on the floor. She wrapped them in a towel. The bundle was bulky. There was no hope of hiding it under the kitchen unit with the other things. Besides, secrecy didn't seem so important now. No one could possibly know about this place and she would only be coming back here if everything went wrong. And if everything went wrong she'd be fighting her way out.

She would love to use the Kalashnikov on Nick Riley. For the twentieth time she imagined killing him. In her mind's eye she saw herself creeping up on him and bursting in with the rifle in her hand. He would stand up and stare in horror. He would raise his hands and look at her imploringly. He would stammer, 'Please don't.' Then she would smile and step forward. He would stumble backwards and start to shake with fear. The sweat would show on his forehead and he would beg her not to shoot. She would let him sweat a little longer, perhaps even make him kneel, then she would tell him what she thought of him. Finally, when he was so scared that he couldn't speak, she would pull the trigger.

She licked her lips. What she would give to make the scene a reality. Anything to obliterate the other vision that kept coming into her mind, the vision of him on top of her, pretending to love her, laughing secretly as he made love to her. She bit back the acid taste of humiliation, and thought: I'll get him one day.

She examined all the possible hiding places in the kitchen and settled on the gap between the wall and the back of the fridge. The bundle sat neatly on the condenser, and could be reached easily by sliding a hand down the wall.

She picked up the empty bag and, locking the flat, went down to the street. She looked carefully around before walking across to the car.

As she got in, Giorgio started the car and asked, 'Where now?'

'To eat. Then to visit your little friend.'

He gave her a curious glance. Pulling out into the King's Road, he laughed, 'She's not little.'

'Maybe not. But she's useful.'

'Oh?'

'Yes. She going to get Max back for us.'

Twenty

It was late afternoon by the time they left London and it took an hour to get on to the motorway. It was raining heavily and very dark, making the road treacherous. The driver, a young detective constable, was silent with concentration. The other man, an inspector with fifteen years' service, made the occasional attempt at conversation, then gave up.

Nick sat in the back, feeling tired and depressed. It had seemed a good idea to make this trip but now he wasn't so sure. What would he find? Proof that Wheatfield had been involved in the robbery? That would be nice, but it wouldn't necessarily get him anywhere. What he really needed was the identity of the others – and that would be a lot to hope for. Cheshire CID hadn't found any evidence, and they'd been working on the case for weeks.

In fact, the trip could well be a complete waste of time. And yet he was intrigued by the hint of inside knowledge. That, and the reason Wheatfield and his friends had chosen such an out of the way place as Chester: somewhere a long way from London, with banks presumably no easier to rob than those elsewhere. There might just be a good reason.

At the same time he was impatient to get back to London, to follow up the explosives lead and the Petrini connection. He decided he would stay in Chester for the night and perhaps two hours of the morning, but no longer.

As the car sped on, he brooded. He had made so many mistakes with this case. Not grabbing Wheatfield at the demonstration. Not getting Black Beard. Finding Wheatfield at St Mark's Villas and then *watching* him buy the ingredients for his bombs. Then losing him again – not strictly his fault, that one, but something he should have prevented. And now a nice comfortable unsuspecting woman who'd had the reasonable expectation of living out her life in peace and fulfilment was dead, blown to pieces in her own kitchen, her only crime to be the wife of the Commissioner.

There mustn't be any more mistakes.

Wheatfield was safely locked up. But Nick wanted to get his friends. Very badly.

They arrived in Chester at eight-thirty. Inspector Morrow had the case file ready for them. He also had the assistant manager of the bank, Mr Chesil, waiting in an interview room.

Nick started with the assistant manager. 'Now, Mr Chesil, I understand you got a glimpse of the driver of the getaway van.'

'Only the *briefest* glimpse.'

'I see. But I'd still like you to look at some photographs for me.' He placed the mug shots of Wheatfield on the table. 'Is this the man?'

The assistant manager stared hard at the pictures and shook his head. 'It *might* be. But I couldn't be sure. It happened so quickly, you see. I hardly had a chance.'

Nick nodded. 'Okay, now I'm going to show you some more photographs and some names. I want you to tell me if any of them are familiar. I mean in any context at all.'

He pulled out a sheaf of photographs of Wheatfield's known associates, a list of their names, and of the organisations that Wheatfield had been involved with.

Chesil went through them slowly, then shook his head.

Kershaw's detectives took over, and Nick returned to the inspector's office.

Inspector Morrow said, 'Some of the other witnesses are coming in during the evening.' He explained who the various people were, and Nick chose to interview Miss Izzard, who was waiting in another room.

She told him about the guns and how she'd identified them as Skorpions. She also described how the first gunman had gone straight to the shopping bag full of money.

'That gunman was a woman?'

'Oh yes,' said Miss Izzard definitely.

Inspector Morrow prompted, 'And the other acted like a gangster.'

Nick asked Miss Izzard, 'Oh? How was that?'

She explained about the 'Shut up or I kill you.' She paused, then added thoughtfully, 'You know, in hindsight I could have been wrong. Maybe I've seen too many films. Now I've had time to think about it, well – perhaps I was *too* certain.'

Nick sighed inwardly. Inspector Morrow had described this lady as a perfect witness and now she was back-pedalling.

'You see,' continued Miss Izzard, 'in actual fact when you come to think about it all he did was to speak like a *foreigner*. Not just a gangster. *Any* sort of foreigner.'

Immediately, Nick thought of Black Beard. Nevertheless, he showed Miss Izzard the photographs and the list of names that he did have. After fifteen minutes she admitted defeat, saying firmly, 'I know none of these people.'

There were no more witnesses to interview for the moment so Nick spent the next hour in Morrow's office going carefully through all the statements in the case file. He kept thinking: There's nothing here. I was wrong to come. After a while his mind wandered. He imagined the remainder of the terrorist cell – perhaps three or four of them – hiding out in London. Would they be lying low? Or would they be busy planning more bombs? He tried to picture them. They would be arrogant, like Wheatfield. And cruel. One failure wouldn't put them off: it would probably encourage them. Even now they were probably planning their revenge.

Uneasy, he phoned Conway in London. Conway told him the explosives had been traced to a batch stolen from the French explosives factory at Cugny the previous June. Ten sticks of Nitramite 19C from the same batch had been discovered in Bilbao, northern Spain, in January, in a raid on the hide-out of some Basque Separatists.

What did it prove? Only what he'd known before; that the terrorists co-operated with each other.

There was no other news.

He rang off and returned to the pile of statements. At ten-thirty Morrow put his head round the door.

'The financial director of Bradbury's has come in. Would you like a word?'

It was Bradbury's payroll which had been in the shopping bag, Nick remembered. Picking up his batch of photographs, he said, 'Yes, why not?'

Morrow led the way down the corridor. 'Well, don't expect too much. He's a taciturn bugger, this fellow. And he says he can only stay ten minutes.'

Kershaw's detectives were already interviewing the man. Nick sat down and listened. The man's name was Leonard Wilson. He was about sixty, thin-faced with grey hair receding at the temples. He was neatly dressed in a grey suit, and sat stiffly in the chair with his hands folded precisely on the table in front of him. It was soon apparent that Mr Wilson was not best pleased at being questioned again. He was quietly but firmly dismissive, and answered the questions as briefly as possible. He obviously didn't suffer fools gladly.

No, he was saying, he had nothing new to add to his statement. He certainly had no idea why some terrorists should have chosen to rob the bank at the precise moment the payroll was being passed over.

After a few minutes he looked at his watch in an obvious way.

Nick stepped forward. 'Would you mind very much looking at these photographs, sir?'

Mr Wilson gave a small but unmistakable sigh of annoyance. 'If you insist.'

He looked at pictures of Wheatfield and raised his eyebrows in vague distaste. 'I've never seen this person before.'

He barely glanced at the other photographs before shaking his head.

'And just a list of names and organisations, if you wouldn't mind.'

The list was quite long, but within ten seconds Leonard Wilson had passed it back across the table.

Nick thought: Oh no, you don't. Pushing the paper back, he said firmly, 'If you wouldn't mind, sir, taking another look. It *is* very important.'

A momentary flash of irritation crossed Leonard Wilson's face, then, pulling the list towards him, he began to read again. Nick watched his eyes travel down the list, flicking from side to side as he read each name.

Half-way down he seemed to pause. Then he started again, reading more slowly, taking more care.

Finally he looked up. 'I'm sorry. I don't think I know any of the people or organisations on this list.'

It was the longest reply he had given that evening.

He stood up to go. Morrow caught Nick's eye and raised his eyebrows as if to say: What did I tell you.

Wilson picked up his coat from a chair. Standing up, he looked unexpectedly thin and frail. As he unfolded the coat a pair of gloves and a scarf fell to the floor. Nick picked them up and handed them to him. He noticed that Wilson's hand was trembling. Well, he was sixty or so; that was old age for you.

Nick helped him on with his coat.

Wilson said, 'Thank you.'

Nick looked up sharply. There was something different about the voice: a warm tremulous quality. Almost as if he were relieved. Or nervous.

The tiniest suspicion crept into Nick's mind.

He opened the door for the older man and walked with him down the corridor. He said, 'The people who robbed the bank are terrorists. Did Inspector Morrow tell you that?'

Wilson nodded. 'Yes.'

'Former students who think they can change the world.' Nick glanced across at him. 'Do you have any children yourself, Mr Wilson?'

'Not any more.' The answer came very quickly.

A child had died, obviously. 'I'm sorry.'

They reached the main entrance of the police station. Nick stopped so that Wilson was forced to pause for a moment.

'It was very good of you to come over. Do you have transport?'

'Thank you. I have a car.' He turned and, pushing rapidly through the doors, was gone.

Nick stared after him. He could swear something wasn't quite right there, although he couldn't put his finger on it.

He went back to the interview room and looked thoughtfully at his list. There was no Wilson on it. And *yet*.

He racked his brains. The name rang a very distinct bell. It was maddening, but he couldn't quite place it. He tried matching it with a dozen Christian names but nothing clicked.

Records would turn it up. He got one of the detectives to phone Conway in London to start the hunt through the files, then he went in search of Morrow.

'Who else can I talk to?'

The inspector thought for a moment. 'Well – there's always our friend Mrs Ackroyd. The lady who carried the payroll. She's worked at Bradbury's for twenty years. But I thought I'd save you an ear-bashing by not asking her in—'

'Would you mind telling her that I'd like to come round?'

Mabel Ackroyd dropped the receiver on to its cradle and raced upstairs in panic. Reaching the bathroom she tore off her hairnet and, grabbing a tissue, rubbed the cold cream mercilessly off her face.

It was important to look her best. Scotland Yard indeed! In the last few weeks it had gone very quiet on the robbery front. She'd told everyone her story, and some of them had been interested enough to hear it several times. But more recently people had started to drift away when she'd mentioned the subject. It was most disappointing. If only Harry, her husband, were still alive. He would have listened. She missed having someone to talk to.

But now! Scotland Yard indeed!

She fluffed out her grey curls and wondered whether to get dressed. No, it was better to stay in her dressing-gown. It would sound more *dramatic* when she told everyone in the morning.

She went back downstairs, turned some lights on, and put on the kettle for some tea. She had butterflies in her stomach.

The doorbell rang and she clasped her hands together in pleasure.

She opened the door with a warm smile. There were two of them. She recognised the nice Inspector Morrow immediately. 'Good evening, inspector,' she said graciously.

She turned to examine the second man and suppressed a deep disappointment. This couldn't be the Scotland Yard detective. This person was frightfully young, with longish hair and blue jeans.

They came in and Inspector Morrow said, 'This is Sergeant Ryder from Scotland Yard.'

So, he *was* from the Yard. But only a *sergeant*.

Never mind. She determined to make the best of it. She led the way into the lounge and asked them to sit down. She noticed that the sergeant was rather good-looking. She smiled, 'How can I help you?'

The inspector began, 'Er, it's a delicate subject, Mrs Ackroyd. It's about Bradbury's. We wanted to know a few personal details about some of the people who work there. About Mr Wilson, for example.'

'Mr Wilson?' she repeated curiously. 'Oh-h-h.'

'Yes. We wondered if you could tell us if he had any children?'

She blinked in surprise. What on earth had this to do with the robbery? 'Well,' she said eventually, 'there was a daughter, I believe.'

'What was her name?' the sergeant asked.

'Her name? Now let me see . . . Yes, Linda. Linda.'

The sergeant put a hand to his eyes and inhaled sharply as if something had just come back to him. Then he exchanged glances with the inspector, and gave him a firm nod.

Mabel Ackroyd felt a small twinge of alarm. 'May I ask *why* you are asking me these questions?'

The young man replied, 'It's very important that we know about Linda Wilson, Mrs Ackroyd. Is she – er – *dead*?'

'Dead? Well, not as far as I *know*. I mean – one would have *heard* if she was. Goodness . . .' She put a hand to her bosom. 'Is she meant to be dead?'

'Can you tell us anything more about her, Mrs Ackroyd?'

The sergeant hadn't actually answered her question. She felt rather put out. 'Well, I don't know the Wilsons well, you understand. They keep themselves to themselves. But I do remember Linda. I used to see her quite often. She was my own daughter's age, you see. Although they weren't friends, as such. She was clever, you see, Linda. She went to a grammar school, and then to university. She was very clever.'

'Anything else about her? What was she like?'

'Oh, quiet. A bit withdrawn, really. She – was very protected, you know. An only child, of course. Always neatly dressed. Always well behaved. Until she was about fifteen.'

'What happened then?'

'She went wild.'

Mrs Ackroyd enjoyed the effect of her words. The two police officers were positively drinking them up.

'Wild? Do you mean with boys?'

'Yes. And in every other way. Her clothes – well, once I saw her wearing the shortest skirt you've *ever* seen. And make-up! Well, you could have scraped it off her face.'

'What sort of friends did she have?'

'Oh, arty types. Layabouts. Not what her parents wanted, not at all.'

'Have you seen her recently?'

'Oh no. She's never been back. Her parents washed their hands of her, you see. When she went away to university. They never forgave her. Never.'

'What for?' the sergeant asked.

'For being so wild. And outrageous. She was very outspoken. They never forgave her for being so – *ungrateful*, I think.'

The young sergeant stood up. 'Thank you, Mrs Ackroyd.'

'But aren't you going to *tell* me what this is all about? I mean, is it about the robbery? Was *Linda* involved in some way?'

The inspector said quickly, 'Something like that.'

She jumped up. 'But you haven't had any tea.'

The sergeant said, 'Another time.' He fixed his gaze on her. 'Can I ask you a favour, Mrs Ackroyd?'

He was giving her such a charming look that she revised her opinion of him. He was obviously very bright and clever as well as being good-looking. It suddenly occurred to her that, despite being a sergeant, he might be important after all. She swelled with pride.

'Of course.'

'May I ask you not to say anything about the – *nature* of our conversation?'

'Oh,' she exclaimed. That was going to be very difficult. She'd already planned how she was going to announce it in the office.

'Just for a day or so. Until we've completed our inquiries. It's important.'

Ah, *now* she understood. It was hush-hush. He was an under-cover man. That explained the jeans. She breathed, 'Of *course*.'

It was only after she'd closed the door behind them that she remembered something else. Good Lord, how could she have forgotten? She threw open the door and called down the path, 'Hello? Hello? Are you still there?'

The young sergeant re-emerged from the darkness. 'Yes?'

'I completely forgot – she once told me that she was *adopted*, Linda did. But it can't have been true. I mean, one would have *heard*. Probably one of her little fancies.'

The young man blinked. 'Thank you, Mrs Ackroyd.'

After they'd gone she made herself a cup of tea and sat up for a while thinking how exciting it had all been.

Then she thought about poor Mr and Mrs Wilson, and how awful it was going to be for them, and felt rather sad.

The house was situated in a quiet residential street, set back from the road behind a tall hedge. It was a house with, Nick guessed, about four bedrooms. There was a light shining in the porch, but otherwise the place was in darkness. A path led from the gate to the front door through a neat ordered garden, the rose beds well dug and covered with manure, ready for the winter.

As they rang the bell Nick noticed a sliver of light showing through a chink in the heavily curtained windows. Someone was still up.

It was a good minute before they heard someone approach the door. Finally a bolt was pulled back, and the door was opened a short way. The face of a woman appeared, but standing well back out of the harsh light from the porch. The woman was small and grey-haired.

Inspector Morrow went through the formalities of identifying himself, then asked if they might come in.

The woman did not reply, but stared at them as if in shock. Nick realised that she had been crying.

She retreated further into the shadow of the hall, and glanced to one side. Suddenly the door was pulled wide open, and Leonard Wilson stepped into the light. He did not look surprised to see them.

He said stiffly, 'You'll want to come in, I suppose.'

They were shown into the living-room, a vaguely oppressive room densely furnished with a brown Dralon three-piece suite, numerous side tables and occasional chairs, lamps with deep fringes, and heavy velvet curtains. Every surface was covered in china ornaments and bric-a-brac. The walls were decorated with a busy beige and tan wallpaper.

The four of them sat down.

Morrow began, 'I believe you have a daughter, Mr and Mrs Wilson. By the name of Linda?'

Leonard Wilson replied, 'Yes.'

'And she's not dead, is she?'

'She is to us.' He closed his eyes for an instant, as if reinforcing an inner resolve.

Morrow paused. 'When did you last see her?'

'Four years ago.'

'And you've had no communication with her since then?'

'None.'

'She – hasn't visited the neighbourhood recently?'

'No. Not that we are aware of.'

Nick said, 'Mr Wilson, you recognised some names on that list that I showed you. Which were they?'

Wilson stared at him. With an effort he replied, 'There were a couple that she might have mentioned . . . Friends of hers at Essex University. Members of that political group – the Socialist League or whatever it was. She brought one of them home once.' His mouth curled up with distaste.

'What was his name?'

For the first time Leonard Wilson's face showed some emotion. He dropped his eyes. 'Wheatfield.'

There was a long silence. Nick asked, 'When was this?'

He shook his head. 'I'm not sure. Probably four or five years ago.'

Mrs Wilson spoke for the first time. 'It was four and a half years ago exactly.' Her voice was thin and tired and defeated. 'In May.'

Nick glanced around the room, searching the tables and mantel-piece for photographs. There were only two, and they were faded pictures of the young Mr and Mrs Wilson taken, he guessed, during the war.

'Do you have any photographs of your daughter, Mrs Wilson?'

She had buried her head in her hand and he realised that she was weeping.

Nick said, 'I'm sorry, but – if you *could* find something . . .'

She dabbed at her eyes and got up. 'I'll go and look. '

'Shall I come with you?'

She nodded her assent, and Nick followed her upstairs into a spare room which seemed to be used as both study and store room. She knelt on the floor and, unlocking one of the desk drawers, pulled out a box.

She started to open it then paused. Her head fell on to her chest and Nick realised she was crying again.

'You'll use this to find her, won't you?' she whispered.

Nick sighed. He could only tell her the truth. 'Yes.'

'And – she'll be locked away.'

'Yes, eventually.'

She shook her head from side to side. 'Nothing but pain. Always. Always the same. Nothing but pain.'

Eventually she blew her nose and taking a deep breath, opened the box.

Nick looked over her shoulder. Baby pictures. A toddler firmly gripping an adult hand. A small girl in a gymslip. The family on a beach somewhere. Then older, about twelve.

Nick stared.

He felt a twinge of alarm.

There was something vaguely *familiar*—

He frowned and very slowly reached out for the photograph.

'The more recent ones are at the bottom,' Mrs Wilson murmured.

Nick's mouth had gone very dry. He stared, horrified yet transfixed, as Mrs Wilson pulled a large black and white portrait from the bottom of the box.

Everything stood still.

Then he heard himself cry, '*Oh Christ. Oh God.*'

For a moment he was incredulous.

Then the shock came to him like a pain, a small ache which grew and grew until it was vast and ugly.

'*Oh God, Oh God.*'

He tried to find another answer, but he knew there was none. And then the realisations came thick and fast, each more ghastly than the one before, each tearing away a new layer of horror like so many layers of skin torn from a wound.

He felt physically ill. He wanted to be sick.

Mrs Wilson's voice came from far away, shrill and frightened. 'What's the matter? *What's the matter?*' He heard her get up and hurriedly leave the room.

He put a fist to his mouth and bit into it until it hurt.

Henry Northcliff dreamed that he was standing at the dispatch box in the House of Commons. He opened his mouth to speak but couldn't think of anything to say. Something ghastly had happened: he'd been caught out in some way, and the members were shouting,

'Resign! Resign!' A member of the Cabinet was shaking him by the shoulder, trying to get him to sit down.

He awoke with a start, and realised he was in bed at home. Caroline was shaking him gently by the shoulder.

He twisted round. 'What is it?'

'I heard a sound. A sort of scraping noise. From downstairs . . .'

Henry listened, but apart from the humming of the wind the night was silent.

Caroline said, 'It's probably nothing. I'm sorry.'

Henry roused himself and, throwing back the covers, swung his legs to the floor.

Caroline said ruefully, 'Oh darling, don't bother. Honestly.'

'I'm up now.'

He pulled on a dressing-gown and went out to the landing. He listened for a moment, then, turning on the light, went downstairs. He noticed it was just after one o'clock. He made the rounds of each room, checking the doors and windows.

Finally he went to the front door and peered through the peephole. In the dim street lighting he could just make out the figure of the policeman at the front gate, pacing slowly back and forth.

He turned back and listened again. Nothing.

He switched off the lights and started to climb the stairs again.

There was a sound. He paused to listen.

From the distance, beyond the kitchen, there was a definite noise, a faint screech.

He retraced his steps and went into the kitchen. He crossed the room and looked out of the window into the garden. The night was very dark. It was impossible to distinguish much apart from the outline of the trees, which were swaying frantically back and forth, pulled by the wind.

The sound came again, more like a wail than a screech. He went to the back door which opened on to the side of the house, and unlocked it.

He put his head out. The wind came whistling down the side of the building and blew at his hair. He peered towards the boundary fence and the dim silhouette of his neighbour's house.

Suddenly it came again. A high screech.

He stood listening.

Suddenly he gave a small snort of amusement.

He closed and relocked the door then hurried back upstairs.

Caroline was sitting up in bed waiting.

'Oh poor darling,' she said. 'It wasn't anything, I suppose.'

'A branch. Rubbing against the Collins' greenhouse. It's the wind.'

He got back into bed and she snuggled against him.

'Poor darling. What an idiot I am.'

'Not at all. I'm glad you woke me. Otherwise you might have stayed awake worrying. You weren't awake long, were you?'

'No. Well – only a few minutes.'

'You should have woken me sooner.'

They lay for a while in the darkness, listening to the wind.

Henry said, 'You don't worry, do you, about these bombers?'

'What? Oh no. Anyway they've caught one of them, haven't they? I mean, very quickly. So they're bound to find the rest, aren't they? Thank God. That poor woman.' She shuddered. 'So dreadful.'

Henry hugged her to him. He suddenly felt exceptionally happy. Here he was in this warm bed with a woman he loved more than anything in the world, secure in a nice comfortable house, with no money worries, and a job that, even if it was causing him worry at present, was on balance most satisfying and rewarding.

'I do love you,' he murmured.

She kissed his neck.

'And you know, I *am* pleased about the baby. *Really*. They always say that late parenthood is an unexpected joy. And I *know* it will be for me too. In fact, I'm very much looking forward to it.'

'We'll still be able to go to Venice. We'll just leave him behind.'

'Yes,' he said. 'That's right. We'll still be able to go.'

A few minutes later, as Caroline's breathing became deep and steady beside him, Henry thought about the baby again and discovered that he had meant every word he'd said. Now that he had got used to the idea, he was most definitely looking forward to it.

Twenty-one

Victoria dreamed that Bella was in the farmhouse kitchen, eating rotten vegetables out of the fridge. The floor was covered in mud and dirt; the creature had obviously been there a long time without food. She walked into the hall. Her footsteps echoed through the cold empty house. The curtains were drawn in the ground floor rooms. She climbed the stairs. The door of Pete and Janey's room was ajar. She pushed it open and looked in. The room was empty. She started up the passage towards her own room. The door was wide open. She hesitated, suddenly sickened. The air was thick with flies. She didn't want to go in alone. But there was no one else in the house.

She woke up, holding her breath. She exhaled with a long sigh. The bedside clock read one. She'd been asleep for less than half an hour. The other side of the bed was empty.

She lay still, trying to shut out the dull ache of the loneliness and the knowledge that he was probably with someone else.

She thought: It's my own fault. I should have known. A man like that was never going to be easy. But the constant uncertainty was hard to bear. It was so wearing. Never knowing when he would be back. If at *all*.

And then there was the awful business of the bundles in the van. If only he could be more definite about what he planned to do with them. He couldn't just *leave* them there. Doubtless he was hoping they would just disappear. But life wasn't like that. He had to *do* something about it. She would make another effort to persuade him. When she saw him. *If* she saw him. She sighed unhappily. What a mess.

There was a sound. She lay tense and still, listening. A window rattled. The wind.

Another sound. *In* the flat.

She got out of bed, her heart pounding.

Giorgio. It must be.

She padded into the living-room. It took a moment for her eyes to adjust to the light spilling in from the hall beyond, and at first she thought the room was empty.

Then she saw something move.

'Giorgio!'

He was standing in the shadows, staring at her, his eyes glinting in the darkness.

She went to him and, reaching up, kissed him. The smell of drink was strong on his breath.

She said, 'You're late. I was worried . . . Is your friend all right?'

He frowned mockingly. 'All right?'

'You said . . .' She trailed off. She could see he was in one of those moods. He was going to pretend he'd never said anything about visiting the friend in trouble. It was one of his favourite tricks, pretending not to remember.

He reached out and, lifting her shift, began to caress her thigh. 'You missed me?' he murmured thickly. 'You want me? Mmm?'

She looked into his face. She sensed he was taunting her. And yet . . .

Closing her eyes, she leant her body against his, and put her arms round him. It was impossible. She just couldn't turn him away. It didn't matter what he thought of her. He brought out strong feelings in her that she'd never realised she had. He made her feel brazen and shameless. He made her feel *alive*.

She laughed, warm and low, and started to unbutton his shirt.

He breathed, 'You want me very badly? Do you? Do you?'

'Oh yes, oh *yes*. *Now*. Every part of you . . . Every *inch* of you.'

'You've been waiting for me, have you?'

'Yes. *Yes*.'

He laughed triumphantly and pulled away. 'Such passion.'

She took his hand to pull him gently towards the bedroom, but he held back.

He was looking at something on the other side of the room.

She followed his gaze.

At first she saw nothing.

Then she jumped back, uttering a small cry.

Somebody was there.

She stared, aghast.

The person moved, coming further into the light. It was a woman, tall and dark.

The memory of what she'd just been saying hit Victoria first, and she flushed with embarrassment. Then came the sickening realisation that Giorgio had staged the whole thing. He had *known* the woman would hear. He had set up the scene just to humiliate her.

She turned on him. 'My *God*!'

Ignoring her anger, Giorgio said smoothly, 'Oh, I forgot. This is my friend Gabriele. She needs a place to stay. I said she could come here.'

Victoria gaped at him. What *was* he trying to do to her? She spluttered, 'Really . . . *Really!* How *could* you?'

Giorgio spread his hands in a wide gesture of surprise. 'She only wants the sofa. I thought you wouldn't mind. She is in need of a bed, that's all.'

Victoria hardly trusted herself to speak. 'You might have told me.'
'I didn't know.'

'That she was *here*, I mean.'

He shrugged. 'She didn't mind. Did you, Gabriele?'

The woman sat calmly down on the sofa. 'No, I didn't mind.'

Victoria thought: This is a nightmare.

The woman lit a cigarette. She said, 'This sofa'll be okay.' She was
very composed. She stared at Victoria with cold assurance, her gaze
steady and unblinking. But there was no warmth in the gaze, nothing
that invited further contact.

She was very good-looking, Victoria noticed, the face dramatically
pale against the dark hair, the features strong and well formed; a
woman who could be attractive to men.

Immediately, a nasty suspicion sprang into Victoria's mind. She
looked from Giorgio to the woman. There was no reason for believing
it, nothing she could put her finger on. And *yet* . . .

Giorgio said, 'She'll need some blankets.'

Sick at heart, Victoria went into the bedroom and dug out a spare
eiderdown and pillow from a box under the bed. She could be wrong,
of course, about the woman. But she knew she wasn't. One got a
feeling about these things.

She took the bedding back to the other room and dropped it on the
floor by the sofa.

The woman said, 'Thanks.'

For an instant Victoria thought there was some warmth in the tone,
then she looked into the woman's face and knew she was mistaken.

Victoria went into the bedroom and closed the door. There was a
pause then she heard the low murmur of voices. They were talking
about her, she knew they were. She wanted to scream. What a fool
she'd been.

A door opened and closed: the bathroom.

Victoria climbed quickly into bed. A moment later Giorgio came in
and turned on the light. She closed her eyes. She heard him undress.
Then the light went off and he got into bed.

After a few seconds his hand came across and stroked her leg.

She hissed, 'Don't touch me.'

He took no notice, and rolled his body next to hers.

'Don't *touch* me!'

He pulled her over on to her back and, pushing her shift up round
her neck, began to kiss her body.

'You're *foul*. You humiliated me. On *purpose*!'

270

He paused. 'Vittoria. No. I was proud of you. Proud. Otherwise why would I have kissed you in front of her?'

She didn't believe him. It was a complete lie. She should have said so, but she couldn't. Instead, she let him continue, hating herself for being so weak, loathing herself for what he must think of her, yet wanting him terribly.

It might be the last time. It *would* be the last time.

And if she was never going to see him again, what the hell did it matter anyway?

The night seemed to have lasted for ever. It was only two-thirty. Nick made himself a cup of coffee and, leaning back against the work top, looked dully around him. The kitchen was old-fashioned: the wooden cupboards of a type popular thirty years ago, the wallpaper old and over-fussy. The paintwork was an oppressive mid-blue, the overhead light inadequate, the effect dim and depressing.

Yet once she had been a child here; once she had eaten her breakfast at the table under the window in the brightness of the early morning. Once she must have run in and asked for sweets, and been given a kind word, and run out again to play. Surely it can't have been so terrible. *Surely*.

The telephone rang in the hall.

He drained the coffee and went to answer it.

It was Conway.

'Cleaned out. Not a sign of life. The forensic people are going over the place now.'

Nick rubbed his forehead. It would have been too simple to find her at the mews house.

'What about the Fiat?' he asked.

'Parked outside. Nothing in it.'

'What about Records? Anything in the passport details?'

'No. Nothing to say she was adopted anyway. Usually they put a special note on the form, don't they? When it's checked.'

'Yes. Let me know if you find anything.'

He rang off, feeling very low. She'd done a bunk. It shouldn't surprise him. It was becoming increasingly obvious that she was a real pro. That was what hurt the most, the way she'd completely fooled him on a professional level. He'd never had a flicker of suspicion. And yet all the pointers had been there if only he'd chosen to see. It made him cringe to think of the things she'd been doing under his very nose – things he could have *prevented*. The bombings. He thought of Mrs McCabe and felt bitterly ashamed.

He'd never *checked* on Gabriella.

He'd meant to. He'd intended to.

He'd just never bloody well *done* it.

There was a footfall on the stairs above. It was Mr Wilson.

Nick met him at the bottom. 'Is Mrs Wilson better?'

'Yes, but she's resting. I'd really rather she wasn't disturbed until morning.'

'Would it be convenient to have those few words now?'

Wilson nodded. He looked tired, but the stiffness, the unrelenting formality, was still in place. Nick sensed that Wilson was not a man who ever let go.

They went into the living-room and sat down.

'She was always wilful,' Wilson began slowly. 'She never wanted to be told what to do. She never listened.'

'When did she first become involved in politics?'

'What? Oh, at university. She picked up all sorts of – *rubbish*. She couldn't stop talking about it. She got very aggressive. Used to shout at us when we didn't listen. It was all complete nonsense, of course. Half-baked theories about this and that . . .'

'About what exactly?'

He made an impatient gesture. 'Oh good God, I can't remember now. I don't think I listened much. It was all about' – he sighed heavily – 'changing the order of things, or something like that. Complete nonsense.'

'Mr Wilson, apparently Linda was under the impression she was adopted. Is that true?'

Wilson hesitated slightly, then said vehemently, 'No! Another of her fantasies. She was always romanticising everything.'

Nick eyed him thoughtfully.

'Was there any particular reason for this fantasy?'

'No, no. She was just over-imaginative. She could never come down to earth. Always felt that the world owed her something. She was – selfish, demanding, difficult. We could never do anything with her.'

'Can you think why she should choose the name Gabriella?'

The slight hesitation again. 'No.' He dropped his eyes and stared at the empty grate.

'Or Schroeder? Or Carelli?' pressed Nick.

'No.'

The denials were being delivered more confidently now, as if he were getting used to a lie.

Nick rubbed a hand over his face. 'Mr Wilson, I don't have much time. Please tell me – is there anything more I should know?'

A woman's voice said, 'Tell him, Leonard.'

The two men turned. Mrs Wilson was standing in the doorway. She said awkwardly, 'I couldn't sleep—'

She came and sat down. Folding her hands in her lap, she said again to her husband, 'Tell him.'

Leonard Wilson stared at her and shook his head briefly and violently.

Marie Wilson raised her eyes to Nick's. Taking a deep breath she said coldly, 'She's not our child.'

'Marie—'

She raised a hand to her husband. 'No, Leonard, it doesn't make any difference now. And I don't want people to think she's our daughter any more. Not when she *isn't* . . .' She looked at Nick again, and continued in a firm voice, 'She's not our child at all. She was my sister's. My sister was what you might call – *wild*. Just like Linda. Very impressionable. She had a boyfriend, just before the war. A German called Schroeder.' She spoke the word 'German' as if it were distasteful. 'He was a writer, an intellectual. Rose, my sister, was quite bowled over by him. She had . . . a strange fascination for those sort of people. Always hanging about them, making a fool of herself. She went to Germany with – this person. But then, in '38, I think it was, there was trouble – he was almost arrested.'

'Why?'

'Why? Oh, I'm not sure—'

'For being a damned communist!' interrupted Wilson.

Mrs Wilson folded and refolded her hands. 'Anyway, he came here as a refugee. When war broke out he was interned. Rose – well, she never stopped making scenes about it. Trying to get him freed. Hysterical, she was. She took a job near the camp in Scotland. He was allowed out in the day to work on a farm. She'd sneak out to – see him. Then – she became pregnant.' She shook her head. 'It was out of the question for her to keep the baby. I mean, she was quite hopeless as a person. Irresponsible. She would never have looked after it. Besides, she didn't *want* the child. She was frightened that the German would drop her. And of course he *did*. After the war . . .' She bristled with righteous indignation.

'Go on,' prompted Nick.

'Well. We decided to – take the child. We couldn't have children of our own, you see.'

'But you never actually adopted Linda?'

Mrs Wilson assumed a look of high moral standing. 'No . . . We didn't want there to be the slightest stain against her name. If anyone had discovered that she was – born out of marriage. Well, we felt it would be terrible for her.'

Or for *you*, Nick thought.

'We decided to make her ours immediately. Rose had the baby in Scotland, in the cottage where she was living. The doctor didn't know Rose at all. It was wartime. People were moving all over the place . . . When we told him her name was Marie Wilson and the baby was to be called Linda, well . . . He took us at our word. And so – *we* brought Linda up. *Properly*. Much better than Rose could ever have done. Anyway – Rose died a few years later.'

Wilson said firmly, 'But the wildness was in her blood. She was just like her mother.' He shook his head. 'Nothing we could do.'

There was a long silence. Nick felt empty and hollow.

Wilson said in an icy voice, 'I suppose this will mean prosecution.'

For a moment Nick couldn't think what he meant. 'For what?'

'For the false birth registration.'

Nick sighed. 'Quite honestly, I have no idea. It was a long time ago.' These people were incredible, he reflected. All they could think about was protecting themselves from something which happened more than twenty-five years before.

'Just tell me,' Nick said heavily, 'how did Linda find out? About her parents?'

Mrs Wilson wrung her hands. 'She discovered a letter. From this – Schroeder man. He'd – written to me, asking about her. I thought he was *dead*. It had been so long . . . And I've no idea how he *found* us. It was awful.'

'When was this?'

'Oh . . . In 1962. Thereabouts. From then on she could think of nothing else. She romanticised him. Saw him as a knight in armour, fighting for freedom . . . A martyr. She became *obsessed* by the story. And as for *us* – well, *we* became monsters. And after all we'd done for her!'

'One last question. Why would she call herself Gabriella?'

Mrs Wilson's mouth pulled back in a grimace of pain. 'That's what the Schroeder man called her. At least, *Gabriele*. In the letter. He seemed to think it was her name. Rose had promised him. That she would call the child by that name. But then Rose always made promises she could never keep.'

Nick stood up to go. Automatically Wilson began to get out of his seat, but, changing his mind, paused and sank back into the cushions. Nick left them sitting in the dark oppressive room, staring at the walls.

Victoria sat up in bed, feeling awful. She'd slept very badly. She remembered waking several times in the night and being unable to get back to sleep. Now, astonishingly, it was ten.

The other side of the bed was empty.

She pulled on a dressing-gown and went to the door. She opened it. There were voices in the living-room. As she went in they ceased.

Giorgio and the woman sat there, looking at her.

Immediately Giorgio rose to his feet and came towards her. He put his arm round her. 'Did you sleep all right?'

She blinked at him. 'No, as a matter of fact . . . I didn't.'

'Ah,' he said without interest. Then, more warmly: 'I make you some coffee.'

He disappeared into the kitchen. Victoria was left with the woman. She was not quite as beautiful as Victoria had thought. There were dark circles under her eyes and in the light of day her skin looked rather sallow. At the same time, there was something magnetic about her, a forceful energy that made it difficult to take your eyes off her.

Victoria immediately felt inadequate.

The woman said, 'We were just talking about you.'

'Oh?'

She uncurled herself from the sofa. Her movements were cat-like. 'You see,' the woman said smoothly, 'you're the only one who can help.'

Victoria sat down in a chair. 'Me? In what way?'

'This awful business with the van. And those people who slipped in the explosives—'

Victoria closed her eyes. Just the mention of those dreadful bundles made her depressed.

'You see, Giorgio knew nothing about them. You realise that, don't you?'

Victoria nodded.

The woman reached down to the floor and took a cigarette from a packet. She lit it slowly and deliberately. She had what Victoria's mother used to call poise.

'These people have used Giorgio. And of course *you*,' she continued. 'And now they want the stuff. We have to decide whether to give it to them.'

It was like a nightmare. Victoria shook her head. 'No, no. That must be wrong.'

'I agree.'

Victoria smiled with relief. 'Thank goodness. We'll give the stuff to the police, won't we? And explain.'

'Well, I don't think it'll be quite as simple as that.' The woman's gaze was very penetrating. 'They'll almost undoubtedly arrest us.'

'Oh God!'

Victoria couldn't even imagine what it must be like to be arrested on a serious charge. After the business with Mel and the farm, and the violence at the demonstration, it seemed that her life was staggering from one horror to another, each worse than the one before.

Giorgio came in with the coffee and put it down beside her. He sat on the arm of the chair and stroked her hair.

'Can't we *go* to someone?' Victoria asked plaintively.

The woman shot a glance at Giorgio, then smiled. 'Why, yes. That was exactly what we thought—'

'Oh good!' Victoria felt the first glimmerings of hope.

'But it must be someone who can put our case – *properly*,' the woman said. 'Someone with legal knowledge that we can trust absolutely. And someone with *influence*. You know how it is – the old-boy network and all that. It's *who* you know that's important . . .'

'There's my solicitor.'

There was a slight pause. 'No, Vittoria, my love,' Giorgio said softly. 'Not important enough. We need someone who can give the best advice. Someone like your friend.'

Victoria felt a small twinge of alarm. 'Who do you mean?'

'Your friend . . . Sir Henry. Now he would *really* know how to handle it.'

Victoria shook her head vehemently. 'Absolutely not. I couldn't possibly. He's been so kind. I couldn't *involve* him—'

'But you wouldn't be involving him,' the woman said in a soft persuasive tone. 'Just *asking* him. That's all. Surely he wouldn't mind giving a bit of advice. And it would make all the difference. Then at least we'd know we were going the right way about things. After all, we're talking about the rest of our lives. We don't want to make any mistakes.'

Victoria stared at her. Suddenly, for no particular reason, she noticed that the woman's hands were shaking.

She looked up at Giorgio. He squeezed her shoulder. 'Please, Vittoria. It would mean a lot. To you and me. And to Gabriele.'

Gabriele leant forward. 'If you just phone and ask if you can see him. We wouldn't come in at all. Just wait outside—'

'Go and *see* him?'

'Of course.'

Victoria felt weighed down with responsibility. Whatever she did would be wrong. She tried to put herself in Henry's place. Would he mind terribly? He was bound to be busy. The last thing he needed was to hear more about her troubles.

And yet – he was understanding, kind. And, as Gabriele had said, they *were* talking about the rest of their lives.

She sighed and heard herself say, 'All right, but – I must go and see him on my own. When he's got a moment. I don't want to *embarrass* him in any way at all.'

Gabriele's eyes flashed. 'Then it'd be best to see him at home, wouldn't it? Quietly. So no one will know.'

Victoria looked at her. Perhaps she'd misjudged her: she was obviously a considerate person. She breathed, 'Yes.'

In a burst of shaky optimism, Victoria thought: Everything'll be all right. It *had* to be.

'Oh yes, that's her all right.'

The car dealer stared at the photograph. His name was Bisley and he looked rather flash, befitting someone who dealt in the more expensive sort of car.

'Rather a sexy sort of number.'

'Yes?' asked Nick painfully.

'In a cool businesslike sort of way, that is. Knew exactly what she wanted. No mucking about.' He whistled through his teeth. 'Boy, did she take me for a ride!'

Nick thought: I know the feeling.

'And all that cash. Thought it was my lucky day.'

Nick gave him a knowing look. Doubtless none of it was destined to go through the books.

They walked towards the door. The rain was pouring down the showroom windows.

'It was a day just like this,' said Bisley. 'She rather brightened it up, I thought.' He shook his head. 'Boy, was I taken for a ride.'

Nick paused at the door. 'Anything more you can add to your statement?'

'To be quite honest, I can hardly remember what I told your colleagues at the time.'

Nick nodded. He hadn't expected anything else really. It was just another bit of the jigsaw that had to be checked. And Manchester was only a few miles on from Chester.

He said, 'Thanks,' and went into the downpour. He got into the car and shook his head at the others. They weren't surprised either.

Without a word, the sergeant started the car and headed for London.

PART FOUR

Twenty-two

Henry put down the phone and went thoughtfully into the hall.

'Jenkins?' he called.

A chair scraped in the kitchen and the Special Branch man appeared in the doorway. 'Sir?'

'I'm expecting a caller. At about seven. A Miss Danby.'

'Right, sir, I'll answer the door, shall I?'

'Oh, thank you. That'd be most kind. Lady Northcliff won't be back till eight or so.'

Henry returned to his study and closed the door. He sat at his desk and wondered what on earth it was that Victoria wanted this time. It was a bit unreasonable of her, asking to see him like this. Surely nothing could be so urgent that it couldn't wait until a more convenient moment. He felt a little resentful. Particularly since, from the sound of it, the problem was serious. Not that she'd said a great deal. But if she couldn't even go to her own solicitor . . . He dreaded to think.

A boyfriend in trouble? Drugs again? Some people were doomed to attract disaster, and she was obviously one of them. Yet in a way he was rather curious to find out what it was. During his many years at the Bar he had never failed to be both amazed and fascinated by the difficulties people managed to create for themselves.

In Victoria's case he must try to be charitable. She was still finding her way in life. It was all too easy for him to mix with successful confident people all the time, and to forget that, for many others like Victoria, life was treacherous and riddled with false turns.

Still, this couldn't go on. She really had to learn to manage on her own.

He would see her. But this, he firmly decided, would be the last time.

Detective Constable Jenkins returned to the kitchen. He wondered whether to make himself another cup of coffee but decided against it. He'd already had five cups that day and they said it did terrible things to your blood pressure. But then the problem was really his weight. He was rather fond of his food.

He sat down at the table and picked up the *Financial Times*. It wasn't something he normally read, but he'd already digested his own copy of the *Mirror* from cover to cover, and Lady Northcliff had kindly left the *FT* and some of the other more serious newspapers out for him in case he got bored. She was a very thoughtful lady. Charming and kind too. And obviously very happy in her marriage. Mind you, what a nice man *he* was. He was everything Jenkins thought an upholder of the law should be: fair-minded, extremely learned, and very hard-working. Jenkins was proud to have been assigned to him.

Not everyone liked this sort of job, of course. That's why one had to volunteer to join the Protection Group. Other coppers liked to be where the action was and were horrified at the thought of guarding one individual for months on end. But Jenkins rather liked it. He was fond of routine and familiar surroundings.

Not that the job was entirely cosy, of course. There *was* a heavy responsibility. This bombing business was terrible. Killing the Commissioner's *wife* – you wondered what the devils would think of next. Nothing like this had ever happened in Britain before. It was appalling to think that these terrorists could get away with it. Well, of course, they *hadn't*. One of them had been caught, and now the identity of a second was known. A woman. He'd seen a rough facsimile of her photograph that morning at the briefing. A woman. Whatever next? It had been the Swinging Sixties that had done it. All that permissive society bit. Moral back-sliding, if you asked him.

Later, when the squad car would be coming to pick him up at the end of his shift, he would have a chance to look at a better print. They were bound to have a batch of posters available by then. As soon as the posters were distributed this lunatic woman wouldn't have a chance. Every copper in the entire country would be on the lookout.

Jenkins settled down to read the *Financial Times*. After a while he felt a bit peckish and reached into his pocket for a Mars bar.

Unwrapping the bar he bit into it, and tasting the thick gooey toffee, immediately felt comforted.

Gabriele rammed the van into second gear and turned into the tree-lined street. Ahead, the tail lights of the Mini slowed a little and she guessed they were almost there.

Beside her Giorgio pulled the holdall up from the floor on to his knee.

The Mini's indicator flashed and the car turned across the road and parked by the opposite verge in front of a large detached house set some forty feet back from the road. A double driveway led up to the house. Gabriele noticed it was particularly well lit.

She drove past and parked in front of the neighbouring house where it was much darker.

Victoria was already walking towards them. Gabriele got out and said, 'We think it would be best if we came with you.'

'But you said . . . *Why*?'

'If he meets us, then he's much more likely to believe us.'

Victoria looked indecisive.

Gabriele waited impatiently. She was tired of nursing this girl along.

Trying to sound reasonable, she pressed, 'We could wait in the hall. While you talk to him. We just thought it would make a difference if he could meet us, just for a second.'

Victoria sighed heavily, 'Oh, dear, I don't know. I really don't. It seems a bit . . .' She suddenly shook her head in defeat. 'Oh, all *right*.'

Giorgio appeared from the other side of the van. Automatically Gabriele glanced down to make sure he was carrying the holdall.

The three of them walked up the driveway to the front door.

Victoria put her finger on the bell.

After a moment clipped footsteps approached across a hard floor. They halted by the door and there was a pause. Gabriele guessed someone was looking through the peephole. She looked away towards the road.

A lock was turned and the door opened.

A voice said, 'Miss Danby?'

'Yes.'

'Come in.' A plumpish young man in an ill-fitting grey suit stood in the doorway.

Gabriele exchanged glances with Giorgio. She had guessed there would be some sort of bodyguard.

They went into the house. The young man closed the door behind them. Gabriele took another look at him. His hair was short, cut in an almost military style. She decided he was definitely a policeman. They moved into the centre of the spacious hall. Giorgio came up beside Gabriele. Keeping her eyes on the policeman she slowly reached down into the holdall and ran her hand over the two Skorpions to be sure they were the right way round.

The policeman was saying, 'I expect Sir Henry will be out in a minute.'

At that moment a door opened and a man appeared.

Sir Henry Northcliff.

Gabriele felt a small surge of excitement.

Sir Henry looked surprised at finding so many people in the hall. With a tense smile, he said, 'Hello, Victoria,' and came forward to kiss her cheek. The policeman watched from a distance.

The moment had come.

Gabriele took a deep breath and reached into the bag. Then, out of the corner of her eye, she felt the policeman looking at her.

She froze, her hand in the bag.

He was staring at her.

Something was wrong.

Shit!

She smiled at him.

He stared back, a look of horror slowly growing on his face.

With a sudden shock, she thought: *He knows who I am.*

In a strange way it rather added to the excitement. She remained perfectly still, her hand in the bag, and smiled at him.

She saw him gulp and wet his lips. Then he began to move slowly towards her.

She felt Giorgio stiffen. His free hand came across his body and slid into the holdall. She felt him grasp the other weapon. The policeman didn't seem to notice: he was still advancing, staring at Gabriele. Victoria and Sir Henry were still talking.

Slowly and deliberately, Gabriele pulled out her gun.

She saw the policeman's eyes drop in astonishment.

Then she yelled, a loud piercing whoop, and jumped backwards to give herself room. Almost simultaneously Giorgio pulled out his Skorpion and shouted, 'Don't move!'

Gabriele went straight into a firing stance, slightly crouched, the machine pistol lodged firmly against her ribs, her thumb against the safety lever, to ensure it was set on automatic. She aimed straight at the policeman's stomach.

Giorgio had retreated until he was covering the other two.

For a split second there was a deathly silence, the five of them frozen in a strange tableau.

Then Gabriele saw the rich-bitch opening her mouth and shrieking, 'What are you *doing*! What are you *doing! Stop it!*'

Giorgio shouted, '*Shut up!*'

The screaming seemed to have snapped the policeman out of

his trance. He began to move forward again, his face twisted with anger and fear.

Gabriele hissed, '*Don't*!'

The policeman said in a low voice, 'Drop that weapon!'

Gabriele clutched the Skorpion more tightly. The policeman hesitated for a moment, looking at the gun, then, making up his mind, stepped deliberately forward and reached out for it.

Gabriele felt the familiar panic surge up in her. She cried out: '*No*!'

He kept coming.

She squeezed the trigger.

It was just the same as in training: the strong feel of the gun in her hands, the juddering as the bullets left the silenced barrel, the soft *thwack! thwack*! as they hit their target. Except it wasn't a dummy now, it was a person.

The policeman staggered backwards, a look of amazement on his face, his hands clutching his stomach.

Then he fell slowly on to one knee, one hand on the floor, the other on his stomach. Blood spurted out all over the place.

Gabriele thought bitterly: That'll teach you.

The girl screamed, an ear-piercing screech that filled the room. She seemed to be able to scream for a long time without drawing breath.

The sound was getting on Gabriele's nerves. She strode up to the girl and thrust the pistol into her belly. The girl stopped in mid-scream.

'Shut up.'

The girl gaped.

Beside her the Attorney-General was very still and very white.

He understood perfectly.

There was a gurgling sound. It was the policeman dying. Gabriele glanced at him and, for a fleeting moment, felt a twinge of doubt. Then she remembered that she'd *had* to do it. She was a trained fighter, and the man had been attacking her. It was no different from a soldier defending himself against the enemy. Soldiers killed all the time.

Now they must hurry. She nodded to Giorgio. He reached into the fallen holdall and took out a roll of strong electrical tape. Putting the Skorpion down, he pulled Sir Henry's arms roughly behind his back and bound them together. He put another strip across his mouth.

Apart from briefly closing his eyes the man showed no emotion.

The girl, on the other hand, was a disaster.

She was gaping, her eyes starting from her head, and wailing loudly. Giorgio looked at Gabriele questioningly. She thought quickly, and said, 'No, bring her.'

Giorgio took hold of the girl's wrists and pulled them behind her back. Immediately she became hysterical.

Gabriele began to regret her decision; this girl was being a pain. Gabriele stepped forward and hit her hard on the side of the head with her hand.

The girl yelped and started sobbing more quietly. Gabriele said, 'Next time I'll use the gun.'

Giorgio grasped hold of the girl's chin and stuck a large piece of tape over her mouth. There was silence at last.

Gabriele went to the door and looked through the peephole. The driveway was clear. She tested the light switches beside the door. One worked the light in the hall, the other the outside lights.

She paused to think. She mustn't forget a single detail.

Going up to the Attorney-General she demanded, 'Is there anyone else in the house?'

He shook his head.

'Your wife's out?'

He nodded.

What else? The girl's shoulder bag. She picked it up and searched through until she found the keys to the Mini. She put the bag over her shoulder.

She had one last thought. She went up to the dead policeman. He was lying on his side in a pool of blood. She pulled open his jacket and searched the pocket. No radio transmitter that she could see. There was, however, a small notebook. She pulled it out and examined it. It was a sort of log. There were entries for each day, saying where the attorney-man had been, and, when at home, what visitors had called.

She looked at the last entry. It was for six-thirty when the attorney-man had arrived home. There was no mention of Victoria Danby.

She dropped the notebook on the floor.

She looked at Giorgio to see if he was ready. He nodded.

While he hustled the prisoners up to the door, she turned off all the lights and took a last look through the peephole.

The road was visible in the faint street lighting.

A car passed. Then nothing.

Opening the door, she listened and, satisfied, stepped back to let the others pass. She closed the door and ran on ahead to make sure there was no one coming along the road.

Behind her there was a slight sound. The stupid girl had stumbled and fallen, but Giorgio was dragging her back to her feet. Gabriele waved them forward to the van and, opening the doors, helped Giorgio to push the girl and the Attorney-General inside.

She ran to the Mini and got it started. As soon as the van moved off she followed. No car passed. No person walked the quiet road.

They had got away unseen.

Caroline Northcliff was tired, and sitting in a traffic jam didn't help. It was solid all the way from Westminster to Regent's Park, and by the time she got on to the Finchley Road the journey had already taken half an hour longer than usual. She couldn't imagine why: it was well past rush hour.

One way and another it had been a trying day. Normally she rather enjoyed going to do's at the House. On this occasion it had been a cocktail party given by the Parliamentary Wives Against Persecution. She'd had to go because she was on the committee. But she'd been feeling distinctly under the weather, and the noise and inevitably intense political conversations had been rather a strain.

Also, these occasions were meant to coincide with evenings when the House was sitting, so that the wives might dine with their husbands afterwards. But Henry had spent all day at his chambers and had then gone straight home to do some urgent work, so he'd not been able to come to the party. Somehow Caroline always felt incomplete and a little lonely when he wasn't around.

And now she was having to deal with all this beastly traffic.

Finally as she approached Hampstead the traffic thinned, and she realised she would be home very soon. What a relief. It was quarter to eight. With a bit of luck Henry would have finished his work, and they could enjoy a quiet evening. She wondered what to make for supper. Something light. There was some cold meat in the fridge, she remembered, and she could throw together a quick salad.

And then she usually offered the officer on duty a snack of some sort. She always felt sorry for the young men who were sent to guard them. It was such a rotten job, having to hang around all the time, knowing you were in the way, yet trying to be as unobtrusive as possible. Today Jenkins was on duty, and he never turned any food down. She smiled to herself.

She turned into the road and felt the tension of the day begin to ease. It was good to be home.

The road ahead seemed strangely dark. She couldn't work it out. Then she realised it was the area in front of her own house which was unlit. Yet she had carefully switched on the lights before going out. Had there been a power cut? No . . . there were lights in all the other houses. Perhaps the house lights had fused. Yet it was unlike Henry not to have fixed them.

She drove straight into the open garage and turned off the engine. As she got out it occurred to her that Henry might have been delayed at work and might not be home after all.

She closed the garage door and looked down the side of the house. The study light was on. Henry *must* be here then. How strange.

In the darkness it took her a moment to fit the key into the front door, but then the lock turned and she was in. She called, 'Hello?'

Light came from the open doors of both the kitchen and the study. She put a hand to the light switch and turned on the outside light. It worked perfectly. Then she tried the hall light.

For a second the light dazzled her.

Then she saw an object on the floor.

A person.

Jenkins.

For a moment she couldn't take it in. There was no reality to the blood, the ghastly open mouth, the silence of death.

Then she had a single appalling thought: *Henry!*

She stumbled to the study door and, terrified of what she might find, looked in. Then she ran across to the kitchen. When she had searched all the ground floor rooms, she ran upstairs.

Nothing.

She called out, 'Henry!' But the silence was final: there would be no answer.

Finally she sank on to the bed and, trying to control her shaking hands, called the police.

Victoria thought: Let me die.

It would be better for everyone.

I'm vermin, I'm evil, I'm sick, I'm hateful, I'm a pathetic *murderess* . . .

There was no limit to her evil.

It was her fault the policeman had been killed, her fault Henry had been captured, her fault that Caroline would be crucified with unhappiness.

It would be better for everyone if she were to die.

The van went over a bump. Her head banged against the floor. Good. She wanted to suffer. Let there be pain.

She cried again until the tears dried up.

Something nudged her leg. *Henry*. Trying to make contact with her. She was lying on the floor, facing away from him. She was glad. She couldn't possibly look him in the eye. She was glad, too, that the tape was over their mouths so they couldn't speak. The nudge came again. Hurriedly she moved her leg away. She couldn't bear it. He was trying to establish communication. But he wouldn't want to have any contact with her once he knew the truth.

She wanted to cry again, but couldn't. She was too disgusted with herself.

Much later, after the van had been going for a long time, a sound made her open her eyes. Someone was singing.

Giorgio.

She imagined him, sitting in the driver's seat, the same person who had touched her, made love to her . . . She had never *tried* to see him as he really was. She had been far too selfish.

Selfish, self-centred, *hateful*.

At one point the van stopped and there was a flood of light. The front door opened and shut again. There were the unmistakable sounds of petrol being put into the tank. Then they were off again, the van droning on endlessly.

She wondered vaguely where they were going. But what did it matter. It changed nothing.

She just wanted to die.

After a long time the van started twisting and turning and Victoria was thrown against the side of the seat, then back against Henry. Instantly she recoiled and tried to jam herself against the seat. A few minutes later there was a great lurch, then a bump and the back of the van did a violent leap. Victoria's head crashed into the floor. Another lurch and bump. The violent movements continued until Victoria was forced to hold her head clear of the floor.

The engine note changed to a lower pitch and they seemed to be going down a hill. There were several more lurches and the van climbed. Suddenly it ground to a halt.

The engine was turned off. The silence was abrupt and complete.

Then it was broken by a familiar sound: the distinctive high-pitched whine of the Mini. This came nearer, then stopped.

Doors were opened and closed. There were voices.

The rear doors of the van were unlatched and swung open with a loud squeak.

She felt Henry being pulled out from beside her. Then a hand grabbed her foot and pulled her roughly across the floor. She was twisted over on to her face so that, when she was half out, her feet fell to the ground.

'Stand up!' It was the woman's voice.

A hard object stabbed at her back, then a hand took her shoulder and pulled her upright.

Reluctantly she made the effort to stand.

Suddenly she tensed.

It was the sounds she recognised first: the murmuring of branches, the rustling of dead leaves, the crunch of the gravel underfoot. The unmistakable scent of damp fertile earth hung on the air.

She jerked her head up.

The shape of the farmhouse loomed black against the night, silhouetted against the pale light of a million stars.

Twenty-three

The road was jammed with parked cars. Nick drove past the brightly lit house and found a space further along. As he walked back an ambulance pulled out of the driveway and came towards him. The driver was in no hurry; they never were when it was a body.

Nick watched it pass and thought: Poor bastard.

At the entrance to the driveway a group of uniformed men were standing guard. As Nick approached, a TV crew came screaming up in a van and wound down their window. The sergeant in charge shook his head firmly. 'Complete embargo on this one, lads. Off you go.'

The newsmen nodded as if a story had been too much to hope for anyway, and drove off.

Nick showed his warrant card and walked up to the house.

He showed it again at the door and went in. The spacious hall was buzzing with men, standing in groups talking or walking desultorily around the sides. No one went near the centre of the room. Here an enormous patch of dried blood sat obscenely on the beautifully polished floor and, to one side of it, an outline of a body had been drawn in chalk.

Nick dragged his eyes away and looked around for one of Kershaw's team. A door opened and a group of men came out of an adjoining room. The first was Straughan, the second the head of Special Branch, Deputy Assistant Commissioner Norris, the third Kershaw, and then some very senior men indeed: the Assistant Commissioner Crime, and finally the Commissioner himself, Sir Peter McCabe. The Commissioner looked very grim. It was hardly surprising: he had buried his wife that afternoon.

Nick was overwhelmed by a sense of despair. He already felt a crushing guilt. This bloody mess got worse and worse. And all because he'd *never checked on her*. Even now he could hardly believe his own stupidity. The blow to his personal pride was bad enough; the way he'd been taken in by her. But pride didn't actually matter. What mattered was his professional failure – and that was unforgivable.

He leaned back against a wall and waited unhappily for the crowd of senior officers to break up so he could talk to Kershaw.

But Straughan spotted him first and glared. After a few minutes the DCS left the group and came over.

'Well, Ryder, what an almighty cock-up this is.'

'Sir.'

'I gather you not only *knew* this Wilson woman, but saw her as recently as *Sunday*. She must have been making bombs under your very nose!'

Nick winced. Salt in the wound. He said unhappily, 'She was a contact, sir – I mean, I *thought* she was.'

'*Thought* she was. Jesus Christ, Ryder, she'd already blown up the Commissioner's wife and injured two other people – and you thought she was a *contact*.' He put his face closer and hissed,

'You're off this job and I don't want to see your face around until I call for you. Understand?' The DSC was shaking with rage. Nick kept silent. It wasn't the moment to argue.

But Straughan hadn't finished. He pointed to the room he and the senior officers had just emerged from. 'Lady Northcliff is in there. Waiting, hoping to hear that her husband is going to be allowed to live. Shall I tell you something? I found it difficult to face her, knowing I had such a blindingly incompetent – *idiot* – on my staff. I found it –'

He broke off as someone cleared his throat. It was Commander Kershaw. He said to Straughan, 'May I have a word?'

Nick moved out of earshot and waited. The two men talked for several minutes then, with a last backward glance of disgust aimed in his direction, Straughan walked off. Kershaw came over.

He said quietly, 'I've said I want to keep you on my team, Ryder.'

'Thank you, sir.'

'It's simply that we've got to find these people.'

Nick nodded. He hadn't thought Kershaw was doing it out of the kindness of his heart.

Kershaw rubbed his eyes. 'It *is* the same bastards, isn't it, Ryder?'

Nick had never heard this soft-spoken man use even the mildest swear word before. He said, 'Yes. It must be.'

'What's going to happen next, then? Presumably there'll be some kind of demand. But what will they want? Money?'

Instinctively, Nick answered, 'No.' He thought of Gabriella and her half-baked philosophies and the intensity with which she believed them. 'Well, not *just* money. They'll want *more*. I think they'll want to humiliate us as much as possible. Publicly.' Nick voiced an idea he'd had when he'd first heard about the kidnapping. 'And I think they'll want their friends back.'

'Wheatfield?'

'And Reardon. And perhaps the woman, Stephanie Kitson, too.'

Kershaw nodded. 'Anything else, I wonder. What about getting out of the country? They can hardly expect to move around freely after all this.'

'I don't know . . .' Nick ventured. 'They've got excellent backup. The Wilson woman had an Italian passport, didn't she?' The agent who'd let Nick the mews house had been positive that she'd shown him an Italian passport in the name of Carelli. 'If they've got one false passport, they've probably got several.'

'But we've got her photograph.'

'We also know she uses disguises.'

'The woman at the delivery firm,' he agreed reluctantly.

Suddenly Kershaw closed the subject. 'Well, all this is conjecture. Let's get back to the office and plan the campaign. By the way' – he paused awkwardly – 'the ACC is taking personal charge of the case. So when we get back it might be wise for you to – er – stay upstairs in your own office. I'll call you when I need you.'

Kershaw turned to go but hesitated. 'I told your boss that I wanted you because you were the only person who understood these madmen. I also said you were a good officer. We all make mistakes at one time or another, Ryder. It's just a pity . . .'

Nick almost finished it for him: a pity that your mistake was so appalling. Nick said quickly, 'Thank you, sir. I appreciate it.'

Kershaw hurried off. Nick stared after him, both cheered and depressed by his words. A good officer . . . Just a pity . . . God, he didn't know whether to laugh or cry.

The least he could do for Kershaw was to give him maximum support. And at this precise moment that meant keeping a low profile.

He walked back towards the door and stopped for a moment to take another look at the brown stain on the floor.

He thought: Here an innocent man died. And I won't ever forget.

He turned to go, then noticed another chalk mark on the floor beside the outline of the body. One of Kershaw's team was standing nearby. Indicating the mark, Nick asked, 'What was that?'

'Jenkins' pocket book.'

'Was there any entry in it?'

The officer shook his head. 'Nothing after six-thirty.'

Nick thought for a moment and said, half to himself, 'I wonder why it fell on the floor?'

The officer shrugged. 'Search me.'

'*Could* it have fallen out of his pocket?'

There was no answer. The officer was giving him a cold look. Nick thought: Ah, I'm overstepping the mark – trespassing on detectives' territory. Then he realised that this alone wouldn't account for the cool attitude.

Of course: everyone knew. Everyone knew that it was Ryder who had ballsed it up.

Dropping his eyes, he nodded his thanks and left.

He didn't care what they thought. All he cared about was getting that woman.

It was eleven. He would go back to the office and work. All night if necessary. He would work until he found something.

Victoria jumped out of an uneasy doze. She was immediately aware of the cold, which had slowly penetrated her body and chilled her into a state of half-sleep from which it was difficult to wake. The earth floor was hard and rough against her cheek. She moved slightly and felt the tape that bound her wrists chafe her skin.

She opened her eyes. A faint grey light was filtering in from the main cellar, giving shadowy outline to the deep recesses of the brick chamber. She and Henry were in a second, smaller cellar, which consisted of two arches supported by wide pillars. The thin grey light emanated from a ventilation brick high up in the wall of the main cellar. Somewhere outside, it was day.

A loud noise: a door opening. Through the archway she saw a block of light. A figure stood silhouetted in the open doorway at the top of the cellar steps.

Giorgio.

Her first instinct was to curl up tighter and make the whole scene go away. But the next moment a bright electric light sprang on and footsteps sounded on the stone stairs. Screwing up her eyes against the glare, she saw Giorgio walking straight towards her. He bent over and reached for her face. She jerked her head away but he grasped the tape covering her mouth and yanked it off. She bit back a cry. He moved off towards the other corner where Henry lay. She made an effort to sit up. She rolled over on to her back and used her elbows to manoeuvre herself upright. Her over-full bladder ached for relief.

There was the sound of tape being ripped away. Victoria forced herself to look at Henry. He sat propped against the wall six feet away. He was blinking rapidly, his eyes smarting from the removal of the tape. His clothes were dishevelled, his hair awry, his face smeared with dirt. He seemed older and somehow smaller.

Suddenly he looked across at Victoria and narrowed his eyes in an unspoken gesture of mutual support.

Victoria's stomach lurched and she looked away.

Giorgio stood back and said to them both, 'The mouth tapes – they go on again if you make any noise.'

Victoria stared at him. She realised without surprise that he was *exactly* the same as before. He hadn't changed a bit. The only difference was in herself: she was seeing him for what he was.

Giorgio repeated, 'No noise. Understand?' He walked back into the main cellar, heading for the steps. He was going to leave them again. In the dark and cold.

Finding her courage, Victoria said, 'Please!' Her voice came out as a high-pitched whine. She controlled it. 'We need water. Please let us have water. And some blankets. And a lavatory.'

Giorgio paused deliberately on the first step and swung slowly round. He said heavily, 'I said no noise.'

She hesitated. '*Please*. Water. And a bucket. Something . . .'

He turned and walked deliberately up the stairs. Through the archway she saw him pause with his hand on the light switch.

She called out, 'And leave the light on. *Please*.'

He made a face of annoyance and, turning abruptly, went out and closed the door. The light was still on.

There was a long silence.

Eventually Henry said, 'Well done. We've got some light at least.' His voice sounded strangely matter-of-fact. He was trying to reassure her.

Victoria couldn't meet his eyes. 'I . . . I don't know what to say to you. It's all my fault. The whole thing. I . . .' She swallowed hard and forced herself to go on: she couldn't bear him to think that she was innocent. 'I – thought they were – *we* were – in trouble. They persuaded me to come and see you. I – had no idea that – they had guns or anything. I – was a complete fool. I—'

'Please stop.' The voice was firm and final.

'I just can't bear to think of what I've done to you.'

Henry said tensely. 'There's just no point in wasting energy on – talking.' He added less sternly, 'We may be here for a long time. We must – husband our resources. We must concentrate on dealing with these people in the only way they understand, which is to be businesslike. I suggest we speak only when we are spoken to, and without aggravating them in any way. We must be co-operative, but without earning their contempt. If we do have to make requests, we should make them politely and firmly. Then – at least we will have done all we can.'

He was right, of course. She could see that. He was being

everything she was not: cool and rational and dignified. He was refusing to be defeated by these people, and raising himself above their ghastliness. The least she could do was to support him. She thought: I mustn't let him down.

'Yes,' she said quietly, 'I agree.'

After a while he asked, 'Any idea where we are?'

She braced herself to speak the words. 'Yes. At – my farm.'

He looked at her sharply. 'Then – someone will find us, surely. Someone will call in, won't they?'

'Only people hoping to buy the place . . . But there haven't been many, so the agent said . . .' She trailed off.

'But people will realise you're missing. So they're *bound* to come here.' There was a note of optimism to his voice.

Victoria shook her head slowly. 'I'm afraid not . . . I don't think anyone will miss me.' She thought: What a thing to be able to say.

'But –' He broke off. Finally he said in quiet resignation, 'I was thinking that, once they realised you'd come to my house, they would work it out from there.'

'Yes?'

'But no one knew. Except Jenkins.'

There was a heavy pause and they did not speak for a long time.

Victoria thought about her life and how different it would be in the future. If she ever got out of this she would be utterly changed. Unselfish and caring. She would spend her life serving other people. She would never be the same again. Never.

The cellar door opened.

The woman came down the steps. A gun was slung over her shoulder, the gun she had used before.

She peered at them, then disappeared, leaving the door open. When she reappeared she was walking backwards, carrying something large and heavy. It was a long wooden box with handles. Giorgio was carrying the other end.

Victoria blinked. She recognised the box: it belonged to the tractor. It contained all the spare parts – the couplings, the tools, the wheel braces. But *why* were they bringing it down here?

They moved with a relentless purpose that filled her with foreboding.

They brought the box into the brick chamber and dumped it on the floor. The woman opened the lid. Victoria saw that the hinged lid had been sawn into two sections, and the interior partitions removed.

296

Giorgio went up to Henry and pulled him to his feet. Reaching behind, he cut the tapes from Henry's wrists. Henry stretched his arms and let out a long gasp of relief and pain.

The woman stood back a little way. She had the gun at her hip, aimed at Henry.

Victoria watched, stiff with dread.

The woman said, 'Get in.'

There was a ghastly silence. No one moved.

'Get in!'

Victoria stared in horror. She meant into the *box*.

Henry drew a long and deep breath. He looked very white. He took a step forward and stared at the box. He whispered, 'I don't think I'll fit.'

'*Get in!*'

Henry swayed slightly, then leant down to take off his shoes.

Victoria said, 'No!'

The woman turned the barrel of the gun on her. 'Shut . . . up . . .'

Henry stood at the side of the box, staring down into it, disbelief on his face. He looked up at the woman questioningly.

She hissed, 'This is the last time. *Get in!*'

Slowly he climbed in and attempted to lie down. The box was too short by at least a foot and he could not straighten his knees. The woman stepped forward and, pushing his knees over to one side, forced the main section of the hinged lid shut. The smaller lid section was left open, so that only Henry's face remained visible.

The woman said, 'That'll do.'

She went back up the steps and disappeared. Giorgio stood back, apparently waiting for the woman to return.

Victoria climbed to her feet and staggered over to him. 'You can't do this! It's appalling and cruel! You can't do it!'

He regarded her calmly. 'Why not? Tell me.'

'Because – it's *inhuman*.'

He shrugged. 'The whole world is inhuman. Especially humans. They are the worst of all. Didn't you realise that?'

'But *he's* not inhuman. He's – a *good* man!'

He was contemptuous. 'You don't know *anything*. You're a spoilt child, Victoria. You're rich and stupid. Yet people like you rule the world. Why should that be? It must be wrong. And you tell me that *I* am inhuman.' He shook his head. 'You try being poor and having nothing, Vittoria, and being shut up in jail by people like *him*!' He shot a glance at Henry. 'Your little world would not be so happy.' He spoke with exasperation and contempt.

She whispered bitterly, 'You're *sick*! You should be *put down*! You—'

The cellar door opened. The woman was returning.

Giorgio said under his breath. 'Get away or she'll kill you.'

Victoria knew it was true. She retreated into the main cellar and shrank back against the wall.

The woman ran down the steps, carrying a holdall. She glared at Victoria, and went past her into the small cellar. She barked at Giorgio, 'Keep the gun on him. In case he moves.' Giorgio aimed it at Henry's head.

Then the woman set to work. Victoria watched through the archway. At first she couldn't understand what the woman was doing. Then Gabriele reached into the holdall and Victoria caught sight of the contents, and felt very sick.

The sticks. The explosives that had been hidden in the van.

Victoria cried softly, 'Oh no . . . Oh no . . .'

The woman worked inexorably on. She taped a bundle of the explosives together and placed them on Henry's chest.

Victoria moved forward. 'Let it be *me*. Please,' she begged. 'Let it be *me* instead. Oh *please*. Let him go. Oh *please*.'

The woman bent down to replace something carefully on the ground. Then she whirled round. The first thing Victoria saw was the gun butt coming through the air, then there was an explosion in her head and she was falling rapidly backwards.

She fell heavily and for a moment lay stunned. She regained her breath and slowly, painfully, pulled herself upright. The woman was working on. She was strapping the explosives to Henry's body. Then she sat down on the floor and remained bent over some intricate task for a long time. Finally she knelt over Henry and, moving very carefully, appeared to complete her work. She gestured to Giorgio to close the lid of the box very slowly. Just before it closed, she peered under it and nodded.

Giorgio put down his gun and, taking some nails and a hammer from the holdall, nailed down the lid of the box. Finally the woman bent down beside the box and pulled at something.

The woman stood up, a length of thread in her hand. She looked rather pleased with the job. She said, 'Right. This thing is booby-trapped. If anyone tries to open it, it'll go sky high. I'm the only one who knows how to defuse it. Understand?'

Then she bent over Henry's face and whispered, 'How does it feel, attorney-man? How does it feel to be locked up like all those kids in prison? Like being in a coffin, isn't it? Soon you'll be lying in your own dirt, in your own coffin. *Then you'll know.*'

Victoria thought: *This is a nightmare.*

The woman tidied away her tools. She was very neat.

Giorgio came towards Victoria. He had a knife in his hand. Victoria held her breath. He reached behind her. The next moment her hands were free. He said, 'You are to keep him alive. I'll bring water and food later.'

Then he and the woman were leaving, climbing the stairs, switching off the light, closing the door.

Victoria crawled slowly back into the small cellar, feeling for the box with her hands in case she should bump into it. Finally she came to it. Kneeling close beside it, she put her head near to Henry's and cried softly, 'Henry . . .'

She paused. There *were* no words. She breathed, 'Oh, Henry, I'm so – desperately – sorry.'

There was no reply.

She began to cry silently. 'If there's anything I can do – I will. I *will.*'

Finally, after a long while, there came a whisper.

'Leave me alone. Leave me – alone.'

Gabriele zipped up the holdall and put it in the kitchen. She glanced at her watch. Eleven. Time was getting on. In Paris it was already twelve.

She took the slip of paper out of her handbag and, going to the phone that stood on the window-sill in the hall, she dialled the number of the dingy offices in the Latin Quarter. She'd already called the number once that morning, but much earlier.

It answered.

'Raymond? Any news?'

'Far, far too soon,' came the reply. 'It will take me many more hours. It is not something that can be arranged quickly.'

'I thought there would be no problem—'

'I am sure there will not, but it is still something that cannot be rushed.'

'When shall I call back?'

'Tonight.'

Gabriele hung up. She hated the uncertainty. She wanted all the arrangements to be made and her retreat secure. But she would have to press on.

She took a sheet of paper from her handbag and unfolded it. Earlier she had spent some time composing a communiqué. She had rewritten it several times until she was satisfied. However she had been forced to leave a blank after the words 'Guarantee free passage to'. Now, reluctantly, she wrote in: 'the country of our choice.'

Then, on the stroke of twelve, she lifted the telephone and dialled a number in London.

Nick's mind felt like a thick soup. It was twelve noon. He'd been at it since midnight and had come up with precisely nothing.

He'd begun with listing everything he could remember about Gabriella. Everything she'd said or done. Everything she'd worn, down to her jewellery, which was one gold chain around her neck. Details of her life history, year by year. Conway and two other Branch men had helped there; they'd been on the task all the previous day, finding out about the missing years between university and the present time. At first there'd been several large gaps in her history, but one by one they had been accounted for. She'd been issued with a permit for a stall at Camden market and had sold second-hand books there; she'd worked briefly at a small publishing company; she'd been involved in a housing action group; she'd spoken at minor anti-Vietnam meetings, she'd applied for unemployment benefit. Gradually the picture had built up.

There was only one large gap remaining, and that was for the time between her escape from the hospital in Paris and her reappearance in London as Gabriella Carelli. The gap was sixteen months. Where had she been in that time? There was no clue.

The French couldn't help. They had no trace of her in the chaos after the student uprising. The Italians? They had never heard of her. The British Intelligence Service, MI6, could offer no suggestions.

It was a mystery.

But wherever she had been, she had learnt to make bombs and kill people.

Next Nick turned to Black Beard.

Wheatfield's friend – and Gabriella's lover?

He had to be. Who else had the clothes in the mews house

300

wardrobe belonged to? And the masculine toiletries in the bathroom?

It was another realisation that made Nick sick with remorse. Black Beard had been close by all the time. A simple check, a surveillance, would almost certainly have led straight to him.

The immigration files had been combed for any likely Italians who fitted Black Beard's description, but thousands and thousands of Italians visited Britain every year. It was like looking for a needle in a haystack.

The Italian authorities had promised to look at their own lists of undesirables to see if they had any who fitted the sketchy description Nick had sent them, but it was pretty hopeless. The situation in Italy was what one might call confused. The authorities didn't really know the nature – let alone the names – of the new left-wingers they were up against.

So much for Black Beard.

Then there were Wheatfield and Reardon. Both had their lips sealed as tight as clams. Barring torture – which was unfortunately banned under the British system – there was no way of getting them to talk.

Dead end. Nothing.

And now his mind was like soup: turgid and thick and utterly useless.

He thought: Damn and hell!

At twelve-twenty a call came up from the incident room.

It was Kershaw. The ultimatum had arrived.

As Nick sprinted downstairs he reflected on Kershaw's choice of word. Ultimatum. He shivered: it didn't bode well.

The message had been phoned to *The Times* fifteen minutes before. It read:

You can dream up all the law and order you like, but you shall be subject to our justice. The attorney-man has been sentenced to death for gross crimes against the people. However, if our terms are met we shall consider leniency. Free Max Wheatfield, Paul Reardon and Stephanie Kitson. Guarantee us free passage to the country of our choice. You have until noon tomorrow or he dies. There will be no negotiation. Print your acceptance in *The Times* tomorrow. We will then contact you. Remember – twenty-four hours and he is dead. It is the people's justice. Signed: The Crystal Faction.

Kershaw went straight off for a top level conference in the Commissioner's office, leaving Nick, Conway and a group of detectives in the incident room. Everyone read the ultimatum several times. Conway murmured, 'We'll give in. We have no choice.'

Nick hoped not, but he could see the attraction for the government. Sir Henry would be returned alive and the terrorists would be out of the country. The only sensible solution ... But *humiliating*. It was total surrender. He thought of the way Gabriella and her friends would laugh. The way they'd be encouraged to do it all over again somewhere else.

Nick rubbed his hand over his face. He was too tired to think any more. He'd had two nights without sleep. He wasn't going to be any use to anyone in his present state. He stood up wearily and said to Conway, 'I've got to go and get some kip. If anyone wants me I'll be back in a few hours.'

On his way out he stared at the story board Kershaw's team had drawn up. On a large sheet of paper that spanned almost an entire wall they had written the sum total of their knowledge, along with various suppositions and possibilities. Thus Linda Wilson's name was prominent in black on the left-hand side, while the words *Soviet-backed? Self-motivated? Allied to foreign group?* were written in blue just underneath.

In the centre was a series of questions with answers, such as: *Why the Attorney-General? Because senior law officer. Motive for kidnap? Ransom or political demands (assumed).*

On the right-hand side there was a scenario: Doorbell rings, Jenkins/Sir Henry opens door, three shots fired, Jenkins falls, hall and outside lights extinguished, Sir Henry abducted. Then there were various unknowns: vehicles used by abductors, route taken, destination.

God, if they knew the *destination*.

Then there were a list of facts: the approximate time the crimes took place, the ballistics details, the wounds suffered by D. C. Jenkins, the location of the pocket book. At the bottom someone had added: *N.B. Blood on underneath of Jenkins' pocket book.*

Nick stared, trying to comprehend the meaning of the cryptic note.

Under? Then the book had been placed on the floor *after* the blood had spread.

What else did it mean? He tried to progress the idea, but his mind wouldn't function. He gave up.

He went back to his office to pick up his coat and took the lift down to the street. It was a blustery day, with heavy black clouds scudding across the sky. London looked very grey.

He walked to the nearest bus stop, intending to take a number 10 over the river. There was a long queue at the stop and no buses in sight. He stood in line and wondered if it wouldn't be better to walk.

Funnelled between the tall buildings the wind came roaring down the street in great gusts. People clutched at their coats. A man left the queue to shelter in a shop doorway. He reached into his breast pocket and pulled out a small map, which he examined and then replaced in his pocket.

Nick stared at him.

Jenkins would have kept his book in his breast pocket. Could it have slipped out after he had fallen bleeding to the floor? Unlikely. In which case someone must have taken it out of his breast pocket and placed it on the floor afterwards.

But *why*?

A half-formed idea flew into Nick's mind, and he grasped at it furiously. Maddeningly, it evaded him and in a desperate attempt to recapture it, he went through each thought one by one.

Why would they want to look at the book? To see what it had in it. So what would it have in it?

Information. Sir Henry's movements that day.

It didn't make sense. Why would they want to know that? Curiosity. *No*. They were in a hurry, they didn't have time to be curious . . .

Come on. *Come on*.

A bus drew up noisily and the queue moved forward. Nick remained still, staring into space. People overtook him and clambered on to the bus.

Then he had it.

The idea came winging back into his mind and he cornered it.

They'd left the book *behind*. So everything had all been all *right*. They'd checked the book. They had checked the book to make sure there was nothing in it.

Therefore it was what *wasn't* there that was important.

Since coming on duty Jenkins had kept a record of Sir Henry's movements, or had appeared to. Except for . . .

The last appointment.

Nick turned and ran back to the office.

As he went up in the lift, another thought fell into place, like a piece in a jigsaw.

Jenkins *must* have opened the door. He would never have stood on one side and let Sir Henry do it. What was more, *Jenkins had opened the door and let the people all the way into the centre of the hall.*

He wouldn't have done that if they had been strangers. He would have challenged them on the doorstep.

Nick pounded into Kershaw's office, but the commander was still in his meeting. Nick spotted Conway sitting in the incident room drinking a cup of coffee, and beckoned him over. Conway caught the mood immediately and hastily followed him into Kershaw's office. Nick scribbed a note and left it on Kershaw's desk.

'What's up?' asked Conway.

'We're going to see Lady Northcliff.'

The room looked over the garden. She sat on the window seat, looking tired and pale in the grey light. Nick hadn't realised how young she would be.

'I'm very sorry to bother you,' Nick began, aware of the disapproving gaze of the other occupants of the room: a chief inspector from Special Branch Protection Group, a senior member of the Attorney-General's staff, and a woman of about Lady Northcliff's age, presumably a friend.

'No, please – I *want* to help,' Lady Northcliff said immediately. 'I'm glad . . . I don't care how many questions you ask me.' She shrugged apologetically. 'If I looked disappointed it was only because I thought it might be news. When I heard the doorbell.'

Nick was silent. He hadn't told her about the ultimatum. That was someone else's job – someone very senior – and, on an entirely practical level, he didn't want her distracted with worry until he'd had a chance to put his questions.

'Lady Northcliff, what I'm about to ask may seem rather strange . . .'

The chief inspector looked even more threatening. The only reason Nick had got in for the interview was by saying Kershaw had sent him.

'The thing is, are you or your husband acquainted with anyone with extreme political views? I mean, even *slightly* acquainted?'

You could have heard a pin drop. Everyone in the room looked vaguely horrified. Lady Northcliff frowned in concentration. 'It's so difficult to say,' she began. 'We meet so *many* people. At receptions and so on. It's very hard to know exactly what their views are. I mean quite a few members of the Labour Party used to be well, *more* left-wing than they are now.'

'Yes, of course.' Nick paused and wondered quite how to phrase the next question. 'What about people you know well enough to see here, in your house?'

There was an awkward silence.

She gulped slightly. 'Oh, you mean . . .' Nick could almost see her thought processes working their way to the inevitable conclusion. 'You mean – the people – last night – might have been known to us.'

The chief inspector frowned at Nick and narrowed his lips.

Nick ignored him. 'Yes, don't misunderstand me. I'm not suggesting that one of your closest friends is involved. I'm just asking if – by any chance – someone's name was used to gain access to the house. Or an appointment was made. Or . . .'

She nodded. 'No, you don't have to explain . . . I understand.' She put a hand over her eyes and thought for a long time. Finally she shook her head and sighed deeply. 'No. I'm sorry—'

'What about left-wing journalists?'

'Well, journalists *sometimes* come here. And it depends what you mean by left-wing . . . Besides, they always make appointments a long time ahead. And Henry wouldn't see one here during a weekday evening. He just wouldn't. Not without telling me.'

'Someone else then? One of these new activists. You know, the sort that go on anti-Vietnam marches?'

'Well, I met that actress once. You know, the one who's always making speeches . . .' She trailed off. It wasn't the sort of information Nick wanted and she knew it.

Nick tried one last stab. 'What about an acquaintance, a friend, the son or daughter of a friend. Anyone who's involved in fringe politics, or pressure groups, or anti-war campaigns. *Anything.*'

A shadow of a smile crossed her face. 'Oh, well, there's dear old Victoria of course.'

Nick waited.

Lady Northcliff suddenly realised he wanted to hear more and continued, 'She's a sort of cousin of mine, and – she dabbles in anti-Vietnam things. But very half-heartedly. She's a bit of a lost soul, one way or another.'

'But she comes here from time to time?'

'Very occasionally. When she needs advice, generally.'

'What's her name, Lady Northcliff?'

'Her name? Oh, Victoria Danby. But really, she's perfectly harmless . . .'

Nick managed to keep his face completely impassive. 'Well – perhaps we'd better just talk to her. Routine, you understand. Could you give me her address?'

'Oh . . .?' Then she shook her head as if bringing herself to her senses. 'Yes, of *course*.' She searched in her handbag and found an address book. 'It's Moscow Road, W2. Number 53.'

He rose to his feet. 'Thank you, Lady Northcliff. Again, I'm sorry to have bothered you.'

Her eyes filled with disappointment at the realisation that the interview was over and that she could be of no more help. She nodded a brief goodbye then turned to stare out into the wind-swept garden.

Twenty-four

It was four-thirty and already dark. Gabriele drove into the airport tunnel and glanced in the mirror. There was no reason to suppose anyone would be looking for her, but it was an automatic reflex now to examine other cars.

The Mini whined its way up the incline at the other end. The sooner she was rid of the car the better. It belonged to the girl and she didn't like the idea of using it any longer. More to the point, it was old and not very fast and probably unrealiable. It had to go.

Also it had been essential to get away from the farmhouse. The place got on her nerves. There was nothing to do there. Except wait. And she was incapable of just sitting and waiting. She had an insatiable need to attend to each detail, to cover each possibility. Everything must be neat and tidy.

Taking a ticket at the barrier, she drove into the car park beside Terminal 2, and parked in a dark corner of an upper storey. She scraped back her hair and twisted it into a knot on the back of her head. As an after-thought she pulled a scarf out of her bag and tied it round her head. She pulled out a deep tote bag and hitched it over her shoulder. In it was the Skorpion: she took it everywhere now. She liked the idea of carrying it into crowded places, as if it were a harmless piece of luggage. The Kalashnikov was far too bulky for this sort of work, and she had left it at the farmhouse.

As a back-up she had a handgun, a Walther 38, in her coat pocket.

She locked the car and dropped the keys in a waste bin some distance away. As she walked across the bridge to the terminal building, she slipped on a pair of dark glasses.

The arrivals floor was thronged with people. There was a long queue at the Hertz desk, so she moved on to the Avis desk. There were three people ahead of her. They seemed to be taking a long time. She glanced around.

A pair of uniformed policemen were walking slowly through the crowd towards her, examining the faces of the people hurrying by. One looked straight at Gabriele. He hesitated in his stride, then continued his professional swagger. But his eyes stayed on her and, inclining his head to his partner, he muttered a few words.

Hastily Gabriele thought: It means nothing. It's just the dark glasses. Or they like eyeing girls.

It means nothing.

The two policemen halted a few yards away. One reached into his pocket and pulled out a sheet of paper. His partner peered over his shoulder to look at it.

Gabriele felt the first flutterings of excitement and fear.

The two men looked at her again, as if comparing her to something on the sheet of paper. She stared back at them through the dark glasses.

They were coming towards her now. Casually she turned her head away and changed her attitude, moving her weight to the other leg, and putting her hand in her pocket. Her hand closed over the grip of the Walther.

'Excuse me, madam.'

She turned slowly. 'Yes.'

'What is your name, please?'

She raised her eyebrows in surprise. 'My name? It is Anneke van Duren.' She put on the slightest accent.

'Your nationality?'

'I am Dutch.'

'Could we see your passport, please?'

She took her hand out of her pocket, and reached into the

shoulder bag. Opening the inner zip compartment, she brought out the Dutch passport.

They examined it, looking carefully at the picture.

'Could we ask you to remove your sunglasses, please?'

Slowly, Gabriele took them off and put them in her coat pocket. She grasped the Walther again.

The two men compared her face with the passport photograph and the information on the sheet of paper. Gabriele craned her neck and took a quick look over the top of the piece of paper. There was a photograph on it.

Her stomach lurched.

She said, laughing, 'Is that someone who looks like me?'

They both stared at her. One said, 'Whereabouts in Holland do you live?'

'Amsterdam.'

'Do you have any other form of identification?'

She shrugged happily. 'Sure.' She reached into the same compartment of her handbag and pulled out a driving licence.

One took it and asked, 'What's the address on this?'

Treating it like some great joke, Gabriele gave them the correct address in a suitably guttural Dutch accent.

The two men glanced at each other. It was obvious that they were uncertain about what to do. Feeling more confident, Gabriele said brightly, 'I'm sorry if I'm not the right person.'

One nodded at her and handed back the passport and driving licence.

Gabriele smiled, 'Thank you. I hope you find the person you are looking for.'

The two men pulled back and stood some distance away, talking between themselves. Gabriele turned her attention to the Avis desk. A second girl was just coming on duty and waved Gabriele forward. Gabriele forced herself not to look at the policemen again until all the paperwork had been done. Then, gathering up the keys of the hire car, she turned to go.

The policemen were nowhere in sight.

Nevertheless she was exceptionally careful. She went to the ladies' washroom and spent several minutes there. Coming out, she took another look round. Then she went by a circuitous route to the hire car pick-up point, going downstairs, through the departure hall, then back along the outside of the building, as if she were slightly lost.

When the Avis bus arrived, she took a seat near the back so she could keep watch on the road behind. By the time the bus dropped her at the Avis depot she was certain there was no one following her.

But it had been a close thing.

Once safely in the hire car – a Ford Escort – she took stock.

The photograph. She had recognised it immediately. It had been taken when she was eighteen.

Linda Wilson.

They knew all about her then.

How? Not through Max. *Never* Max.

How?

She went through all the possibilities – but there was really only one.

Nick Riley. It had to be.

Just the thought of him made her wince.

He must have gone to the mews house, and guessed she had done a bunk. He must have combed his records, just like the filthy little spy he was, and finally linked her to Linda Wilson.

He must be gloating at his success.

Or was he?

Suddenly she saw the other side of it. He'd had a terrorist right under his nose, *in bed* . . . And never realised. What a humiliation for him. What a fool he must look to his colleagues. He must be sick at having been taken for such a ride.

The thought took some of the edge off her anger and made her feel slightly better.

And as for the police having her identity – in a way she was rather pleased. Now they knew who they were dealing with. No one would ever take her lightly again. They would broadcast her name on television. Petrini would hear about it, and the Lotta in Milan, and Raymond in Paris. From now on her name would be synonymous with active struggle . . . And that pleased her.

She drove on to the A4, heading west towards the farmhouse.

A new worry nagged at her mind.

It was a potentially serious one. It would be unwise to use the Dutch identity again. Which left just one passport – the Argentinian one hidden in Chelsea – to get her out of the country. A single passport. And no margin for error.

It was all a matter of control.

Dear God.

The longing to move was so powerful that Henry had to grit his teeth to stop himself from trying to break out of the box. His mind had accepted the necessity to stay still, but his body hadn't. The muscles in his legs were burning with a terrible energy that was independent of his brain. He had the awful feeling that, if he stopped concentrating for a moment, his legs would spring out from his body and force open the lid of the box.

After a while he tried moving his toes in the hope that this would alleviate the pressure on his legs. But it only encouraged his leg muscles to scream out for action, and the burning sensation was almost more than he could bear.

Control. He must *not* lose control.

In the wild rangings of his imagination the loathsome package on his stomach seemed, at one moment, to be benign and incapable of causing the slightest harm, and the next moment, to be so evil that he could almost feel it burning a hole in his stomach, like a ball of virulent acid.

Reaching for lifelines, he tried concentrating on work, on a new bill the PM wanted ready for the next session. He made himself go through the proposed clauses one by one.

On the fourth clause his mind wandered to Caroline . . .

With an effort he brought his thoughts back to the bill, but her image floated into his mind again.

Yielding, he indulged himself for a moment, and thought of her sweet face and her lovely smile and how much he loved her.

But thinking about Caroline was a slippery slope. He imagined her now, worried to death and having to face the full horror of the situation without him, and he felt so angry at the savage inhumanity of these people that he wanted to assault them physically.

But that of course was exactly what they wanted: to provoke him. Whatever happened, he must never give them that satisfaction.

Control.

Oh, but it was hard . . .

Thinking about Caroline gave him a desperate appetite for life. It was impossible to face the idea of death with any equanimity at all. Death would be an outrage, an appalling waste. The thought was so painful that he had to clench his fists to force the emotion out of his mind.

The voice, when it came, seemed to float on the air. 'Henry – would you like some water?'

Victoria.

He opened his eyes. The light was on. She was kneeling beside him. He said, 'Yes, a little . . .'

She held the water cupped in her hands and dripped it into his mouth. She said, 'They left the water in a bowl. I didn't want to risk spilling it all over you.'

'Thank you.' He took a little more, then shook his head. He didn't want to take too much liquid. He had already had to relieve himself where he lay. A singularly unpleasant experience, but a necessary one which was surprisingly easy when one had no choice in the matter. Since then he had deliberately ignored the uncomfortable wetness of his clothing; as a matter of principle he refused to let it bother him. None the less, it was something he would rather not have to repeat too often.

'Have you managed to sleep?' Victoria asked.

'Not really.'

'I left you – in case.'

She offered him food, but he refused.

She said, 'Do you want to talk?'

He looked at her. She was much more composed now, as if she had made an enormous effort to suppress her feelings. The expression on her round freckled face was cool and concerned. He remembered his own word: businesslike.

He said, 'Yes, let's talk.' Talking would be useful; it would help take his mind off the object on his stomach.

She looked relieved. She asked rather formally, 'Is there anything in particular that you would like to talk about?'

He could think of a dozen things he *didn't* want to discuss. He sighed deeply. It was all too much.

She said immediately, 'What about talking about all the things the police are doing at this very moment to find us?'

The place was in darkness but they took no chances.

First ultra-sensitive listening devices were put against the walls. Then marksmen with Enfields were positioned on the roofs opposite. When they finally went in, the first men through the broken door carried Smith and Wesson .38s.

They had taken no chances. But they need not have bothered. The flat was empty.

Nick went in behind Kershaw and Conway. As soon as the armed men had withdrawn, Kershaw's detectives got silently down to work.

Nick went quickly from room to room. Everything was neat and tidy. There were no signs of hurried departure. Nor had Victoria Danby been away for very long. The milk in the fridge was fresh, the soft fruit on the small dining table was not overripe. There was only one letter lying on the mat inside the front door, and that had been posted the day before.

The flat looked so normal that Nick had the dreadful feeling he'd got it all wrong again and that Victoria Danby bore no connection to anything at all.

He wandered around the living-room. Behind the sofa a pillow and eiderdown lay carefully folded in a neat pile on the floor.

An extra guest.

In the bedroom the bed was made and the coverlet smoothed over without a crease. In the bathroom the towels were folded over the hot rail and some women's underwear was drying on a rack in the bath.

All horrendously normal.

Back in the living-room Kershaw was on the phone, a letter in his hand. He gestured Nick towards an expandable cardboard file which someone had put on the table. Covering the mouthpiece, Kershaw said, 'Go through the rest of this lot, will you, Ryder?'

The concertina-type file had twenty compartments. The Danby girl was very orderly. Each was carefully marked with a category. Nick began with cars. There were two registration documents: one for a camper van, one for a Mini. He waved them in front of Kershaw just as Kershaw said into the telephone, 'Is this Mrs Danby? My name is Commander Kershaw of the Serious Crimes Squad at Scotland Yard . . .'

Nick placed the papers in various piles. There was a passport – the details matched those obtained half an hour ago from the passport office; three sterling travellers' cheques for ten pounds each; an outer folder showing that two cheques had been cashed only a week before, in Paris. Some French money. A ferry booking – again for only the week before.

Kershaw was saying, 'So you have no idea where your daughter might be, Mrs Danby? We wouldn't find her at work somewhere?'

Another compartment contained bills, marked 'Paid' with a date scribbled underneath. Another, bank statements. There was certainly no shortage of money. Nick wondered where it all came from.

Kershaw was asking patiently, 'May I ask, Mrs Danby, does your daughter still have two vehicles, a Mini and a – VW camper van?'

Nick went to the next compartment marked: Hunter's Wood. In it were more bills for a property somewhere in Wiltshire. There were also letters from a firm of solicitors called Makepiece & Makepiece, concerning the purchase of the property in May of 1968. Then another series of letters, which were much more recent, relating to a sale.

As Kershaw said, 'It is vital we find your daughter, Mrs Danby, to eliminate her from our inquiries,' Nick put one of the solicitor's letters in front of him and pointed to the Wiltshire address.

Kershaw said, 'Mrs Danby, does your daughter have any connection with a property in Wiltshire, a place called Hunter's Wood?'

Nick went quickly through the last few papers: letters from someone who might be a sister; an old diary; some invitations to weddings and parties – all very grand, he noticed.

Kershaw was bringing his conversation to a close, murmuring the appropriate thanks and apologies. He put the phone down.

'Nothing much,' he said, 'She doesn't work. Money of her own. The mother has no idea where she is. Oh, and that place, the farm, has been sold. The girl hasn't lived there for some time.'

Nick had a sinking feeling in the pit of his stomach. This was getting nowhere. He couldn't believe it. The Danby girl had been at the pre-demo meeting that Wheatfield and Black Beard had attended. And she knew the Attorney-General. There had to be a connection. *Surely*.

He wandered round, watching the team of men at their work. They were taking the place apart, ripping the bottoms out of the sofa and chairs, pulling up the floorboards, emptying all the food out of containers ... Kershaw's orders had been simple: he wanted information at any cost, even if it meant losing fingerprints.

In the bathroom a man was bent over the bath removing hairs from the surface enamel with a tweezer. He said, 'Straight black hair here. Isn't the Danby girl fair?'

Nick nodded. So she had a friend with dark hair ...

Another man was emptying tins of talcum powder on to a sheet of polythene. Three tubes of toothpaste lay waiting to be given the same treatment. In the bathroom cabinet a few items remained: a woman's shaving kit, some medicines and ointments, suntan lotion. On top of the cabinet were bottles of half-used shampoo.

A sponge bag in a bright floral pattern lay on top of some boxed-in pipework beneath the sink. He unzipped it: nothing special.

A rubbish bin. He poked through it with one finger. Dirty face tissues, pieces of cotton wool, a razor blade, and –

His heart stopped with a thud.

He whispered, '*Jesus!*'

He reached slowly down and picked out an empty bottle.

The bottle had contained eau de cologne. Brand: Rocco. Made in Italy. Legend: *Per uomini*.

Nick thought: Don't get excited. But he did.

It *couldn't* be coincidence.

Holding the empty bottle by the neck he took it into the living-room and, catching Kershaw's eye, held it up.

Giorgio brought food again in the evening. He put it next to the cheese and bread that remained untouched from the afternoon.

Victoria ignored him. She wasn't going to give him the satisfaction of begging. That was all in the past. She sat stolidly beside Henry and waited for Giorgio to leave.

But he lingered, standing by the archway, watching her.

She realised he wanted to talk.

'Poor little Vittoria,' he murmured. 'Life is not so beautiful . . . But soon you will be home in your big rich house.'

She said unbelievingly, 'I will?'

'Of course. The pigs will give in. Completely. They have no choice.'

She'd imagined that the motive for capturing Henry was something to do with revenge. The idea of bargaining was unexpected. Glancing at Henry, she got to her feet and beckoned Giorgio into the main cellar.

'What are you asking for?' she whispered.

'The release of our comrades. Free passage.'

Victoria felt a spark of hope. They weren't asking much. The government was bound to give in.

'And Henry? You'll let him go free, won't you? And you'll let him out of that thing as soon as your people are free. *Won't* you?'

Giorgio shrugged. 'If the pigs do as we say . . . And in time.'

'In time?'

'They have twenty-four hours.'

'And then?'

'Then –' He gestured a sudden explosion with his hands.

Victoria had a desperate need to know precisely what he meant. 'Then *what*? What do you *mean*?'

Giorgio gave a small secretive smile. 'The box will go bang. He will be dead.'

She gaped at him. Finally she breathed, 'When?'

'When we choose. Midday. Maybe before.'

A timer. A remote switch. Midday. Tomorrow. It wasn't very far away.

She said, 'You can't – please say you *can't*.'

Giorgio gave a short contemptuous laugh, as if such a question was unworthy of a reply, and, turning on his heel, climbed the steps and was gone.

Sick at heart. Victoria went back into the small cellar and resumed her seat next to Henry.

She felt him watching her.

'What exactly did he say?' he asked painfully.

It was impossible to tell him the truth. Already he was visibly more distressed than before. For the first time she saw fear and despair in his face. She smiled at him confidently. 'They've made their demands – the release of their friends and safe passage. The government are *bound* to give in. It's only a matter of a few hours, I'm sure.'

Henry frowned in concentration then closed his eyes as if a great weight of responsibility were descending on him.

Victoria repeated quickly. 'They're *bound* to give in.'

Henry whispered. 'They shouldn't. It would be quite wrong to do so.'

'But – they *must*.'

Henry made a last effort to speak. 'There's no *must* about it . . .' He trailed off and turned his head away.

Victoria sat back unhappily. He obviously wanted to be left alone. She had the awful suspicion that he might have overheard what Giorgio had said. In which case he knew about the twenty-four hour deadline. And the dreadful appalling timer on the bomb.

The knowledge brought Victoria to a decision. That she would stay with Henry. Whatever happened. She would not leave him alone.

It was a surprisingly easy decision to make. She thought: It'll be the first decent thing I've done.

She sat close by the box, in case he should need her. After a while he dozed a little and muttered in his sleep. She kept a hand close to his shoulder to wake him in case he had a nightmare and started struggling to get out of the box. But finally the mutterings ceased and he slept.

She left her hand on his shoulder, for the slight reassurance it might give him, and because it made her feel closer to him. She was very calm, now that she had come to her decision.

At one point she stared at her watch. Eight in the evening.

Time was passing. Fast. The night would slip away, then it would be morning . . .

And here she was, totally helpless. Someone cleverer would think of something. But she wasn't clever. No brains, no sense, never did have.

She made an effort to think everything through, calmly.

Removing her hand from Henry's shoulder she got up and went into the main cellar. She looked up the steps to the door.

Think. *Think.*

He must be alone. Otherwise why had he come to chat? And why had he been so relaxed. He was never relaxed when the woman was around.

But was he *still* alone?

She climbed the steps and put her ear to the door. Nothing.

She tried the handle, just in case. It turned, but the door wouldn't open.

Think. *Think.*

She would only have one chance. She mustn't foul it up. At the worst the woman *would* be there after all, and would shoot her. At the best, she might escape and save Henry. Either way, it was better than sitting and waiting. *Anything* was better than that.

But when she tried to work out exactly how she was going to escape, her determination faltered. There *had* to be a way, but she couldn't think what. The phrase 'play it by ear' came into her mind, and she clung to it as a temporary prop.

She listened again. Still nothing.

Then there was a sound. But it was only Henry, moaning softly. She heard him inhale deeply and guessed he was waking. She

316

suddenly realised that she would have to tell him something.

She hurried back into the small brick cellar and knelt beside the box. He was awake, staring upwards, a look of faint horror on his face as if he'd just woken from a nightmare.

'Henry?' she whispered. He focused on her, the nightmare still in his eyes. She said, 'I'm going to try to get out. Now, you mustn't worry.'

He looked horrified. 'Victoria, don't do *anything*. I forbid it.'

'I must, I'm sorry.'

'But *what* are you going to do?'

'Er. Well, I don't quite know . . .'

He sighed with exasperation. 'Victoria, these people will *kill* you. Without a second thought. I forbid it. It can only make things *worse*.'

She touched his shoulder. 'I'm sorry, Henry . . .'

Before he could speak again she got up and, taking the water bowl, emptied the last of the contents into a corner.

'Victoria?' Henry's voice was urgent, pleading.

She took a last look at him, the pale haggard face showing in the window of the obscene coffin-box, and her stomach lurched. She cried, 'I'm sorry, Henry. For everything. I really am . . . so sorry.'

She turned quickly and, holding the empty bowl in her hand, climbed to the top of the steps again. Taking a deep breath, she beat on the door.

Twenty-five

Nick shouted into the phone, 'It's very urgent!' then held the receiver away from his ear. The babble of voices boomed down the wire. He waited impatiently. This was the fourth restaurant he had tried. The flatmate hadn't been certain which one Diana Danby had gone to and had named five or six possibilities. Each restaurant appeared to be staffed by Italians who took a maddening delight in failing to comprehend straightforward English.

But it was worth trying. This girl, Victoria Danby's sister, might have some idea of where she was.

He waited for what seemed like a long time, but which was

actually four minutes. Around him was the clatter and buzz of the incident room where a team – now more than fifty strong – was based. Someone at the next desk shouted across the room. Nick flinched; all noise seemed unnaturally harsh. It was the tiredness. He didn't think he'd ever felt so tired in his life.

He pressed the receiver back to his ear. Finally he heard a clunk as someone picked up the phone at the far end.

'Hello?' It was a female voice.

'Miss Diana Danby?'

'Speaking.'

With relief Nick introduced himself. 'I need to find your sister, Miss Danby. She's not at her flat. Have you any idea where she might be?'

'Oh gosh! She's not in trouble again, is she?'

'Miss Danby, *please*. Do you know where she might be?'

There was a pause and the clatter of the diners echoed down the wire. 'Oh dear, I can't *think* . . . Quite honestly, I haven't seen her for a while . . . I mean, I only know about her *flat* . . .'

'What about boyfriends?'

'She didn't tell me about any. Not new ones, anyway.'

'Relatives. Friends. Anybody—'

'She used to be involved with a whole lot of people in a commune. Did you know that? Well, ever since then she's been a bit on her own really. It all broke up, you know. *Maybe* she still sees some of them – the commune people, I mean. Have you tried them?'

'No. What were their names?'

'Oh. There were a couple called Martin and Janey, I think. But I never knew their *other* names . . . And as for the rest – no, I haven't a clue, I'm afraid.'

Nick rubbed a hand over his face. This was getting nowhere.

'But they might still be living at the farmhouse,' she continued. 'Though I'm not sure.'

Remembering Kershaw's conversation with the mother, Nick said, 'But I thought the farmhouse was sold?'

'Oh no. Not yet. For some reason it didn't sell. So it's going to auction. Next month, I think.'

'But your mother – she seemed very definite.'

'Oh, she knows *nothing* about it.' Her tone was scornful. 'Don't take any notice of what *she* says. It isn't sold yet. I know it isn't.' There was a pause. 'Hello? Are you still there?'

Nick had been miles away, thinking of the unoccupied farmhouse.

He gave Diana Danby the number of the incident room, in case she heard from her sister, and rang off.

He went straight to Kershaw and gave him the news.

The brief look of excitement that passed over the commander's face was quickly replaced by one of anxiety. Momentarily, he plunged his face into his hands. He came up looking very tired. 'It's definitely worth a look, of course. We can mount a discreet watch on the place – but we can't search it.'

'What do you mean, sir?'

'I mean, I've had a directive from upstairs – and it comes from Downing Street itself. There's to be a hands-off until negotiations have been successfully concluded and the Attorney-General safely returned.'

Nick sat down and tried to absorb the implications.

'Surely we can approach with caution?' he asked.

Kershaw looked uncomfortable. 'Apparently we must do nothing that might jeopardise the situation . . .'

Nick sensed that the commander didn't like the directive any more than he did. He shook his head. 'Seems crazy to me, sir.'

Kershaw raised his eyebrows in silent agreement, and said heavily, 'The argument is that if we go nosing around and the terrorists get wind of it then – the feeling is that they are perfectly capable of murdering Sir Henry. And that mustn't happen.'

'But if the terrorists *are* there, then it would be a real chance for us to get the upper hand. Show ourselves. Surround the place so that they realise there's no point in killing anyone. In fact, it would be Sir Henry's best chance of staying *alive*.'

'Maybe. But would you like to be the person responsible for putting that argument to the test?'

Nick hesitated. The image of Lady Northcliff came into his mind. He saw her at the window, staring out into the garden, despair behind the pale composed face . . .

He nodded slowly. 'Yes, I see what you mean.'

'This is a new type of criminal, Ryder. And we don't know how to deal with them yet. We can't go blundering around finding out.'

'But giving in entirely? Pandering to them? It'll just encourage them! They're not going to go away.'

Kershaw sighed, 'I know, I know.' He stood up and made for

the door. 'But don't let's get excited about anything yet. Let's find out if there *is* anyone at that farmhouse first.'

Nick got hastily to his feet. 'What sort of party were you thinking of sending, sir?'

Kershaw pondered. 'Very small. Six men.'

'And an indirect approach, sir. On foot over the fields. I'll get an ordnance survey map right now. We can be ready to go in five minutes.'

For a moment Kershaw eyed him quizzically then, giving in gracefully, nodded his agreement. 'Okay, Ryder, you're on. But' – he raised a forefinger – 'you're to keep your distance. Look for signs of life – lights showing and vehicles parked outside – no more, no less. And if you *do* find anything, report straight back to me.'

'Do we tool up?'

Kershaw shook his head. 'I daren't, Ryder. Not in the present climate.'

Nick wasn't surprised. The Met, like the county forces, was proud of its long tradition of not carrying firearms. It was considered a virtue to approach dangerous armed criminals with no more than a truncheon in your hand. Nick was one of many younger officers who believed the policy to be ridiculously out of date.

It took fifteen minutes to muster the rest of the party – Conway and four of Kershaw's top men – to draw walkie-talkies, binoculars, cameras, maps and extra-warm gear, and to get down to the cars.

They set off with eighty miles and well over two hours' driving ahead of them. At first Nick was unnaturally alert and jumpy, a dozen thoughts ricocheting around his head, thoughts which, maddeningly, refused to connect in any sensible pattern. He realised that his mind was increasingly muddled. He'd be no good to anyone if he didn't get some sleep.

It wasn't until the car sped into Middlesex that a deep aching weariness finally overtook him and, resting his head against the seat, he was instantly asleep.

Victoria pounded on the door again. There was no sound. Where was he? Perhaps he'd gone away. Perhaps she and Henry were alone in the house. In which case it was just a matter of getting *out*. She rattled the handle and pulled violently at the door, but it wouldn't budge. It was a heavy door, made of thick wooden planks with solid crossbeams.

Defeated, she leaned back against the wall. The plan probably wouldn't have worked anyway.

Suddenly there was a sound. She put her ear to the door and listened.

A door closing. Footsteps in the distance . . .

She pounded on the door.

More sounds, closer. Footsteps coming across the hall.

Victoria retreated quickly to the foot of the steps and waited, trembling.

A key turned. The door swung open. It was Giorgio. 'Yes?' he demanded.

She held up the empty bowl. 'We need more water.'

Giorgio looked irritated. 'You use too much.'

'I need a wash.' She indicated Henry in the far cellar. 'And now he's thirsty.'

With visible annoyance, Giorgio came half-way down the steps and reached out for the bowl. He went out again, locking the door behind him.

Her heart thumping wildly, Victoria ran up the steps and pressed herself against the wall. When he returned she would be hidden behind the open door. Or would she? There wasn't much room. If he flung the door open it would probably bounce off her body. He was *bound* to realise that there was someone there.

She thought: Dear Lord, why couldn't I have been *thin*?

And her *feet*. She suddenly realised that, standing as she was two steps below the threshold, her feet would be visible beneath the open door. But she couldn't *get* any higher.

It was hopeless. Why had she ever thought any different?

Footsteps sounded in the hall.

She hesitated, torn with indecision.

The footsteps shuffled to a halt.

Too late.

She turned her feet sideways, pulled herself in and held her breath.

A key sounded in the lock. The handle turned. The door swung open fast. It swung towards her face. It came up against her body. She sucked in the last of her breath.

The door was bouncing back off her body.

She grabbed the door knob and pulled the door hard against her. She almost cried out. *He must realise!*

There was an agonising pause.

Then, unbelievably, Giorgio appeared. Walking slowly down the steps, the bowl in his hands, peering curiously towards the far cellar, wondering where she was.

He hadn't realised.

For a moment she was frozen with amazement.

Then she knew she had to move. Now – while his back was turned. Before he reached the bottom of the steps. Before he turned to walk across the cellar and spotted her out of the corner of his eye. Before he discovered she was not in the far cellar after all.

She began to move her weight down on to a lower step, to manoeuvre herself round the open door.

He was almost at the bottom.

She hesitated. Had she left it too late?

She eased herself round the door.

He had reached the foot of the steps. He turned towards the far cellar.

She moved clear of the door.

Then his face flicked round.

He saw her.

The fear leapt into her throat.

For a moment he was motionless, a look of black rage on his face.

Then, throwing the bowl of water aside, he coiled himself and sprang up the steps.

She let out an involuntary cry and pulled herself up the last two steps. She reached out for the door handle. He was half-way up and coming fast. She pulled the door shut. He was almost there. She grasped the handle tight and held it fast. She fumbled at the large metal key that protruded from the lock. Suddenly the handle twisted violently under her hand and, with a desperate gasp, she gripped it with all her strength to prevent it from turning.

She jerked at the key and almost screamed.

It wouldn't turn!

Finally there was a firm click.

It was locked. She fell back with relief.

The knob twisted violently from side to side. Victoria stared at it, mesmerised.

The next moment, there was a crash and the whole door shook.

God!

Another crash. The door vibrated but held firm.

She retreated fast across the hall, watching the door.

She looked longingly at the telephone and hesitated. There was a momentary silence from inside the cellar. She reached for the phone.

Suddenly there was a deafening *bang!*

She sprang back with a gasp.

It came again: *bang!* A gun. The door was splintering around the lock.

And then she realised there was no time. *He was almost out.*

Scrabbling at the front door, she pulled it open and ran out into the night.

The darkness was impenetrable, a mantle of black that enveloped itself around her. She ran blindly forward, away from the house in the direction of the drive.

She stumbled once but regained her footing. Then she hit a bump and felt herself pitching forward. She threw out a hand and caught her fall.

And kept running.

Gradually her eyes became accustomed to the darkness; she could make out the pale surface of the road and the shadows cast by the ridges and pot-holes. But the soles of her boots were hopelessly slippery, and the slight heel made her ankles keep twisting over.

She cried inwardly with frustration and ran on, glancing over her shoulder, looking for him. She felt the blind fear of the pursued, the panic of a thousand nightmares.

Her lungs were hurting, her legs maddeningly heavy.

God, give me strength!

She stole another look behind.

Nothing – or *was* there?

She pushed desperately on, half running, half walking. The road was curving upwards, steepening between the open fields. Ahead she could make out the deeper blackness of the woods and the archway of chestnuts on the brow of the hill.

Soon there'd be somewhere to hide.

She staggered forward, her heart crashing in her ears, her legs like lead. She pulled at the air, trying to breathe, but her lungs wouldn't *draw*.

The trees – if only she could get to the trees.

Then she heard it.

The sound of an engine. Coming from behind. Roaring into motion; followed by the grating and squeaking of a van being driven hard over a rough road.

She looked wildly about her.

There was no cover here. Only the woods ahead – but they were too *far*. Or the woods away to the left. Yes, *nearer*. Her only chance.

Then she saw the beam of the headlights, swinging slowly round, reaching out towards the woods, illuminating the trees, arcing towards her . . . And she realised the lights would catch her, pin her fluttering to the darkness behind.

To the right, then. There was nowhere else to go.

She dived for the barbed-wire fence and forced herself between the middle and upper strands. Her sweater caught on a barb. She pushed her body through the wire and yanked furiously on the sweater. The headlights were swinging round, almost upon her.

She screamed, '*Come on.*'

With a final wrench the sweater gave way and she was free.

She ran desperately. It was downhill, a little easier now, down into the valley. *Back* into the valley – the wrong direction. Almost back towards the farmhouse. Yet she *had* to get away from the road.

Her legs were weak now, wobbling violently over every tussock and undulation.

Behind her the vehicle was roaring up the hill. The reflection of the approaching headlights illuminated the ground around her. She could almost feel Giorgio's eyes boring into her back. She ran at a crouch, looking for cover.

There was a slight rise in the ground. She threw herself behind it and lay flat, gasping for breath.

The engine noise rose to a crescendo then faded as the van passed by on the road above. She thought: Perhaps he didn't see me after all. She pulled in great gulps of air then lay still, the grass cool and soothing against her cheek. She wanted to stay there, lying against the damp ground, for ever.

She stiffened.

The engine note had changed. She raised her head slightly, listening hard. The engine was idling, the van stationary . . .

Suddenly the engine spluttered to a stop. There was an unearthly silence, broken only by the pounding of her heart.

She craned her head. The headlights had been extinguished. There was only darkness, a great expanse of black where the light had been.

Where was he?

She peered forward. The deep shadows merged one into another until they formed an elusive mosaic of shimmering dots. The patchwork shifted constantly until there was an illusion of movement in every fragment of grey, a dark racing figure in every shadow.

She *must* move.

With an enormous effort, she raised herself into a crouch, her senses reaching out into the stillness.

Distant sounds ... An owl's hoot ... The faint whispered undertones of the wood.

Where was he?

She began to creep away crabwise, down the hill, away from the road, further into the valley.

A sound.

The crunch of feet on pebble. Up on the road.

She accelerated down the hill, down on to the flat meadowland.

Ahead was the stream, gurgling faintly. She reached the bank and, pausing for an instant, looked back.

Darkness. Nothing. *Where was he?*

She gasped.

There.

A dark shadow up by the road, detaching itself from the surrounding grey.

Running.

Running straight down the hill. *Towards her.*

She leapt into the stream, dragging her feet through the clutching water, and stumbled up on to the bank. She ran up the slight incline, her stride ragged, her ankle turning on a hump.

Ahead, the rolling pastureland climbed towards the steep valley side and the distant ridge. To the left, fields, open and exposed. *Nowhere to hide.*

She swerved to the right, towards the black familiar mass of the farm buildings. There, at least, there would be somewhere to hide.

She willed herself on but her body wouldn't respond: it was a sluggish weight, pulling her back, dragging her down. Her lungs ached with pain, the breath coming in long whooping gasps. She was incapable of running any more. She staggered forward at an untidy lope, forcing one foot in front of the other, her arms swinging uselessly at her sides. She couldn't bring herself to look behind. Then, suddenly, she didn't need to. She *heard* him.

She heard the pounding of his feet on the turf, the scrape of his shoe against a stone. The sound of panting, faint at first, growing louder, coming up behind her.

The panic gave her a last burst of strength. She pumped her arms, forced her legs into a run, pushed herself forward over the ground. The sheds loomed up ahead. *Not so far*. The sheds . . . The house beyond . . .

But what was this ahead?

The *gate*.

She'd forgotten. The gate. Barring her way.

She heard a short pant, the rasp of his breath, close behind.

Then she knew: this was the end. Nothing would save her now. She could almost feel his hands on her back, dragging her down. She screamed inwardly.

The gate was coming up fast. As she reached out for the latch, she suddenly realised – *the gate was slightly open*.

She reached out a hand and swung herself round the end of it and half fell through the gap, pulling the gate closed in an instinctive attempt to delay him.

She gave a violent start. To the right a dark shape was vaulting the fence. Jumping high, a hand on the gate post. She veered to the left, across the yard. The solid blackness of the tractor shed loomed close ahead.

Behind her there was a thud and a muffled shout.

She reached the shed and ran blindly along the side until she came to the back wall. She stopped, gasping for breath, and listened. She could hear nothing but the hammering of her own heart. She put her head round the corner and looked back down the side. The eaves cast deep inky shadows on the narrow pathway between the shed and the rising ground. Was he there? It was so difficult to be sure.

What had the thud meant? The cry? He must have caught a foot on some wire and fallen.

She took another careful look.

Nothing.

Then she remembered the *other* side. The house side.

He might be creeping up *there* . . .

Go and look! But suppose she met him at the corner?

Oh God!

She forced herself to creep along the back of the shed to the opposite corner. Bracing herself, she thrust her head out.

Nothing.

What now?

Should she wait here – or go back to the other corner?

No: stay still. Wait for him to make a sound. *Wait.*

She kept as still as she could, her senses reaching out into the darkness, listening for him, watching for him. She had a desperate need to know *exactly* where he was.

The silence grew, punctuated only by her own breathing and the rustle of the grass in the wind. Somewhere far away a night creature called.

She thought: Perhaps he's gone. Perhaps he's hurt himself. But how was she to know? He might be waiting at the far end of the shed, waiting for her to reappear, or he might be circling in a wide loop, expecting her to make a run for it across the kitchen garden. Or he might have returned to the house. He might be – anywhere.

Perhaps she should move. Perhaps she should try to reach the house and find a gun. Immediately she thought: Hopeless. There wouldn't be guns lying about. Not just like that.

No: she *had* to know where he was.

She had a terrible urge to run into the middle of the yard and shout, so as to end the appalling uncertainty.

She stiffened.

A faint snap.

Where from?

She took another look down the side of the shed facing the house. Definitely not there.

Infinitely slowly, she moved herself round the corner.

Again.

A footfall.

Where?

From the *other* side.

The fear leapt into her throat. She moved quickly away, down the side of the shed nearest the house, until she was back in the yard.

Where now?

The interior of the shed, gaping blackly, beckoned to her: a place to hide. She slipped inside. The tractor sat hugely in the centre. She went deeper into the darkness, feeling her way quickly round the bulk of the vehicle, taking small anxious footsteps in case of obstacles.

At the back of the tractor she paused, listening hard. Almost immediately, she heard him. Through the side of the shed, the faint crunch of feet on earth, moving slowly, following her route, heading for the yard.

The footsteps faded then halted altogether. And restarted.

And then he appeared, a black figure silhouetted in the wide doorway.

He was coming in.

Very slowly, she began to move, keeping the bulk of the tractor between her and the slowly advancing figure. The footsteps halted again. She pressed herself against one of the massive rear wheels.

There was a long silence which seemed to whine and jangle in her ears.

Another footstep, but very faint. He was treading more carefully.

She put out a foot to move further round and began to transfer her weight. Her heel pushed against something – something *loose* – something she had inadvertently shifted slightly. She began to withdraw her foot. *Too late*. The object rocked back, making a minute sound. She froze. The sound seemed to hang for ever in the roar of the silence.

She clenched her teeth.

She heard him coming round the back of the tractor. She ducked down behind the immense wheel, retreating under the body of the machine. In the faint light from the doorway she became vaguely aware of what her foot had touched – a heap of objects on the floor beside her: metal, abandoned tools, cog wheels.

The outline of a long metal bar showed grey in the darkness. She reached for it, grasped it, and felt a tiny spark of confidence. Yes – he wouldn't get her without a fight!

A sudden wild courage made her pick it up and back quickly under the tractor until she was standing on the other side. Her footsteps echoed loudly. There was a moment of electrified silence, then he moved.

He moved quickly, darting towards the doorway to cut her off. But she sprang round to the back of the tractor again. And waited.

He came more confidently this time. He called softly, 'Vittoria, I have a gun – come out or I must kill you.'

She thought: He still thinks I'm a fool.

She waited for him behind one of the large rear wheels. As he approached, she braced herself, then, with a small cry, she leapt out at him, swinging the metal bar wildly from side to side, viciously, violently, advancing on him, wanting only to hurt him, hating him. She caught him off-balance and he retreated slightly, his arm up to deflect the blows. Then, finding his feet, he brought a hand up, pointing something at her. A weapon.

She thought: *No! No, you bloody don't.*

She swung again with all her strength. She felt the bar glance off his arm. There was a clatter as something hard hit the ground. He gasped and his hand went up to clutch his head. Exhilarated now, she swung again, scenting the possibility of another hit. But she missed. He grabbed for the bar. She spun it downwards, out of his reach and up again the other way, up until it was raised high above her head. With all her might, she brought it down again. He reached for it, ducking at the same time, but she pulled sideways, so that the downwards motion became an arcing sideways loop. His hand snatched at the bar and missed. In the split second before the bar hit him, she realised with a raging triumph that he had not ducked far enough.

The bar hit him. He fell back.

Then she swung the bar with cold calculation, going for his arm, and then his back, and then a part of his head that he wasn't covering with his hands. Recovering, he lunged for her, but she sprang out of his reach. She felt all-powerful now, as if the bar in her hand was a mighty weapon quite independent of her. She swung wildly, back and forth, back and forth. Suddenly there was a soft thud. She'd got him again! She could have laughed. It was a satisfying feeling, hitting him. She wanted to do it again.

He was on one knee now, moaning loudly.

She danced behind him and, with one last massive effort, she raised the bar and brought it winging down on to the top of his head. He toppled over and fell to the ground. She swung the bar back and forth in the air, waiting for him to come up, longing for him to try to catch her again, so that she could *hit him harder*. Massively hard.

'Come on, come on!' She hovered impatiently. *'Come on!'*

It was only after several minutes that the wild elation left her and she realised that he was not going to move. She felt a sharp disappointment.

Eventually she became aware of the silence and the passing of time. She looked down at the hunched outline on the floor. He was utterly still. She blinked, not understanding . . .

It took several more moments for her to realise that she was free, and there was nothing to stop her leaving. But something nagged at her mind, something that she had to do. What was it?

Henry.

She staggered out of the shed towards the back door of the house. She heard a clacking sound and realised it was her teeth chattering. She was suddenly very cold.

The door was open and she lurched into the kitchen. She was shaking like a leaf. She felt very disorientated. She leant against the dresser. No – that was wrong. She must get on. She realised she still had the metal bar in her hand. Putting it on the kitchen table, she went through into the hall. The door to the cellar was open, the light still on.

She must tell Henry. No – *first* she must telephone. That was by far the most important thing.

Leaning heavily against the wall, she picked up the receiver and listened. A comforting buzz sounded in her ear. She put a shaking finger in the nine and began to dial.

She dialed the final nine and allowed herself a small glimmer of hope. In some extraordinary way everything was going to be all right after all. She sighed shakily, half-way between tears and laughter.

A split second later she knew nothing was ever going to be right again.

Her hair was being wrenched backwards off her skull. It must surely come *off*. She screamed out in pain and fell heavily backwards, falling aginst the doorframe.

As she fought for breath she heard the receiver being dropped firmly back into its cradle.

Twenty-six

Gabriele took hold of the girl's hair and pulled hard. 'Where's Giorgio?'

'I don't know.'

Gabriele let the girl see the short grey barrel of the Skorpion and repeated in a low voice, '*Where is Giorgio?*'

330

'He went away.'

'How do you know?'

'He said so.'

'Did he give a reason?'

'No. He just said he wanted to go away. He didn't say why.'

Gabriele thought furiously. *Why* would he have gone away? It didn't make sense. She asked through tight lips, 'But why would he bother to tell *you* that he was going?'

The girl shook her head violently. 'I don't know, I don't know. He just *did*.'

How did you get out?'

There was a whimper. 'I – I just did.'

Gabriele pulled the hair harder, jerking the girl's head from side to side. The girl yelped with pain. 'I – used a wrench.'

The girl was lying. There had been no wrench. She gripped the hair more tightly. 'Try again. This is your last chance.'

The girl's mouth moved, but no sound came out. Gabriele loosened her grip. Eventually the girl gasped, 'There *was* a wrench. I found it in a corner – when we first came. I hid it – and then when Giorgio left I levered the lock off. I *did*.'

Letting go of the girl, Gabriele considered. It was just possible, about the wrench: the lock was dented and pulled at an obtuse angle to the wood. It was *possible* . . . 'Where is it now?' she demanded.

'I – left it in the kitchen.'

Gabriele went into the kitchen, dragging the girl behind her. A metal bar lay on the table. The food Giorgio had bought earlier in the day sat on the draining board, along with the whisky and cigarettes. Most of the weapons were still there – her own Kalashnikov, as well as Giorgio's. However there was no sign of either Giorgio's Skorpion or his handgun, a Makarov. He must have taken them when he went out.

If he had gone out.

She desperately tried to think. Nothing made *sense*.

·The van . . .

What was the van doing abandoned at the top of the hill?

Something must have happened. He must have been on his way somewhere when the van broke down. But where had he been going? There were plenty of booze and cigarettes. And why, when the van broke down, did he set off on foot? This bloody place was miles from anywhere: he couldn't have gone far without transport.

None of it made sense.

Unless –

There was a pub in the village. Brightly lit, inviting. But she immediately dismissed the thought. Not even Giorgio would go wandering off to a pub at a time like this. Going back into the hall, she turned off the lights and, pulling open the front door, stared into the darkness.

The night was silent. She looked up towards the woods where the road passed through the avenue of trees. She had left the car up there beside the van. When she'd first seen the van she'd thought something really dreadful had happened: that the police had discovered them and Giorgio had been trying to escape. But there had been no signs of life, no other cars, nothing else to suggest that something had gone wrong. So she had run silently down the drive, the gun in her hand. As she'd neared the house she'd heard a sound – a door closing – and thought it must be Giorgio. But then she'd looked through the window and seen the girl at the telephone and realised something *had* gone very wrong after all.

But *how* wrong, that was the question?

She snapped on the hall light and put the barrel of the gun to the girl's forehead. 'How long have you been out? Did you make any other calls?' She pushed the barrel hard into the girl's head. The girl shrank against the wall and closed her eyes.

'I was only out for a minute,' she blabbed. 'I didn't make any other calls, I swear it. I swear it . . .'

Gabriele prodded with the gun once more. 'The truth!'

'It is, *it is*. It's the truth, *honestly*.' She started to cry, sobbing quietly, her face contorted like a small child's. She was pathetic, Gabriele decided. And probably telling the truth.

But even if there was no immediate danger Gabriele was filled with a deep instinctive unease.

She came to a decision: she had to get out. It was too risky to stay here. She would go to Chelsea. And Giorgio would meet her there, sooner or later.

This place would have to be tidied up then, made secure. Gabriele eyed the girl. She was a nuisance. Gabriele had never wanted to bring her; it had been Giorgio's idea. Now the girl was a threat as well as a nuisance. She might break out again. She would have to be dealt with.

Gabriele considered the alternatives but there were none. The knowledge reassured her. She was only doing what any commander would do when covering his retreat. A matter of logistical necessity.

It would have to be done in the cellar, so as to be out of the way. Just in case a casual caller came to the house.

She hesitated; she hadn't thought *that* possibility through. What *would* happen if someone came? The risk was slight, and yet – if someone did come they might find the attorney-man. Then the disposal people might dismantle the explosive before the deadline ran out and then she'd have nothing to negotiate with. That mustn't happen. No one must discover what was in the cellar.

Turning on the cellar light, she examined the door again. Apart from the lock there was nothing wrong with it. It must be possible to seal it in some way. She'd look into it when she'd dealt with the girl.

Yes: first things first.

'Get up!'

The girl looked at her in terror. Gabriele thought: She knows.

She repeated furiously, 'Get up!'

The girl got unsteadily to her feet, her face very white.

'Get in there.' Gabriele waved the gun towards the cellar.

The girl walked slowly across the hall and started down the steps. Gabriele followed. A sudden spasm of nervousness hit her. She wished Giorgio or Max were here. Yet it shouldn't be hard. Everyone had told her it wasn't. Provided you didn't look them in the eye when you did it. She would turn her head as she squeezed the trigger. And then, once it was done, she would close her mind to it and everything would be all right again. A logistical necessity.

She reached the foot of the steps and ran her tongue across her lips. The girl was staring at her again. Gabriele blinked and, raising the gun, took a step forward.

Something caught her eye. A movement from the far cellar. It was the attorney-man, lifting his head out of the box.

Then, suddenly, the germ of an idea came.

Gabriele gave it a moment, letting it develop. She looked up to the cellar door and then the idea crystallised.

Of course. Simple. She smiled a wild ragged smile. The girl's jaw dropped open.

Gabriele turned on her heel and ran up the steps. She called down to the girl, 'Stay right there or I'll blow your head off!'

The holdall was still in the kitchen. She scooped it up and went back to the cellar door. Putting the Skorpion down, she sat on the top step and thought for a while. Then she removed some plastic explosive from the bag, cut off a small section and placed it in an empty fuse box – a small container of hard plastic. Burying a detonator in the centre of the putty-like explosive, she wired it to a small 1.5-volt battery and, keeping the positive and negative separate, led the wires out through a hole which she made in the lid of the container. She put in a safety device: the usual clothes peg with a stiff piece of card in between the contacts, and a length of strong thread attached to the card.

She was rather enjoing herself. She had never made anything quite like this before.

Now to set the whole thing up.

She chuckled with excitement. Better and better.

She looked down at Victoria and beckoned. 'Come here.'

The girl advanced uncertainly up the steps.

'Arms in front of you.' Gabriele tied her wrists together with wire, then passed the wire round her waist, so that her hands were held firmly in front of her. Then she taped the plastic box with the wires hanging from it on to Victoria's back. The girl staggered slightly. Gabriele snapped: 'Don't move!'

Now for the interesting bit.

Gabriele fixed the wires to a simple pressure release switch. Now only the card caught in the clothes peg prevented the device from being live. She passed the thread from the card loosely under the half-closed door.

Leaving just enough room to squeeze through the door, she turned the girl round and pulled her down on to the edge of the top step. She taped the pressure release switch on to the stone step, facing upwards.

She squeezed through the gap in the door, out into the hall and pulled the door closed, leaving Victoria on the other side.

She called. 'Sit right back against the door!' Through the crack under the door she saw the girl's shadow move as she obeyed.

'Can you feel something on the step? Are you sitting right on it?'

There was a silence, then the faintest, 'Yes.'

'Well, you'd better be, otherwise you'll go up with a bang in a minute. Understand?'

The girl groaned.

The adrenalin shot into Gabriele's veins. This was it then.

Paying the thread out through her fingers she moved away from the door and sheltered round a corner. Very carefully she pulled on the thread. She felt it tauten. She increased the pressure. The card was resisting. She jerked it slightly and felt it give a little. She swallowed nervously, then pulled again. Suddenly the cord was free. She pulled it until the card appeared under the door.

She allowed herself a moment of satisfaction. Very neat. Now only madam's weight was keeping the pressure switch down. If anyone tried to get in, or if the girl tried to move, her back would be blown off.

Of course they might still get in *through* the door. She'd forgotten that. Her mind searched for a solution – she imagined herself in *their* place, imagined someone like Nick Riley looking for a way in.

Then she had it. Going into the kitchen she tore up a grocery bag and, using a pen from the holdall, wrote a message on it. She put the message in front of the cellar door.

Gabriele glanced at her watch. It was nine. Late. She must go. This place was a trap. Coming here had been a mistake, right from the beginning. Giorgio's idea.

Giorgio – where the hell *was* he?

She hurriedly repacked the holdall and took it with the Skorpion to the front door. The telephone sat silently on the window ledge. She snatched it up, and referring to the slip of paper in her bag, dialled the number in Paris.

Eventually it connected and the number rang. She waited tensely. It didn't answer. She dialled again. This time the call did not connect. Impatiently, she dialled a third time. It rang once more. There was no reply.

Angrily she reached down and pulled the cable out of the wall. She turned off the hall light. The house fell into darkness apart from a sliver of light gleaming under the cellar door. That light should have been turned off. She swore under her breath. There was nothing she could do about it now.

Taking the spare explosives and her Kalashnikov, as well as the Skorpion, she stepped out into the darkness and listened for a moment before closing the door quietly behind her. The atmosphere was eerie and still. She thought: How I loathe this place.

She set off up the drive, a cold dread pulling at her mind. High on the hill a breeze sighed softly in the trees. She quickened her pace.

Finally the van came into view and, beyond it, the hired Ford.

She put the holdall and the gun into the car, and then approached the van. Apprehensive, she hesitated for a moment then, opening the back doors, climbed in. She felt around with her hand. Then, impatient, she risked the interior light. Everything was there still: sleeping-bags, clothes, ammunition clips, spare explosive. Giorgio had not taken anything. *Strange.* She gathered some of her own gear.

She glanced over the back of the driver's seat into the front.

She stiffened.

Giorgio's Skorpion lay on the front seat. She stared at it for a long time.

Picking up her gear she turned off the light and went round to the front. The keys were in the ignition. She sat in the seat and tentatively turned the key. The starter whirred noisily, shattering the silence. The engine burst into life.

There was nothing wrong with the engine at all then. She put it into gear to make sure. The van leapt forward.

She turned off the engine and looked at the machine pistol again. Its presence worried her deeply. *He would never have gone anywhere without it.*

What should she do with it? Leave it in case he returned?

She couldn't think. Part of her was filled with a deep foreboding. She had the feeling Giorgio would never return.

Picking it up, she got out of the van and stood quite still for a moment. The echo of the engine still rang in her ears and she strained to hear. Slowly the sounds of the night returned: the whisper of the woodland, the murmur of the wind. The faint hum of a car sounded in the distance, somewhere on the main road.

Making up her mind, she threw the Skorpion back on to the front seat and hid it under a sleeping-bag. Just in case. It would be terrible if he did come back, only to find it gone.

She ran to the Ford and drove quickly to the main road. It wasn't until she was through the village that she began to relax her grip on the wheel.

As she neared the A4 the traffic gradually increased. She barely noticed the two Rovers that swished rapidly past her, one behind the other, going fast in the direction from which she had come.

'Wake up.'

Conway's voice. Nick opened his eyes and for a moment couldn't remember where he was. He rubbed his aching temples.

The sleep might have been a mistake. He wasn't sure he felt any better at all.

The car was travelling fast through country lanes. They rounded a bend and, coming into a small village, slowed down.

'We're about half a mile off,' said Conway, shining a penlight at the map on his knee.

A few minutes later the car slowed to a crawl and turned left into the gateway of a field. The second car followed. They parked them both well back from the road, in the shadow of a hedge. When they had sorted out their gear they split up into three groups of two men each: one, including Conway, to stay with the cars and form the radio link with the nearest police HQ at Swindon; the second to go along the road and keep watch on the lane leading to the farmhouse; the third – Nick and a man called Williams – to go across the fields and do the recce.

Before setting off, Nick took a good look at the map, memorising the layout of the farm and, as far as he could decipher it, the topography.

The sky was overcast and it was very dark. Nevertheless they made fast time across the fields and soon came to a belt of woodland which had been clearly marked on the map. Presumably Hunter's Wood. Not far to the right was the lane that led to the farmhouse, but Nick wanted to stay well away from that. They looked for a path through the woods and found a small trail which started well but soon evaporated into a tangle of undergrowth.

They fought their way through with difficulty, then, reaching an area of more mature trees, the undergrowth thinned and they were able to press on. Through the pitch darkness Nick caught the glimmer of open sky ahead and, after negotiating one more dense patch of brambles and a barbed-wire fence, they were through into an open field. They now kept to the edge of the field, following the line of the trees. To the left the ground sloped down into a valley. Nick reckoned the farmhouse must be only a short distance away, a little further up the valley.

The outline of some fencing came up ahead, and beyond it a road: the driveway to the house. Nick whispered to Williams, 'Better head off down into the valley and round.' The other man nodded and they altered direction, going straight downhill. They crossed a narrow stream and climbed half-way up the other hillside before changing direction again to continue their journey along the valley.

Suddenly Nick put out a hand and they halted. Immediately below them, only fifty yards away, were the dark shapes of several buildings. The farm. But they had got rather close. Nick waved to Williams to retreat a little. Once safely out of earshot they took a long look through binoculars. There was no light showing, not even a glimmer. They had a hurried conference and decided to make a large circuit of the property, to examine it from different angles. Climbing higher up the valley side they passed behind the house and made a wide detour until they had reached the woodland immediately above the drive and overlooking the front of the house.

Nick took a long look through the binoculars and felt a deep disappointment.

There was nothing, not even a suggestion of life. No light, and as far as he could see in the darkness, no vehicles parked outside. There might be something parked in one of the outbuildings, of course. But somehow he doubted it: the whole place looked utterly lifeless.

His heart sank. Another dead end.

He took one more look, then made a large sweep with the binoculars from one end of the silent valley to the other. He examined the track in its long traverse from the farmhouse across the field immediately beneath him to the dark woods two hundred yards to his left, where the track disappeared into the trees.

He paused, took the binoculars away from his eyes and stared. There seemed to be something on the track at the point where it disappeared into the trees. A gleam ... The suggestion of shape ...

He nudged Williams and they walked cautiously along the treeline, keeping to the shadows. As they got closer they approached at a crouch.

It was a van.

They halted and watched it for a while.

A van. The Danby girl had owned – *still* owned – a van.

What was it doing here, Nick wondered. Abandoned perhaps? It was a funny place to park ...

He remembered his orders not to approach the house. Well, this wasn't the house, was it? This was a vehicle and it was clearly unoccupied. There was no risk of putting the wind up any terrorists just by taking a little tiny look.

He indicated to Williams to stay put, and crept forward. The van was parked at an odd angle, as if it had been left in a hurry. Nick felt a small spark of hope.

He listened hard, then climbed through the barbed-wire fence and went up to the van. He peered in through the windows, then tried the passenger door. It was not locked and the handle gave easily. He began to open it. There was a loud creak. He winced. Trying not to open it any further, he put his head in.

There was something lying on the seat. He couldn't quite make out what it was and ran a hand over it. A bulky padded fabric. Something hard beneath. He slipped his hand under and grasped metal.

He shivered with excitement.

He pulled the object out and held it up until it was silhouetted against the windscreen. A machine pistol. With silencer.

He replaced it carefully on the seat. He felt around the floor. Nothing. Closing the door as quietly as possible, he went round to the back of the van and pulled open one of the rear doors. He thrust a hand in and felt clothing, shoes, a polythene bag.

He decided to risk a little light. Taking a penlight from his pocket he shone it over the floor. A sleeping-bag, pillows, clothing . . . And in the polythene bag five magazines of ammunition.

And a stick of explosive.

He flicked off the light and closed the rear door.

Returning to Williams, they retreated a short distance into the trees and radioed back to Conway.

Less than fifteen minutes later there was a reply from London. No one was to move until further notice. Under no circumstances was the house to be approached. Nick found a tree trunk with a good view of the house and drive and, pulling his collar up, settled himself against it. He might as well make himself as comfortable as possible. It was going to be a long cold night.

Gabriele lay on the bed in the darkness, knowing she would never sleep. Once or twice she almost dozed off, only to be woken by the distant hum and click of the nearby lift. She kept thinking about Giorgio, wondering if he was caught, wondering if he was even now in some pig-hole. If so, she would get him out, with the others. She would demand it.

As the long night drew on she finally dropped into a fitful sleep, and saw Giorgio in her dream, a Giorgio who was very distant and strangely uninterested in what was happening. She called out to him, but he was separated from her and somehow couldn't hear . . .

She awoke, troubled, and heard the sounds of early traffic rising from the street outside and realised it was almost morning.

At seven she got up and tried the Paris number again. It rang for a long time without reply: the loneliest sound in the world. Gabriele suppressed a feeling of despair.

Going to the window, she watched the street for several minutes. The first glimmerings of dawn delineating the grey outlines of the small but expensive Chelsea houses. The Ford was just opposite, parked under a street lamp. Apart from the occasional passing car, nothing stirred.

She kept thinking about the Paris number. Why didn't it answer? Raymond knew how urgent it was. There were only a few hours to the deadline. When had she first phoned him? Yesterday morning. So he'd had twenty-four hours to contact people. It *must* be long enough.

Eventually she went to the kitchen and, searching the cupboards, found some coffee. There was no food. As she waited for the kettle to boil, she unwrapped the bundle she had left behind the fridge so many days before. She had already brought all the weapons up from the car. The Kalashnikov gleamed at her, sleek and deadly.

She levered open the plinth beside the cooker and pulled out the parcel she had hidden there. She opened it, pleased with her own resourcefulness. Her planning had paid off.

She examined the Argentinian passport, checked the money, and laid out the change of clothes, ready to put on.

Still time to kill. There was no radio to listen to. She sat drinking coffee as the minutes dragged by. At last it was seven-thirty; in Paris eight-thirty: all the offices would be open by now.

Trembling, she dialled the number yet again.

It answered straight away. She felt a warm flood of relief. It was a man's voice.

'Raymond?' she breathed.

Raymond was not there, the voice replied, but he was expected in at any moment. Did she want to leave a message?

It was vital to speak to him direct, she told the voice. Could he call her?

'What is your name and your number?' the voice asked.

She told him and rang off, bitterly disappointed.

Then she remembered that she *had* to go out and buy *The Times*. Supposing he rang back while she was out? Would he give up and never call back again? Stay calm. *Stay calm*.

Giorgio would have helped her to think. *Giorgio* . . .

She suddenly felt very alone.

She pulled on her jacket and hurried out into the street. There was no one about; she looked over her shoulder a couple of times to make sure. She found a newsagent in the King's Road and, picking up a copy of *The Times*, leafed quickly through it.

Where would they have put it?

She tried the Personal Column. She felt a shiver of excitement. It jumped out at her: the first item, prominent in block capitals.

It read: 'CRYSTAL. OFFER ACCEPTED. PLEASE CONTACT SOONEST. 01-875 2289.'

Henry's body was icy cold, but nothing could ever feel so cold as the chill in his heart. The minutes passed ruthlessly, and with each moment he became more bitterly aware that in all probability he would die quite soon.

He had until midday. He knew that. He had heard the man telling Victoria.

And now Victoria would probably die too.

As long as he had believed that only the lid could trigger the explosives he had been able to cope; there was a strange security in being locked in the box with the means of one's own destruction. But then had come the bolt from the blue: the realisation that he had a finite amount of time; and then he had discovered a fresh and more incisive fear. Though he tried not to, he couldn't stop himself from imagining the final moments. Though he might be unaware of exactly how long remained, there was the ghastly possibility that he might know – *sense* – the final moment approaching. He would probably be overcome by panic of the most debasing and loathsome kind, he would probably sweat or – even worse – call out. And he couldn't bear the idea of any of that. Better to go quickly, thinking of Caroline . . .

She would be all right in time. She was so young. And she would have the child. What a blessing that would be. What a consolation. And, though she would find it hard to believe at first, she would find someone else in time, someone to take care of her.

The thought was reassuring. Though not half as reassuring as being able to tell her himself. That would be his great regret. Not having the opportunity of a final word or a last message.

He thought about Victoria. He must tell her that he bore her no grudge: that he forgave her. It wasn't quite the truth. He didn't think he could ever completely forgive her. But he must make his peace with her; and he must tell her soon before it was too late. It was the right thing to do, and he very much wanted to do the right thing.

There were no other sections of his life that he could tidy up. It would have been marvellous to tell Caroline how much she had meant to him, but then she knew that already. He had said it often enough. So many people went through life *without* saying these things, but he had never been embarrassed by emotion. Quite the contrary. How very glad he was of that now.

The thought brought him a transitory peace and for a few moments he lingered in the memories of that warm and simple love.

Nick drifted out of a dream. He was dimly aware that he had slept for an unusually long time. A sound disturbed him, something scratched at his face. He sprang awake. There was a branch against his face. He pushed it away and thrust his watch up to his face. Nine. *Christ!* He sat upright and looked wildly about him.

But it was all right. The three officers who had relieved him and Williams in the early hours were just moving away, and a new team were taking over, crouching in the undergrowth, their rifles across their knees.

Kershaw had put men everywhere: behind the ridge, throughout the woods and hidden beside all the access roads to the village. The place was sealed tight. But what were they waiting for? As far as Nick could tell, they were waiting simply to watch helplessly as the terrorists left the farmhouse and got clean away.

If they were there at all. There still hadn't been a sign of life.

Nick wondered whether to head back towards Kershaw's base, which had been set up at a neighbouring farmhouse. Quite apart from anything else he was wolfishly hungry.

He went to tell one of the men that he was leaving and began to retreat through the woodland. But a sound came from behind and he stopped. One of the officers was speaking into a walkie-talkie. Nick retraced his steps. The officer turned to him and whispered, 'Car approaching.'

They waited silently, watching the track where it emerged from

342

the avenue of trees. But they heard it long before they saw it, the innocent sound of a car being driven along at a moderate speed.

The engine note slowed a little, then it appeared: a red Morris 1300. It carefully negotiated the stationary van, then progressed down the drive towards the farmhouse. Nick followed it with the binoculars. There was a single occupant: male, youngish, collar and tie. A picture of respectability.

The car drew up in front of the farmhouse. After a moment, the driver's door swung open and the young man got out. He slammed the door shut and stood still for a moment. Then he sauntered about. He turned his back to the farmhouse and stared back up the hill.

Looking at the van.

After a moment he turned away and leaned against the car bonnet.

Waiting. Very relaxed. Who on earth?

Then Nick shook his head. He called up Kershaw on the walkie-talkie and reported: 'I think we've got ourselves one estate agent.'

Twenty-seven

Archie Pinker looked at his watch. Five past nine. He always gave clients a reasonable time before giving up on them – at least twenty minutes, sometimes longer if he was in a good mood.

It was a lovely morning. He would give this one until nine-thirty. Probably too generous. Some people could leave you waiting for hours without feeling a moment's remorse.

It occurred to him that he should open the house up. It had been empty for quite a time and probably smelled musty inside. Women were always on about throwing windows open and airing rooms. Maybe they had a point.

He sorted through the bunch of keys in his hand and selected the one that looked most promising for the front door. He tried it in the lock but it wouldn't turn. He was a little put out: he usually prided himself on matching keys to locks.

From hard-gained experience of the perversity of people who fitted locks to doors, he twisted the key the other way.

To his surprise it turned. He tried the knob. The door wouldn't budge. Finally he realised: he had just *locked* the door. When he had first tried the key, it had been *open*.

Perhaps that mad hippy girl who owned the place had been down here. Or her equally mad friends. That would account for the open door and the van parked half-way up the track.

He went in and walked through the hall into the kitchen. He tutted. Just as he'd thought: food and drink on the draining board. How one could be expected to sell a place when there were hippies coming and going, he didn't know.

On his way to the living-room he passed through the hall again, and noticed a scrap of paper on the floor. Typical, he thought. Litter all over the place. He scooped it up. It had writing on it. KEEP AWAY. FROM BOTH DOOR AND GIRL. THE SLIGHTEST VIBRATION AND BANG! THE CRYSTAL FACTION.

Some weird game they'd been playing, no doubt. Quite mad. He screwed the paper into a neat ball and threw it in a waste bin in the living-room. He drew back the curtains and opened a window. The room certainly needed the air: it smelled of spilled drink and old cigarettes.

He wandered back into the hall, humming softly to himself.

A sound startled him. A muffled female voice.

'Hello?' he called cautiously.

The voice came again. This time he heard the words quite distinctly: 'Who is it?'

Archie Pinker advanced slowly towards the door which, he remembered from the details, led down to the cellars.

'Hello?' he said again.

'Whatever you do, don't open this door!'

Archie blinked. The voice sounded – *awful*. And what on earth was someone doing in the *cellar*? 'Um – is there anything the matter?' he asked uncertainly.

'Yes! Please phone for the police. Straight away. *Please*. It's desperate. *Please*. Tell them it's a matter of life and death and that they must come *immediately*.'

There was a pause.

Archie was a bit taken aback. What *was* going on? Good God – *of course*. It must be another drug orgy, like the one in which the chap had died. Lord. What a nasty thought. And now *he* was being dragged into it. It really was most unreasonable. At the same time, it would be quite a thing to inform the police. A good story to tell in the pub.

The voice was saying, 'Please, please, are you still there?'

'Yes.'

'Are you from the estate agents?'

'Yes. Archie Pinker.'

'Well, please tell the police it's to do with the Attorney-General. *Please*. They'll understand. You will tell them, *won't* you?'

'Oh . . . Yes . . .' Archie felt a pang of disappointment. The girl was obviously nuts. The Attorney-General indeed. And as for the police understanding, he was beginning to be uncomfortably certain that they wouldn't.

Nevertheless he looked around for the phone. Seeing one by the front door, he picked it up to dial 999. The phone was dead. He looked at it crossly. Silly girl hadn't paid the bill.

Blast. What a nuisance this all was.

'Hello?' he called through the door. 'Your phone's been cut off. I'll have to go into the village or something.'

'Ohh.' The voice sounded very distressed. Archie was not very fond of emotion, especially in women. He said briskly, 'Right. Well, I'll be off now.'

'Please – make sure they realise. They mustn't – absolutely mustn't – open the door!'

'Right ho.' Archie retreated fast. He got straight into the car and tried to decide what to do. It was nine-fifteen. No client in sight. If he left now he'd probably miss him. Really, this was too much.

Finally he decided to whizz quickly up the road to the nearest phone box and then whizz straight back. He drove quickly up the drive, or as quickly as it was possible to go on the dreadful road surface, and three minutes later arrived in the village.

He was looking for a phone box – there was always at least *one* in these small villages – when a car appeared from nowhere and forced him to brake sharply to a halt. Brimming with righteous indignation he wound down the window, ready to give the driver a piece of his mind, when he saw four men getting out of the car and approaching in what he quickly appreciated was a serious manner.

'Mr Pinker?' the first man asked.

'Yes,' he replied, wondering nervously how they knew his name.

'Could you tell us, please, what you saw at Hunter's Wood just now.'

Archie looked at the card the man was holding in his hand and realised that, due to some strange stroke of providence that he didn't quite understand, the police were already here.

How long would it take? Victoria imagined the estate agent driving up to the village, finding the phone box, having to wait while someone else finished a call, then getting through to the local police station. They wouldn't believe everything he told them, of course . . . But they would send someone anyway, just to check. A local man. In a slow car . . .

How long?

At least half an hour, she decided.

She must be patient. Another half-hour was not very long. Not after a whole night of biting pain from the wire on her wrists, and the nightmare of trying to prevent herself from falling asleep.

She called down to Henry again. 'Another half-hour, I should think. Then they'll be here!'

A faint 'Yes' came up. His voice sounded flat and uninterested, as if he didn't quite believe what she had told him.

She couldn't quite believe it herself. Everything had gone wrong for so long. She was still kicking herself for not having picked up Giorgio's gun. It must have dropped on to the floor of the shed, but she'd never even stopped to look for it. If only she *had*, then she might have been able to stop the woman. Shot her if necessary. It couldn't be that hard to aim and fire a gun. She could have done it, she *knew* she could.

After all, she'd stopped Giorgio.

For most of the night she'd been in terror of him returning, injured and viciously angry, and barging in through the cellar door. But as the long cold hours had dragged by she'd realised he would not return. Instead he had come to her in vivid appalling dreams which leapt into her mind as soon as she dozed. The nightmare always ended in the same way – with her falling forward, off the step. Then she awoke with a terrible start, her heart thumping, her mouth dry.

Now, as she waited, the memory of what had happened in the tractor shed had become just another vague half-realised horror that jostled with all the others in her tired mind. If she had hurt him badly she felt no remorse at all.

There was a sound. She was instantly alert.

The creak of a hinge. A footfall in the hall.

She gasped, 'Hello?'

A slight pause, then a voice close to the door. 'I'm a police officer. My name is Nick Ryder. Is that Victoria Danby?'

'*Yes.*'

'Is there anyone else in the house, Victoria?'

'Just us – me and Henry.'

'Sir Henry Northcliff?'

'*Yes.*' Victoria felt a wonderful relief: he *knew*. She wouldn't have to explain. She shouted the news down to Henry and he acknowledged it briefly.

The voice continued, 'Why mustn't we open the door, Victoria?'

'Because – there's a bomb. And another on Henry. And' – she whispered, putting her mouth close to the crack in the door – 'it's going to explode at midday. That's what they said. You will – be able to stop it, won't you. *Won't* you?'

'I'll have to get help, Victoria. Straight away. Can you hang on a minute?'

'You're not going?' She couldn't bear the thought of being alone again. He had such a reassuring voice.

'No,' he said quickly, 'I've just got to speak into my radio, that's all. I'll be straight back.'

She heard his voice, muted and efficient, and the tinny sound of amplified voices coming back in reply. While he was busy she called to Henry again. He replied in a voice that was stronger, more certain. He, too, was allowing himself to hope.

'Victoria?' It was the calm voice at the door again.

'Yes.'

'The bomb disposal people are on their way right now. They'll be here as soon as possible.'

'Thank you. Thank you.'

'Victoria, listen – what can you tell me about the people responsible for this? Where have they gone to – have you any idea?'

'There were two of them. A woman, Gabriele – I don't know where she's gone. She left last night.' She paused. 'Then there was a man. Giorgio. I think – I'm not sure – that he may be in the shed.'

There was an electric silence. 'In the shed!'

'I hit him,' she said calmly. 'I think he's still there.'

He was still there all right. Stone cold. Nick touched a hand. He'd been dead for some time. A Walther pistol lay on the floor some yards away. And the girl had killed him. Extraordinary.

He had known it would be Black Beard. There was no one else it could have been. Giorgio: he turned the name over in his mind. Italian then. He still didn't know his second name. He shook his head: there should have been a way of finding out before now.

In the yard behind him more cars were drawing up and men appearing from their stake-out positions.

A breathless Kershaw came up beside him and stared down at the body. 'One of *them*?' he asked.

'Yes. Our friend from the demo. Wheatfield's mate. The user of that Italian cologne.'

'How many does that leave then?'

Nick ventured, 'Just one. Just the Wilson woman. Unless –'

'Yes?'

'Unless she's got more friends.'

Kershaw grunted sharply. Waving a couple of his men forward he barked, 'Right, no pauses for snaps. Give him a good going over.'

They rolled the body on its back, and went through the clothing. As the contents of the pockets came out, Kershaw examined them and passed them to Nick.

Wallet . . . Money . . . Door keys . . . An Italian passport in the name of Riccardo Enrico. Crumpled receipts, a restaurant card, small change. And, folded in a back compartment of the wallet, a small slip of paper.

It had a list of five numbers on it, four of them with seven digits, the last with eight.

'Phone numbers?' Kershaw suggested. 'Right, let's go and try them.'

As the detectives cut the jacket off the body and tore the lining out, Nick followed Kershaw back towards the house. 'There's an army bomb disposal unit in Salisbury,' Kershaw said. 'They're on their way by road.'

'We only have till noon, so the girl says.'

'Ask her how she knows. Ask her *everything*. It'll be good for her to keep talking anyway. Meantime we'll get going on these numbers.'

Nick returned to the cellar door where another detective was crouching, his ear to the crack, talking softly.

Taking over, Nick said, 'Hello, Victoria. It's me again. Nick.'

'Hello.' She sounded pleased in a breathless panicky sort of way.

'Victoria, I'd like to have a long chat with you. About

everything. About how you got involved in this. Everything that might help us. Just until the bomb disposal people get here. Will that be all right?'

'They won't be long, will they?'

'Not too long. They're coming as fast as they can.'

'It's just – there's so little time.'

Nick looked at his watch. It was ten to ten. God!

In what he hoped was a comforting voice he said, 'Don't worry. If you could just—'

'But tell me,' she interruped firmly, 'did you find him in the shed?'

Nick hesitated for a moment. He didn't want to upset her – or did she already *know*? He said, 'He was there all right—'

'Tell me.'

Her tone was insistent. Hoping he was doing the right thing, Nick said, 'He was dead.'

There was only the slightest pause. 'Good,' she said matter-of-factly. 'I'm glad. He was a terrible person.'

'Yes.' So she had known. 'Now, Victoria. Please tell me what you know, about these people's contacts, their friends—'

'You want to find that woman—'

'Yes.'

'She was a terrible person too.'

Her words turned in his stomach; a knife-like memory that had lost none of its sharpness. He said, 'Yes, I know.'

She talked for a long time, first in great bursts, then more slowly, with greater effort. He could hear the tiredness in her voice as she dredged her memory for any small detail that might be useful.

He pressed her for more and more facts about the trip to Paris. She tried hard to remember the address where the van had been loaded, and the two streets where she had waited while Giorgio went to his appointments.

'He went into a door beside a newsagent's . . . There was an antique shop on the other side of the doorway. And then at the other place not far away – he came out of a second-hand bookshop – I *think*. Oh dear. I memorised the name of one of the streets. I really did. It was *Rue* something . . . But I can't remember!'

He could hear the exasperation in her voice. They had talked for thirty minutes. He guessed she was near her limits.

Some men in army uniforms were coming into the hall. Nick

said, 'Look, don't worry now. 'We'll try again later. The bomb disposal people are here. And they'll want to talk to you. I've got to go and make a phone call—'

'I was no use, was I? I'm *sorry*.'

'You were! You are! Really. And I wouldn't just say that.'

She started to speak, but her voice quavered, and he sensed that she was on the point of tears.

He said, 'Please don't – *worry*. You've been doing so well.'

There was a sniff and she said in a deliberately calm voice, 'You'll come back again, won't you?'

'Yes, of course.'

'I – feel so . . .' The voice trailed off and her silence hung painfully in the air.

'I'll be back,' Nick repeated softly. 'I promise.'

The bomb disposal men moved in to talk to her and Nick went to the phone, which a uniformed man with a screwdriver had just succeeded in reconnecting. Nick called Desport at the DST in Paris and gave him the details, such as they were, of the places the girl had visited. He also gave him the name of the girl, the name on the Italian's passport, details of the van, and the dates when they had been in Paris. It might not find Gabriele for them, but it could lead to the people responsible for helping her. And he wanted to know who they were, very badly.

He found Kershaw in his car, speaking into the radio mike. The commander clicked it back into its cradle. 'Nothing on those numbers. I've given them to a cypher bloke but . . .' His voice was heavy with pessimism.

Getting out of the car he added, 'We've heard nothing from the remaining terrorists, either. No contact at all. And only an hour and a half to go. If that bomb *is* on a timer, it doesn't leave much leeway.'

They walked towards the house. The head of the bomb disposal unit, a Major Phipps, came up. He was a typical army type, Nick observed. Short schoolboy haircut, crisp no-nonsense manner. 'We're going through the door,' he announced. 'Cutting a hole in it. Then we can get men inside and start work on both devices simultaneously.'

'It's safe, is it? To go through the door?' Nick asked.

'Should be. I've had a long talk to the girl. The device is strapped to her back. And the initiator is underneath her behind, so it is reasonably safe to assume that her weight is the critical factor.'

Nick gave an involuntary shudder. He remembered the jolly,

plump girl at the Vietnam United Front offices. Naïve, unworldly, pathetically enthusiastic. He had been scornful of her then. But, looking back, she hadn't been guilty of anything more than gullibility. She had trusted the first man who'd given her a good time. She wasn't the first to have fallen into that trap. She certainly didn't deserve this.

He looked into the hall and, seeing there was no one at the cellar door, he ducked under the tape that the army had slung across the front doorway and hurried across.

An army sergeant intercepted him. 'We're sealing this place off. Could you keep clear now, please.'

Nick waved him impatiently away and put his mouth to the door.

'Hello, Victoria.'

'Nick, is that you?' She sounded hopeful. Dangerously so. 'They're coming through the door, they said.'

'Yes. Any moment now. Be brave a while longer. You *have* been very brave, you know.'

'No. No. I haven't. I've made a complete mess of everything.' Her voice was full of anguish. 'I can't believe how *stupid* I've been.'

'Well, no point in brooding. It's in the past now.'

'I never realised, you know, who they were. Not until I found those sticks in the van.'

'I know.'

'The trouble was' – there was a pause – 'he made me happy. I never *thought* about – I just wanted to be happy. For a while. He was so – *different*. I'd never known anyone like him before. I didn't think about what or who he was or what he was doing. I just – wanted to be happy.'

'I understand.' There wasn't much else he could say.

'Everything's my fault—'

'You must stop thinking about it. You must think about helping the lads when they get through to you.'

'Yes. So sorry. Of *course*.' She added, 'I'm glad you're here. You – make me feel it's all going to be all right. You'll be staying, won't you?'

'Yes, of course.' He hated himself for being so definite; it was a promise he wasn't sure he would be able to keep.

'I – I feel – you'll think this is silly' – she gave a nervous high-pitched laugh – 'but I feel that you really *understand*.'

He thought: Better than you'll ever know. He said, ruefully,

'Yes. I – got involved with people like this myself once. Without realising it. So – I know how easy it is.'

'Oh.' She sounded surprised. Then, taking comfort from what he had said, she added, 'Thank you for telling me. Thank you.' Then, a tinge of worry returning to her voice: 'Are they coming soon?'

The army team were even then unrolling cable and preparing cutting tools.

'Any moment.'

She sighed softly.

Nick had a sudden thought. 'Victoria, we have met before, so don't be surprised when you see me.'

'We have?'

'Yes . . . Off the Holloway Road, at the VUF offices. I came in one day to ask for information.'

'Oh.' She sounded bewildered.

'It was in the line of duty,' he added apologetically.

'D'you know, I had the feeling I knew you. Isn't that odd?'

They made him move away then, out into the drive. He went to join Kershaw by the cars.

Suddenly there was a shout from inside the house. He spun round. He'd thought he was the last of the team to leave, but he could see Conway in the hall, talking urgently with Major Phipps. The next moment Conway hurried out into the yard, his face very grave. He was holding a piece of crumpled paper in his hand.

Nick took it from him and read the faintly written message.

KEEP AWAY. FROM BOTH DOOR AND GIRL. THE SLIGHTEST VIBRATION AND BANG! THE CRYSTAL FACTION.

A bewildered Archie Pinker confirmed he had found the paper in front of the cellar door and thrown it away. Which meant that the message was intended to be found straight away. It could be a bluff, of course. Everyone realised that.

Major Phipps questioned the girl again, to ask if she had seen anything attached to the door. She didn't remember. And she couldn't see very well without moving . . .

Then she did remember something. There had been a string . . . something the woman had led under the door.

Major Phipps withdrew his team from the door. The string might mean nothing. On the other hand it might have been used to arm an initiator attached to the door itself. It was too risky to go in that way. For the moment at least. They would have to try something else.

And someone would have to tell the people in the cellar.

It was ten forty-five.

Gabriele stared at the telephone, hating the very sight of it.

She'd called Paris again, half an hour before, but the impersonal voice had reported that there was no news. They had not yet called back.

Now she couldn't delay any longer. If all the arrangements were to be made by noon, she must communicate them to the pigs.

She pulled *The Times* towards her and prepared to dial the number in the ad. She imagined a circle of men, sitting by a telephone somewhere in Whitehall, waiting for her to call. They must be in a sweat. Running around like chickens with their heads cut off. Perhaps the whole British government was waiting for her call. It was an intoxicating thought.

She dialled the number and aware of her thumping heart, picked up the piece of paper on which she had prepared her message.

The number connected and began to ring. It was answered immediately.

'Hello?' A clipped male voice.

She began to read: 'A plane is to be prepared at Heathrow airport for immediate departure. It is to have maximum fuel and a full flight-deck crew. Wheatfield, Reardon, Kitson and the Italian known as Giorgio are to be taken to the airport straight away and put on the aircraft. If these terms are not met, you know the consequences. You are to have a radio link set up between the plane and this number so that we can speak to our comrades.'

'But how do we know –' the voice began to protest.

She quickly broke the connection. She knew their tricks. Trying to get you to talk so they could trace the call. Well, they wouldn't catch her that way.

She went into the kitchen and made herself another coffee. She'd already drunk several cups. Her hands were shaking and she was as jumpy as a cat. She should go out and get something to eat, but she wasn't hungry any more.

She went to the window and stared down into the street. She wondered if they really did have Giorgio. Well, if so, she'd get him on to the plane with the others, and Nick Riley and his friends wouldn't be able to do a thing about it.

But her optimism was shaky and she didn't dare examine it too closely. Somewhere in the depths of her mind there was a nagging sense of abandonment. She had the feeling she would never see Giorgio again; already she was distancing herself from the memory of him.

Ever restless, she picked up the Kalashnikov and, unclipping the magazine, checked the mechanism.

Nick tried to make light of it. 'They just think it would be safer to go through the ceiling, that's all.'

'But it's so thick. It'll take hours.' Her voice was high and fearful.

'Well, they're going to *try*. They just think it would be safer,' he repeated.

'But – I don't understand. It would have been so *easy*.'

'I know. But, give them a while. If it doesn't work, they'll come back and try the door again. Okay?'

There was silence. After a while he realised she was not going to reply. He said, 'Chin up, there's a brave girl,' and then wished he'd kept quiet. He felt, instinctively, that it had been the wrong thing to say.

He stood up, heavy-hearted, and watched the army moving equipment into the dining-room which was situated above the cellar.

Conway appeared in the front doorway and beckoned him over.

'I've got an idea about those numbers, the ones our Eyetie had on him.'

They went and sat in the back of a car. Conway indicated the fourth number. 'See this one? It's got all the same numbers as the Danby girl's phone number. They're just in a slightly different order, right?' He pointed at a combination he had written alongside and Nick saw that the numbers were the same, but with the first four in reverse order.

'Now the third one has the same numbers as the service flat in Weymouth Street, but again in a different order. The *same* different order, if you see what I mean.'

Nick felt a shiver of excitement.

'And the others? What about the mews house?' he asked.

'I was going to ask you for the number. To save me getting it from London.'

Nick reached into his pocket and pulled out his address book. Looking under 'C' for Carelli, he read it out.

'Bingo,' said Conway quietly. 'It's the first number.'

Nick grasped Conway by the shoulder and gave him a rough shake of delight. 'You clever sod!' he exclaimed.

'Now, now, don't say things you might regret later,' said Conway. 'Right, let's get a make on this second number then, shall we? Must be a London number like the rest. Seven digits. But this last number – somehow I doubt we'll get much on that. Eight digits. An odd number of numbers, if you see what I mean.' Conway got out and, climbing into the front seat, called up Wilts HQ on the radio.

Nick went in search of Kershaw and found him talking rapidly to some of his men. Kershaw caught sight of him. Even before he spoke, Nick knew that something was up. 'Ah, Ryder, there you are. The terrorists have made contact. And a decision has been taken.' He sighed. 'They're to be allowed to leave. Unimpeded. From Heathrow, I want you to come with me in the airport party. We leave in five minutes.'

Nick stared in dismay. The government seemed to be caving in without a fight. And without a single guarantee for the safety of the two in the cellar. What a fiasco.

A minute later Conway had an address for the second phone number: a flat in Chelsea Manor Street. Kershaw hurried off to the phone to organise an immediate raid.

Nick waited for Kershaw to finish. Before leaving for the airport he must call Desport back. And the office. And then – then he would have to have one last talk with the girl, to tell her that, despite his promise, he couldn't stay after all.

Twenty-eight

It was five to eleven. Gabriele began to get ready. She put the Kalashnikov, the ammunition clips and a few personal items into the large holdall along with fifty pounds of the money. She placed the holdall by the door. She washed briefly, splashing water over

355

her face, then brushed her hair. It was important to look good. She eyed herself critically in the mirror. She changed her clothes and jammed the Makarov into her jacket pocket. The rest of the cash and the precious Argentinian passport also went into the jacket, in an inner zip-up pocket.

That left the Skorpion. She wanted to keep it handy. In the past she'd always carried it in the tote bag, but another bag would be cumbersome. Best to abandon the tote bag altogether. She put the Skorpion in the top of the holdall, where she could grab it easily.

But she wasn't sure if she had done the right thing. It was the nervousness. She must calm down. And make some more decisions.

Eleven. The airport was half an hour away. She would leave at quarter past eleven and arrive just before noon. Whether or not Raymond phoned. It was impossible to leave it any longer.

Somewhere near the airport she would stop and phone and talk to Max on the radio link to make sure everything was going all right.

Once at the airport she would take a hostage and walk on to the plane. For perhaps the twentieth time that morning she conjured up the scene in her mind: the plane waiting on the tarmac, the others already inside, the pig-police watching but helpless to do anything about it. Then she imagined herself, walking out on to the tarmac, a slim dramatic figure holding the Kalashnikov at someone's back.

She had a sudden doubt. Would it be wise to do it that way?

There might be marksmen on the rooftops. They might pick her off.

And yet – they wouldn't dare, would they? She would still hold the trump card: the attorney-man, and where he was, and how to de-rig him. They daren't touch her until she'd given them the information.

In her imagination she resumed the scenario on the airport tarmac. She would walk slowly, confidently . . . All those watching would notice her poise, her command of the situation. Perhaps there would be TV cameras and pressmen. Yes: there were bound to be. They would record the whole thing. Perhaps she would turn at the top of the steps, so they could get a good view of her. They would love that. They would call her the beautiful gunwoman, or something similar – they always called a woman beautiful if she was half decent-looking and if it would add to the drama of the story. Her picture would be on the front page of every newspaper in the world. The headlines would express outrage at this unthinkable event: blatant terrorism in Western Europe, the stronghold of law and order. And, most galling of all for them, they would have to report that one person – and a woman at that – had outmanoeuvred the entire British police force (not difficult, admittedly) and the might of the British government.

A real coup.

She reminded herself: When it happened.

If only Raymond would phone. She loathed hanging around.

She attempted to read *The Times*, but her eyes skimmed the words without taking anything in. There was, of course, nothing about the disappearance of the Attorney-General. She wasn't surprised: they were bound to hush it up if only to save face. But they wouldn't be able to hush it up much longer.

She walked to the window. The street scene was becoming irritatingly familiar.

The silence was split by the jangling of the telephone.

She jumped violently, and stared at it as if it had struck her. Tentatively she walked over and picked it up.

'Yes?'

'This is Raymond.'

She felt a surge of relief. '*Oh*, Thank God—'

'That special friend of yours,' he interrupted, 'the one you're hoping to see. He's in Damascus. I'm sure he'll be very happy to see you there. But why don't you surprise him? Don't tell anyone you're going – just drop in. Do you understand what I mean?'

Gabriele thought rapidly. She must get this right.

'Yes. You mean – make it a total surprise.'

'Absolutely. In fact, if he knew you were coming he might put you off – you know how it is. So many commitments and pressures. But if you just arrive, I'm fairly sure he won't turn you away. So my friends tell me.'

'I understand.'

'Goodbye then.'

She put down the phone, elated. She'd known he would fix something. She'd known that he would move heaven and earth. There was a bond of commitment and loyalty between them: a bond that was strong and pure and enduring; something the money-grabbing materialists could never understand.

The thought lifted her, and she felt a new optimism.

It was only five past eleven. *Think*. Should she go yet? She didn't want to hang around the airport. They'd be looking for her there.

Wait then? She didn't like that either.

She decided to call *The Times* number again, to make sure everything was going to plan. She would drive to a phone box some distance away and make it from there. That would use up the time nicely.

She checked the flat to make sure she hadn't left anything behind, then went to the window to take a last look out.

The Ford was parked in its usual place. Another car was manoeuvring into a space just in front of it. She watched it park. A girl in a very brief mini-skirt got out and, locking the door, walked jauntily off along the pavement. A youth coming towards her gazed openly at her legs and, passing by, stopped to watch the rear view wiggling ridiculously away.

A delivery van roared along the road and turned into an adjacent street.

Nothing. Nothing to worry about at all.

She was about to turn away when another vehicle caught her eye. It was stopping some way up the street to the left, almost on a corner. She watched it park and waited for the driver to emerge. A minute later the door still hadn't opened.

She glanced impatiently at her watch. It really *was* time to go now. She looked back at the car. She was worrying too much. It was just someone waiting.

She went to the door, put on her jacket and lifted the holdall. It was heavy. Perhaps she should have abandoned one of the weapons. But it was too late now.

Checking that she had the car keys handy in her pocket, she went out into the communal hall. Everything was quiet. She slipped down the stairs to the street and paused in the doorway. She eased her head out and looked up the road. That car was still there. It was hard to see if there was anyone in it. Maybe the driver had got out while she was on her way down.

She looked the other way, to the right. A Harrod's van was growling up the street towards her. She waited for it to pass. Some distance behind, a car was approaching normally.

She glanced back to the left. Nothing to worry about. She walked across the pavement and paused between two parked cars to look for traffic. The approaching car was fifty yards away and braking suddenly. She kept perfectly still, watching. It swerved violently into the opposite kerb and stopped.

Unusual. Swerving suddenly into the kerb. Not many people drove like that.

She pulled back a step. No one was getting out of the car.

That made two cars that no one had got out of.

It meant nothing. *Surely*.

She waited motionless, staring at the second car, dark blue and ominous, gleaming darkly. She caught a glimpse of movement inside. The driver. And someone else. Perhaps even a *third*.

Her stomach turned. She looked across the road to the Ford. So near. The width of the street. All she had to do was walk over. Yet a warning bell screamed in the back of her mind. If she moved it would invite disaster . . .

Better to stay still and uncommitted . . .

The faint chug of a diesel engine sounded in the distance. Beyond the second car, a taxi was approaching. The cab came parallel with the car. It was moving between her and the mysterious watching figures.

She had only a split second.

She reached into the holdall and, pulling the Skorpion out, thrust it under her jacket.

Not enough free hands.

The cab roared past. She followed it with her eyes as if checking that the absence of a For Hire light had told the truth and that it was indeed occupied. Then, as if searching for another cab, she looked back.

Behind the windscreen of the dark car something caught the light and gleamed.

Binoculars?

She looked again at the Ford. It would seem odd if she suddenly walked across to it and got in. Or would it? She could easily have given up the idea of taking a cab and decided on a car instead . . .

But a *car*. A car was something which could be followed and stopped. A car was a trap.

Before she could change her mind, she turned and stepped back on to the pavement. She made herself walk casually along the pavement, away from the second car and towards the street that ran down the side of the block of flats. Diagonally ahead of her was the first car. She could see two people in it.

Keeping her elbow tight against the Skorpion, she reached the corner and turned left down the side street. Out of the corner of her eye she saw the door of the first car start to open.

This was it then.

She quickened her pace and examined the street ahead. On the right, there was an estate of council flats whose blocks were connected by a honeycomb of courtyards and archways.

She crossed the street and risked a quick glance behind. A man wearing a raincoat had appeared at the corner, hovering, eyeing her uncertainly, as if he wasn't absolutely sure.

Ignoring the archway leading into the estate, she hurried on, walking fast. Ahead was another street. If she turned right, it would take her along a second side of the council estate. She came to a decision. Making a supreme effort not to look behind, she walked on. She reached the corner, rounded it—

Now.

She burst into a sprint.

It was difficult to run with both hands encumbered. The holdall bumped maddeningly against her leg. She held it up, clear of her leg, and felt her arm complain. The other arm she kept firmly jammed against the Skorpion under her jacket. She pushed on, running wildly, her eyes on another archway ahead. She could almost feel the man behind her, rounding the corner, his eyes burning into her back.

She came to the archway and, diving in, stopped. She put her head out and took a quick look back.

He was just appearing at the corner, looking round in alarm, beginning to run with no clear idea of where he was going.

He hadn't seen her.

Immediately she darted off into the courtyard. Ahead was another achway, leading to a second courtyard. She sped towards it, trying to work out how long it would take the raincoat man to reach the archway and see her.

Once through, she wheeled to the left. Ahead was an archway which would bring her out on the third side of the estate. She approached it cautiously. She put her eye to the corner and looked both ways.

Nothing.

Rapidly, she pulled off her jacket, draped it over the Skorpion and walked out into the street. Her jacket was black, her sweater green. If she was seen, the difference might just be enough to confuse them.

She turned left, heading back towards the street where she had last seen raincoat man.

This was the tricky bit. The fear rose in her throat.

If she'd got it right he would be chasing through the network of yards and passages inside the estate. If she'd got it wrong, he would even now be loping along the street and they would meet face to face on the corner . . .

She grasped the butt of the pistol. *God, but she felt so much better with a gun in her hand* . . .

The corner came up. She slowed and inched forward.

Nothing! Exultant, she hurried away, heading for the King's Road. She could see it ahead, busy with traffic and shoppers. Once there she could lose herself in the crowds and find a cab to take her out to the airport . . .

No more than a hundred yards now. She looked behind. Clear. She hurried on, almost sick with apprehension.

Coming to a junction, she glanced automatically down the side street. And froze.

God.

The dark car. Right at the far end, *coming.*

She forced herself to continue her journey across the street to the next corner. She heard the car accelerate suddenly. *They had seen her.*

Time to stop running.

Dropping the holdall on the pavement and throwing the jacket aside, she grasped the Skorpion in both hands and, flicking the change lever on to automatic, crouched behind a parked car.

The engine roared up noisily, then slowed as it braked for the corner. The car shot into view. She stood up. The surprised faces stared out of the car windows at her. She gave it a short burst. The driver's hands fought the wheel, the car shot on across the junction. There was a loud crash of colliding tearing metal, and the dark car was at a halt against a parked car.

Gabriele reached for the holdall, ready to run, but hesitated. A man, completely unhurt, was getting out of the back of the police car, poising himself to run at her. Bracing herself again, she aimed slightly to the right and squeezed the trigger, intending to fire the burst across his body.

The pistol vibrated in her hands, spitting its muted cough.

Then silence.

She squeezed the trigger harder.

Nothing.

A *jam!*

She looked wildly from the gun to the man. The man was staggering and falling, grasping his side. She'd got him then, after all.

She paused, scenting the wind. Sirens sounded in the distance, coming closer. Far down the street she saw a running figure coming rapidly towards her, raincoat man. She felt a flutter of panic. Impossible to shoot it out, even with the Kalashnikov. Take a hostage? Run?

She threw the Skorpion down and, picking up the holdall, started to run. Crossing the road she darted into a small side street. She kept running, glancing over her shoulder. She rounded another corner into another street of small Chelsea houses, zig-zagging her way gradually towards the King's Road. The wail of the sirens grew steadily closer. She began to tire.

She glanced over her shoulder. Nothing. *Yet.* But a siren was coming closer all the time. From behind.

Ahead, the King's Road, tantalisingly close. Yet too *far.*

Gabriele thought: I can't bear it.

Two yards ahead, a woman was standing outside the front doorway of her home, looking out into the street, irritated at all the noise in her quiet expensive neighbourhood.

Without slowing her pace, Gabriele swerved in through the metal gate, up the steps to the door and, before the surprised woman could utter a word, had yanked her inside the house and slammed the door.

The siren wailed to a crescendo, hovering in a high-pitched scream which filled the air, then slowly faded.

Gabriele leant against the door for a moment, panting hard, letting the relief flow through her, before turning her attention to the woman. The woman was making a lot of noise. She was sixty-ish, with tightly curled hair rinsed a pale shade of blue, and several rows of pearls over a massive bosom. She was squawking indignantly, her bosom swelling like a set of massive bellows. She reminded Gabriele of a ludicrous turkey, gobbling and parading.

Gabriele said, 'Shut up.'

The woman gaped and said, 'Well *really!* I'm going to phone the police!'

Gabriele saved her breath. The wobbling gobbling mouth would clam shut once it saw the Makarov.

She reached down to her pocket.

The jacket.

In the holdall. *It must be.*

But even as she bent down and thrust a hand into the bag she *remembered*.

Throwing the jacket on to the pavement.

Leaving it.

She cried out, 'Oh *no*! Oh G-o-d!'

The Makarov.

Then she froze in disbelief as the realisation dawned that it was much, much worse.

The money. The passport.

She had nothing but fifty pounds. And the Kalashnikov.

They'd said it was urgent. Nick sat in the car, waiting impatiently to be connected through the radio link-up. He might as well be calling Mongolia as Paris for the time it was taking. And he only had a few minutes before the last car left for the airport; minutes which he needed to make a brief explanation to the girl.

He was just about to give the call up when the number finally rang and he was through to Desport.

Nick listened to the DST man with growing incredulity.

'What do you mean the camper van was *seen* outside this organisation?'

'It was logged by our man.'

'Then this Aid and Solidarity place is well known to you?'

'Yes.'

'Why weren't we *told* – about the van, I mean.'

'You were,' replied Desport. 'The information was passed on in the normal way, to our liaison man who would have passed it on to your Security Service.'

Bloody Box 500. Bloody Reece-Jones. Doubtless the information was filed away in some dust-coated archive and no one had thought it worth disseminating to Special Branch. Secretive and incompetent to the bloody end. Nick thought: Sod them all.

'So tell me, Claude,' Nick asked bitterly. 'Who are these people, Aide et Solidarité?'

'They help political refugees, particularly Third World people. With accommodation, contacts, that sort of thing.'

'So what would our Italian be doing there?'

'Well, there's a possibility they provide other services.'

'Like?'

'Papers, false passports . . .'

'And?'

'And maybe even more.' He was sounding a little defensive. 'But – that is not certain.'

Nick ventured, 'Arms and training?'

There was a pause. 'It's possible.'

Nick thought: Marvellous. A subversive organisation operating under the noses of the French. 'And did these people realise they were helping terrorists to operate in Britain?' he asked.

'Ah, yes. I was getting round to that. We have already notified your headquarters that there was a telephone call made from Aide et Solidarité just a short time ago which could be of interest. It was to England. A veiled conversation. But there was a mention of Damascus. It is possible this is the destination that has been arranged for your terrorists.'

Nick absorbed the information. So they'd been tapping the organisation's phone for some time. Pity nothing of 'interest' had come up before. Nick said coldly, 'Thanks. You'll keep us informed?'

'Of course. We don't like these people any more than you do, you know.'

Nick rang off and thought: I wonder.

Now – Victoria.

He hurried across the drive and into the house. The loud whine of an electric saw sounded from the dining-room. Major Phipps was crouching by the cellar door, talking urgently. He was not looking happy with the conversation. As Nick approached, the major flung him an imploring glance.

'It's very difficult to be certain,' he was saying. 'I'd have to know how much explosive there was. But if it's a tiny quantity like you say, then it's *very* unlikely.' He added hastily. 'Look, I've got to dash now. But Sergeant Ryder's here. I know he wants to have a word with you.'

He stood up and whispered to Nick, 'She's asking all sorts of questions about the devices. Seems to be worried about one setting off the other. Anyway – I've reassured her as best I can.' He indicated the dining-room. 'Got to get back. That floor's made of ship's timbers with enormous cross-beams. It's taking longer than I thought to get through.' He strode off, looking immensely relieved to be returning to the job in hand.

Nick sat down and put his mouth to the door. 'Hello, Victoria.'

'Hello. I'm glad you're here.' Her tone was brisk. 'There's something I want to ask you.'

'Yes?'

'Promise to tell me the truth?'

Nick hesitated. He didn't want to be put in an awkward corner. He murmured reluctantly, 'I'll try.'

'Tell me why they're not coming through the door.'

So that was it. He couldn't see any reason why she shouldn't know. It couldn't make things any worse, and the uncertainty was obviously bothering her.

'A note was found. Saying the door was booby-trapped.'

'But it *isn't*. I would have seen.'

'Well – it isn't that we don't believe you. It's just – we don't want to take any chances with your safety.'

There was a silence.

'They'll be through the ceiling in no time. It's safer this way. You *do* see?'

'Yes.'

'How's Sir Henry?'

'He's all right. I spoke to him a moment ago.'

Now for the awkward bit. 'Victoria, something's come up. The terrorists have asked for a plane to be laid on at the airport. And – I have to go.'

A pause. 'I understand.' Her voice was so low he could barely hear it.

'Believe me, I would stay if I could. I'm sorry.'

He could imagine her, sitting there on the step, feeling alone. He had promised to stay, and now he was breaking his word.

'I'll come back and see you just as soon as I can. The minute the airport business is over. And that's a definite promise. You'll be out of here by then.' He struggled on, wishing she would reply and ease the moment along. 'And then I'll make sure you're looked after. I promise.'

'That's all right.' Her voice was ragged and uneven. 'I'll see you later. When you get back.'

He sighed. He felt a bit of a heel.

'Goodbye then, Victoria. Remember, I'll be thinking of you.'

'Tell me, have you got fair wavy hair? Longish?'

Her question took him by surprise. 'Yes.'

'I remember you then. I remember what you look like.'

He laughed, 'You'll know who to be angry with then.' Looking at his watch, he said a last goodbye and hurried away.

Henry wondered if it wasn't better to be without hope. Then at least you knew where you were. But he dismissed the thought almost immediately: better to live with the uncertainties of hope than to die alone and in despair.

The hum of the saws was getting louder by the minute. They should be through very soon now. Then—

Then, he reminded himself, it could still end in disaster. The only difference was that other people would die with him. That worried him. It was unnecessary.

At the same time, the hope that everything would end well had grown steadily in his mind. He had resisted it at first, but now he let it lift and sustain him. It could do no harm. It took his mind off the fact that he was exceedingly thirsty and that the pins and needles which had plagued his right leg for some hours had given way to a dull aching numbness. No: hope could do no harm . . . Better to pass the time thinking of a future with Caroline than to brood about having no future at all.

He imagined himself and Caroline sitting on a beach. The baby was playing in the sand nearby. He noted that the beach was nowhere near Venice. Venice didn't seem important any more.'

The three of them were bathed in a glow of warm yellow light. The light of happiness. He had always doubted that people's hearts could swell with love, but he felt it happen to him now.

He pulled himself up. He was getting dangerously sentimental. It wouldn't do to be in an emotional state.

There was an especially loud noise.

Were they through?

If only he could see into the main cellar. But he must be patient.

'*Henry*?' Victoria's voice was hardly audible above the noise.

He drew breath to reply but the sound grew louder and the effort was too great.

The next moment there was a crumbling sound and the patter of falling plaster.

Suddenly the patter grew to a deep rumble and a great whoosh of air blew across the box, bringing a dense cloud of fine white dust in its wake.

366

Henry coughed and tried to turn his head away, but the dust was everywhere, filling his nose and lungs.

He coughed more violently, but with each gasp he sucked in more of the dense, choking dust. He couldn't *breathe*. As he fought desperately for the air that wasn't there he felt the beginnings of a cold remorseless panic.

Victoria raised her head from her chest. The fine white dust hung suspended in the air like a cloud. Coughing violently, she peered down into the cellar. It was almost impossible to see.

'Henry? *Henry?*'

She called until she was hoarse but there was no reply. In exasperation she turned to the door and shouted for help. Why wasn't anybody *there*?

At last someone replied. She recognised the voice of the army man.

She cried, 'Quick – *quick* – you must help.' She could hear herself babbling. 'Henry – I think something's happened to him. Please – *help*.'

'We're not quite through yet.' The man was using the tone that adults use to placate small children. 'In fact, I'm afraid there may be a lot more dust. We can't quite see – but it looks as though the entire ceiling may come down. It's obviously a bit dicky. Can you hold on in there?'

She coughed harshly, trying to clear her lungs. Regaining her breath, she begged, '*Please* – why don't you come in through the door?'

'Er – well, we might end up doing that. But we're going to press on with the ceiling. Just for the moment.' He spoke with finality.

She shook her head. It was a nightmare. A sort of Mad Hatter's tea party where, for no apparent reason, everyone did the opposite of what they should. Through the depths of her tiredness she couldn't work out why.

She called to Henry again. *Nothing.*

The hearty voice was still there. 'Just hold on, won't you!' it said, full of forced optimism. 'All right?'

'What time is it?' she asked.

'Ah. Don't you worry yourself about that. Plenty of time yet. Got to go and see how the lads are doing. Back in a mo.'

Victoria knew then. *Of course.* He hadn't dared tell her. That there wasn't much time at all. How long? Half an hour. Ten minutes. *Less?*

There was still no sound from Henry. She couldn't bear it. He *had* to be all right. That was the whole *point* of everything ... The reason for making all this effort: this keeping going for hour after hour, this good behaviour, this talking through the door as if everything was normal. She couldn't *bear* it if all that had been for nothing. Henry *had* to be all right. Without him, nothing would ever be the slightest bit right again.

Her own future tightened round her like a band. She could feel it encircling her head. In time it would crush her. There would be no escape from what she had done. No forgiveness. People would always remember: she didn't blame them. The shame would be with her always. Unbearable. And lonely. And she *would* be alone. Alone and lonely. She was fat and ugly, she could see that now. Men might be kind, like that police sergeant, but no one would ever want her. Not really. No. She could see that now.

She felt ashamed to think about such things. What mattered was the poor young policeman lying in the pool of blood, appallingly dead because of her, and Henry suffocating in that dreadful box.

A sudden vision of Giorgio came into her mind. She saw herself swinging the metal bar like a mad animal, the blows crushing his head. Then in some extraordinary way he was all right again and getting up and coming towards her, smiling secretly, knowing he could make her do it all over *again*.

The thought was loathsome because it was *true*. Or was it? What was true? She couldn't think. It was all getting very strange. Nothing was quite real any more. A deep weariness pulled at her, confusing her thoughts. And yet one idea remained vividly clear.

Someone *must* get to Henry. If anything happened, she would never forgive herself.

Tears slipped down her round cheeks. She knew what she must do.

It should be safe, the army man had said so. The small brick cellar was far enough away ...

She gave herself a moment to let the intolerable pressure of thoughts subside. Then she grasped at two simple, comforting ideas. That she would soon be released from the burden of what she had done. And that Henry would be all right.

Then it was easy.

She screwed up her eyes and, uttering a loud cry, stood up.

Nick cried, '*Pull over!*'

The driver beside him didn't need any encouragement. He was white as a sheet. Finding a lay-by, he swerved in and braked to a halt.

The four of them sat in silence, listening to the flat monotonal voice on the radio.

'. . . The second subject is okay. The army is through and working on him now. Over.'

The mike lay forgotten in Nick's hand. The driver took it from him and acknowledged.

Nick put his head in his hands.

One of the detectives in the back said, 'Thank God for that. Only the girl. I thought for a moment—'

'Yeah,' said another. 'Lucky they didn't both go up. At least there's a chance now. For *him*.'

'I wonder what happened,' murmured the driver. 'Think it was on a timer?'

'No. She probably panicked and thought she could run away from it.'

Nick flung open the door and, walking a few yards away, drew in some deep draughts of cool fresh air.

Twenty-nine

'Thank you, sir. That seems to give me the picture.' Captain Edwin Harris, Royal Engineers, specialist in bomb disposal for more than twenty years, spoke cheerfully, not only because he wanted to reassure the pale tense figure lying in the box, but because he *was* quite cheerful. This was going to be a challenge, and if one didn't like the idea of meeting challenges then one had no business being in bomb disposal.

He sat in thought for a moment, going over what Sir Henry had told him, trying to picture the form that the infernal device – as it was known in the trade – might take. Possibly a time–delay fuse, if Sir Henry had overheard the terrorists correctly. Four or five sticks of explosive, nine or ten inches long. Possibly this mixture of TNT and ammonium nitrate called Nitramite 19C, if the terrorists were using the same stuff as before. Not that the exact make was vital. All explosives went bang.

The exact make and type of detonator didn't matter that much either. What really counted was the initiator. If it was a delayed-action fuse, as the terrorists had suggested, then the delaying mechanism might be electrical or chemical. If electrical, there must be a timing device, and a sophisticated one at that – not an ordinary clock and certainly not an egg-timer – since it had been set over twelve hours before. A chemical delay was unlikely but not impossible. The method favoured by anarchists involved filling a rubber contraceptive with acid which slowly burnt its way through on to a highly combustible substance. But it was unreliable, since one could never be sure how long the process would take.

No. If it was a delayed-action fuse, then he was pretty sure it must be electrical. First thing, then, was to have a good listen. From his box of tricks he took out a device not unlike a doctor's stethoscope, except it was powered by batteries which amplified sounds up to five times. He listened for a good three minutes, moving the sensor from place to place on the surface of the box. He was listening for any sort of ticking, or the click of an electrical timer. Around the stomach area, where the device was apparently located, all he could hear was Sir Henry's laboured breathing. It was possible that a faint sound could be lost behind it.

So – it could still be anything. At this stage it was important not to rule anything out. He must keep his mind open to every possibility.

One possibility – and quite a strong one, he believed – was that it wasn't a delayed-action fuse at all, but a mechanical initiator that would be triggered by the opening of the box or the handling of the device itself.

One thing was for sure: it wasn't vibration activated. Otherwise the blast five minutes ago would have set it off and blown up not only Sir Henry, but a lot of the house as well.

'All right then,' he said brightly. 'We'll get going. Anything you want to ask before I start, sir?'

Sir Henry coughed violently. He wasn't sounding at all well. His breathing was heavy and laboured. The shock of the explosion can't have helped. The poor bloke had probably thought he was going up too. Lucky he didn't.

The coughing ceased. He was trying to say something. 'She died instantly, did she?'

Captain Harris said gravely, 'Yes. Instantly.' In fact she had lived for a minute, but only in a technical sense; her heart had kept beating, pumping blood out through the massive hole in her back. But she had been unconscious, so it had hardly counted. The body was still here. No point in removing it and endangering more lives. Harris had thrown a coat over it.

Now there was just Sir Henry and himself. Harris wondered how long Sir Henry could withstand the strain. At the moment he was still calm and composed. It was vital that he didn't panic.

Although he generally preferred to work in silence, Harris said, 'Look, if at any time you're worried, feel uneasy, or just want to talk, do so, won't you? And of course you will tell me if you feel anything move or click or whirr or anything like that. Are you with me?'

'Yes, I understand. The only thing is, I may not be able to stop myself coughing.'

'That's all right. But perhaps you could give me some warning.'

'I'll try.' Sir Henry managed a weak smile. Harris smiled back. They were going to get on fine.

Harris began by taking a good look at the box. He crawled round it, minutely examining the wood for signs of holes or fittings. He stopped on the right side, where Sir Henry had said the girl had been sitting while setting up the device. There was a small hole. Of course it might have been there before. On the other hand it could have been used to remove a safety device and arm the bomb.

The lid itself was fixed down with nails. There might easily be a spring mechanism jammed underneath; the lid was definitely *not* the way to approach the problem, then.

He shone a torch down past Sir Henry's shoulder and had a look with a mirror. However, the poor man's body was jammed so tight up against the lid of the box it was hard to see beyond his chest.

Sir Henry was lying with his knees pushed over to the right, so he had said. The obvious approach was from that side. However, it would be wisest to start from the end of the box, as far away from the device as possible, and see what he could discover from there.

After asking Sir Henry exactly where his feet were located, he cut a small hole in the end, well away from the lid and hopefully from Sir Henry's feet, and removed the offcut. Nothing untoward in sight. Cautiously he slipped a finger into the hole and felt gently around. When he was satisfied, he made the hole a little larger. Eventually, the hole was large enough to take a really good look.

As far as he could tell there was nothing in this end of the box at all. Unfortunately, however, Sir Henry's thighs were twisted across to the right and, apart from the area by the knee, jammed up against the lid, so that he could not see beyond to the stomach area.

But what was that by the knee? Something screwed on to the side of the box, just under the lid.

And a wire leading from it.

Ah.

He cut a hole in the side of the box below the knee, where he knew it was clear, and had another look. Ah yes, more and more interesting. A pressure release switch, which would be activated by the opening of the lid. Two wires led from it but were lost to view between the clothing and the lid.

Part one of the puzzle.

He asked, 'As far as you remember the entire device is on your stomach?'

'Yes.'

'Nothing on your sides?'

'Only the tape she fastened it on with.'

'And where is your right hand, sir?' he asked.

'Against my right leg.'

'And your arm is pressed hard against the side of the box?'

'Yes.'

'I'm going to take a section of the side away in that area. You may feel the saw but hopefully not the cutting edge.'

'Right.'

Harris cut into the side of the box half-way along, where he judged Sir Henry's stomach to be, and made a six-inch hole near the bottom so as to keep well away from the lid and from the small hole which might or might not be significant. He removed the offcut. Nothing but clothing in sight. He slipped his fingers inside the edge of the hole and felt around. No wires. He pushed his entire hand in. Nothing. He listened. No unusual sounds.

He enlarged the hole to within four inches of the lid. Ah, that was more like it. He could see over Sir Henry's arm to the area of his stomach. He shone a torch in. *There*. The side of the device: two sticks of explosive visible. Plus . . .

Bother, he reflected mildly. He couldn't quite see.

He pressed gently down on Sir Henry's sleeve so that he could aim the torch beam higher up into the box.

There.

Wires.

Right. The wires could belong to a simple electrical circuit connecting the charge to the pressure release switch. In which case a simple cut of the wire would deactivate it. On the other hand, the wires may be part of a collapsing circuit which, if cut, would complete a second circuit and fire the device. A sophisticated booby-trap. The firm rule was: do nothing until all the components of the device have been identified.

Often easier said than done.

Cautiously, he pushed his hand in through the hole and felt up the side of the box. This was fairly safe, since Sir Henry had, according to his story, wriggled his arm on several occasions.

Nothing so far. He pushed his hand further up the side until the tips of his fingers came to the join with the lid. He ran his fingers along the join. Nothing.

Checking with his hands to make sure it was safe he enlarged the hole still further, the whine of the jigsaw shattering the eerie silence. He peered in.

Ah. More of the wires were visible. They ran away from the infernal device along the underside of the lid towards Sir Henry's hip. One of them was hidden between the lid and the hip, the other dipped back down towards the floor. To the very thing he had been looking for.

A clothes peg. The wires connecting across two drawing-pins. On the floor beside it a piece of card attached to a strong thread. The safety device.

From the clothes peg the wire ran straight back up to the area where he had seen the pressure release switch.

Harris ran his fingers further along the join where the lid met the side. Yes, there it was. He barely touched it with the tip of his fingers. Two wires, one to a metal washer, the other to the plunger.

He felt a small satisfaction.

Two parts of the puzzle in place.

Now he must check that the second wire, which was caught up against the lid, did indeed run straight to the explosive charge. Very gently he pulled on the wire until it was free.

It did run straight to the charge.

He took a breather.

Then he cut into the other side of the box. He examined the explosive charge. No more wires in sight.

He'd got almost all the information he needed. There was only one unpleasant possibility. That there was more to the device than met the eye – a second circuit hidden *under* the explosive itself, next to Sir Henry's chest, which he couldn't see.

But that would be pretty sophisticated stuff. From what Sir Henry had said they had made this device fairly rapidly. Also, each bomb-maker had a style, a *modus operandi*, and this girl had done nothing before to suggest she was into clever booby-traps. Careful, *yes*. But sophisticated, *no*.

Sometimes one had to make a judgement. He made it now.

Taking some small wire cutters he reached in. At that moment Sir Henry made a sound and, drawing in a rasping involuntary breath, coughed loudly. Harris held still. The coughing fit lasted for a good thirty seconds. He gave it another minute to make sure Sir Henry was over it. The man was looking agitated now. Yes: this business would be over none too soon. Giving Sir Henry a comforting smile, he reached back into the box and felt for one of the wires.

He snipped it.

And blinked.

The great thing about getting it wrong was that, though something happened all right – and how – you would know nothing about it.

Next, he carefully capped off the two severed ends of wire with plastic tape. You could never be too careful.

Time for another breather. Sitting back on his heels, he said cryptically, 'Well, I think we've made progress. But still a few more things to check.'

'Well done.'

'You okay?'

'Oh yes,' he whispered. 'Don't – consider me. I've been here so long that . . .'

In his mind Harris finished the sentence for him: A little longer won't make any difference.

He turned his mind back to the job in hand.

He cut another hole in the left side of the box, near the feet. Nothing. He tried the other side, looking into the triangle formed by Sir Henry's bent knees.

Nothing.

Eventually he had cut enough away to have examined the entire lid where it met the wall of the box. No more pressure release switches anywhere.

It was still possible that there was some kind of initiator sitting directly on top of the charge. Very carefully he reached in and felt the device itself. He tried to slip his fingers over the top, but it was pressed up very close to the lid. However, by squeezing the device downward into Sir Henry's stomach, he eventually managed it.

There was nothing. He came to a decision. It was time to open the box. He took a wrench and began to lever open the lid. At each stage he checked the rim. Then, as soon as he could get to it, he taped back the plunger on the pressure release switch, just to be doubly sure. When he was satisfied, he prised the lid completely free of its nails. And swung it open.

There was a small gasp from Sir Henry, but Harris was too busy taking a good look to pay attention. No horrid surprises in sight.

Sir Henry's face was contorted with pain.

'Best stay as you are, sir,' Harris said. 'I've still got some checking to do.'

He thought: Very much so. He had to check the tape that bound the device to Sir Henry. This he did very carefully, looking for wires and triggers. Once satisfied, he cut it, keeping a steadying hand on the device itself.

A nasty mind would have put another pressure release switch underneath the device, next to Sir Henry's body. With exceptional care he examined the device from every angle then probed very gently underneath.

Two minutes later he lifted the device off Sir Henry's chest.

It still wasn't over.

'You sure nothing was put underneath you, sir?'

Sir Henry was obviously in a bad way, but he managed: 'Pretty sure.'

Harris checked anyway.

Five minutes later he called in his team to take the remains of the device away, and the stretcher party came down soon after. Then it really *was* over.

Harris shook Sir Henry's hand. He was a brave man. Strangely, the fellow didn't look very relieved, just dazed. Probably hadn't hoisted it in yet. And then there was the delayed shock. Harris guessed it would take him a long time to recover from his experience.

For Harris it was a lot easier. He was trained for it. Nevertheless, it did sometimes cross his mind that one day, for no good reason, the grand lottery in the sky might throw up his number. As usual he was rather pleased that today had not been the day.

Gabriele paid off the taxi at a phone box on the airport perimeter.

It was a quarter to twelve.

There was a petrol station further along the road. A good place to take a car-driving hostage. And she could still get into the airport by twelve.

She pulled *The Times* out of the holdall and propped it up in front of her. Her hand was shaking. She felt hot and feverish.

She put the money in and dialled, preparing her speech.

The number rang three times.

It answered. The same clipped voice. 'Hello?'

She pressed the button. The money dropped. She began, 'We will arrive at noon. You have fifteen minutes to complete the arrangements. Once we are safely in the air I will give you directions on how to locate the hostage and defuse the explosive. Now let me speak to my comrades.'

'I'm afraid it hasn't been possible to fix up the link—'

'*You have two seconds to get them on the line.*'

'Er – can you give us a little longer?' The voice was confident and strangely unperturbed.

She thought: They're just stalling. 'You don't *have* any longer!' she snapped. 'The attorney-man dies in half an hour. And I'm going to take more hostages! And if you haven't got that line open when I call back again the first hostage dies. *Understand*?'

There was a pause. Gabriele felt a burning impatience. Even now they must be tracing the call. She was about to slam the phone down when the voice came smoothly back.

'In that case the deal's off.'

Gabriele's heart gave a great lurch. The voice was very cool. Something was dreadfully wrong.

The voice continued, 'Sir Henry is safe and sound. The bombs are all defused. The deal's off. Although we are prepared to discuss surrender—'

'*Give me proof.*'

Another pause, as if the voice was conferring. Back it came, calm and controlled. 'Hunter's Wood Farm. In the cellar.'

Gabriele slammed down the phone, raging with anger. For a moment she couldn't grasp the enormity of the disaster.

Max, Stephie, Reardon. *Success.*

All gone. All gone.

Failure hit her like a punch in the stomach. She had been massively outrageously cheated, and the bitterness rose like bile in her throat.

Then she realised: they would be coming for her. Trying to catch her, trying to put her away.

Grabbing her belongings, she stumbled out of the box and walked rapidly away, looking over her shoulder. She crossed the A4, went past the petrol station, until she came to a residential road. She cut down it and lost herself in the network of roads beyond.

She came to another phone box. Someone was in it, a large homely woman who looked as though she was going to chat for hours. Gabriele paced up and down outside then beat on the glass. The woman gave her a withering look. Gabriele flung open the door. 'It's urgent!' Using all her strength she pulled the woman out.

'How dare you! Who do you think you are!'

Another squawker, like the woman in Chelsea. Gabriele had left that one tied up in the bath. To this one she merely snapped, '*Fuck off*!' The woman retreated, looking outraged.

Gabriele pulled the door shut behind her. Fumbling, she found her list of numbers and getting through to the international operator, asked for a transfer charge call to Paris, person to person.

Asking for the number restored some of her confidence. Raymond would know what to do. He would send her papers and money. He would get her out of the counry.

At last she heard the number ring and answer and the operator cut in, asking if they would accept the charge. With vast relief Gabriele heard Raymond's voice.

In the fraction of a second before she spoke two dull clicks sounded on the line.

*

Nick got back to the office in a mood of rage and disbelief. They had missed her at the hideout in Chelsea and now they had missed her at the airport.

Unbelievable.

The airport had been the perfect place for a trap. She could have been lured in under the pretence that all was well, and then been caught. Somehow. But the plan had been vetoed. Too dangerous. Innocent people might have died.

Now the intention was to seek her out in the normal way: plaster her picture over every air and seaport, watch for her on the streets, offer a reward for information. But it wasn't enough, not by a *long* way. They knew of two false passports she had used. She probably had others stashed away.

The more he thought about it the more convinced he was that she *would* escape. The idea filled him with bitter anger.

In a side room off the main incident room the items found near the scene of the shooting in Chelsea had been laid out. He recognised the jacket immediately. She'd worn it the evening they'd gone to dinner in Chelsea. It was strange to see it again now, familiar and harmless, beside the two chilling weapons. A machine pistol and a handgun. He didn't recognise the types and looked at the tags tied to the butts. Skorpion. Makarov. Russian or Czech presumably.

Then there was money. New notes in sequence: the bank job.

Finally, there was a passport. Argentinian. He picked it up and flicked through the pages. A very good fake. He paused at the photograph. The sight of her still had the power to unsettle him. That look – so intense, so antagonistic; the small angry abandoned child.

He snapped the passport shut and put it back on the table.

Conway put his head in. 'We're wanted.'

'The DST have been in touch,' Kershaw said as soon as they reached his office. 'They've just telexed a transcript of a phone conversation which took place half an hour ago.'

Nick grabbed the telex. Attached to it was an English translation. It read:

Call logged at 12.55 French time. Reverse charge from England to premises of Aide et Solidarité, Rue St Médard, 5th Arrondissement. Person to person: Gabriele to Raymond:

Female voice: Raymond? I need help. I – things have gone wrong. I've got to get out—

Male voice: I'm so sorry, this is not in fact Raymond. He's out at present. Could I ask you to call him later on the other number?

F: What? But I . . . (*Pause.*)

M: He'll be on the other number in about one hour's time. You have the other number?

F: Er . . . Yes, I have it. Yes, I understand. I'll call then. In one hour. He will be there won't he? It's very urgent.

M: Yes, he'll be there. Goodbye.

F: Goodbye.

(*Conversation ends.*)

'Have they got a tap on this other number?' Nick asked excitedly.

'How *can* they when they don't know what the number is?' Kershaw demanded shortly. He looked tired and irritable. He said more reasonably, 'They *have* got a tap on this Raymond's private number, so they say. But apparently he knows perfectly well that it's tapped, so . . .'

So, Nick thought, there wasn't a cat in hell's chance of them using it. His excitement evaporated.

He asked, 'Don't the DST have any contacts inside this Aid and Solidarity place?'

Kershaw raised his eyebrows slightly. 'We've requested all possible assistance. That's all we can do—'

'We might ask bloody Box 500 and the other lot what else they've been sitting on,' Nick exclaimed hotly. 'If the van incident is anything to go by, they've known about these people in Paris all along.'

Kershaw rubbed a hand over his face. 'I've got their report in front of me, Ryder. It doesn't add a great deal to what we already know.' He regarded Nick thoughtfully. 'Why don't you go home and get some rest? You look as though you need it.'

Nick opened his mouth to speak but something in the commander's face made him shut up.

He went up to his office and sat at his desk for a while. There was no question of his going home. Not while Gabriele was out there. Free. He couldn't bear to think of her getting away. The idea made him so angry that he had to get up and move around.

There must be *something* he could do. Even if it was only to go out and search the streets.

Ridiculous. *Think*.

He sat up again and eyed the telephone, deep in thought. An idea came to him. He turned it over in his mind. It was worth a try. *Anything* was worth a try.

Picking up the receiver he dialled Paris and, after some discussion with Claude Desport's office, not all of it amicable, managed to get Desport called away from his lunch.

'Sorry to ruin your meal, Claude. Nothing special, I trust?'

'Hah! With the time available? A sandwich, my friend.'

'Do you owe me any favours, Claude?'

'Well, I like to think we come out even, Nick. Fifty-fifty. Eh?'

'I want to use them up all at once.'

'Ah.'

'We've asked the DST for assistance in the matter of this girl. Right? Where do you think that's going to get us, Claude?'

'We will of course do all we . . .' There was a silence. 'Not so very far perhaps. Not directly.'

'Quite. That's why I'm asking you. To do what you can. It means a lot to me. Maybe even my job, Claude.' Nick mentioned the job as a weapon of persuasion, instinctively trying to add a touch of drama, but even as he said it he realised it was probably true. 'I was thinking,' he continued. 'There must be something you could pressurise them with. Something you've got on them. They've been operating for quite some time. Surely —'

There was a sharp intake of breath. 'Nick, these people are not just – *anything*. They're not just a political group. They have contacts. Links. Perhaps all the way to Moscow. You ask more than I can give.'

'All we want is a lead to the girl, Claude.'

'You ask too much.' But there was a thoughtfulness in his voice. 'But your job . . . You mean it?'

'I mean it.' Nick made a feeble attempt at humour. 'I got everything ever so slightly disastrously wrong.' He gave it a moment then pressed: 'It will mean more than I can say.'

There was a deep sigh. 'I promise nothing. You hear? Absolutely nothing.'

From the closed door of the darkroom in the Studio Vincenne came the occasional sound as the photographer worked at his task. He had promised to produce two passports in one hour. There really couldn't be anyone better, not only for speed but for quality.

From stolen blanks the man could produce a finished passport complete with personal details, photograph, embossing, and stamps so near perfect that only a real expert could tell the difference. He was the organisation's greatest asset.

Bernard Duteil waited, thoughtfully smoking his cigarette, and wondered which courier he should send to England. There were several young people who were glad to do little jobs for him in exchange for trips abroad. He never asked them to carry anything really compromising. No arms. Only money, papers – things that would never get them into serious trouble. Most of them enjoyed doing their little errands.

This time, however, he must choose carefully. There was quite a risk involved. It was possible he might be sending someone straight into the arms of the British police. When Gabriele had made her second call – to the priest's number – she'd sworn that she'd take care not to be followed. But she was sounding nervous and frightened. Capable of error.

He had known she was in deep trouble. He had heard the radio news. The kidnapping idea had been quite clever, but she had obviously made some very basic mistakes. Two of her group dead. And the hostage discovered before she'd got away.

It could have been bad luck, of course, but he was beginning to believe otherwise. She had failed in both her tasks: in subverting British society and in forming a group capable of continuing the work. It had turned into a fiasco.

And after all his hard work arranging the welcome in Damascus. He felt justified in being irritated. He had used a few favours there.

But if the Damascus business was annoying, the interest in Gabriele's telephone calls was worrying. The phone taps were back in full swing and, by the number of clicks on the line, they didn't mind letting him know. It was a not-so-subtle warning. And yet he owed some sort of loyalty to the girl, if only to get her out and away before she did any damage. And, more importantly, to cheat the British government of total victory. He didn't want them to gloat. If the entire group were imprisoned it would be a bad example to those who might one day follow in Gabriele's footsteps.

So he would send her the passports and some money, with the suggestion that a ferry to the Irish Republic and a plane from Dublin to Stockholm might be the safest route out of the country.

He had already told Gabriele where to meet the courier and how to recognise him. Now he must choose the right person.

He finally decided on a bright young art student who, though very new to the organisation, had a way with him: an apparent naïvety and endearing loquacity which could fool anyone into believing he knew nothing about the contents of the envelope.

As soon as the passports were ready, he would send a message to the student asking him if he wanted a trip to London. Duteil was confident he would agree. The only important thing was that he should wear a red scarf. A rather ridiculous device as a means of recognition, but serviceable enough.

Finally the photographer emerged. He was not a man to boast about his skills, but Duteil could see that he was satisfied with the results of his hour in the darkroom. Duteil did not need to inspect the finished products.

He made his way back to the Rue St Médard. It was necessary to get the details tidied up as soon as possible. The student had to be on the ten o'clock plane to London the next morning.

As he approached the door beside the newsagent's shop a car door opened and a man emerged.

'Monsieur Duteil?'

Duteil knew immediately. The man had authority written all over him. DST? Yes, he decided: DST.

He gave a small nod.

The man said, 'There is something of interest I would like to bring to your notice. May we talk? In the car?'

Duteil considered. These people had absolutely nothing on him, nothing they could ever make stick. He could refuse point blank to talk either in the car, at the station or anywhere else. At the same time the man's opening remark suggested there might be something in it for him.

'Not in the car. In the café.' He indicated a small place up the street. He preferred neutral territory.

They settled at a corner table.

'Monsieur Duteil,' the officer began carefully, 'you have managed to live quietly in this country for some time. A visitor who has respected the laws of France and up until this moment has given us no reason to believe you will not continue to do so.'

Duteil stayed silent. He could guess where this was leading to.

'However, we have reason to suspect that – *inadvertently* – you are about to transgress one of the more important rules. Which would be a great pity, as I'm sure you would agree.'

Duteil continued to stare. There was really no need for him to speak.

'The thing is, we are quite *generous* about many things. But we do lose our – what should I say, ability to overlook matters? – when we are dealing with a person wanted on a serious charge. I refer to a certain foreigner who was active in the Troubles. We have been looking for her for some time.'

Duteil narrowed his eyes at the mention of a serious charge. It seemed unlikely. She had only done what all the other students had done. Lobbed a few cobblestones.

The DST man saw his doubt. 'She is wanted for subversion against the state,' he elaborated. 'There was also another matter – she tried to kill a police officer. Took a knife to him. He was stabbed in the shoulder. This cannot be overlooked.'

Ah, now he was beginning to understand. Gabriele was perfectly capable of having stabbed someone. And yet why hadn't he heard about it? Why hadn't she told him?

'The thing is,' the officer continued smoothly. 'We have good reason to believe you aided and abetted this person at that time. And may indeed be considering doing so again. As a peaceful organisation dedicated to a worthwhile cause' – he said it with only the faintest sarcasm – 'you will not want to commit an offence which will have serious consequences for you.'

'What exactly are you asking?'

'Help us find the girl. We want her. The British want her. If you lead us to her you will be left in peace. On this matter at least.'

'Are there *other* matters?'

'Not at present.'

Duteil tapped his fingers thoughtfully against his mouth. 'A man's reputation is everything in life, wouldn't you agree?' he murmured. 'Suppose I knew someone who could help you – which I'm not saying for a moment that I could – what would happen to that man's reputation? Particularly if he was known for assisting refugees and victims of oppression. Would this man be trusted any more? I think not.' He laughed ironically. 'What would a man's friends think?'

The DST man whispered, 'Ah, but no one would ever know. This man could complete the arrangements and merely let slip a small detail. The meeting would go ahead in the normal way.'

'And the messenger?'

'Would be untouched. You have my guarantee.'

Duteil thought very carefully. He wondered how serious this threat to the organisation really was. He didn't believe this story about the stabbing. If it was true he would *definitely* have heard about it at the time. But he realised that the truth was irrelevant. If he did not respond to the pressure they would merely find another way of making his life difficult.

He sighed inwardly. This would teach him to break his own rules. He should never have helped the girl in the first place.

At the same time he strongly resented this pressure being exerted on him.

He commented, 'Blackmail is not a very pleasant development.'

'I would call it a mutually convenient arrangement.' The DST man leant forward. 'And be certain that this is a very important matter.'

The whole thing could be a great big bluff, Duteil realised. There was no guarantee that they would keep to their promise.

The DST man pressed home his argument. 'The government is being pressurised by the British. They are looking to *us* for an explanation of how aid to a terrorist group could be emanating from Paris. Either we must produce culprits or we must produce information. It is one or the other. There can be no compromise. Do you follow me?'

Duteil followed all right. He had also made up his mind.

The girl had failed. She was unlikely to be of much use in the future.

Regrettable. But it was the way of the world. One had to be prepared for sacrifices in the service of the greater cause.

Thirty

Darkness was going to fall early, even for November. Yet it had been a long time coming. Gabriele had spent the afternoon freezing in a dreary place called Gunnersbury Park, a meagre patch of green in the western suburbs, half-way between the airport and central London. She detested killing time in this way, but the empty park was the safest place she could think of. For a while she had dozed on a bench, which had made her feel better: the jittery nausea left her stomach, and her hands became steadier. But then cold and lethargy crept over her and she realised she must force herself to move.

The meeting was still many hours away, hours that stretched out before her, fraught with difficulties. Somehow she had to find shelter for the night. And food. And a place to hide until noon the next day.

The meeting was set for two the next afternoon, on the bridge in the centre of St James's Park. Thank God for Raymond. She had known he wouldn't let her down. He was the one constant factor in the appalling run of uncertainty and bad luck.

The moment she had the papers and the money she would be as good as free. She would go to Paris first, of course; then to Milan to see Petrini; and then . . .

Back here. In time.

A grey cheerless twilight enveloped the monotonous rows of suburban houses; it was time to move. She went down to the main road and caught a 27 bus to Hammersmith and Notting Hill. She sat next to a window, examining fellow passengers in the reflection of the glass. For a while she was convinced the conductor was staring at her and gripped the edge of her seat, ready to run. But then he chatted to another passenger and, without a second glance, climbed up the stairs to the top deck.

She left the bus at Notting Hill Gate and went into a large chemist shop. The lighting was very bright. She kept her head down. There was a great craze for synthetic wigs and a large stand of them stood in the centre of the shop. She chose one in auburn with a deep fringe. She also bought sunglasses and make-up. She kept an eye on the shop assistant but the girl didn't give her a second glance.

In a nearby side street Gabriele pulled the wig hastily over her dark hair and put on some lipstick. She re-emerged into the brightly lit street with more confidence.

Now food. She'd had nothing since the previous day. It had got to the point where she didn't feel hungry any more. But it was essential to force something down. There was a Wimpy Bar further along the road on the other side of the Tube station. She set off, keeping her head down as she approached the Tube exit. It was almost five: the rush hour. People streamed out of the station.

Someone bumped into her. She veered away, stepping into the street to circle the crowd. As she stepped back on to the pavement she halted, face to face with her own picture. Duplicated dozens of times. All over a newsstand.

The headline screamed: WANTED!

She felt a sudden thrill, an extraordinary burst of exhilaration.

She turned away, then, changing her mind, reached into her pocket for some coins and bought an *Evening Standard*.

Tucking the newspaper under her arm she approached the Wimpy Bar and looked in through the window. It was fairly crowded but she spotted a seat in the far corner. No one took any notice of her as she walked in. She ordered a double cheeseburger and chips then, unfolding the paper, started to read.

She gave a small snort of disgust and amusement. They'd decided to call her the 'glamorous gunwoman'. How transparent and cliché-ridden. But worse, the story bore no relation to the truth. They talked of 'fanatical extremists'. What rubbish: the fanatical extremists were closer to home – the people who owned newspapers that printed distortions like this.

She flicked on through the story.

Then stopped.

And read the section again. Two deaths at a remote farmhouse. Both believed to be members of the terrorist gang. A girl killed in an explosion. A man found dead in an outbuilding. *A man*.

Giorgio.

He had been there all the time. Dead.

She felt no sadness, only a chilling sense of aloneness. And a strong sense of betrayal, as if he had somehow died on purpose in order to make life more difficult for her.

God! How could he have been so *stupid*. And *how* had he managed to get himself killed? By the *girl*?

But her mind soon veered back to the present.

She was really alone now. Everything would be harder. She would have to be doubly careful. She would have to find somewhere safe to hide.

The food arrived. As the waitress put it in front of her she noticed a man looking at her. Her heart gave an unpleasant lurch. She stared back. He dropped his eyes.

Keeping an eye on him she stuffed the food into her mouth and discovered that she was ravenously hungry after all. She picked up the newspaper again and read on: A watch was being kept on the ports . . . Linda Wilson believed armed and dangerous . . . On no account were the public to approach . . .

Distortion again: they made her sound like a madwoman who'd shoot anyone on sight. *Definitely* not true. She only had one target: the oppressors. These filthy lies were making her sick.

Then she almost choked. In the centre of the paper there was a double-page spread headed: Attorney-General Freed at Eleventh Hour. Brilliant detective work – it read – had led to the location of the remote farmhouse a bare two hours before the terrorists' dead-line ran out . . . Army disposal rushed in . . .

Brilliant detective work. The phrase rankled. It suggested Nick Riley and his friends had outmanoeuvred her. Well, they may think they had, for the *moment*. But the war wasn't over, not by a long way.

The thought of Nick Riley still had the power to fill her with an uncontrollable rage. What she would give to get him face to face. The memory of his cold cynical manipulation of her was like a knife turning in a wound; it gave her no peace.

The man at the other table was looking at her again. She wrapped the second burger in a napkin and stuffed it in the holdall. She went to the cash desk, paid, and hurried out. She went down a side street and doubled back into the main road. The man did not follow her.

She headed north up Ladbroke Grove. Her route took her past a police station. She hesitated, but it was completely dark and there was no one outside. She walked on.

The holdall was getting very heavy. She felt stupidly weak but forced herself on. The rise of Notting Hill seemed endless until finally she reached the top and headed down the gentle slope towards North Kensington.

Beyond the Westway she found the road she was looking for, the street where Max's friend Bet lived: Tulip Street. Through Bet she should be able to pick up some old contacts – someone like Wally Bishop, who'd been on the Linden House demo and was a close friend of Reardon's. He was sure to be okay. He would have a place to go.

She approached the house cautiously, watching it for a good five minutes before climbing the steps and ringing the doorbell. A man opened the door. She asked for Bet and waited outside while the man shouted upstairs.

Eventually a girl came crossly down the stairs to the door, wrapping a towel round her dripping hair. 'Yes?' she demanded.

Gabriele kept back from the door, away from the pool of light. 'I was looking for Wally Bishop. Can you tell me where to find him?'

'Sure,' Bet began. Then she paused and peered more closely at Gabriele. She stiffened.

There was a nasty silence. Gabriele could almost feel the other woman's animosity. Bet looked back over her shoulder, then scanned the street.

She whispered, '*Go away*! They came asking about you this morning. And they've been to *Wally's*. And they're coming back, they said they were. *We* can't help you. You *must* go away!' The girl swallowed nervously. 'Look, I won't say a word about you having been here. Not a word. Honest. Just go. *Please*.'

Wordlessly, Gabriele turned and walked away into the darkness.

Back in Ladbroke Grove she headed south. After a while she hailed a taxi. 'Where to?' the cabby asked.

'Earl's Court.'

Gabriele hardly knew the Earl's Court area. Which was the whole point of going there. No old haunts, no friends, no way of tracing her. Just the anonymity of street after street of rooming houses used by thousands of visiting Australians – the area was commonly known as Kangaroo Valley.

The cab dropped her in the Earl's Court Road. She set off down a side street and came to the first of a long row of rooming houses and cheap hotels. She hesitated outside a place with a 'Room to Let' notice in the window, suddenly wary. Something about this idea was making her deeply uneasy. It was the prospect of sitting in a box-like room, with no means of escape, not knowing who might have recognised her, not knowing if the police were closing in. A rat in a trap.

But she forced her doubts aside for a moment and, going in, knocked on a door marked 'Enquiries'.

A smiling Pakistani emerged. The terms were two pounds a week and the room was on the third floor at the back. He offered to show it to her and went back into his room to fetch a key.

Gabriele moved forward until she could see him through the open door. She watched him pick a key off a hook. He was not suspicious. It was going to be all right. She looked down. There was a low table in front of an easy chair. Evidently he had been reading the evening paper. Upside down and at a slight distance her picture seemed to fill the whole of the front page.

He was turning, the key in his hand. She pulled her eyes quickly away from the newspaper.

She tried to smile. 'I'm sorry – I've decided it wouldn't be suitable.'

The Pakistani looked surprised. 'But you haven't *seen* it!'

'It's the stairs. Too far up. Thanks anyway.'

He gave her a long hard stare. She turned hurriedly and went out into the street.

She could have kicked herself. That had been very stupid. There must be no more mistakes.

She walked rapidly away from the area, heading south. She racked her brains for somewhere to go. There *had* to be somewhere. It was just a case of thinking it through. She just wished she wasn't feeling so tired.

She plodded on into Chelsea. A chill hung over the misty river. Battersea Bridge loomed up ahead. There was a park on the other side where it might be possible to stop for a while; but it was another cold, damp, desolate, godforsaken place. She felt a bitter resentment. She couldn't believe it had come to this. She'd had nothing but bad luck. Then the *others* had let her down so badly – Giorgio. And Max . . . And then of course *him* – the spy.

Suddenly she had an idea and grabbed at it. She stopped in her tracks and gave a small exclamation of triumph. Of course. It was so perfect she couldn't imagine why she hadn't thought of it before.

A man could give his soul for this, Nick decided, no trouble at all. A warm flat – at least it would be in a moment, when the electric fires had done their job – fish and chips from down the road, and a hot bath within half an hour. Already the geyser was hissing and roaring, spitting its thin jet of steaming water into the tub below.

But most important of all – *vital* – the prospect of catching Gabriele. By this time tomorrow it should all be over. And, though it never paid to count one's chickens, there was reasonable hope for optimism.

Two. At the bridge in St James's Park. A man wearing a red scarf. With a bit of luck they'd pick him up at the airport and tail him all the way there, just to be sure. In his mind he gave Desport another pat on the back. It was quite a coup. And, since Desport had passed the information direct to Nick, some of the credit would undoubtedly rub off on him.

If all went well.

One thing was certain: once in the trap Gabriele would never escape. The place was going to be crawling with men – and marksmen. Would she try to shoot it out? If so, she'd be dead in an instant. All things considered, it might be for the best. He caught himself thinking: What's one more death?

Yes. They would get her. One way or another.

God, he was going to sleep like a baby tonight. The tension that had gripped him for days had eased, leaving him pleasantly languorously weary. He dug into the grocery bag and found himself a beer. The phone rang.

It was Conway. 'A possible sighting in Earl's Court, at a cheap rooming house. Had second thoughts about a room and scarpered. But the ident is far from certain. The geezer thought the face was right but the hair was the wrong colour. Could have been a wig of course. Anyway, Kershaw's put ten cars in the area and started a house-to-house.'

Nick considered. It *could* have been Gabriella. Although a cheap rooming house in Earl's Court was hardly her style. Which might have been the reason she tried it. Perhaps she had nowhere else to go.

'Keep me posted, will you?' he asked Conway, and rang off.

He wandered across to the record player, deep in thought. Eventually he selected *Norma* with Callas and Corelli, and listened to the familiar melody of the overture. He turned up the volume – to hell with the neighbours for once. He placed the next disc – which went to the end of Act II – on the spindle, ready to drop, so that he would have a good hour's listening while he was in the bath.

He took the beer into the bathroom and stripped off. The water was only about eight inches deep. Good enough.

He stepped in and uttered a sigh of bliss. He lay back and felt the water creep up his body. It was so deliciously hot it was almost unbearable. He knew what was going to happen; he was going to fall asleep. But he didn't care. It was irresistible.

'*Sediziose voci, voci di guerra* . . .' Norma's entrance. Callas's raw sensual voice filled the flat, rising effortlessly above the belches of the geyser. He shivered. He couldn't begin to imagine how it must feel to sing like that.

At last the water covered his body. He turned off the geyser and slipped into a doze that glowed with warmth and peace. He reflected that this was the closest to heaven he was ever likely to get.

Yet a deep unease nagged at him. It was the stake-out, of course. He would worry about it until the very last moment, until he actually saw her walk into the trap.

There was a lull in the music. A sound intruded. Reluctantly he opened his eyes and tried to identify it. It came from downstairs somewhere. Then he had it. Someone was at the street door buzzing the flat below. That was the trouble with these houses. You could hear everything.

He woke once, briefly, when side one came to an end, but then the next disc dropped and the rich music swelled into the room and resonated through his mind, expunging all thought, and he slept again.

Gabriele stood on the front steps. She took another look at the names by the door. Flat 3: Ryder.

Riley. Ryder.

It *had* to be him.

She went down the steps and examined the house from the street. Lights were burning on the second floor and she could hear the faint sound of opera music. It *had* to be him. Right there. And not expecting her. *Hardly*. He'd probably forgotten that she had this address. The knowledge gave her a curious thrill.

Now, to get in. She'd tried ringing the bells of the other three flats, but there was no one in. She purposely hadn't rung his bell: he might call out of the window. Or there might be a scene at the door. People might notice.

Besides, she wanted to surprise him.

There was no obvious way up the front of the house, which was anyway too public. The narrow street was residential, with rows of small working-class houses on either side: the sort of street where people were nosy.

Even at that moment there was the sound of voices and a noisy group emerged from a house two doors away. As they passed they gave her a curious glance.

It would have to be the back then.

The house was on a corner. She went down the side and had a good look. Rows of back yards stretched out behind the houses. Easy. She hoisted the holdall over the wall and, gritting her teeth, let it drop. There was a dull thud. With an effort she pulled herself up and over the wall. The holdall was lying on concrete. Taking the rifle out of the holdall, she strapped it over her back.

As an after-thought she tore off the hot uncomfortable wig and jammed it in the holdall with everything else.

She examined the back of the house. There was a door. She tried it. Locked. She looked up. At the first floor level there was an open window and, just to the left, a drainpipe. She hid the holdall behind some abandoned sheets of wood in the yard and, with only the rifle against her back, pulled a dustbin across to the drainpipe and climbed on top of it. The window wasn't far. She gripped the drainpipe and slowly began to pull herself up.

Suddenly a door opened and she froze. It was next door. There was the sound of scurrying paws and a dog started yapping noisily. A shaft of light sprang out into the darkness. A voice called, 'Bisky? Bisky? Come here! Good girl!'

The dog stopped yapping. Gabriele twisted her head round and looked down. The dog had its nose up, sniffing the air, trying to catch her scent. It growled threateningly, then thought better of it and scampered inside. The door closed. Gabriele took a couple of deep breaths and continued her climb.

She pulled herself up level with the window and reached a foot across to the sill. So far so good. Now she had to find a handhold. She put her arm out and grasped the rough brick corner of the reveal. Not good enough. Still holding on to the drainpipe with her left hand she shifted her weight as far as possible across to the sill and stretched her hand out further. At last she managed to get two fingers over the top of the open window. It wasn't much. With her heart in her mouth, she pushed away from the drainpipe and pulled herself across. For one moment she swung outwards, her left foot scrabbling for the sill, her weight hanging over the yard below. But then she managed to get her left hand over the window and pull herself in. She stood on the sill, shaking and hot with fear.

She gave herself a moment, then pushed the sash window fully down and climbed in. As she descended into the dark room her foot upset an object which fell with a great thud to the floor. She remained still, listening, but there were no lights showing and no one came.

She dropped to the floor and found her way across the room and into a tiny hall. She listened at the front door and, satisfied, turned the lock and opened the door a fraction. Light streamed in from the stairs and communal landing. There was no one about.

Putting the door on the latch she stepped out and pulled the door to behind her. She ran lightly up the stairs. There was only the one door on the top landing. Flat 3. The music was very loud.

She examined the door. Strong, with a Yale lock. She felt along the top of the door frame, in case there was a key hidden there. There wasn't.

She padded back downstairs and into the empty flat, closing the door. There was two options: force her way into the flat by shooting open the door – which was out of the question because the whole street would hear – or simply knock and wait for him to come to the door. But it *wasn't* the way she wanted to do it.

She gritted her teeth. There had to be a way.

She went back to the window and, climbing on to the inner sill, stuck her head out.

Ah. The *next* window.

She dropped down again and, going quickly into the next room, pulled open the window.

A back extension – traditional in many mid-Victorian terraces – abutted the wall just inches from the window. As usual, the extension was only two storeys high. The roof was just inches away. The roof pitched up to a ridge – a ridge which ran very close to a second-floor window. She examined it carefully. The only problem might be the window itself.

She went back into the flat and, risking a light, rummaged through the tiny kitchenette. Thrusting a collection of knives, tin-openers and skewers into her back pocket, she killed the light and went back to the window.

Getting across to the roof was the tricky bit. She had to put a foot on the open window frame, lever herself up, and scrabble across to the roof, trusting her weight to some ancient guttering.

Once safely on the roof, the worst was over. She waited for her heart to stop pounding before climbing upwards to the ridge and the waiting window.

She pushed the handle of a tin opener under the window frame and levered it downwards.

The window gave a fraction. She pushed the lever further in and got her fingers underneath the frame.

There was no resistance. The window slid up several inches.

The exhilaration pounded in her chest. Carefully, she pushed it completely open and climbed in.

The dream had been going so well. He was somewhere nice, somewhere warm and cosy. There was a fleeting image of Coniston, in the Lake District, where his parents had once taken him on a rare holiday. They were sitting in some tea-rooms which they had reached after a long tiring walk in the hills. He remembered the strangeness of those rugged hills and his feeling of puzzlement at the sight of all that wilderness. Nothing in his life had ever suggested that such places existed.

But then the memory was slipping and the mood changed. There was a coldness around him, and a deep worrying silence. He was back at the farmhouse. The army chap was announcing that more bombs had been discovered: it wasn't over yet, he said in his rather pompous voice, not by a long chalk. This time there were many more hostages. Nick discovered more and more of them in the bedrooms upstairs, each attached to some even more ghastly device. Time was running out but there appeared to be no way of helping them. It was extraordinary, but no one seemed to be concerned. All they were interested in was getting organised. More and more equipment kept arriving. Nick shouted out: For God's sake can't we save *anybody*? And the army chap replied: Shouldn't think so. Better get clear.

The feeling of impotence was infuriating. He wanted to *make* these stupid people do something, to shake them until their teeth rattled, to scream at them.

Suddenly something made him wake. He opened his eyes for a moment.

He took a deep breath. It was only a dream . . .

The water had gone cold. The music had stopped. In a moment he would get out. He dozed again, trying to channel his thoughts away from the morass of the nightmare.

Christ – !

Something jabbed into his head, cold and uncomfortable.

For a split-second he convinced himself it was part of the nightmare.

But then he woke with a violent start that sent his body arcing out of the water.

Christ!

He didn't need to look round.

He *knew*.

His heart pounded in his ears. His mouth hung open. One thought leapt burning in his mind.

It was *her*.

And she was going to kill him. In cold blood.

He stayed completely still, his mind racing.

She spoke. He gave another involuntary start.

'*Frightened*, are you?'

He forced himself to speak. 'Yes. Of course.' The gun was pressed hard against his head. He couldn't see her: she was to one side and slightly behind.

'Think I'm going to kill you?' The voice was low and ragged.

He whispered, 'Probably.'

'Too right. Nasty little gigolo. Sell yourself for anything, wouldn't you! Cheap bastard.'

He licked his lips and said carefully, 'I didn't know who you were when . . .'

There was a nasty silence. '*When you screwed me.*'

'I never looked on it like that.'

'*Like what?*'

'Like just a screw.'

'No? Well, *I* did! *I did!* It was just a screw!'

He blinked agreement. She had to be humoured, but not too obviously.

'*Well?*' she demanded.

He thought desperately, trying to guess what she wanted him to say. But it could be *anything*. He stayed silent.

The voice came from close by his ear; he could feel her breath. 'Don't you want to know how long you've got?'

Thoughts flashed through his mind: a yes and she might say five seconds in which case he'd rather not know; a no and she'd tell him anyway. Better to say nothing.

She prodded the gun barrel further into his temple. He cringed, his eyes tightly shut.

She said, '*Now!* Yes, why not! How's it feel, you bastard, to be on the point of having your brains splattered over the wall?'

Nick felt sick. His stomach turned to water. He began to tremble violently.

Christ – he couldn't cope with this.

She was still speaking. 'You were my unfinished business, you cheap bastard. I didn't want to go without attending to you. Just so you couldn't screw anyone ever again.'

The gun was pulled away from his head. Out of the corner of his eye he saw the barrel travelling down over his stomach. *Down.*

He stared in horror.

Dear God, she was going to kill him in stages. The pain. And it would take a long time to die.

She was putting the gun barrel into the water. On to his flesh.

He closed his eyes, trying to shut out the wall of fear. Then, through the panic, a part of his mind rallied. *Say something! Something to distract her!*

What was it *she'd* said. Some words echoed in the back of his mind. He clutched at them. *I didn't want to go without attending to you.*

Sure that even now it was too late, he babbled, '*You can't go!*'

'What do you mean!' She gave a nervous contemptuous laugh. 'I'll go just as soon as I've finished with *you*, bastard!'

He took a few deep breaths. He had her attention. He said more steadily, 'They know all about it.'

There was an electric silence.

'Know – *what*?' Her voice was high-pitched and unsteady.

'You're meeting a courier. Tomorrow at two. In St James's Park.'

Nick gave it a moment, then risked a slight turn of his head.

She was staring through him, grey with disbelief. She looked very different: ravaged, drawn, older. She stood back, letting the gun barrel fall slightly.

She hissed, '*How*?'

He made his voice more relaxed. 'A tip-off. From Paris.'

'*Paris?*'

She seemed to dissolve before his eyes, swaying slightly, her shoulders falling forward.

'*Who in Paris?*'

He must be careful here; she mustn't know the truth or his instincts told him she'd kill everyone in sight including herself. He said, 'I don't know.'

The gun came up and jammed into his temple again. '*You do! Tell me!*'

'The courier! The courier was a traitor!'

She breathed, 'The *courier!* I don't understand . . .'

He said quickly, 'I'll offer you a deal. I'll get you out of the country in return for my life.'

The gun was pulled away from his temple. He turned and looked straight at her. He had to make her believe him. He repeated, 'I'll get you out.'

At last she seemed to absorb what he had said. She shook her head. 'I could never trust you!'

'Why not? It's a fair deal. I've only got my job to lose and I've lost that already.'

'Your job?' she asked vaguely.

'Of course. Because of you.'

She was hardly listening. She was clutching her forehead, a deep frown of concentration on her face. Her mouth opened and closed, but no words came.

Suddenly she exclaimed, 'No! You bloody bastard! You'll try to trick me! You're a pig, just another pig!' Her mouth was screwed down at the corners in an ugly grimace. 'You're out to kill me. Just like the rest! You think you have the right to persecute and rape and *humiliate* people.'

He thought: She's mad.

What should he say next? He wasn't sure any more.

He ventured, 'I know ways of getting out of the country. Places where they don't check too closely—'

'*Where?*'

'The Liverpool–Belfast Ferry. Once in Northern Ireland it's easy to get into the Republic. From Dublin you can fly to lots of places.'

She glared at him with an expression of deep uncertainty. He wished she would believe him; it was undoubtedly the safest route.

She whispered, 'What about papers? A passport?'

'Surely your friends can get you one. Send it to Dublin?'

'And money?'

'I can get some. Take a chequebook anyway.'

'Transport?'

'There's a friend's car that I often borrow.'

'How do I know it isn't a police car?'

'There's no radio in it.'

She nodded slowly, the fear beginning to recede from her eyes. She appeared to be coming round to the idea.

'Why do *you* need to come along? Why shouldn't I go *alone*?'

Nick thought: Because if you leave me here, you'll leave me dead. But aloud he said, 'You'll need someone to drive you on to the ferry in Liverpool. They'll be watching it. And again, possibly, at the Irish border.'

'But they'll have missed you by then!' she accused. 'They'll be looking for you too!'

'Not if I phone and say I've got flu.'

Suddenly she laughed nervously. 'I like the idea of you getting me out. It seems *right* somehow. After all, you got me into this mess. *Bastard!*'

He tried to make light of it. 'It was my job—'

'That's what the SS used to say when they sent the Jews to the gas chambers.'

'I never meant to harm anyone . . .' It was a nonsensical remark. But anything to keep the conversation going.

There was a shrill jangling.

They both jumped.

The telephone rang again.

It would be Conway.

Gabriele was pointing the gun at him again.

He said quickly, 'If I don't answer they'll know there's something wrong. *They know I'm here!* And it would be a good time to tell them I've got flu!'

She seemed to be thinking frantically, her eyes darting from side to side. Finally she shouted, 'All right! *All right!* But one – *one* – wrong word and I'll blow your head off!'

The phone kept jangling.

Nick climbed slowly out of the bath. Gabriele retreated a little, both hands on the rifle. His flesh crawling, Nick walked carefully out of the room. He felt Gabriele taking up station behind. He advanced to the phone and stood dripping in front of it. She nodded. He picked it up. As he put the receiver to his ear the gun jabbed into his temple.

Conway's cheery voice said, 'What were you doing – getting well-earned rest or something?'

'Having a bath.'

'About time too. Anyway, here's the latest. The ID in Earl's Court looks a little more positive. She had a holdall which tallies with the one she was carrying when she left the flat in Chelsea Manor Street. I'm going up there now. Wanna come along?'

'No, I'm too tired, old boy. In fact I'm not feeling too well. Flu or something. I think I might have to crash.'

'What's with this "old boy" business? You gone posh or something?'

Nick said coldly, 'No. Er – when are we due back on duty?'

'God – don't ask me!' Conway exclaimed. 'Since when did we ever work *hours*.'

'Oh. Seven o'clock, was it?' Nick nodded gravely.

'What on earth? You're not making any sense, old mate. Don't tell me,' Conway exclaimed conspiratorially, 'you're otherwise engaged! Why didn't you *say* so?' He chuckled, already losing interest. 'Don't know how you find the energy.'

Nick's heart sank. The gun jabbed into his head. She was signalling angrily. He had a last attempt. 'Look – can you get Andrews to fill in for me tomorrow?'

There was a short silence. Nick could almost hear Conway working things out. Nick thought: Come *on*. Come *on*.

'Who the hell's Andrews?' Suddenly Conway got on to the right track. 'Is everything all right?'

'No, not in the slightest,' Nick said casually. 'Bye. Got to go now.'

Nick put the phone down. He noticed his hand was shaking. For something to say, he murmured, 'I got rid of him as quickly as I could.'

'Who was it?' she demanded.

'A colleague.'

'How do I know you haven't warned him?'

'You heard what I said—'

'Get dressed! We're going this minute!'

Nick thought: Conway, dear plodding Conway. Please understand. May God beam down a great shaft of illumination upon your brain.

Thirty-one

Old boy, indeed. Conway thought: Huh!

But then it had been a strange conversation all round. Ryder was obviously overtired. What *had* he meant with that seven o'clock business? There was no chance that Conway was going to be around at seven the next morning. He was going to be in his bed, snoring loudly, and nothing but nothing was going to get him up any earlier.

Besides, like he'd said, when did they ever have fixed hours? And Andrews? Who the hell was he? Perhaps there was someone of that name in Kershaw's team. Because there certainly wasn't in Special Branch. Or was there?

Conway couldn't think straight any more. No sleep. Bad food. Small brain. He left his office and went to the nearest coffee machine. Blasted coffee. Never knew if it was going to do you any good. He sipped at it. It tasted like old cardboard. Or maybe that was the cup.

He went back to his desk and started sifting through some papers.

After a moment he gave up. It was no good. That conversation kept coming back into his mind. It worried him.

Why would the presence of a woman make Ryder sound so strange? Even allowing for the astonishing possibility that, after a week without sleep, Ryder was capable of a romantic evening?

And that proper tone. The 'old boy'. It wasn't in character. Normally, he would have expected Ryder to give him a polite 'Sod off' or something similar. After all, they were good friends.

And why, in their earlier phone call, had Ryder asked Conway to call back if he knew he was going to be busy?

Finding a piece of plain paper, Conway jotted down what he remembered of the conversation. Then he underlined the remarks that had seemed strange. Particularly that one when he'd asked: Everything all right? And Ryder had answered: No, not at all. Or was it: No, not in the slightest.

That damned seven o'clock.

What *could* he have meant?

He looked at his watch. It was seven. In the evening.

Now.

He should ring back.

He reached for the phone then hesitated.

Extremely nasty thoughts had whistled into his mind. And if they were in the slightest bit right, then the last thing he must do was call back.

Getting hastily to his feet, he grabbed the piece of paper and made for the stairs at a run.

He could be making a fool of himself, of course. This might be the largest dose of egg that he'd ever got splattered on his face. But better that than—

Anyway, he had a feeling about this one.

It took a moment for him to identify what it was that made him so sure. Then he had it.

It wasn't just the oddness of the answers, nor even that dreadful 'old boy'. It was that appalling *politeness*.

Not Ryder, not Ryder at *all*.

Nick dressed as slowly as possible, but even then he couldn't draw it out for longer than five minutes. She watched his every move, getting increasingly impatient. He tried making conversation but she silenced him with a motion of the gun.

As he picked up his wallet she demanded, 'How much is there?'

He counted the notes. 'Fifteen pounds.'

'*God*! That's not going to get us very far, is it!'

'I *told* you, I've got a chequebook.' Immediately he realised he'd used the wrong words and the wrong tone. She wouldn't like remonstrations. He braced himself.

'I *know* you've got a bloody chequebook!' she said furiously. 'But is it going to *work*? What happens when we try to get cash? They'll phone your *bank*, and then they'll know *exactly* where we are!' She paused for breath. 'Give me a jacket!'

He found an old denim one and threw it across the floor to her. Picking it up, she draped it over the rifle. 'Now where's this car?'

'It's usually parked further up the road, outside the friend's house.'

'Will it *be* there?'

'He only uses it at weekends.'

'What about keys?'

'I have some. They're in the hall drawer.'

She gestured him into the hall. She said, 'Pull the drawer out slowly and empty the contents on to the floor.'

He did so and the keys fell out, followed by a flurry of papers and library tickets.

Slowly he bent down and picked up the keys.

'Have you got a gun?' she demanded suddenly.

He shook his head.

She gave a short laugh. 'What, not even to use against dangerous terrorists?'

'There's a firearms squad. They're specially trained . . .'

'Okay. Let's go.' She waved the gun in the direction of the door, and stepped back. She was no fool. She always kept her distance when he was about to move. Not that he felt like being brave. Not yet anyway.

As he opened the front door he tried to think of a reason to delay her.

He said, 'I might have some more money in the bedroom. I'm not sure . . .'

She was instantly suspicious. 'Get out!'

He almost argued, but sensed it wouldn't be wise.

As he stepped into the hall the gun jabbed into his back.

He tried to work out how long it would take to reach the car. No more than three minutes. Even if there *was* a team on the way they'd never get here in time.

Hopeless.

They began down the stairs. There was a sound from below. They both stopped dead. There were noises of doors opening and closing, then silence. The occupant of the ground-floor flat. They started down again, passing the first-floor landing, down to the ground floor. The beat of rock music suddenly bellowed from the ground-floor flat. As they passed the door Nick willed it to open, but it didn't.

At the street door, she hissed, 'Stop!'

She came up close behind him, holding the gun to his ribs. 'Can we get out to the back from here?'

'The back?'

'The *yard*!'

'No. It belongs to the guy in there.' He indicated the door of the ground-floor flat.

She prodded him forward. 'Okay. Open it slowly.'

He turned the latch and swung the door open. She made him halt in the doorway. He guessed she was looking up and down the street.

She wasn't the only one. He searched desperately for signs of life. But it was quiet as the grave.

Even now Conway was probably packing up his desk and heading for Earl's Court, blissfully unaware, imagining merely that Nick had flu and had gone appropriately strange in the head.

The thought filled him with quiet despair.

'Move!'

They set off down the steps. He was about to turn left, towards the car, when she pulled him the other way. 'I've got to collect something first!'

Nick felt a small flutter of hope. It was a delay. More time. And time was what he wanted.

*

Gabriele pushed him forward. She hated the delay. But she *had* to get the holdall. There was the spare ammunition. The wig. The make-up. The sunglasses. And the tote bag with her few remaining belongings. She'd feel naked without them.

At the corner she prodded him to the right then made him stop by the wall.

This was the hard bit. She hadn't allowed for this – having to retrieve the holdall with *him* around. She looked up and down the side street. A car approached, slowed at the junction, turned left and drove off. Another car passed in the road they had just left then another. At last there was nothing. She pulled the jacket off the Kalashnikov and let it fall to the pavement.

She said, 'Give me a leg-up.'

He looked surprised but obediently cupped his hand. She put a foot in it, careful to keep the rifle at his head, then said, 'Push me up!' She added harshly, 'If you try to drop me, I'll kill you! So don't even think about it!'

Grunting with effort, he pushed her up. With her spare hand, she gripped the top of the wall. 'Higher!'

He gave a last heave and she levered herself on to the top. She swung a leg over until she was sitting astride.

'Now you!'

He took a deep breath then scrambled up until he too was on top of the wall.

'Go down and find my bag. It's in that corner.' She pointed in the approximate direction.

He dropped down and searched for it. She watched him, thinking hard. He might even now be planning something. But if he imagined she was relaxing her guard for one moment he was making a big mistake. No chance. In fact she was feeling much better now: more alert, more in control. The shock of discovering they knew about the courier, that had been appalling. Like being hit in the face. It had taken a bit of getting over.

But she'd still get out all right. She knew she would. The pigs were stupid. One had to bear that in mind all the time. It was simply a question of keeping one's nerve.

He was standing up. He had the holdall in his hand.

Another car passed along the adjacent road. She reached down and took the holdall. She gestured him to climb back on top of the wall. He pulled himself up and sat astride, facing her. She was about to tell him to drop down into the street again when she caught a movement out of the corner of her eye.

Someone was walking along the street towards them. An old man wearing a cap. Doubtless a nosy old man. He was even now looking up. He couldn't fail to see them sitting up on the wall.

She could kill him, of course. But the *noise*.

The passer-by had almost reached them. He was slowing, inclining his head to peer up at them.

Gabriele wavered. She should do something . . .

Then it came to her. Jabbing the rifle into Nick's ribs, she leaned forward and, putting an arm around his neck, drew his head towards her. He pulled back in alarm, but she kept the pressure on until she felt his cheek come up against hers.

She squinted down at the passer-by. He was gawking up at them. He muttered a vague, 'Blimey . . .' Then shouted, 'There are safer places, yer know!' Muttering to himself, he finally began to move off.

She gave it a moment. In the silence she was aware of Nick's breathing, the touch of his flesh, warm against hers. The contact sent startling echoes reverberating through her mind: memories of friends, of feeling a warm sense of belonging; of good times in Italy; of the weeks when Giorgio and Max had been there to support her; of times when she hadn't been so horribly alone.

Times when—

She pulled away angrily. The touch of him almost made her choke. She said with difficulty, 'You make me sick! Now – get down!'

'Gabriele.' His voice was soft. 'I *did* care.'

She hissed, 'How *dare* you think it matters to me one way or the other. I don't care a damn!'

He looked away.

A ghastly loathsome self-pity overwhelmed her and, with disgust, she heard her voice break. 'Well, if you care so much,' she managed bitterly, *'why the hell aren't you getting off this wall and getting me out of here!'*

With satisfaction, she saw him draw back. Silently, he manoeuvred both legs over the wall and dropped to the pavement.

'Move away from the wall.' She wiped a hand angrily across her eyes, then, letting the holdall fall, followed it to the ground. She threw the jacket back over the Kalashnikov and picked up the holdall.

In the distance a siren sounded. She glared in horror at Nick. A flicker of excitement seemed to pass across his face. She thought: *He was hoping for this! He's just been playing for time! The speech on the wall – just for time!* Jerking the rifle up to her hip, she trained it on him. 'If that's anything, you're *dead*!'

'It's just the local police.'

Was he telling the truth? *God!*

They waited tensely. Slowly the siren faded into the distance.

She breathed again. Throwing him the holdall, she gestured him forward. He moved cautiously. She prodded him roughly to make him go faster.

Retracing their steps, they turned the corner and passed in front of the house again. She looked around nervously.

Nothing. No cars.

Nothing.

She felt jumpy again.

His fault. He had unnerved her. She wouldn't let him do it again. There'd be no more talking.

The shadows seemed darker, longer. Up towards the end of the street she thought she saw black shapes. *Moving.*

Shit!

She'd just got the jitters. That was all.

Suddenly she realised why. It was so goddam *quiet.*

Nick drew in an involuntary breath. Hardly even a gasp. Yet for an awful moment he thought she'd heard it.

He waited in an agony of suspense.

But there was no sound from her. They walked on. It was all right.

He breathed again. Then took another look at the van parked some way up the street. Between two pools of lamplight. A darkish van. But it was so hard to see – *damn* it! He squirmed with frustration. It *looked* very like it but—

Suddenly he caught a glint.

The glint of metal. A whip aerial.

Yes!

His heart almost burst through his ribs.

A whip aerial. It *must* be.

Some of his exhilaration evaporated.

What *now*, for Christ's sake? The training manual didn't cover this. Desperately, he tried to think.

Suddenly she spoke and he jumped.

'Where's the car?' she snapped.

The car. He looked. Not far. He recognised the shape of the Vauxhall Viva just ahead. They were almost there. *Too near.*

Gulping, he lied, 'It must be further on. I can't see it yet.'

'Well, find it!'

'I think I can see it, just up there.' He indicated vaguely towards the end of the street.

His mind raced: now he was committed to a lie he had to find a way out of it. He looked for the next street lamp. It was about fifteen yards ahead.

Not far from the van.

As they approached the lamp, he could feel himself trembling.

'Just over there.' He pointed across the road to a Hillman Minx which he'd never seen before in his life. He thought: Dear God, let me be right about this. Otherwise when he failed to open the car she would realise that he had tried to trick her. And then he knew what she would do. She would kill him.

He stepped off the kerb between two parked cars and automatically looked for traffic.

Then it suddenly struck him – and then he *knew.*

There *was* no traffic. There had been none for some minutes.

It seemed to have stopped everywhere. Only the faintest hum rose into the night air high above the city. Somewhere nearby there was the muffled beat of music.

But the street itself was silent. Their own footsteps echoed large in the stillness.

Suddenly there was a sound. From up the street. Like metal against metal, the *clonk!* exaggerated in the silence.

He was jerked to a halt by his collar.

'*What was that?*' She was sounding frightened. There was a quaver in her voice.

He kept still, pretending to listen. Eventually he whispered, 'Nothing. A cat perhaps.'

He could hear her panting, her breath coming in short uneven gasps. Then she thrust him forward again, into the road.

He eyed the Hillman Minx, gleaming innocently. And stepped out.

He crossed diagonally, keeping as close as he dared to the pool of light around the lamp-post.

Surely something would happen now. *Surely.*

She wasn't too close. There was at least a foot between the two of them. She *must* make a good target. *Surely*.

They reached the centre of the road. He braced himself for the crack of a rifle shot.

Surely . . .

The Minx was getting close. He couldn't believe it.

He reached the car door.

Nothing happened.

Didn't they realise!

Fumbling in his pocket, he reached for the keys.

She came up close behind him.

Christ. Now it was too late.

He pulled the keys out and started sorting through them. His hand was shaking. The keys fell with a loud jangle on to the road.

'*You stupid bastard!*' She was spluttering with rage, all the arrogance back in her voice. 'Pick them up!'

'Sorry,' he murmured.

Then he knew what he had to do.

As he bent down and grasped the keys, he braced himself, and thought fleetingly: Dear God, let me have it right!

In the split second before he moved he glanced sideways. Her attention was distracted; she was looking nervously up the street. He tried to judge the distance.

Her eyes were coming back to him.

Then he sprang, twisting round, uncoiling himself from the ground.

He caught the rifle barrel with the first swing of his arm. It jerked out of his vision. He saw the surprise leap into her face.

Then he raised his foot, pulling his knee high up to his chest, and gave an almighty kick in the general direction of her stomach. It went home: he heard her suck in a great rasping breath as his shoe went punching into her body. He fell back against the car. Gabriele shot backwards, wheeling one arm, trying desperately to regain her balance. She tottered for a moment then fell in the middle of the road.

But she was rolling over, pulling herself quickly up on to one knee.

She was coming up again.

Then he saw – *she still had the rifle in her right hand*.

Her eyes were blazing at him, vicious with shock and hatred. She was regaining her balance, bringing the barrel up.

He should have moved. He felt the car hard against his back.

It was too late.

She was pulling the rifle back against her hip.

He caught a glint of cold determination in her expression, and felt a moment of total disbelief.

Then it came.

A loud booming amplified voice that split the silence.

'Drop your weapon! You are surrounded! Do not attempt to fire!'

Gabriele gave a violent start and dropped her weight forward as if poising herself to run. But then she hesitated, her eyes swivelling wildly, suddenly aware that she had nowhere to run to.

She was in the centre of the road. She hadn't got a chance.

He could see that she knew it.

She remained frozen like an animal, her eyes on Nick, but filled with a huge unimaginable terror.

The voice echoed between the houses.

Drop your gun! You are surrounded! Drop your weapon immediately! We are police officers! We have orders to fire!

There was a silence.

Nick urged, 'Do it! Gabriella – *just do it!*'

She blinked at him questioningly, a look of bewilderment on her face. Then her expression sank into bitterness and despair.

'Do it!' he whispered. 'Just drop the gun!'

She gave a small cry of anguish and shook her head. Very deliberately, she tightened her grip on the rifle.

He cried, *'Don't!'*

But she was already dropping. Quickly, so quickly. Down into a crouch, hunched over the rifle. For a moment he thought she was going to aim at him, but she swung the rifle away. The air filled with noise, a staccato of loud cracks as she sprayed the street, ranging the rifle back and forth across the width of the road.

She made no attempt to run.

Then it happened. In the noise, he never heard the other shots. He just saw her. Hit by some powerful force.

The rifle jerked. The force plucked her upwards and back. For a moment she seemed to hover, twisting round in the air. Then she crumpled. Neatly. Going at the knees first, then sinking gracefully to the ground. Her head falling back on to the road. The mass of dark hair falling . . . Her face a pale oval, deathly white in the lamplight.

There was a silence.

Nick walked slowly forward. He knelt beside her.

She was already dead, her eyes sightless and half-closed.

He knelt there for some moments.

She'd made the decision, when she'd raised the rifle. She'd made the decision to die.

Yet she hadn't tried to kill him. Perhaps she hadn't hated him so much after all.

There was the sound of running feet. Soon a circle of men stood staring down at her.

A voice said, 'Thank God.'

He knew what they were thinking: That she was dead and it was right that she was dead because she had got to enjoy killing, and there was nothing worse than that.

They were right, of course. That was the only way to look at it.

And he tried to lock the confusing blend of bitterness and guilt and pity out of his mind.

Thirty-two

The drizzle fell in unremitting grey curtains, cloaking the car park in a mantle of gloom. The group of pressmen – well over twenty of them – huddled under the porch of the crematorium, stamping their feet, chatting desultorily, their breath hanging in white clouds on the damp air. The local newsmen wore a slightly pained expression, the consequence of being heavily outnumbered by the national boys, and having a correspondingly slim chance of getting anything of their own into the dailies. Two television crews, enveloped in voluminous waterproofs, adjusted and fussed over their equipment. While sustaining necessary journalistic appearances of boredom and disinterest, everyone maintained a firm eye on the long drive that snaked down between bare lawns to the gates at the bottom of the hill.

It was almost ten to two, but no mourners had yet arrived. It was going to be a quiet funeral.

Suddenly there was a subtle change in the atmosphere, a buzz of interest. The photographers started manoeuvring for position, tucking their cameras inside their raincoats and trotting out into the wet.

A black car had appeared and was slowly climbing the hill. The TV cameramen raised their cameras to their shoulders; the soundmen dusted their cans. There was silence as each man peered forward, trying to identify the occupants.

The car rose over the brow of the hill and swung in a slow arc into the covered area in front of the doors, its dripping black metal momentarily glistening in the flash of the camera lights.

The car halted. The newsmen pressed in closer. Someone whispered. 'The parents!'

The driver got out and opened the passenger door. There was a pause then a woman in a black hat with a heavy veil emerged. The light danced with the blinding flicker of flashbulbs. She lowered her head and put a hand up to shade her eyes. The photographers jostled in front of her, crouching to get shots of her face.

She swerved, but they pressed in on her. She gave a small cry of rage or anguish and ran forward into the sanctuary of the chapel.

The father came next, an upright figure in a military tie, his face set in an expression of British impassivity. He did not attempt to hide his face, but took the bombardment of lights with a series of fierce blinks and a firm set of the jaw.

Finally a girl in her mid-twenties. The sister. The hacks had all her details: name Diana, age twenty-four, Sloane Square address, seen around London with the minor aristocracy. She too wore a veil, but not a thick one, and the boys knew that, by getting up really close to the face, they'd get a good shot through the thin gauze. As she stepped forward someone called, 'Were you close to your sister, Diana?'

The girl gulped, and her face completely crumpled. The photographers fired off a cacophony of shots and silently thanked the guy who had shouted the question. An anguished face was always good front-page stuff.

As the sister stumbled in through the doors of the chapel, the journalists scribbled away happily on their pads. They'd have no trouble building their notes up into something substantial. This was a gift of a story – had been ever since it had broken five days before. There were so many punchy phrases that sprang to mind.

Heiress to fortune. County set. Wealthy land-owning family. Hints of connections in high places. Educated at top school. Turned hippy. Despair of her parents. Country commune. Drug orgies. Sex orgies (not established, that, but a good hint added a lot of spice). Italian terrorist boyfriend. Trips to France. Gun-running. Putty in his hands. Leads gang to victim's home.

Poor little rich girl.

The story had all the ingredients you could ever hope for: sex, drugs, murder, intrigue, lost innocence. And of course, the best of all, a sudden and violent end. In the pubs of Fleet Street it was being said that a severed foot had been found days later, stuck in a corner of the cellar. Couldn't print that, of course. None the less they wished they got stories like this every day.

Another car appeared in the gateway at the bottom of the drive. It didn't look very promising. A dark blue saloon. Nothing special. There was cautious lack of interest among the watchers.

The car did not drive up to the doors, but parked beside a grass verge some distance away. Two men got out, one with fair collar-length hair, snappily dressed in casual dark slacks and jacket, and an open-necked shirt.

Immediately there was a rekindling of interest. Looked the type who might be a friend of the dead girl.

One of the experienced newsmen, a hack of twenty years' standing and now a feature-writer with one of the tabloids, inched his way forward. He knew exactly who these two men were.

As they approached he stepped forward and introduced himself to the fair-haired young man. 'You talked to the Danby girl through the door, I believe, sergeant. Can you tell me what she said?'

'No comment.'

'And I believe that you were the police officer taken hostage by the Wilson woman. Is that correct?'

The young policeman spun round angrily. 'We're not allowed to give interviews, as you well know. And you can't publish my identity either.'

The photographers, who had been snapping away, came out from behind their cameras. They were getting the gist of the conversation.

The second police officer shouted, 'Forget the pictures, boys! I'm a Special Branch officer and you're not permitted to publish pictures of me or my colleague here.'

The fair-haired officer gave the hack a last angry look and turned on his heel.

They all muttered amongst themselves. The trendily dressed

one was the undercover man of course. They pretended that they'd known who he was all the time. Pity they couldn't use him. But at least they were all in the same boat.

An electricity suddenly gripped the crowd.

Their eyes were riveted on the end of the drive.

Was it too much to hope for? It *looked* promising. My God, if it *was* . . .

There'd been rumours, of course. But none of the official government sources would confirm or deny it. And unofficial sources were apologetic, but equally unhelpful. A purely personal decision, the sources said, so not something they were likely to hear about.

But, oh boy, if it *was* . . . What a complexion *that* would cast on the story! Victim comes to mourn girl-terrorist. Terrific. It suggested that he had kept some sort of affection for the girl.

It also suggested he had been deeply affected by what had happened, that he had lost his detachment . . .

There might even be a resignation.

The group stood, for once completely silent, their eyes locked on the black chauffeur-driven car rolling up the drive.

Caroline gripped Henry's hand. 'Oh *darling*! There are thousands of them.'

'Yes. I knew there would be.'

'Why couldn't they—'

Henry shook his head briefly. 'Inevitable, I'm afraid. Just remember – keep your face impassive, even if they tread on your toes. And stay close to me. Anderson will force a way through, won't you, Anderson?'

The Special Branch man nodded firmly. 'Yes, sir.'

The car climbed inexorably up the hill. Even as they swung in towards the covered porch the cameras were up against the car windows. Henry gripped Caroline's hand. They exchanged fleeting smiles of encouragement.

The car pulled up. Anderson leapt out and fought his way round to help the driver, who was trying to clear some space by the passenger door.

The door opened. Henry got out first, then turned to help Caroline. There was a babble of voices. 'Sir Henry! Can you tell us why you're here?'

'Sir Henry – what is your attitude to terrorism?'

'Sir Henry! Sir Henry! How do you *feel* at this moment?'

He ignored all the questions, especially the last one. They weren't enquiring after his health. They just wanted some raw emotion for the front page.

Tucking Caroline's arm firmly into his, he walked slowly forward into the space cleared by Anderson. The pressmen fell back. They knew better than to badger a politician if he wasn't in the mood to talk. Politicians and newsmen knew the game too well.

Henry led Caroline into the sudden calm of the chapel's anteroom.

Caroline breathed, 'My goodness. What hyenas.' She gave him a sudden, anxious look. 'Are you all right, darling?'

He nodded and they walked into the body of the chapel.

It contained just five people. The large black hat, he rightly guessed, belonged to Mrs Danby. A brief greeting would have to be endured at some point; he might as well get it over with straight away.

He and Caroline approached and stood by the pew.

Mrs Danby looked up. An expression of horror crossed her face and she gasped audibly. Then it all seemed to become too much for her, and she buried her head in her hand.

A wave of sympathy overcame Henry and, bending down, he murmured, 'You know, she was a fine girl. I really believe that. And I'm sorry that . . .' Henry broke off. Mrs Danby had raised her head. Her mouth was open, her expression aghast. She whispered fiercely, 'After what she did to *you*? Well, *I* can never forgive her! *Never*!'

Henry stared, taken aback. 'But you must understand – she did try to make amends. And you know, she was very brave, right to the end.'

Mrs Danby shook her head vehemently and looked away.

Caroline tugged at Henry's sleeve. She was right; there was no point in discussing it. Not here and now. He nodded briefly to the sister and the father, and turned away.

He didn't know the others. Two young men. Their eyes met, established a fleeting contact, then slid away.

Henry and Caroline chose a pew and sat down. Almost immediately Henry began to wonder about the two young men. He examined their profiles, his curiosity roused. The furthest one was dark and soberly dressed in a suit, the nearest one was fair, wearing dark but casual clothes. He thought he knew who they might be. He would find out later, after the service.

The chapel was cold and bare. There were no flowers. Some trestles stood in front of the altar, ready for the coffin. On one side of the altar was a long rectangular stand on which the coffin would eventually be placed. At one end of this was an opening covered by black curtains: the road to the cremation chamber. Henry suppressed a shiver. It was all so depressingly sinister.

There was a mild commotion outside, the sound of doors swinging open. Recorded organ music suddenly filled the chapel. The meagre congregation stood up.

Henry turned. A parson was walking slowly up the aisle in front of a plain wooden coffin borne by professional pallbearers, their faces grave with superficial and well-polished solemnity.

The coffin came level. Henry's heart gave a small lurch. He was always hopelessly sentimental on these occasions. He tried to control the surge of emotion, but all he could see in his mind's eye was the cellar and the pathetic heap under the hastily arranged coat and the blood, the appalling scarlet blood, splattered everywhere like a slaughter room in a ghastly abattoir . . .

He closed his eyes. When he opened them again he found himself looking at the fair-haired young man. His face was turned to the coffin, his expression serious. Or perhaps it was closer to remorse: it was difficult to tell.

He thought: At least someone else cared enough to come.

The coffin was placed on its stand. The service began. It was obviously going to be brief and to the point. The parson announced a hymn – 'The Lord is My Shepherd' – normally one of Henry's favourites, but with the pre-recorded music, so few voices and those raised half-heartedly the hymn sounded thin and joyless.

They knelt to pray. Tears came to Henry's eyes. He couldn't help it. He was still deeply tired. And the memories of the long hours in the cellar were still clear in his mind. Moreover, since the rescue, he'd been feeling strangely depressed, guilty almost, as if the suffering that had been visited on Caroline and everyone around him was somehow his fault. It was all nonsense of course, he realised that. The doctors talked knowledgeably about shock and reaction, but he was still finding this period of adjustment difficult and confusing. Time, everyone kept telling him; time would heal . . .

Caroline touched his hand. He nodded to show that he was all right, and took her hand in his. It had been hardest of all for her.

She still couldn't believe he was safe. Nor, sometimes, could he. Each day was a miracle.

He put his mouth to Caroline's ear and whispered, 'Bless you . . .' Then: 'I'm glad we came.'

She smiled her agreement, and then they rose to listen to the address. It was brief in the extreme. A few platitudes. The parson obviously hadn't known Victoria.

The pallbearers moved forward and, lifting the coffin, slid it on to the rollers. Almost immediately the curtains opened, the music swelled – to cover the whirring of the electrically operated rollers, Henry realised – and the coffin trembled and rocked its way into the black void.

Henry stared blankly. His emotion was spent.

He was only sorry that it had been such a poor, sad, lonely funeral. Somehow *shameful*. And no one deserved that.

He thought again: I'm glad we came.

The service was over. The family went out first. Henry and Caroline followed.

Henry paused in the ante-room and waited for the two young men.

He approached the fair-haired one with his hand outstretched. 'Henry Northcliff.'

The young man shook his hand and replied, 'Sergeant Ryder, Special Branch. This is my colleague, Sergeant Conway.'

Henry shook Conway's hand then turned back to Ryder. 'I thought it must be you. The Commissioner kindly sent me some of the reports.'

Ryder dropped his eyes. 'I'm sorry I couldn't do more to prevent what happened.'

'No, no.' Henry gestured to show that he had no wish to discuss it. The two men strolled to one side of the ante-room. Henry paused. There was something he wanted to ask this man, but the question wouldn't form clearly in his mind.

'I wondered – at the farmhouse, when you talked to her through the door – did she seem . . .' He trailed off. He didn't know how to phrase it.

'She was surprisingly calm, really,' Ryder volunteered.

'Yes, but ' Henry knew what he must ask. But he hesitated for a moment, to prepare himself for the answer. 'Was she worried – about time running out? About the explosives going off at a certain time?'

Ryder shot him a look of sudden comprehension. There was a long pause. He said reluctantly. 'She was aware of it. Yes . . .'

Henry nodded slightly. It was as he had thought all along.

'It was a pity she never realised,' he said softly. 'I mean . . . That there was plenty of time after all.'

The two men exchanged glances, then looked away. There was not a lot to say.

They strolled back towards Caroline who was waiting by the doors.

Henry shook Ryder's hand. 'Well, at least we know. How brave she was. That's something, I suppose.'

Tucking Caroline's arm in his, he took a deep breath and facing the doors, prepared himself for the barrage of pressmen who, he knew from experience, would still be waiting patiently outside.